"A larger-than-life hero

Jade

Treasure of the Golden Cheetah

"Suzanne Arruda brings the flavor and flare of the golden era of silent movies and colonial Africa into each scene and chapter. This book is certainly a page-turner." —*Wichita Falls Times Record News*

"Cinematic in its descriptions of Africa, compelling in plot—this is a true whodunit—and skilled in characterization, *Treasure of the Golden Cheetah* is the best so far of an outstanding series. And Arruda's cliff-hanging ending will have readers yearning for the quick appearance of Jade's next adventure." —*Richmond Times-Dispatch*

"What an adventure! Jade is one strong, savvy woman, and her cheetah sidekick, Biscuit, makes a striking companion. If you like excitement, romance, and exotic locales, this book will spirit you away." —Sandi Ault, author of the Wild Mystery Series

The Leopard's Prey

"Melds [Isak] Dinesen's evocation of a bygone Africa with [Agatha] Christie's ability to fashion a sharp whodunit. . . . Arruda writes with flair, creates an intriguing puzzle, and plays fair with clues. But the main attraction of this series is Jade herself—sometimes reckless, never feckless." —*Richmond Times-Dispatch*

"Great characters, careful plotting, and an unusually beautiful depiction of Africa." —*Library Journal*

continued . . .

"A lively mystery adventure with a strong sense of both its historical period and its exotic locale." —*Kirkus Reviews*

The Serpent's Daughter

"[A] rollicking tale of adventure and suspense . . . stellar."
—*Library Journal*

"Captivating . . . Jade's escapades should appeal to fans of Elizabeth Peters's Amelia Peabody series or the Indiana Jones movies."
—*Publishers Weekly*

"Jade del Cameron . . . is closer to Indiana Jones than Miss Marple in a book that is part adventure story, part mystery, part travelogue— and overall a rattling good read." —Rhys Bowen, author of *Royal Blood*

Stalking Ivory

"Suzanne Arruda is fast creating her own unique and popular niche in mystery fiction. With deep research and rich imagination, she gives us Africa in the 1920s and a bold new heroine in Jade del Cameron. This is a series that deserves a long life."
—*New York Times* bestselling author Nancy Pickard

"The resilient Jade will charm readers as she asserts her independence in rugged Africa." —*Publishers Weekly*

"British East Africa is the seductive setting of this sequel to the author's exuberant debut, *Mark of the Lion*. . . . Like its predecessor, this book is deliberately over the top, and great fun to read."
—*The Denver Post*

"Another top-notch mystery. . . . Fans of Ernest Hemingway and Agatha Christie alike will find this second tale of Jade's exploits a ripping good yarn." —*Richmond Times-Dispatch*

Mark of the Lion

"*Mark of the Lion* sweeps the reader along with an irresistible narrative and literary drive. If you're looking for a fresh new mystery series, a vivid historical setting, and an especially appealing heroine, look no further. One of the most memorable mystery adventure stories I've read in a long time." —*New York Times* bestselling author Douglas Preston

"Jade del Cameron . . . brings new meaning to the word 'gutsy.' Vividly portraying the long-ago age of shooting safaris and British stiff-upper-lip attitudes, this novel is filled with appealing characters."
—*The Dallas Morning News*

"This debut novel delivers on its unabashedly romantic premise and for good measure throws in a genuine mystery. . . . It's storytelling in the grand manner, old-fashioned entertainment with a larger-than-life heroine far ahead of her time." —*The Denver Post*

"*Mark of the Lion* is historical mystery at its best, with a dynamic amateur sleuth and well-drawn supporting cast of quirky characters. First-time author Suzanne Arruda hits the reader with a gripping opening and builds tension, twists, and turns from there . . . a compelling premiere performance." —Karen Harper

"There's something for everyone in this new series debut—mystery, history, adventure, travel, even a bit of romance."
—*Library Journal* (Starred Review)

"Arruda's debut is an enjoyable romp through a colorful place and period in which the heroine has a Douglas-Fairbanks-in-a-split-skirt charm." —*Kirkus Reviews*

"An exciting, well-paced debut." —*The Philadelphia Inquirer*

THE
CROCODILE'S
LAST EMBRACE

A JADE DEL CAMERON MYSTERY

SUZANNE ARRUDA

AN OBSIDIAN MYSTERY

OBSIDIAN

Published by New American Library, a division of
Penguin Group (USA) Inc., 375 Hudson Street,
New York, New York 10014, USA
Penguin Group (Canada), 90 Eglinton Avenue East, Suite 700, Toronto,
Ontario M4P 2Y3, Canada (a division of Pearson Penguin Canada Inc.)
Penguin Books Ltd., 80 Strand, London WC2R 0RL, England
Penguin Ireland, 25 St. Stephen's Green, Dublin 2,
Ireland (a division of Penguin Books Ltd.)
Penguin Group (Australia), 250 Camberwell Road, Camberwell, Victoria 3124,
Australia (a division of Pearson Australia Group Pty. Ltd.)
Penguin Books India Pvt. Ltd., 11 Community Centre, Panchsheel Park,
New Delhi - 110 017, India
Penguin Group (NZ), 67 Apollo Drive, Rosedale, North Shore 0632,
New Zealand (a division of Pearson New Zealand Ltd.)
Penguin Books (South Africa) (Pty.) Ltd., 24 Sturdee Avenue,
Rosebank, Johannesburg 2196, South Africa

Penguin Books Ltd., Registered Offices:
80 Strand, London WC2R 0RL, England

Published by Obsidian, an imprint of New American Library,
a division of Penguin Group (USA) Inc.

First Printing, September 2010
1   3   5   7   9   10   8   6   4   2

Copyright © Suzanne Arruda, 2010
All rights reserved

OBSIDIAN and logo are trademarks of Penguin Group (USA) Inc.

Library of Congress Cataloging-in-Publication Data:
Arruda, Suzanne Middendorf, 1954–
The crocodile's last embrace: a Jade del Cameron mystery/Suzanne Arruda.
p.   cm.
"An obsidian mystery."
ISBN 978-0-451-23117-8
1. Del Cameron, Jade (Fictitious character)—Fiction. 2. Women private investigators—Kenya—
Fiction. 3. Americans—Kenya—Fiction. I. Title.
PS3601.R74C76   2010
813'.6—dc22   2010019147

Set in Granjon
Designed by Alissa Amell

Printed in the United States of America

This book is dedicated to Bryan (PNut) Peters and Jeff Scott.
Semper Fidelis and Semper Paratus, gentlemen.
I'm proud of you.

ACKNOWLEDGMENTS

My THANKS TO the Pittsburg State University Axe Library Interlibrary Loan staff for their tireless efforts; Dr. Steve Timme, biology department, Pittsburg State University, and Serita Stevens, coauthor of *Book of Poisons*, both for their assistance with potential toxins; Dr. John Daley, history department chair, Pittsburg State University, and James Williamson, roving editor for *Gun Week*, for their advice on firearms; Bryan (PNut) Peters for field-testing a .45-caliber bullet on oak; author and writing buddy Terry (Tessa) McDermid, for her help bouncing ideas; my Border Crimes Chapter of SInC, especially Cami Litchfield for helping me understand con artists; James Arruda, for assistance with early parachutes; Michael Arruda, for the inspired help with the final title; my publicist, Megan Swartz, for all her hard work; my agent, Susan Gleason, and my editor, Ellen Edwards, for their continued belief and efforts in the series; all my family: The Dad, James, Michael, Dave, Nancy, Cynthia, and Emily, for helping me shamelessly promote the books. I especially wish to thank Joe, the greatest husband and webmaster a writer could ever want, for all his help and support; and Wooly Bear for continuing to keep her hairballs off the keyboard.

Any mistakes are my own, despite the best efforts of my excellent instructors.

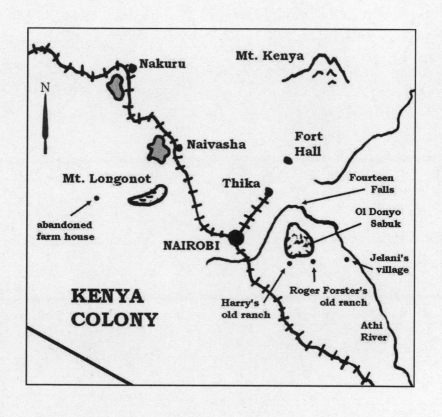

THE
CROCODILE'S
LAST EMBRACE

CHAPTER 1

*Hunters speak of the dangers of the "Big Five," the deadliest animals they
encounter in Africa. Lion, buffalo, rhino, elephant, and leopard top the
list. I would add the crocodile and, of course, the human.*
—The Traveler

FROM HIS HIDDEN VANTAGE POINT, the man watched the young
American woman called Simba Jike. The name fit not only
because she moved with the unconscious fluidity and grace of
a lioness but because she held herself with a lion's assurance
as well. Only once had he ever seen her truly vulnerable, the
day she stood in the deluge of rain at the train depot, watching the American leave her behind. He'd watched, too, rec-
ognizing that his opportunity had come.

A slight sound escaped his lips, half sigh, half groan, born
of both desire and sorrow.

He'd heard about her and her exploits before he'd ever
met her. All the colony talked about her unconventional behavior and attire, and she might have been shunned by Nairobi society but for the approval she'd received from old Lord
Colridge and Lord and Lady Dunbury.

Simba Jike in her dusty tan trousers, scuffed boots, khaki
shirt, and that worn-out old slouch ranch hat seemed to

embody Africa more than the British women in their Paris frocks and flowered straw hats. He'd also heard of her from his lover, who told a different tale. No grudging admiration there, and that was the source of his sorrow.

He could almost feel the strength radiating out of this American, see the pent-up passion. It smoldered inside her, flaring and flashing like green fire from eyes that could be as hard as emeralds or as soft as spring moss. Eyes that inspired desire.

He recalled that passion in his lover, but they'd been apart for so long, his memory was as remote as a real person was from a photograph. And now her passion had flared into anger and hatred. Other men might have freed themselves, moved on, perhaps towards someone like this human lioness, but he was bound to his mistress, tied by want and need and the remnants of love as well as by their past deeds.

When he'd first met this Jade del Cameron he'd expected most of the stories to be exaggerations, embellished tales told by needy people longing to draw everyone's attention. Instead, he found the tales fell short of the reality, and he'd come to admire her.

That made his job all the more difficult.

He'd been ordered to break her.

THE ANTLER HILT FELT COOL IN HER HAND, the well-polished knobs and curves as familiar to her fingers as a sweetheart's face. The hilt nicely balanced the length and heft of the blade. In short, the knife promised no surprises, provided the body did its part. It would. She'd practiced often enough and once, years ago, had pinned a rattler that had been menacing her sheepdog.

Her gaze locked on the target, gauging the distance, calculating the number of rotations before the blade struck. She stepped back a half pace and raised her right forearm even with her ear, willing a connection between her vision and her hand. She took a deep breath and dropped her arm on the exhale at the same time that she shifted her weight to her left foot. Her arm shot straight out in front of her, wrist taut, making one perfect line and freezing in position as abruptly as it had moved. As her fingers splayed, the blade spun twice in a graceful somersault like a diver teasing the air before piercing the water.

Jade del Cameron heard the satisfying *thunk* as the blade bit into the wood and stuck, quivering slightly. A smattering of applause followed.

"Bravo, Jade," called Beverly Dunbury. "Spot on the bull's-eye." The speaker was British, classically lovely with shimmering corn-silk hair, watercolor blue eyes, and the fair complexion generally associated with English ladies. She presented an interesting contrast to Jade, whose olive complexion, short, wavy black hair, and green eyes spoke of her exotic bloodlines.

Beverly nodded towards the target board. "Did you all observe how Lieutenant Jade kept her focus on the target? That's what *you* are supposed to do with your sling."

Lady Dunbury addressed a small herd of eleven girls ranging in age and deportment from three gangly, restless ten-year-olds to a pretty, well-mannered brunette of thirteen. All were dressed in khaki blouses and dark blue serge skirts that came more or less to their knees. Beneath the skirts were dark blue knickers and black woolen stockings. Each had an indigo blue campaign hat held in place with a chin strap. A powder blue neckerchief hung knotted around each neck. Most of the girls had tied additional knots on the dangling ends, a reminder to do the daily good turn. The two oldest girls' knots were already undone. A brown belt around each waist completed the military uniform of the 1st Nairobi Company Girl Guides, Ivy Leaf Patrol.

To mark their patrol allegiance, an ivy leaf was embroidered on each blouse's left-front pocket. Mary Postlewaithe, who would turn thirteen in a week, had lobbied extensively for the patrol to adopt a native flower—in particular, the fireball lily. The flower was spectacular, with its globe of hundreds of slender red florets exploding outwards like some aerial fireworks. And Jade had to agree that most of these girls were more like fireballs than the lilies and roses that had also been up for consideration. But in the end, no one could manage to embroider the complex fireball lily flower on her shirt or paint it on a banner without making it look like a squashed bug. Beverly suggested that they adopt the ivy leaf in honor of the 1st London Company.

"Will you teach us how to throw like that, Lieutenant Jade?" asked Helen Butterfield, the oldest girl. The daughter of a recently arrived settler, she boarded at the English school and showed the most interest in outdoor lore.

Jade winced at the title. "Please, Helen, you do not have to address me as lieutenant. I'm only assisting your, er, captain," she said, casting a sidewise look at Beverly. Her friend wore a simple walking dress of blue cotton serge and a campaign hat similar to the girls', only Beverly's hat sported a cock's feather plume and no chin strap. A whistle hung around her neck from a white lanyard. A Girl Guide was supposed to dress plainly, not call undue attention to herself, which, ironically, was what the uniform did.

Jade had proudly worn a similar skirt-and-trouser uniform as an ambulance driver for the Hackett-Lowther unit during the Great War, but she refused to truss herself up like a soldier now. She'd agreed to help Beverly with the newly founded troop only if she could still wear her usual trousers, white shirt, and boots. It was the knife scabbard on her boot that had started this knife-throwing demonstration.

"I'm certain Miss del Cameron will be happy to teach the older girls in due time," said Beverly, "but for now, you had better concentrate on using the sling. Besides being handy for chasing vermin out of your garden, it can be very useful in bringing down small game if you're lost and in need of food. And it will help you develop hand-to-eye coordination."

Jade retrieved her knife and slid it into her boot sheath as the girls each selected a small stone and pushed it into the pocket of her leather sling.

"Miss Jade, have you ever killed someone with your knife?" asked Elspeth.

"Elspeth Archibald!" scolded Beverly. "Is that how a Girl Guide talks?"

"I'm sorry," Elspeth said, although her expression suggested she was sorrier that she was being reprimanded. The downcast look vanished as quickly as a dewdrop under the hot Nairobi sun. "It's only that I've heard all sorts of exciting stories about Miss Jade. How she's captured criminals, and roped wild animals, and how she's flown a plane, and—"

"Is it true you've been traveling the globe these past months, looking for your lost love?" asked Mary. The other girls' heads all snapped around in unison to stare wide-eyed at Jade.

"Where in the name of Saint Peter's goldfish did you hear that load of . . . ?" asked Jade.

Undaunted, Mary persisted. "My mother heard from Nancy, the telephone girl, that your sweetheart died in the war. But Uncle Steven said that your sweetheart left you and went away." She put a finger to her lips and crinkled her brow as she tried to reconcile the conflicting accounts.

"Uncle Steven?" Jade asked.

"Steven Holly," said Mary.

"Oh," replied Jade in a flat tone. She remembered Mr. Holly only too well. During her first visit to the Muthaiga Club, he'd made a drunken pass at her and she'd punched him in the face. And if the telephone operator was spreading stories, everyone in the blooming colony would know by now that her beau, Sam Featherstone, had left her at the train station.

Jade pulled her own sling out of her trouser pocket and picked up a small stone. "Shall we get back to your practice? Perhaps Mary would like to emulate William Tell's son, put a tin can on her head, and let us try to knock it off."

Mary hung her head. "I apologize, Miss del Cameron." Her head popped back up as though on a spring. "It's just that both you and madame here," she added, addressing Beverly in the approved Girl Guide manner, "have led such exciting lives driving ambulances and traveling, and we'd dearly love to hear about some of it." All the girls' eyes opened wide in expectation.

"No!" Jade's voice was low, but firm. "Now, if you are ready, we'll continue with your sling practice."

She put an empty canned-meat tin on top of a fence post and lined up the girls from youngest to oldest. "Remember what I taught you. Keep one strap wrapped around your hand; hold the other end loosely. Swing around several times to get the proper speed but keep your eye on the target, not on your sling. Release at the top of your downswing and let the stone fly."

Each girl took a turn. A few stones smacked straight down into the dirt by the girls' feet. Others made great sweeping arcs up and down, falling short or long, depending on the girl's strength. One stone went straight up before plunking down on the thrower's hat. Jade explained to each girl what had gone awry: releasing too late or too soon or without enough speed and force. The last girl, Helen, stepped up and flung the stone with enough accuracy to graze the tin and make it jiggle.

"Very good, Helen," said Beverly. "It really is just a matter of practice."

"This is harder than archery," said Gwendolyn Walker, a plump little blonde. "I can't see where I'm throwing with the sling."

"That's part of practice," said Jade. "Teaching your hand to obey your eyes. It's not much different from throwing a ball." She told the girls to continue practicing, and let her mind drift while keeping half an eye on them. Beverly joined her.

"It's no good, Jade," Beverly said softly. "I'm not going to let you stand alone over here and brood. And," she added when Jade arched one eyebrow as though to express her disagreement, "I know you too well, love. You keep stealing off to be alone, and when I find you, you're in a dismal mood. I knew I shouldn't have let you wander off to France for the Armistice remembrance. It simply was not healthy."

"I couldn't stay here, Bev. You know that."

"You could have gone to your home in the States and voted in that election. And you know you always have a home here with Avery and me."

Jade didn't argue. It wouldn't have made any difference anyway. Beverly had always been protective of her friends, and now that she was the mother of a little girl, her maternal instincts had kicked into high gear. Jade had known she had to come back to Nairobi when Beverly had written to her in France, pleading for her help in getting the Girl Guide troop into operation. The four months that Jade had given Sam Featherstone to return to her had been over and she wanted to be here when he came back. The desire had grown into a need, as vital as that for water or air.

If he comes back.

She shook her head to chase out the dark thought that had clung to her like a parasite. Since Sam had left in September to sell his motion picture in the States, Jade hadn't heard a word from him. He'd intimated that he wasn't the right man for her, that she should forget him, but that was as impossible as forgetting how to breathe.

After the first two weeks of trying to keep busy, she'd turned her pet cheetah, Biscuit, over to Madeline and Neville Thompson on their coffee farm and taken a boat to Europe. She'd wandered through France, visiting the battlefields and searching out some old friends from the countryside. Then, at her mother's insistence, she'd spent Christmas with a distant cousin in Andalusia. Over the holidays she'd sent a telegram to Sam, care of his parents in Battle Ground, Indiana.

It read simply, *I love you. Haul your horse's patoot back here. Jade.* She had no idea if he'd ever received it.

"Your house is crowded, Bev," Jade said. "Between baby Alice, her nanny, and now your sister, Emily, I wonder you don't kick me out for the space. It's time for me to find a place to stay somewhere in town."

"Nonsense. Emily's doing her level best to snag a husband in the colony. I should have her out of the house in no time."

Jade laughed. "I think you're actually more fond of her than you let on, Bev."

Beverly chuckled, a musical laugh like a gently rippling stream. "I suppose she has improved of late. For as long as I can remember, she's been my bossy, bullying, proper older sister. But she's had her own rough times, taking care of Father after Mumsy passed. Or perhaps all it took to temper her was knowing that I'm all the family she has left." She paused and watched as one of the youngest girls, Clarice, accidentally clunked herself in the head with her sling as she spun it around. "Or maybe it took that same knowledge to temper *me*."

"Don't look at the sling, Clarice," Jade called. "Look at the target."

Bev laughed and turned back to Jade. "You never did tell Avery and me about your time in France. I'm happy to listen if—"

"There's nothing to tell, Bev. But since you won't let the matter drop until I do, this is the short of it. I went back to each of our corps shelters to do a story for *The Traveler* about the changes in the countryside since the war."

"A terrible choice of articles," muttered Beverly.

"Do you want to hear this or not?" Without waiting for a reply, Jade pressed on, eager to get it over with. Much like removing a splinter, it wasn't any easier for going slowly. "I thought writing the article would help me think."

"You mean help you to *forget*," said Beverly. "You thought that seeing places where you hadn't known Sam would get him out of your mind. And all it did was confuse you more, didn't it? You thought about David instead. You probably went back to the place where his plane crashed, didn't you?"

She had lowered her voice when several of the girls turned to watch and listen. Now she raised it to tell them, "If you are finished with your sling practice, then you may go inside and practice sitting quietly."

As one, the girls returned to their throwing, but Jade heard snatches of whispered phrases. "So tragic" and "How romantic" drifted back to her.

"Wonderful," said Jade. "I'm sure that will make the gossip rounds now. Don't the Kenyans have anyone else to talk about besides me and my dead or absent loves?"

David Worthy had courted Jade during the Great War, proposing to her three times, and each time Jade had laughingly said no. After each refusal David had worked that much harder to impress her, flying deeper into enemy territory. On his last run he crashed defending her ambulance. He died in her arms, tasking her to find his missing half brother. Jade had never completely gotten over her guilt concerning his death.

How do I recover from holding him as he died, knowing I fueled his death? Or that his mother tried to kill me in the belief that I had murdered her son?

She walked back towards the girls. Biscuit, who'd been napping in the shade of a lush rosebush, stood up and stretched before ambling over to Jade. The beautiful cheetah chirped once in greeting and butted his head against her thigh. Jade responded by stroking his broad head. Since her return, the cat had been very attentive to her, rarely leaving her side. It was as if he'd grown more sensitive to her moods, much like a pet dog.

Or he's just making sure I don't go off and leave him behind again.

The girls' attention, having already been diverted by Jade's previous comments, was now engaged by the sleek cheetah. Each girl insisted on stroking his back or scratching him behind his ears. Biscuit endured it all with regal indifference, but even he had his limits. After a few minutes of receiving the giggly attention, he padded back to his rosebush and lay down.

"Perhaps it is time to put away the slings, pick up the stones and tins, and get ready for your mothers," said Beverly.

As if to illustrate her statement, a black Fiat driven by an Indian chauffeur pulled into the Dunburys' drive. He opened a rear door and an elegantly dressed lady stepped out. More motorcars, a taxi, and a rickshaw arrived soon after. The women in the latter two were neatly but more plainly dressed than those arriving in the motorcars, but every woman wore a hat and white gloves. Beverly advanced to meet them.

"Ladies," she said, "you are just in time. The girls were about to organize afternoon tea."

"Lady Dunbury," said Mrs. Archibald, the first woman to arrive, "Elspeth has spoken of nothing else since you took on this Girl Guide company. At first I assumed that Lady

Northey herself would be in charge, but I'm delighted that it is headed by such a charming lady as yourself. Good breeding is so important for the girls, you know."

"Thank you, Mrs. Archibald. I'm sure it is, but of course, the Girl Guides are founded on the principle that young ladies can and should serve king and country in a variety of ways."

"Mother," said Elspeth, tugging on her mother's sleeve, "come and see what we're learning today." She ran back towards the firing line, took her leather sling from her skirt pocket, fitted it with a small stone, whirled the sling, and let the stone fly. It smacked the tin straight on, knocking it to the ground. Elspeth turned towards her mother, her eyes bright with pride in her marksmanship.

Mrs. Archibald and two of the other mothers each gasped in unison, gloved hands covering their open mouths. The other women said nothing, waiting perhaps to see how Lady Dunbury would respond.

Beverly pretended she hadn't heard the shocked gasps at all. "Very good, Elspeth! Very good, indeed. Now please join the others inside and prepare for tea. I think we might take it on the veranda."

Elspeth, still oblivious to her mother's horror, said, "Yes, madame." She raised her right hand in the guide salute with the three middle fingers upraised and the thumb and pinkie crossed over the palm. Then she joined the others as they lined up, eldest to youngest, and went into the house. When they were out of hearing, Beverly turned back to Mrs. Archibald.

"Are you all right, Mrs. Archibald?" she said. "I thought I heard your breath catch a moment ago."

"I am shocked, Lady Dunbury! Shocked and horrified that my only daughter is engaged in such . . . such outlandish activities." The woman's gaze turned towards Jade and her brows arched. "It is most *unladylike*. Of course, I presume *you* are not to blame for this choice of activity. I shall speak to Lady Northey."

Jade walked over and stood beside Beverly. She knew that Mrs. Archibald's statement was meant as a slap in her face. She didn't care about this woman's opinion of her, but she *was* prepared to defend her friend. Beverly believed strongly in the Girl Guides, enough to begin a company years before her own infant daughter would be able to participate.

Beverly drew herself up straighter, maintaining her benevolent—if no longer warm—smile. "I'm sorry you feel this way, Mrs. Archibald. Your disapproval can only be a result of your lack of knowledge, knowledge of the brave deeds performed by some of the finest women the world has ever seen. Women with whom I had the honor of serving in the late war." Her chin rose a notch higher. "The women of the Hackett-Lowther ambulance corps were brave, bold, quick-witted, and able to repair their own vehicles. *They* would have applauded a skill in stone throwing, and they were *all* ladies down to the last one, including Miss del Cameron."

Jade cleared her throat. Her own mother might have disagreed with Beverly on that last point. She'd sent Jade to London to become a lady. It never took. Jade remained what Sam termed a varmint, through and through.

"It's also very practical," Jade added. "After all, this is Africa and one never knows when a cobra will appear in your garden. We don't want the girls to be afraid in their own homes."

"Well, I'm certain . . . I mean to say, I never," stammered Mrs. Archibald.

Beverly smiled. "Apology accepted. I knew that once *you* were informed of all the facts you would certainly agree with me." She made a gathering motion with her left arm while her right pointed the way to the veranda. "Ladies, shall we take tea?"

Jade stayed where she was. The daughters were an affable group by and large, if a little giddy at times, but Jade didn't wish to spend more time with the mothers than was absolutely necessary. Several of them reminded her of the arty set that in recent years had taken over Taos, New Mexico.

"Aren't you coming, Jade?" whispered Beverly. "I won't serve coffee, you know. It isn't good for you. You are jumpy as it is. But you could have some cake."

"No, thanks, Bev. It's enough that I have to see these mothers in two days at Mary's birthday party. If Mrs. Archibald isn't happy with me now, imagine how she'll feel when she learns that we taught the girls how to cauterize a deep wound as a last resort by igniting black powder in it. If it's all the same to you, I'm going to wait by the lane for Emily to return with the mail."

Beverly laid a hand gently on her friend's shoulder. "Jade, dearest. I do hate to see you waiting for word from Sam. It breaks my heart to think that he might never come back, but it saddens me even more to see you so expectant, and then so disappointed." When Jade didn't reply, Beverly persisted. "Going to France was a mistake, Jade. All you did was mix yourself up even more. Now you have your feelings for Sam and whatever guilt or loss you still carry for David battling it out in your heart."

Jade fingered the sapphire ring that she wore on her right hand. Every time she gazed into it, she saw herself aloft in the blue with Sam in his plane. It was impossible to look at the sky without searching for him, without listening to the familiar purring drone of the engine. Sam's engagement ring didn't belong on her left hand, since he'd broken off their engagement right after Jade had finally accepted him.

"I will always mourn David," said Jade, "but as I mourn for any good friend and for all those brave young men who died in that horrid war. But Sam *has* to come back. Because if he doesn't, Bev, then I have no home. Africa will be dead to me, and if I return to the States, I'll be trying to find him there. I'd lose more than him, Bev. I'd lose my home, my friends, my family." She hugged herself against a gnawing emptiness and looked past the rose garden and the stables as if she might see the grasslands far beyond, where the great herds and the prides still roamed. "He's coming back, Bev. I'm not giving up hope."

"It's still early," said Beverly. "Your four-month edict was hardly enough time."

"One month to travel, two to sell his motion picture, and one month to return. More than enough," said Jade. She called to Biscuit to join her and walked down the drive. She chose a shady bench under an arched arbor of bougainvillea and sat to wait for Emily. Bev's sister had driven off into Nairobi earlier in the day when the local newspapers had announced that the mail boat had docked in Mombassa two days ago. If one assumed a speedy unloading and sorting, the mail could have arrived on yesterday's afternoon train. Jade doubted that the mail would actually appear in the post office for pickup until tomorrow, but Emily had seized the excuse to do some shopping.

And perhaps accidentally run into one of the gentlemen she has her eye on.

Biscuit butted up against Jade, turning his head for an ear scratch. Her left hand did the job as she kept her gaze on the lane. The cheetah's raspy purr erupted in the stillness, and in it Jade imagined she heard the Jenny's purring motor. She stopped her caresses, and Biscuit settled sphinxlike at her feet.

Maybe Bev was right. Maybe going to France had been a bad idea. But staying here would have been worse. Still, things had happened on that trip that Jade hadn't told Bev. Beverly had been afraid that Jade's nightmares would begin again. They hadn't. In fact, sleep had been her one respite. But awake? Awake she'd been pursued by living nightmares. Twice she'd had unnerving experiences, too insubstantial to be real, too corporeal to be dreams. Once, she swore she heard the cries of the wounded drifting up from an old battlefield.

And another time . . .

She hadn't been in France for more than a week when she'd had her vision. She'd encountered several veterans of the war making their own pilgrimage and many wore their uniform, or part of it. So when Jade first spied the RFC pilot sixty feet in front of her, she didn't think much of it, except to wonder whether he might have also been a friend of David Worthy's.

Then he turned!

Jade's arms tingled anew at the memory.

David!

His face was a mask of tragedy and perhaps shame. And then, when she'd blinked, he was gone. She couldn't explain that to herself. There was no sense in trying to explain it to Beverly.

The chug of a motorcar brought Jade's mind back to the present. She stood and looked down the lane. *Good, Emily's back.* Bev's sister drove the Hupmobile over to the garage built beside the stables and parked beside Avery's Dodge truck. Jade went to meet her. As Emily walked to the house, she cradled several parcels in her arms and gripped a cluster of envelopes in her left hand. She was a paler version of Beverly, a description that went beyond milk white skin and hair the color of unbleached muslin. Emily lacked her sister's self-assurance and her ebullient if sometimes ornery personality. An attractive woman in her own right, she'd suffered from constant comparison to her beautiful younger sibling. Now, at twenty-six, she'd made peace with herself and Beverly and had come to the colony in search of a life.

And a husband.

"It seems most of the mail is still being sorted," said Emily, "but I have some good news, Jade. There's an envelope for you."

Jade hurried to join her. "From America?" The question was rhetorical. The only mail she ever received was from either her parents or the editor of *The Traveler*, both in the States. What she really wanted to ask was, "From Sam?"

"Actually, I believe the postmark is Paris." Emily thrust a letter into Jade's hands. "I must get these inside. I suppose my darling sister is still entertaining?"

Jade nodded but didn't reply. She was too engrossed in

the envelope before her. The handwriting was elegant and somehow familiar, but it wasn't Sam's tight hand. She pulled her knife, and neatly sliced open the flap. Jade took out the paper inside and shoved the envelope in her pocket after replacing her knife in its sheath. But when she unfolded the single sheet of white paper, she felt her legs turn to rubber. Shaking, she found a bench and plopped onto it.

Clipped to the paper was a newspaper obituary for David Worthy. And on the paper were written the words:

Why did you let me die?

It was signed, *David Worthy*. Even more unsettling, it was written in his hand.

CHAPTER 2

The region around Nairobi is blessed with water and beautiful waterfalls.
The one on the Athi River called Fourteen Falls is the loveliest.
It sits near Ol Donyo Sabuk Mountain, one of God's many seats.
—The Traveler

AVERY FOUND JADE FIRST. After recovering from the initial shock, she'd slipped away, avoiding the house and its people. She'd wandered first to her rooms, then past the darkroom and through the gardens, seeking a hiding place. Only she couldn't find a way to escape from her inner turmoil.

Her rational mind didn't believe that David's spirit was reaching out to punish her, but after all she'd seen and experienced in the past few years, her heart wasn't so certain. By the time Avery found her, Jade was at the stables, stroking a mare's soft nose. Biscuit stood beside her.

"Jade," he called, "are the junior Amazons finished for the day? Is it safe for me to enter my own house?"

Jade started. She'd forgotten that Avery had gone to work the horses. From the look of his dusty jodhpurs and riding boots as well as his rolled-up sleeves, he'd been engaged with them for a long while. "They're having tea," she replied. "Or at least, they were."

"And you'd had your fill of the little darlings?" He chuckled and retrieved his jacket from a fence post, pulling a pipe and tobacco from one of the pockets. He leaned against the post and filled his pipe. "I commend Beverly for taking them on. It gives her something purposeful to do and it ensures an active company when little Alice is old enough to take part."

"I like to think that it teaches the girls some self-reliance and skills other than arranging roses in a vase," said Jade. "All the girls attend Nairobi Government School, but two, Helen and Clarice, board there while their parents are starting up farms. They could benefit the most."

"I wondered why you agreed to help Beverly," said Avery.

Jade shrugged. "I helped because Bev's my friend. When she sent for me, her appeal sounded rather desperate, as though she'd bitten off more than she could chew, though I've come to suspect it was all a ploy to bring me back here."

Avery lit his pipe and puffed at it for a few moments. "Don't expect me to agree or disagree with you there, Jade. But we were worried about you."

"Were?"

"Fair enough. Still are. For instance, right now you look as though you've received your death sentence." He pointed with his pipe stem to the paper sticking out of her shirt pocket. "I say, how stupid of me. You've heard from your family. Bad news?"

Jade studied her friend from under lowered eyelids. The paper made him nervous.

He's hiding something.

"Not from my family." She handed the brief note and obituary to Avery and waited while he read them.

"This must be a hoax. It can't be—"

"From David? One wouldn't think so, but it is his hand."

"It's a foul, dirty joke," said Avery, anger edging his voice. "Someone's done a good job of playing the forger, that's for certain." He turned the note over, looking for any clue on the back. "Did you see anyone in France? Someone perhaps who was suffering from shell shock?"

"No." Jade didn't tell him she thought she'd seen David. It *had* to have been a trick of the mind. "You flew in David's squadron. You would know if any of the other pilots in your group blamed me."

"And no one did," he said. His pipe hung forgotten from his fingers until he raised his hand to stroke his chin. "Blast, it went out," he said, and relit it. "I would suspect David's mother, Lilith, was behind this. A retaliation of sorts for breaking up her smuggling ring in Morocco, but there's been no word of her doing anything from prison."

"You haven't heard from your contact in London?" asked Jade.

"No, but I asked him to send word only if she did something major: relocated, received a caller. There's been nothing since that clergyman visited her in August."

"What are you talking about?" asked Beverly as she joined them. "Something very serious by the looks on your faces."

Avery leaned over and kissed his wife on the cheek. "All through with the Junior Amazon Society, are you?"

"Yes, so you are safe to come back to the house, my dear. Now, what is going on?"

Jade handed the note and obituary to Beverly. "This came in today's mail," she said.

Beverly's eyes widened in surprise, then quickly narrowed in anger. "How dare someone do this to you, Jade. You should take this to the police immediately. Perhaps they can find some fingerprints on it."

"Yes, the postal clerk's and ours," said Jade. "We've all handled it. And it's hardly likely that Inspector Finch would have any record of prints on file from France. I think Avery was closer to the mark in suggesting this is Lilith's work. She probably paid one of her confederates to do the job, imitating David's hand." Jade took back the letter and shoved it into her trouser pocket.

"We've never been able to find out just how many people she employed in her criminal network," said Beverly. "You've run across some of them, but there must be more."

"A feeble attempt to frighten you, made by a caged woman," said Avery. "If she had anyone close at hand, they would have attempted to harm you by now, I should think. But I'm happy to know you haven't received bad news from your family."

Jade looked at Avery from under hooded eyes. "You knew it wasn't from Sam, didn't you? You've heard from him, though."

"Well . . . it's only that . . ." Avery coughed. "Oh, blast! It's been months. Not since he arrived in California, no."

"This is all a lot of horrid nonsense," said Beverly. "And, Jade, you've been wound as tightly as a watch spring since you came back from France. It's high time you told us what happened there."

"What makes you think something happened in France?" asked Jade.

"Because I know you. You've had a faraway, haunted look in your eyes ever since your return."

Jade grimaced. "Haunted is right. I thought I saw David."

"Blast and damn," muttered Avery. "When?"

Jade briefly explained the encounter.

"Jade," said Avery, "you held a dying man in your arms, one you cared for, and under horrific circumstances. Men still relive those experiences in their minds."

"He was trying to tell me something."

"It was the fog and another man in uniform," insisted Avery.

Beverly put a comforting arm around Jade's shoulder. "I knew I shouldn't have let you go. You're overwrought. You need a diversion. Alice is asleep just now. Come with me into town. I have some shopping to do."

Jade rolled her eyes. "Bev, I love you dearly. I'll do nearly anything for you, including help you lead those female firecrackers of yours, but I draw the line at shopping. I think I'll take Biscuit for a good run and go out to see Maddy and Neville."

"Splendid. Fresh air and activity," said Avery. "Tell them hello for us. Ask Neville how his new coffee machine is doing."

"And ask Madeline about little Cyril. And remind her that she promised me a start of her blue ribbon cabbage rose," added Bev as Avery checked the bolts connecting the sidecar to Jade's Indian Power Plus.

Jade waved away their requests and called to Biscuit. She took off towards the Thompsons' coffee farm near Thika, Biscuit loping alongside her. Once she'd crossed the Nairobi

River and left the city's residential districts behind, she cut her cycle across country, giving the cheetah a chance to open up and run without fear of vehicles.

Even then she had to mind where she rode the bike. So much of the surrounding area was farmed and fenced, but she'd already discovered a route that cut across strips of open grassland, still green from the rains that had continued long past the "short rains" that year. Despite the lush grazing, Jade saw none of the large herds that still marked the Serengeti. These had moved farther away from the town and habitations, and with them had gone most of the great predators: the lion and the leopard. Now the danger lay in African wild dogs and roving jackals. Jade despised them. The dogs were vicious, eating their prey alive. They reminded her of humans who preyed on simple, trusting folk with schemes and promises of wealth.

The February summer sun had begun its downward run for the day, casting shadows in front of the occasional flame tree. The wind brushed Jade's exposed cheeks and tousled the hair that peeked from beneath her leather helmet. It felt cleansing, sweeping away the dread and horror of that letter. Biscuit raced just ahead of her, guessing her destination. His long, slender legs stretched ahead, then drove into the ground as the rear ones came forward to join them. Over and over his lithe body lengthened and contracted like a piston, and Jade rejoiced inwardly at the cat's beauty and grace.

To the left, a lone male antelope—a gerenuk—stood on his hind legs and browsed a thorn tree branch. He spotted them and galloped away, his long neck raised high. Biscuit swerved towards him momentarily, but the cheetah had already spent most of his energy and dropped back into a trot, then a walk. Jade slowed her machine to allow him to jump into the sidecar for the remainder of the trip. All too soon, they'd reached the edge of the Thompsons' farm. She spied Maddy taking down wash from a line. Her adopted son, Cyril, played with a ball by the clothes basket. Jade waved and pointed towards the makeshift thorn brush airplane hangar north of the house.

Maddy cupped her hands and shouted, "Come back to the house for supper."

Jade nodded and puttered off to the hangar and Sam Featherstone's Curtiss JN-4 "Jenny." Leaving Biscuit to forage up a mess of hapless rodents for a snack, Jade immersed her mind in tending to Sam's plane. She drained the radiator, refilled it, oiled the multitude of points that called for attention, twanged the wires to check for tension, and adjusted the bolts where the wires had loosened. She inspected the struts, the wing fabric, the engine, and anything else she could see before the long shadows made it impossible to distinguish one part from another. The plane had to be ready for Sam's return.

It was a task Jade both loved and feared. Tending to any machine took most of her concentration, so the job became an escape from her trials. But in another sense, it added to them. What if Sam didn't return? It was impossible to tighten a rusting cable bolt and not hear Sam's gravelly voice, to caress the wing fabric and not feel his hand. She caught herself looking up from a task, expecting to see his angular face with his long, slender nose that seemed to grow out of his brow and the thin mustache that underscored it. The deep sigh that shuddered out of her throat made Biscuit look up inquiringly.

She put away the tools and locked the toolbox. "Let's go, Biscuit. We'll see if Maddy's got something more for you to eat than those mice."

Maddy had several soup bones for Biscuit. She served a large meal to Jade and Neville consisting of chicken roasted with various root vegetables, and a platter of steaming mealies, as corn on the cob was termed. A loaf of freshly baked bread completed the dinner. Cyril had eaten earlier and was asleep in his room. Conversation lagged while everyone ate; then Jade passed on Bev and Avery's regards and questions. Neville told about the growing number of nearby farmers interested in his coffee-washing service as well as the advance orders for the washers from farmers farther afield. Madeline set out a pudding for dessert.

"We were a bit surprised to see you today, Jade," said Madeline. "You worked over the plane just five days ago."

Neville looked up from his pudding, his eyes alight with expectation. "I say, does this mean that you've heard—"

"No," said Jade, cutting him off. "I'm sorry, Neville. That was rude of me. No, I haven't heard from Sam. I just needed to get away and I wanted an excuse to visit you."

Neville smiled, accepting the compliment. Madeline, however, pursed her lips and studied Jade's face with the practiced eye of a mother looking for unspoken hurts.

"You never need an excuse to visit us, Jade. You know that," Maddy said. "But you do look a little drawn. I suppose those girls are running both you and Beverly ragged."

"They are active little creatures," Jade said with a chuckle. "I suppose it's nothing less than I deserve after the trouble I gave my mother."

"Hmm," mused Madeline. "Oh, did you know that

Harry is back in the area? He stopped by yesterday on his way to look at his old ranch property. Surprised he hasn't sold it."

"He should," added Neville. "He's off on safari so much that he just stays in some rooms above Newland-Tarlton's offices when he's in town."

"He asked after you," added Madeline.

Jade frowned. Harry Hascombe, rancher turned safari guide, had been a thorn in her side on several occasions. His interest in her, coupled with Maddy's tendency to play matchmaker, made Jade wary.

"Maddy, thank you for the delicious meal and for giving those soup bones to Biscuit. It was nice visiting both of you, but I'd better collect my cheetah and head back. It's late."

"You could stay the night," Maddy offered.

"Thank you, but no. You have a full house without us." She looked around for Biscuit. "Where is he anyway?"

They found the cat lying next to Cyril on the boy's bed. Neville smiled. "The little chap's got his arm tight around Biscuit's neck. Let Biscuit stay the night. We'll bring him back tomorrow. I've got errands to run in town and it will give Maddy a chance to take that rose to Beverly."

Jade agreed and headed back to Nairobi by way of the road. Her motorcycle's light lit her path, leaving the rest of Kenya drenched in a velvet blackness that reminded her of Sam's eyes. There was no moon tonight. Jade longed to look up at the thick sweep of stars above her, but she didn't dare take her eyes from the road. To prove her point, a little civet darted across her path, its eyes shining back at her from its raccoonlike mask.

Stay away from Maddy's chickens.

Over the Power Plus' engine, she heard a distant *bwaa!* as a lone jackal called out, seeking its pack. The only reply came from a spotted hyena. Its ascending *whooo*, repeated more than a dozen times, told Jade that a single male, ignored by the matriarchal pack, was also seeking company.

All of Africa is lonely tonight.

She understood the animals' mood. She longed to cry out herself. She crossed the Getathuru River, a tributary of the Nairobi River, and felt as if she'd crossed a moat and entered the castle keep, with all its sordid noise and business. Suddenly, she didn't want to return to the Dunburys' house or to her silent rooms. Not yet.

I need to see that sky.

On an impulse, she turned off the Fort Hall Road and onto the Limuru Road back out of town. Ahead of her stood the Limuru Bridge. She maneuvered her motorcycle in the deep, dry ruts made during the last rainy season, now baked to a bricklike consistency. Once across the bridge, she rode another hundred feet. Jade pulled her motorcycle to the side of the road and shut off her engine and the light. Then she gave herself to the night sky.

At first she faced north, seeking Ursa Major, the Great Bear. One of the better-known constellations, especially to a pilot, he was her link to Sam wherever he was. The bear's nose and foreleg pointed up to the Lynx. But his body, which formed the Dipper, barely cleared the horizon.

After finding the bear, she turned east and located Leo, a constellation she'd come to associate with Africa. The great cat, too, climbed skyward tonight. Near his feet sat a bright orb. *Jupiter.*

Jade sat down on the grass close to her motorcycle and

watched the sky, drinking in the deep black. Only Nairobi's glow diminished the gems of light winking out of the ebon veil. The bridge's embankment shielded her from much of the town's lights and most of the noise, although on a Thursday night, even the Muthaiga Club would be subdued.

A deep *hoo-hoo* sounded from a spotted eagle owl in one of the nearby trees. When Jade turned her head to better hear him, she caught sight of two streaks of light pitching across the sky. She'd forgotten there was to be a meteor shower. She waited, attentive to her peripheral vision as well. Within a few minutes, three more meteors sped across the sky, burning themselves up in their run. Jade felt as if the fireballs had coursed through her, searing her lungs and heart with an overwhelming need to see and touch Sam until her desire and loneliness threatened to suffocate her.

Time to get back to my bungalow.

Jade rose when a slight noise from the bridge frightened the owl and alerted her. She expected to hear an approaching engine, see a pair of headlights. She stepped farther back from the road, lest the sudden sight of a person standing alone startle the driver. But no lights appeared, which was odd. The Nairobi police were fully intent on enforcing their headlamp law. Jade listened more closely. The engine noise sounded labored, but muffled, as though something between her and the vehicle was blocking the sound. Then the engine noise lessened and she heard a car door shut.

At first, she wondered whether someone was having automobile trouble. She took a step towards the road to see whether she could offer her help as a mechanic. The sharp crack of snapping wood arrested her in midstride. It was immediately followed by the groan and crunch of metal and a soft splash.

They've gone over the bridge!

Jade hurried back to her motorcycle and rummaged in the dark for the flashlight in one of her panniers. She slid the switch on, and used the beam to find her way down to the car and its driver. Hopefully, someone was still alive. Farther away from the bridge, the bank wasn't as steep as it was under the bridge. If there was a route to the driver, it would be there, following the river back upstream to the car. As she scrambled down the embankment, she heard another sound, but it wasn't the expected moan of an injured victim.

It was the soft putter of a car slowly backing away in the darkness.

CHAPTER 3

During the rainy seasons, Fourteen Falls flows as one thick cascade,
red from the soil. Fish now move farther upriver, seeking food
that was flushed out along with the land.
—The Traveler

JADE SNAPPED OFF HER LIGHT and froze.

This was no accident!

She waited, listening for footsteps, a cough, anything to alert her to another presence—to danger. All she heard was a faint grinding of gears coming from the bridge. Then silence.

Someone pushed the car over the bridge! Her hope of finding someone alive in the car disappeared. Instead she wondered how many bodies had been dumped.

She turned on her light and hurried up the shallow river to the wreck, at times sloshing through ankle-deep water when it was easier than plowing through the scratchy brush and large rocks that bordered the steep bank. Something small rustled through the debris nearby, but other than the frightened rodent, all was silent.

Jade reached the car, a Dodge, resting on three tires; the fourth was hung up on a rock. The car's hood was crushed where it had struck the rocks below before righting itself. Peering through the broken windshield, Jade spied one occupant, a man, slumped over the steering wheel, motionless. A very thin dab of blood stained his forehead. She moved around to the driver's side and opened the door, careful to cover her hand with her sleeve. If the police were going to search for fingerprints, she didn't want hers on the handle. The smell of alcohol wafted out of the car. Jade put her index and middle fingers to the driver's neck. No pulse. She wasn't surprised, only saddened.

"Sorry," she said to the victim, and crossed herself, reciting a brief prayer for the man. Then she headed back to her motorbike and into town.

One lone police constable sat at the desk on duty, reading yesterday's newspaper. Jade recognized some of the headings: *Another Plague Victim in the Indian District* and *Limuru Road Bridge a Danger to Life and Limb*.

It certainly was tonight.

The constable, a young Englishman, jumped to his feet. "How may I help you, miss?"

"I'm reporting a death, possibly a murder."

"A death? I say. Where?" He ran his gaze over Jade's muddied shirt and trousers. "Are you all right?" He took a sheet of paper from a desk cubby and pulled a pencil from his shirt pocket.

Jade pointed to the newspaper lying on the desk. "At your Limuru Bridge. A car went over the rails. The driver is dead."

"Then it's an accident."

"I doubt it. I heard another car drive off slowly. There were no lights."

"Well, if someone was driving with no lights on that bridge, it's no wonder that they went over. That is a violation of the law, you know."

Jade sighed. "You misunderstand me, Constable. I suspect the car was pushed off the bridge intentionally, made to look like an accident."

Her statement suddenly struck home and the constable momentarily ceased scribbling on his paper. "And what were *you* doing there at this hour, miss?" He studied her again. "Were you in the vehicle?"

Jade noticed that he didn't specify *which* vehicle, the one that went over or the one she reported hearing leave. "Neither. I had stopped my motorcycle on the north end of the bridge before going into town." When she noticed his arched eyebrow, she added, "I wanted to look at the stars."

"Alone?"

"Alone!"

The constable bent down and made some notation. "Your name and residence?"

"Jade del Cameron. I'm a guest of Lord and Lady Avery Dunbury near Parklands."

She answered a few other basic questions regarding where she'd been and again why she was alone at night near the bridge. Jade replied patiently, wishing for a cup of coffee. When she'd heard the crash and reacted, it was with the nearly instinctive reflexes that had carried her on her ambulance runs during the war. Jade was certainly no stranger to death there. Several of her runs had ended in unloading a deceased soldier whose wounds had been too severe to withstand the long trip from the lines to an evacuation hospital. But the aftermath was always the same, sitting with Beverly and the other women in some farmhouse basement, drinking tea, cocoa, coffee, or Bovril—whatever someone had received in a package from home. She felt the need for that now, only she knew she'd be drinking alone. It wouldn't be right to disturb Beverly.

The constable's voice startled her out of her reverie. "I rang up the inspector, miss. Gave him all the particulars. He'll send some men out to the spot to fetch the body tonight."

"Did you tell him that it might be murder?"

"I did. Funny thing, miss—when I gave Inspector Finch your name, he didn't seem at all surprised. He said you had best go home now. Inspector will contact you tomorrow if he has any questions."

Jade nodded, thanked the constable, and went outside to her motorcycle. Her hand shook as she gripped the handlebars and it took all her presence of mind to steer the machine north through town to the northern edge of Parklands and to her rooms. She recognized the symptoms as a type of aftershock that hit after the initial surge of energy came in times of danger. While she was on the riverbed or by the car, her mind felt as clear as the African night. Her leg muscles had carried her willingly up and down the embankment, her arms assisting by pulling on low branches. But whatever extra strength she'd gained, she paid for now with trembling limbs and an exhausted, foggy brain.

One light burned in the Dunburys' windows. Bev, Jade knew, would either keep watch or have Farhani keep watch and alert her once she had safely returned. For a moment, Jade considered knocking on Bev's door, but decided against it.

No sense waking the baby. As she turned on her own house lights, the one in the big house across the yard went out. Beverly would retire now. Jade headed into her bathroom and took off her filthy clothes. It was too late to heat water out in the main kitchen for a hot bath, so she settled for a cold sponge bath and shampoo at the bathroom basin. She put on a fresh camisole and drawers and tossed the dirty clothes onto a chair. While she toweled her hair, she looked on her supply shelf for coffee. The can was not beside her little spirit burner.

My coffee's gone!

She moved aside some tinned meats and, not finding it, looked to see if it had fallen onto the floor. There was only her wooden chop box, where she kept her camping supplies. That was when she spied a tin on her little table with *Miss del Cameron* printed on a tag. Two notes lay beside it. One simply read, *Please give this to Miss del Cameron with my compliments. It's a spiced South African red tea. Quite delicious and purported to be very healthful, more so than her coffee. Your friend, Major Anthony Bertram.*

Jade recognized him as Avery's friend who was visiting when she'd returned from Kilimanjaro last September. The other note was from Beverly.

To that effect, I confiscated your coffee can. Love, Beverly.

Jade sighed. More mothering from Bev. "I hate tea," she muttered. Jade opened the tea and sniffed the contents. A fragrant blend of cinnamon, cardamom, nutmeg, and some other spices wafted up to her. She sneezed. *And pepper, too!* For a moment she considered trying a cup when a great yawn erupted from her. *Tomorrow.*

She barely remembered her head hitting the pillow, but in her dreams, it was a rolled-up blanket under her head and her bed was a bundle of straw stuffed into old ticking in a farmhouse basement the day that David crashed.

*   *   *

JADE ROSE FORTY MINUTES BEFORE SUNRISE, dressed in last evening's clothes, and settled herself at her table for a Spartan
breakfast of a stale scone dunked in a cup of the tea, which,
to her surprise, was good once she added a dose of honey to it.
Not only didn't it remind her of dried oak leaves steeped in
ditch water, as did black tea, but the pepper provided a pleasant jolt to her palate. She knew that Beverly would expect her
to join her and Avery at the main house, but Jade didn't feel
like facing an interrogation so early in the morning. At least,
not from Bev. Jade was expecting one anyway, but from a
different quarter. Finch arrived just as the sun rose, the long
morning shadows sprouting in the golden light.

"Miss del Cameron, it seems I need to speak with you
about a body," said Finch. "Again." His gaze drifted down to
her dirty trousers and stocking feet and snapped back up to
her face. "My apologies for disturbing your breakfast. However, I presumed you would be an early riser, as I need to see
this accident right away. It appears you've anticipated me."

"Won't you come in, Inspector?" said Jade. "Have some
tea while I put on my boots. It's South African and not bad.
The pepper in it is very stimulating."

Finch stood at her door, his hat in his hand. "Thank you,
no. I need you to accompany me straightaway to the Limuru
Bridge and tell me everything that happened last night. I want
to be finished before there are many people on the road."

Jade set her empty cup on the table, grabbed her boots
and hat, and headed out the door.

"You do not lock it?" Finch asked.

"Should I?"

"There have been the usual burglaries by natives, miss.

Don't think that because you are part of Lord Dunbury's estate, you are immune."

Jade took the hint and went back inside to find the house key and lock her door. Finch held the rear door of the Crossley staff car open for Jade, then slid in beside her. An Indian constable sat behind the wheel. At Finch's nod, they drove to the bridge. Jade finagled her boots on in the rear seat. She saw Finch look at the knife hilt peeking out of the sheath on her right boot. He said nothing and looked out the window again.

The car stopped on the Nairobi side of the bridge, about fifty feet back. A second, even older car was already waiting for them. Constable Miller stood beside it, stiffening to attention when Finch stepped out.

"Inspector!" said Miller with a salute.

"At ease, Constable," said Finch. "You've been here all night?"

"Yes, sir, Inspector. Traffic very light. No one's been by since two o'clock, sir, excepting one farmer."

"Very good," said Finch. "We'll look at the scene now. Constable Singh," he said to the Indian, "take photographs, but get the fingerprints when we get the car back to police grounds. Miss del Cameron, show me where you were last night."

Jade pointed across the bridge. "On the other side."

"Where, exactly?"

Jade led the way across the bridge, keeping to the rail opposite the break. As she walked, she studied the ruts in the dirt road. On the other side of the river, she found the place where she'd sat.

"Here," she said. "It was near to ten thirty when I stopped on my way back from the Thompsons' farm."

He arched his brows and frowned. "Then you'd have been on the Fort Hall Road, not here. Why did you come here?"

"I wanted to see the night sky. I couldn't look at it very well while I was riding my motorcycle, so I turned off onto this road." She didn't look at Finch when she explained. To her ears it sounded pitiful and she didn't want to see his reaction.

"Continue, if you please."

"I heard an engine coming up from the south. I stepped back farther away from the road so I wouldn't startle whoever came across, but no one did come. That's when I heard the wood snap and the car go over. I can't be certain, but I thought I heard the car door close just before it went over. But it was soft, not a slam."

"What did you do next?"

"I went east, downstream, to find an easier way to get down to the car."

"Do you mind showing me? You needn't fear seeing the body. My men removed it early this morning."

Jade pointed to her filthy trousers. "As you said, I anticipated you, Inspector." She took him along the route, wondering if he'd follow her into the river. He did, as did the Indian constable who carried a box camera.

"By the way, you won't find my prints on the door," she said. "I used my sleeve."

Finch's thin lips twitched in a half smile. "Don't worry, Miss del Cameron. I didn't plan to arrest you." He looked up to the bridge and the splintered railing. "Nearly a straight drop."

"Not what one would expect if someone was speeding along and broke through the rails," said Jade.

"But you saw no lights," said Finch. "And the man had been drinking. The smell of the alcohol inside the vehicle was quite strong. So it's not inconceivable that he was drunk, forgot to put on his headlamps, and drove off the road. You've seen the papers, I'm sure. The railings are merely tacked in place in some spots, giving the illusion of safety. Public works has done nothing about the bridge."

Jade considered this a moment. "Even drunk, he'd have put his arms up defensively when he went over. They were at his sides, as I recall, and I didn't see much blood, which suggests he was already dead before he hit. And did you notice the ruts up top?" She stepped over the rocks to the back of the car.

"Yes," said Finch. "I did. Deep from the last rains but nearly parallel to the railing."

"Exactly," said Jade. "One would have to be driving very fast to skip out of those ruts."

"In which case the automobile should have flown even farther before landing," finished Finch.

"This rear guard is scratched," Jade said.

Both Finch and Singh joined her. The latter took several pictures of the scratches as well as the position of the car relative to the bridge.

"Pushed," said Finch. "The man on duty last night said that you heard someone drive away."

"Slowly, with lights off," added Jade.

"Blast and damn," muttered Finch under his breath. He straightened and motioned for Jade to lead the way to the top. "The body is in Dr. Mathews' office, awaiting an autopsy. It will be only a matter of time before the jackals from the newspapers descend on my office. I will, of course, do what I can to keep your name out of this, Miss del Cameron, at least until there is some formal inquest."

Finch and Jade trudged up the bank to the top, leaving the Indian constable below to guard the car. Finch waved for Constable Miller to join them. "I shall send you back to town. Take Miss del Cameron with you. Then find something to haul up the car; block and tackle if we have to, or try Messrs. Childs and Josephs to see about borrowing that Bates Steel Mule tractor of theirs. We'll have to drag the motorcar back to town, I'm afraid. Doubt it's in any condition to . . . Oh, bloody hell."

Two vehicles pulled up behind Finch's car and a man jumped out of each. Both wore tweed suits and straw boater hats. One sported large sunshades the size of motoring goggles, and wide sideburns. He stood aloofly to one side of his car. The other was barefaced, sunburned, and approached with the aggression of a hungry dog. Each man carried a notepad and a pencil.

"I think the reporters are here," said Jade.

"Miller, keep them back!" ordered Finch.

"Is it true that someone drove through the rails last night, Inspector?" shouted the red-faced man.

"Was it suicide?" asked the one with the dark glasses. His voice, more subdued, carried the question with a practiced gentility, as though this were a garden-party conversation.

Both suddenly noticed Jade standing just behind Finch. The red-faced reporter pounced. "Miss, were you in the car at the time?" he demanded. "Tell us what happened!"

"All *I* can tell you," said Finch, "is that a motorcar did go off the bridge last night. The driver is dead. Everything else is purely speculation and I refuse to speculate to the press." He tugged on Jade's arm. "I'll take you back myself. Miller!" he called to the constable. "Stay here with Singh. I'll send some men to help get the car. And don't let any of these civilians down there. Arrest them if they try."

Miller saluted. "Yes, sir, Inspector."

Finch pulled Jade towards the Crossley. "Do you mind stopping at headquarters again, Miss del Cameron? I'll see that you get home right enough."

"I suppose not. But what else do you need me for?" She fidgeted with her hands and rubbed her arms, feeling her skin prickle.

Finch started up the car and drove them back to town. "You've got a sharp eye and a clear mind. You raised some interesting points back there. I'd like to discuss them with you. By now, one of my men should have found our deceased friend's rooms and been through them for any information. Your insight may be useful."

Jade rubbed her arms again and nodded. What was it about sitting in the car with Finch that made her skin crawl? He wasn't accusing her or her friends.

"Are you cold?" Finch asked.

"No. It's nothing."

"I'm not going to ask you to see the body again, if that's what is troubling you."

"I've seen bodies before," Jade replied, looking out the window. Government Road was still fairly empty at this hour, only the usual settler or two doing business at Whiteaway and Laidlaw. Finch parked in front of the dilapidated-looking galvanized-tin structure that still served as the police headquarters. While the rest of Nairobi was growing into dignified stone structures, Jade thought the police headquarters looked more like a place where a crime might take place rather than where it would be solved.

"Yes, I know you have," said Finch. He held the door to the headquarters open for her, then ushered her into his office.

"Smith!" Finch called. "Bring the Limuru Bridge case materials in here."

A young constable, looking to be no more than eighteen and gleaming with all the spit and polish that a fresh face and a clean uniform could give, dashed into the office with a box. "Will there be anything else, Inspector, sir?" he said, saluting.

Finch waved him out with a flip of his hand, his attention on the box. Jade pulled her chair closer to the desk, finding herself more than a little curious. She waited, however, for Finch to begin.

"Seems our man was a Mr. Clyve Stockton, recently arrived in the colony. His motorcar was hired locally. Usual belongings one would expect: shaving kit, assortment of clothing for roughing it, suit, watch, that sort of thing." As he spoke, he extracted a worn, thin leather case.

"A man's pocketbook?" asked Jade. "I presume he had some papers. Did you find any letters from a mother, a bank?"

"A sweetheart?" added Finch. "Here's his pocketbook but there are no letters. If Mr. Stockton had any relations, he didn't carry any tokens of them. No lock of hair or any other such treasures. He had money. Not much, but enough to get by until he found a position somewhere." He looked up at Jade, measuring out his next statement. "We did find something unusual."

Jade waited, playing his game by showing equal patience. Finch shrugged slightly and reached into the box. "We found this." He pulled out a small ring-sized box, opened it, and took out a gold nugget the size of a small pea.

Jade whistled, long and low. "Saint Peter's bait bucket! That *is* gold, isn't it?"

"Yes. It is. And we did find one paper in his pocketbook. It seems our Mr. Stockton had become a secondary partner in a gold mine up in the northern territory."

"There's gold up there?"

"If there is, it will be news to a great many people, including the commissioner of our own Land Department."

"Well, there's a motive for murder," said Jade. "If he talked about this with anyone, someone might have killed him to steal his gold."

"Perhaps." Finch replaced the nodule of gold in the ring box. "Judging by your surprise, you haven't heard anything of this before today."

"No," said Jade. "Did you think I might have? Are you trying to get me to do your work for you again?" she asked, referring to the time when he'd tricked her into solving the murder of a local businessman.

"Not at all. But you are an astute young woman and you do travel in a wide circle of people. Of course, if you do hear anything—"

"I'll let you know. I would be interested in learning how he died."

"As will I. I am sorry to say that those reporters will likely have recognized you, Miss del Cameron. I might suggest that you make yourself unavailable for the time being. Visit Mombassa, perhaps. That is, until we need your testimony for an inquest."

"I'm afraid leaving is not possible. I have to be at Mrs. Postlewaithe's garden party tomorrow, of all places. The Girl Guides are giving an archery demonstration. Perhaps they can shoot the reporters."

"Indeed. At times I'm inclined to agree with you. Let me get one of the constables to take you home."

Jade rose and Finch stood with her. "That won't be necessary, Inspector," Jade said. "I think a walk will do me good. Help me clear my head."

Jade initially intended to turn north towards Parklands. Then she remembered what Emily had said about the rest of the mail being ready today. *Maybe there's a letter from Sam.* She turned south to the post office and set off at a brisk pace, hoping to lose some of her on-edge feeling.

The postal clerk told her that someone had already come by that morning to pick up the mail. Suddenly she felt the need for haste and decided to find a taxi to get back sooner.

"Thank you," Jade said. "Sorry to bother you for nothing."

"Wait a moment," called the clerk as Jade turned. "Miss del Cameron, right?" Jade nodded. "Ah, good. I *do* have something for you. The package must have fallen into some mud, because the address was barely legible. However, after some brushing, I was able to make out the name Cameron. Only finished cleaning it now." He handed over a very dirty parcel wrapped in brown paper and twine. As the clerk had said, "Cameron" and "Nairobi" were the only words clearly readable amid the grime and the blurred letters. If there had been a return address, it was obliterated.

As soon as the package touched Jade's hands, she shivered. A nauseating fear gripped her and her heart pounded. Beads of sweat broke out on her brow. For nearly a minute, she stood rooted to the spot, unable to will her legs to move.

"Miss, are you all right?" asked the clerk. "This is yours, isn't it?"

Jade nodded and noticed two businessmen staring at her. "Thank you," she murmured, and went outside. The sun's heat and the noise of the now bustling city helped to chase away some of the dread that had struck her. She found a quiet bench down the street and attacked the string with her knife as though she were attacking someone intent on harming her.

Get a hold of yourself. It's just a package. Probably something from Mother.

It wasn't.

Inside was a silk neck scarf, the sort that aviators wore, only this one was splattered and stained rusty red with dried blood. A note written in David Worthy's elegant but masculine hand read: *I won't let you go. You belong to me!*

A cold sweat broke out on Jade's arms. Her hands shook, and her heart hammered in her ears as she dropped the packet to the ground.

CHAPTER 4

*The Athi River teems with fish and many of them are not only tasty
but make very good sport for the fisherman.*
—The Traveler

By all appearances, Beverly was chatting with Mrs. Archibald and Lady Northey, but Jade knew that her friend was also keeping an eye on her. Ever since Madeline had found Jade sitting on the post office bench, the silk scarf lying at her feet, they'd all been worried about her. Madeline had come into Nairobi as she'd promised, bringing Biscuit to the house before going into town to shop. After she saw Jade, Maddy escorted her back to the police headquarters and insisted on having the scarf and the paper it was wrapped in fingerprinted before taking Jade home. Since then, Bev hadn't let Jade out of her sight. Now, a day later at Mary Postlewaithe's birthday garden party, Jade could feel Bev's eyes on her back as she gave the girls an impromptu lesson on observing footprints on Mrs. Postlewaithe's lawn.

"Gwendolyn, Clarice, you girls pick someone at the party and see if you can follow where they've been," Jade said. The girls set off, searching out their quarry, leaving the other girls behind. Jade, in deference to Beverly's position in the colony, had worn a loose, calf-length walking skirt over her trousers and boots, as she'd done in the ambulance corps. If the skirt wasn't fashionable, it at least hid the pants and her knife and suited the approved attire for a Girl Guide lieutenant. Of course, the slender cheetah standing beside her caused more of a stir than her costume. Jade watched the first pair of girls for a while, eavesdropping on Beverly's conversation with the governor's wife while she waited.

"The girls are going to give an archery demonstration later, Lady Northey," Beverly said. "I'm sure you'll agree that archery is splendid physical exercise for young ladies. Even our late and beloved Empress Victoria practiced archery."

"Indeed," said Lady Northey. "I'm certain *you* would never allow the girls to do anything improper."

Jade smiled. *No, but she's worried that I might.* She looked at the girls in front of her, who were practically quivering with excitement while they awaited instructions. She gave them. "Now see if you can follow their tracks." They skipped off in the direction that their friends had taken, slowing to a walk as they studied the ground.

"Then if you'll excuse me, Lady Northey, Mrs. Archibald, I'll just see to the girls," said Beverly. Bev hurried to Jade's side and grabbed her by her sleeve. "Oh, that woman is an insufferable snob. Her attitude towards single women in the colony is positively antiquated."

Jade didn't ask which of the two women Bev meant. Everyone had read Lady Northey's scathing article in the papers, decrying single women trying to farm or work on their own. Only women of means or married women had a right to live here, according to her.

"How are you feeling?" Bev asked Jade.

"I'm well enough," Jade answered, avoiding Beverly's eyes. Bev could spot her in a fib in an instant. "I can't seem to shake this feeling that my skin is crawling and that someone is watching me."

"I'm watching you."

"Besides you, Bev."

Beverly scanned the attendees, an assortment of adults related to the Girl Guides. "Well, several men have had their eyes on you, love, despite that horridly outdated skirt you have on."

"It's what I wear to church, Bev. And I thought as Girl Guide leaders we weren't supposed to dress to attract attention." She nodded at Beverly's own costume, a pretty but simply cut buttercup yellow dress with only a touch of lace at the collar and at the ends of the elbow-length sleeves. Compared to Lady Northey's rose-colored silk, it was definitely plain but far more becoming.

"We are, but I'm telling you that even in that outfit you look quite fetching to the men and *that* explains this feeling that you're being watched. It's common gossip that Sam left, and you know there are several eligible gentlemen in the colony. Shall I tell you who is looking?"

"No! Introduce them to Emily."

"I have, but don't be surprised if Steven Holly comes over."

Jade made a low growling noise. "Can't your sister keep him occupied?"

"Emily's busy with that new missionary gentleman, Dr. Landrake Dymant, and the postmaster, Mr. Hamilton. We could join them if you like." Beverly nodded towards her sister, who wore a powder blue linen dress and a wide-brimmed straw hat trimmed in matching satin roses. She was speaking with a middle-aged man with hair the color of wheat. His bushy beard bore traces of gray strands amid the golden brown. He matched Emily's height of five feet, five inches, but looked shorter because of his disproportionate build. Somehow his legs looked unable to support his expansive chest.

Bev led the way and Jade followed, preferring to stay by her friend and have some hope of intelligent conversation rather than risk Mr. Holly's silly, self-centered attempts at repartee. She gave a slight tug to Biscuit's leash and the cat immediately fell in step beside her. They joined the group as Dr. Dymant was explaining his reasons for coming to Kenya Colony.

"I spent several years in India and have acquired a certain respect for the Hindu," Dymant explained. "But I felt I should look to those Indians who have made their home here in this colony. I have heard that they are not as well looked after as one might hope, but I intend to take care of that *dreckly*," he said, slipping into an old dialect.

"Their houses and shops are atrocious," declared Hamilton. "Do you realize that there were four more instances of plague in the Indian district last month? It's shameful."

"So much disease in Africa," said Emily. "Although I understand that Kenya Colony is much healthier than the interior. Why, I read that leprosy still haunts parts of the Belgian Congo."

"Leprosy is the least of the Congo's troubles," said Hamilton. "I fear they'll never recover from Leopold's rule. He encouraged every villain to brutalize and torture the natives in order to extract the last ounce of gold that he could wring from that land. Some of the atrocities! And not all from Belgians either. I heard tell of an English overlord who routinely cut off the ears of the laborers and branded them—"

"Ahem," said Dymant. "Such topics are probably not appropriate for a lady's ears." He nodded towards Emily, Bev, and Jade.

"That is what is most curious," persisted Hamilton. "Some claim that it was an English*woman* in charge—"

Emily gasped and Hamilton blushed. "My apologies. I forgot myself."

"You are forgiven," said Emily. She beamed at Dr. Dymant. "It is so good of you to come, Doctor. I'm sure Kenya can use a fine medical man such as yourself."

Before Dr. Dymant could reply, Hamilton chimed in again. "The colony is a splendid place, to be sure, but it seems to be attracting a considerable amount of riffraff," he said. "Er, not meaning yourself, Doctor. I was speaking of this latest news in the paper. Death on the Limuru Bridge, no less. The medical examination said that the man had consumed far too much alcohol. That smacks of an accident due to overindulgence."

"Most tragic," said Dymant. "Perhaps a suicide?"

"That is what the *Leader* hinted at," said Hamilton. "Of course, the police have been very closemouthed about it. But the *Leader* even suggested there was a woman involved. One was spotted at the bridge with the inspector but he bundled her out before anyone could speak with her. All they could say was that she wore trousers." Hamilton looked pointedly at Jade when he said this.

"If you are implying that Jade was the female, Mr. Hamilton," said Emily, "then you should remember that she's never without her cheetah, and the paper failed to mention seeing one of those."

"But did you hear what they found?"

Everyone turned to the new speaker, Steven Holly. The banker wore a belted jacket in a pale brown plaid with a golf-style cap, and looked every bit the dandy he was. Jade stifled a groan. Holly, a notorious womanizer, had pursued her on several occasions, and more frequently since Sam had been gone.

"Yes, Mr. Holly," said Beverly. "They found a pea-sized piece of gold. Hardly a fortune."

"No, indeed," said Holly, "but it wasn't the nugget that was important. It's what it represents. I know, because I'm a part of it, too."

"Part of what?" asked Hamilton and Emily simultaneously.

"Part of a gold mine in the northern territory, of course," said Holly. He wore a big grin plastered on his face and rocked up and down on his toes as he watched their reactions.

"A gold mine?" asked Beverly. Skepticism riddled her words.

"Yes, Lady Dunbury," said Holly. "I shall be a rich man." He smiled and winked at Jade. "But I doubt this was any more than an accident," he continued. "Dr. Mathews performed an autopsy and could find no obvious cause of death aside from hitting his head in the accident. The man was quite gassed, you know."

"Dr. Mathews, did you say?" asked Dymant. "I knew a Mathews in medical college. A year ahead of me. Pleasant fellow. Wonder if it's the same man." He threw one arm across his broad chest and balanced the other on it, his fingers tapping his lips as he thought. "Can't remember his first name, something biblical. Peter?"

"Paul?" suggested Emily.

"Yes, I believe it was."

"Then that's your man," said Hamilton. "He does a good bit of work for the police department, when he's around. But he's gone extensively, visiting the military outposts and some of the native villages."

"Yes, quite," said Holly, impatience edging his voice. "But as I was saying, I'm sure this dead Stockton chap had shares in the same mine that I have. It would be too much of a coincidence to have two such mines up north, wouldn't it?"

"Indeed," said Inspector Finch, who'd just arrived. "Pardon me for intruding, but I'm trying to find out more about our friend Stockton. I'm making the rounds of several social functions in the hope of speaking to as many people in one place as possible." He gestured with one hand towards Mrs. Postlewaithe. "I've asked our hostess and she's agreed to let me disturb the party for a few moments, provided I don't let the children hear about this."

"Perhaps I'd better see that they keep out of the way," said Beverly. "Jade, will you come with me?"

"Miss del Cameron should stay here, if you please, Lady Dunbury. I'd like to speak with her, too."

Jade caught Hamilton's smirk, as if he'd been vindicated in thinking the woman mentioned in the papers was Jade. Finch noticed. "I need to speak with Miss del Cameron about a strange parcel she received. Perhaps, since it came through the post, Mr. Hamilton, I should interview *you* as well."

Hamilton colored and coughed. "I don't handle the posts myself, Inspector. You should know that. And I don't know anything about the man who went off the Limuru Bridge, so if you'll excuse me . . ." He touched his cap and made a slight bow to Emily and to Jade before drifting off to a more amiable group.

Finch ignored him. "Then you knew this Stockton, Mr. Holly?" he asked.

"Never met the chap," said Holly. "I only supposed that he and I were partners in the same mine. Rather a surprise actually. I didn't know there was another investor when I came in on it."

Dr. Dymant cleared his throat to cut in. "If you'll excuse me as well, Inspector, I don't have anything to tell you and I must get back to town. I've an appointment at three o'clock to see about a possible office space and that just leaves me time to make my excuses to our hostess."

He bowed to Emily, nodded to Jade, and left. Emily hesitated only a second before accompanying him to his automobile.

"Well, I seem to have lost some of my audience," said Holly. "I trust you won't desert me, Jade."

"If you have any news for me, Inspector, you can find me *after* you're finished talking to Mr. Holly. Come on, Biscuit, let's find Bev."

"I say," said Holly as Jade hurried off.

She found Beverly directing the two oldest girls, Helen and Mary, to set up their archery target on the lawn, away from the party.

"Is Uncle Steven talking about his gold mine again?" asked Mary.

Jade nodded. "Yes, he's very excited about it." She looked over her shoulder to see him accost yet another victim. This time it was Dr. Mathews, who'd just arrived, apparently look-ing for Finch. He wore a belted tweed jacket and motoring gloves, a golf-style cap on his head. Mathews was listening politely as Holly expounded on his good fortune, his voice gaining in volume until Jade could overhear snippets of the monologue. Words like "collateral" and "nugget" reached her. The volume increased as Holly, Finch, and Mathews all joined her.

"You didn't hear this part, Jade. I was just telling the doc-tor here and Finch what a stroke of luck when a chap named Waters came into my bank. Wanted a loan for equipment. Naturally I was intrigued. Interesting fellow. A bit taciturn at first. Actually travels with a parrot. Tragic about that other fellow, Stockton, but I should think my shares will be larger now."

"Uncle Steven!" scolded Mary. She put her hands on her hips and shook her head. "This is *my* birthday party and I do not want to hear any more about your silly mine. Will you please help us bring out our archery target? It is in the gar-den hut." She turned to Jade and Beverly, her eyes wide with anticipation. "Oh, wait until you see it. Helen and I made it ourselves. It's really splendid." She scampered off with her uncle and Helen to fetch it. Finch moved on to speak to someone else.

"Mr. Holly is quite enthusiastic, isn't he?" commented Mathews with a chuckle.

"That's the polite way of putting it," said Jade. Biscuit wound himself around her legs, impatient after having sat so long in one place. Jade reached down and stroked his head after extricating him from his leash.

"Such a beautiful cat," said Mathews. "May I pet him?"

"Let me introduce you to him first." She showed Mathews how to hold out his gloved hand in a relaxed fist, palm down, for Biscuit to sniff. "Biscuit, friend." Biscuit looked at the glove and at Dr. Mathews before gently butting his head on the knuckles. "That should do it, Dr. Mathews."

He extended his fingers and reached for the broad head, his fingertips barely skimming the top of Biscuit's fur. "He's very soft."

"I'm not sure you're actually making contact, Doctor. You don't need to be afraid. He won't bite a friend."

"Ah, yes, of course," said Mathews, and he slowly lowered his hand until it rested on Biscuit's head before lightly stroking it. "Very nice."

"There was someone here at the party earlier who thought he knew you, Dr. Mathews," said Beverly. "You can't have missed him by more than a quarter of an hour. He's a new medical doctor come to treat the Indian population."

"Oh?" asked Mathews.

"Yes, his name is Dr. Dymant. Landrake Dymant," said Beverly. "Do you recall him?"

Mathews' brows furrowed as he puzzled over the name. "Cannot say that I do. He said he knew me?"

"He said he was a year behind you in medical school," said Jade.

"Ah, well, that would explain why I don't recollect him. One tended to stay within one's own ranks, you know. Still . . ." He closed his eyes as he tried to recall a name or face. "Yes, I think I do remember someone by that name. Cornish, as you'd expect with a surname like Dymant. Tall fellow, slender, dark. Very penetrating blue eyes."

Beverly laughed. "Just the opposite, Dr. Mathews. Shorter

than you by several inches, straw brown hair, beard, brown eyes, strongly built chest. But he *did* sound Cornish."

"Ah, possibly a brother or cousin, then, of the man I knew."

Emily joined them, accompanied by Mr. Lippincott, a clerk in the land office. His thick spectacles gave him a serious, scholarly appearance, especially with his graying temples. Holly returned at that moment with the girls, a big straw lion in his arms. At least, Jade assumed it was a lion, with the mass of straw protruding at all angles from the head end. A red heart was pinned just behind the shoulders, or what passed for them. Holly set it down with a sneeze and dusted the loose straw from his coat. Mary and Helen giggled as they adjusted the wooden limbs supporting the straw beast while Holly hurried back towards Jade.

"Lippincott," Steven Holly called, "you're just the man to tell me about this gold mine. I'm sure you've seen the papers that Mr. Waters filed."

"I don't recall, but then I don't always handle the mining paperwork," Lippincott said.

"That's quite enough, gentlemen," said Beverly. "The girls are going to demonstrate some of their woodcraft skills for us."

She took a whistle and lanyard from the pocket of her dress and blew it once to gather the girls together. It also served to gain everyone else's notice. Conversations ceased or dropped to a murmur as people speculated on what was about to transpire. The girls clustered around Jade and Beverly, each taking a turn at petting Biscuit.

"Girls," Beverly said, "get your bows. Mary, you may bring out the arrows." When the girls ran off in various directions to fetch their weapons, Beverly addressed the adults. "Ladies and gentlemen, as you know, in keeping with the Girl Guide manual, the Ivy Leaf Patrol has been working hard to gain a wood-lore badge. They've studied tracking and bird identification—"

"And how to bring down an ox with a stone," said Clarice Chivell's father. He had made the trip into town with his wife just to see his daughter, who boarded at school, as did Helen.

A round of laughter followed his little joke. Jade noticed that Lady Northey didn't join in and her smile looked pinched and forced.

"Yes, indeed. David defended his flock with a sling, and the girls are learning its value, too," said Beverly.

Jade knew that Beverly was referring to the biblical David and not her former beau, but at the mention of his name, she shuddered. Perhaps it was the crowd and the noise, but all through this party she'd fought the urge to bolt for safety, sometimes imagining she saw shadows out of the corners of her eyes. She caught Dr. Mathews' concerned look and fought for self-control.

"But today we have a treat. The girls are going to demonstrate their newest skill, archery. Bear in mind that they've only had one lesson, but I believe with practice we shall have a set of proficients. Girls, are you ready?"

The patrol stood ramrod straight in a line, bows in one hand and quivers of arrows slung over their backs. Jade saw a larger bow, the one she'd used to demonstrate with, leaning against a tree.

The parents and family friends gathered behind Beverly to watch the girls. Helen, as the patrol's senior member, announced that Mary would have first crack at the target, since it was her birthday. Mary stood thirty feet from the straw lion, nocked her arrow, and assumed the proper sidewise stance. Jade noted with approval that she kept her left elbow slightly flexed and the wrist gripping the bow straight. Mary drew the arrow's fletching to her cheek and let fly. The arrow pierced the dummy's head and exited the other side.

Cries of "Bravo" and "Well shot" followed. Mary made a slight bow before returning to the end of the line. One by one, the younger girls took their turn, some standing closer to the target. They hit the dummy in the rump, the nose, and the leg, but none pierced the heart. As far as Jade could see, the parents couldn't have been prouder anyway, and each girl received her share of applause and accolades.

"That will teach old simba to attack our girls, won't it?" said Mr. Gault after his daughter, Lily, landed an arrow on the target's nose.

Helen, who shot last and hit the straw cat in the hindquarters, walked up to Jade holding the large bow. "If you would please demonstrate for us again, Lieutenant Jade," she said with a salute.

Jade took the bow with a smile while Beverly shooed everyone farther back, explaining that Jade would shoot from where she stood at nearly one hundred feet. Mary handed Jade an arrow and stepped aside, joining Helen. Jade thought she detected a knowing look pass between the girls and dismissed it as troop pride in their instructor.

Better make this one count then.

Jade turned sideways to the target and drew back her bow, her fingertips barely grazing her cheek. She took one deep breath, held it, and released the arrow. It flew true and struck the paper heart dead center.

Polite applause followed, but Jade paid it no mind. All her attention was focused on the paper heart. It pulsed softly, as though the arrow had brought it to life. She could almost hear it, beating in time with her own. The red shifted in a creeping mass until it coalesced into thick blood and dripped onto the ground just as Jade dropped her bow.

CHAPTER 5

But with the fish also come the crocodiles.

—The Traveler

"Jade, are you all right? Jade!" Beverly's voice came from a distance like a memory, one of an abandoned basement, a bloodstained scarf, and David's cryptic ring—the ring that held the clue to his father's murder. Jade looked at her hands, expecting to see that ring there. It took Finch's hand gripping her elbow to snap her back to the present.

"It's just paint," he whispered. "Nothing to be alarmed at. Only the girls having a lark, it seems."

Dozens of voices chattered around her. No one else seemed to notice her reaction. A few mothers with hands over their open mouths expressed shock over such a horrid stunt. Others tittered and most of the men laughed outright. The girls, watchful of their parents' reactions, suppressed giggles or openly expressed their delight in the joke.

It's a good one at that. And now that she'd picked up her bow and walked over to the target, Jade saw that the spreading red puddle was nothing more than paint.

"Mary! Helen! Was this your idea?" she asked.

They nodded. "Yes, but Uncle Steven helped," admitted

Mary. "We couldn't think what to use to hold the paint until I remembered those bags made from a goat's stomach that the natives use for carrying milk. Uncle Steven bought one for me."

"Were you surprised, Miss Jade?" asked Helen.

"Very."

"You're not angry, are you?" asked Helen. "You looked . . . well, rather queer just then."

"I'm not angry and I'm fine. But I don't believe that Lady Northey appreciated the joke."

The girls looked past Jade to the governor's wife and paled. "Oh, dear," said Mary.

"I wouldn't worry about it too much," Jade said as Beverly approached Lady Northey. "I'm sure your leader will smooth things over, but in the future, you might think twice before doing anything like that again." She saw how downcast each of them looked and smiled at them. "If it's any consolation to you, it's a trick much like I used to pull when I was a girl."

"Really?" asked Mary. "And did *you* ever get in trouble?"

Jade recalled the paddling she'd gotten on her backside when she'd put a dead snake under a parlor chair just before her mother's library committee meeting. She grinned. "Yes, I did. But it was worth it."

Jade called to Biscuit and went off to wait for Beverly away from the crowds. Even though the girls had come up with this prank, it didn't lessen Jade's unease. That paint had looked too real to her, throbbing with a life of its own. She wanted to escape the noise and go home, something she couldn't do without Beverly, since they'd arrived together. Dr. Mathews followed close by as though reading her mind.

"If Lady Dunbury is unable to leave now, I'll be happy to see you safely home," he said. "Indeed, it would be best if you did go. I saw how you reacted. You're not well."

"I'm only tired," Jade said. She caught Beverly's eye and waited while her friend excused herself from Lady Northey.

"Are you ready to leave?" asked Beverly. She studied Jade's face.

"Yes. How much trouble are the girls in?" asked Jade.

Beverly grinned. "The little darlings created quite a stir with their prank. I shouldn't wonder if I was deposed as patrol leader soon. But I believe we can drive home now. I've already made my good-byes to our hostess. Having a baby waiting at home with a nanny is a wonderful excuse for leaving early."

"I'm glad Miss del Cameron has a good friend to watch out for her," said Mathews. "But I am still happy to follow. I could prescribe a sedative for you."

"Thank you, but no, Dr. Mathews. I'll be fine. I just want to sit on my porch, put my feet up, and drink a cup of coffee." She looked at Beverly during the last part, hoping her friend would take the hint. She didn't.

Mathews frowned. "I would not advise it. That would only agitate you more. You must get some rest. I'm leaving early tomorrow for Fort Hall and some of the native villages. I'll be absent about a week, but I intend to look in on you as soon as I return." He bowed to both of them.

"He's a good man," said Beverly after he'd gone. "Though I'd advise caution, Jade. It's entirely possible that he's interested in you as more than just a patient."

"All the more reason for not letting him tend to me."

*   *   *

JADE'S REST PERIOD, once she was home, lasted three-quarters of an hour. She'd changed out of her skirt, made a cup of the spiced tea, and settled herself on her porch with Biscuit at her feet. The tea wasn't half-bad, but she still missed her coffee. She'd have to talk to Bev about that or just sneak off and buy some without telling her. But try as she might to relax, she couldn't stop fidgeting. She kept envisioning the pulsing red liquid that had flowed from the target.

Jade decided to get her camping gear together instead. Most of the older girls were counting on a little safari, and Jade and Beverly planned to take them next weekend to Fourteen Falls, on the Athi River. Jade intended to leave after tomorrow's Mass to scout out a good spot. The falls were also near enough to Jelani's village to allow a visit. She owed one to the young Kikuyu healer whom she'd befriended on her first trip to Africa.

She pulled out a thin bedroll, her cooking kit, a tin mug, and her coffeepot, then stowed all but the bedroll in a canvas rucksack along with her tin of tea, matches, and a long-handled fork. She set the bundle beside her wooden chop box, which already held a small cast-iron skillet, a tin of flour, baking powder, a bit of lard, a wooden bowl, and a few tins of beef. Jade took her fishing rod from the wall along with her Winchester, a newer model that her father had given her for a birthday gift. Not that she planned on hunting for game. But this was Africa and it didn't hold to go out unprepared. She set her tackle box atop the chop box. With any luck, she'd have some fresh fish to go with her biscuits. If not, she'd have the canned beef.

Biscuit padded through her open door and sniffed the boxes.

"Don't worry. You're coming, too. But if I don't catch any fish, you're going to have to hunt for yourself." The cheetah brushed lightly against her exposed forearm, and Jade felt her skin prickle. A vague shadow darted just out of view and she turned her head to see if a rodent had come in through the open door.

Not likely. Not with Biscuit on patrol. She turned to her packing and shivered again. This time her back irritated her, as though she had returned to the war and was living in that flea-bitten farmhouse cellar.

"I need some air," she said as she stepped outside. She spied Beverly and Avery walking her way. "I thought you two were going to the theater tonight," Jade said.

"We are," said Beverly. "And we're dining at the New Stanley first. I wanted to see how you were before I dressed for dinner." She studied Jade's face. "You didn't rest very long."

"Didn't try to." She pointed to the pile inside the door. "I've been busy."

"Ah," said Avery. "So you still plan to scout out a camping spot for the junior Amazons?"

Jade nodded. "Getting out of this crowded city will do me good. I plan to see Jelani, then do some fishing." She sat down on the step and motioned for her friends to join her. "What did you think about Steven Holly's gold mine announcement? Do you really think there's gold up north?"

Avery shook his head. "I shouldn't think so, but then, in point of fact, I have no idea. There's gold in the Belgian Congo and I believe someone found traces in the Tanganyika Territory, but no one has ever found much in the way of minerals in Kenya Colony. I'm wondering if Holly didn't invest in a pig in a poke."

"Oh, dear," said Beverly. "He may be a bit of a scamp, but I'd hate to see someone take advantage of him."

"Aren't you both jumping to conclusions?" asked Jade. "We know nothing about this gold mine beyond Holly's boasts."

"You're probably correct, Jade," said Avery. "It's just that I think it would be rather simpleminded for Mr. Holly to enter into something unproven. He's a bank clerk. I'd expect him to know something about business."

"But he said that this man Waters had samples," said Beverly. "Isn't that proof?"

Avery smiled at his wife. "You are too trusting, my dear. Anyone could carry in a bit of gold he had purchased and say it came from his mine. Mr. Holly would have done better to go to the site himself and take a sample of the area for assay."

Jade rubbed her arms and twitched her shoulders. Beverly frowned. "You're very agitated this evening, Jade. You might be catching something. Are you feverish? Have you been drinking your tonic water and using the mosquito netting?"

"Bev," said Jade, "I love you dearly, but I'm not sick."

"I could call old Dr. Burkitt in," Beverly said. "Malaria is nothing to be sneezed at."

"I don't want or need a doctor."

"Then at least stay at the house tonight. Let our cook prepare something for you. Matthew *mpishi* makes lovely chicken soup."

The left side of Jade's mouth twitched. "I don't have malaria. I need solitude, Bev, not mothering. And I don't need a personal *mpishi*. I can cook for myself. I plan to scramble some eggs over my little spirit stove, butter up a slab of bread, and call it an early night."

"You're not riding your motorcycle on the trip tomorrow, are you?" asked Beverly. "I don't think——"

Avery coughed and shook his head, hinting to his wife to drop the matter. "Our Jade knows that she can have the use of my new motor truck anytime she wishes. I shan't need it for a few days. I'm sure Biscuit will be much more comfortable riding in it than running alongside the motorcycle for such a distance. There won't be room in the sidecar with the gear."

"Thank you, Avery. I thought about going into town to hire a truck."

"Nonsense. It's too late in the day for that. And she's full of petrol and ready to go." He stood and gently raised his wife to her feet. "Come along, darling. Time to get ready. Jade's a big girl, you know."

Beverly laughed. "You're quite right, Avery. I've been horrid. It's motherhood, you know. I suddenly want to fuss over everyone. Forgive me, Jade?"

"Nothing to forgive, Bev. You're a good friend. Have a lovely time and if I don't see you early tomorrow morning, I'll see you when I return."

She watched them stroll arm in arm back to their house, waiting until they were inside before she gave in to the shudder that she'd tightly controlled. Her right eye twitched twice. "Some peace and quiet is all I need, Biscuit. That and a good night's sleep."

She got neither.

She tried reading, but the letters on the page jiggled like crawling bugs. Jade put aside the book, a Jack London adventure, and undressed. She lay on her bed, wearing her camisole and linen drawers, and prayed for her skin to stop creeping before she shed it like a snake. Waking reality blended with her sleeping dreams. The very walls of her bedroom shifted and moved, sometimes receding, sometimes closing in on her.

Her heartbeat echoed in her ears, and a cold sweat broke out on her forehead. She felt as she had when she'd sat in the bait half of a leopard trap. Jade's fingers clawed at the bed frame, fighting for a way out. Her chest tightened as her lungs struggled to pull in enough air.

Maybe I do have malaria! Jade struggled out of bed, intent on pouring a glass of tonic water, but she spilled half the bottle onto the floor.

Then she heard Biscuit's soft growl, an agitated churring sound. She froze, listening.

Something moaned outside, and her nose caught the faintest whiff of smoke.

Fire?

She stumbled into her trousers and stepped outside in her bare feet. She looked first to the main house, then to the stables. Nothing. Biscuit churred again and she followed his gaze. Her darkroom stood several hundred feet away, and the hazy white smoke of a smoldering fire wafted in front of it.

Jade started for the tool hut, intent on finding a shovel, when a flickering movement caught her eye. Out of the haze emerged a figure, shifting and shimmying with the smoke.

David!

He wore his leather flying jacket and a silk scarf, and raised his hand in greeting. Jade blinked twice, then a third time, hoping each time that the vision would disappear.

It didn't. Instead, as she watched, his face melted into nothing and, in its place, a skull grinned back at her. The apparition moaned again.

Jade collapsed to the ground, her own anguished cry ringing through the night.

CHAPTER 6

The irony is—it's not safe to fish when the fishing is good.
—The Traveler

BISCUIT NOSED JADE, prodding her with his big head. She felt him, but didn't move. She was too terrified, frightened in a way she hadn't experienced since she'd fought the rising panic when a shell-shocked victim had broken into insane laughter in the back of her ambulance. A hyena's warbling laugh had triggered the reaction, too, at least until she'd faced it and fought it down.

She lay on the ground huddled in a ball, clutching herself and trembling, afraid to open her eyes for fear of seeing that hideous apparition. She'd seen soldiers react to firecrackers popping or to wafting scents. Some became belligerent; others cringed. Many never knew what set off the attacks. Why was she seeing apparitions *now*? What was triggering *her* terrors?

Am I going insane? She recalled Sam's violent ravings during a recent illness. *Maybe I do have malaria.* At present she'd take the disease over losing her mind.

Biscuit's raspy tongue scraped her cheek, and Jade drew reassurance from the cheetah's solid presence. She raised her head and risked a glance at the darkroom. Nothing. Barely a remnant of smoke.

Suddenly, Jade felt embarrassed. "Sweet Millard Fillmore's bathtub, what is the matter with me?" she muttered. "Overreacting to nothing!"

Well, not entirely nothing. Someone had sent her the bloody scarf and the first letter. Those items were real, and Jade had an idea who was behind them. David's mother, Olivia Lilith Worthy, hated her and had tried to kill her once before. That she was in prison in London only meant she must have a confederate in Africa doing her bidding. A minion could be dealt with. Jade had done it before. The problem was in discovering who it was. And it still didn't explain her hallucinations.

So what's wrong with me? The problem lay in her mind, in seeing crawling letters, shifting walls, and creeping blood. *And David.*

She knew what Beverly would say, that she should see Dr. Burkitt or talk to the French priests at the Ngong mission. But Jade dreaded doctors and she'd avoided the holy fathers, attending the Catholic church in town instead. The last time she'd been to the mission, they'd invited her to bring Sam to visit. *And Sam's not here.*

Her jaw clenched with a twinge of anger. *He ought to be here, blast it!*

Jade got to her feet and stroked Biscuit's back, building up her resolve to inspect the darkroom. After a few moments' hesitation, she took a step towards the structure. "Let's go, Biscuit. If I don't face this now, I never will."

There was little to see. Jade squatted and pawed at some damp straw. It felt warm to the touch. Underneath it were a few blackened patches. She picked up a handful and sniffed. Definitely burned. Nearby were a spent match and a cigarette butt.

"It looks as if the cook or one of the kitchen help decided to have an evening smoke, Biscuit." She held up the remnants of the hand-rolled butt. Biscuit sneezed and took a step back. "It's a good thing some of this straw was still damp or we might have had a serious problem."

And the vision? Jade put it down to a lack of sleep.

She stood, wondering if she should leave a note for Bev and Avery to find when they came home, then decided against waking the rest of the household. "I'll be back in a day or two anyway."

In the end, Jade returned to her bungalow, and the next morning, after early Mass at St. Joseph's, loaded up Avery's truck with her gear and Biscuit and drove towards Ol Donyo Sabuk. Immediately after Thika, she left the main road and cut southeast on a smaller road towards the mountain. Recently, a bridge spanning the Athi had been built, making the trip to Ol Donyo Sabuk easier. Jade wasn't surprised. Sir William Northrup McMillan's farm, Juja, sat near and, in part, on it. Game was good and many people, including President Roosevelt, had hunted there. A bridge was inevitable. But as far as she knew, McMillan himself, in all his seven-foot glory, was abroad now, his health failing.

The first time Jade had made this trip she'd been on horseback, on her way to Jelani's village to hunt a man-eating hyena. She'd forded the river below the falls, watching for crocodiles. Everything she'd seen had inspired awe, from the lone antelope bounding away to the sight of Mount Kenya looming in the distance. Mount Kenya's imposing grandeur still moved her and she wondered why she'd never yet made a trip to it. Perhaps she could go there. It was one place that held no memories shared with Sam.

Two kudu, startled by the truck, darted out of the thicket where they had been browsing. Jade admired their gracefully spiraled horns and their beautiful tawny coats. The thin white stripes that ran down their sides from their spines reminded her of icing drizzled on a cake. Biscuit wriggled in the seat beside Jade, his head hanging out the open window.

"They're too big for you, boy."

The kudu stopped several hundred feet away and looked over their shoulders at the truck with an air that said, "You cannot catch us." Farther on, a family of baboons watched them, the nearby thorn tree promising them a safe haven should they need it. One juvenile hid behind his mother, peering over her back as Jade drove by.

Jade slowed to take the bridge, amazed at the volume of water that still gushed underneath, remnants of the longer rainy season. Not far downstream, the flow met with large blocks of blackened igneous rock that divided the water and sent it cascading in an arc of waterfalls, enough to earn the area its name of Fourteen Falls.

A mile downstream on the south side of the river sat Jelani's village, but Jade skirted the mountain towards Harry Hascombe's old cattle ranch at the southern end. Jade had stayed there in a guest hut after killing that hyena. A hankering to see both Harry's ranch and that of his deceased neighbor, Roger Forster, seized Jade. She couldn't have explained why the sudden need except that both men had been involved in that first search for David Worthy's missing half brother. With David haunting her waking hours, it was reason enough. The detour might supply her with some answers.

Biscuit chirped once, his eyes intently searching the landscape.

"You recognize your old home, boy? You know Harry doesn't live there anymore."

She found the ranch, or rather, what was left of it. Harry's house still stood, but the outbuildings had long been stripped of every usable scrap of wood or galvanized tin by neighboring tribes. Most of the mud and thatch guest huts had crumbled and collapsed. Jade found the one she'd slept in once. It still stood, but the door was gone and the thatch roof had decayed and fallen into the interior. A mouse scurried off as she kicked at the pile.

"There's not much left, is there, Biscuit? All the old animal pens are gone."

Biscuit padded softly around the grounds, pausing to inspect some rubble.

"Come on, boy. I don't know what I hoped to see here, but we're wasting our time." She led the cat back to the truck and drove away, steering the truck towards Roger Forster's farm, which adjoined to the east. Again, she had no real reason to go there, just a feeling that she needed to see it. Forster's farm had been sold to a woman after his death, but when a fire destroyed the house, no one had ever taken up residence. Like Harry's land, it had reverted to wilderness as the forested slopes of Ol Donyo Sabuk, the mountain of the buffalo, crept down to reclaim their rightful realm.

Jade had never seen Forster's farm. If she had expected old ostrich pens and a great blackened char where the house had stood, she was bound to be disappointed. Grasses and a few seedlings sprang from one spot, where the house had probably stood, but the fire ash had long since been absorbed by the ground and seedlings starved for nutrients. Orange, bronze, black, and white swallowtails flitted and supped at invisible flowers tucked into the dense forest. The thick green hardwoods were broken only by black-and-white-banded boulders like petrified zebra.

She had no idea how many outbuildings Forster had possessed, but like those on Harry's farm, most had collapsed or stood as hollow shells without roofs. Only one remained intact, a small shed or kitchen made of masonry. A thorn tree that grew directly in front of the door explained why no one had managed to scavenge that wood.

She heard a soft noise as dried leaves rustled and a twig cracked. Biscuit heard it, too, which gave Jade a feeling of relief. The way her mind had been working lately, she didn't know if she could trust her senses. Wary of the buffalo that roamed this region, she slipped her rifle from her shoulder. A vervet monkey, her black face prominent above her white chest, had left her treetop to scavenge for food on the ground. She'd found what looked like a creamy white tuber and was turning it over in her hands. Then she spied Biscuit and screamed. Biscuit gave chase, but the little monkey was quicker. She leaped onto the stone building, dropping her prize. Jade picked it up and was surprised to see it was a candle stub. She dropped it onto the ground.

"Leave her alone, Biscuit. It's time to leave and go see Jelani."

At the sound of the youth's name, Biscuit trotted back to the truck and jumped inside. Next to Jade, the cheetah loved Jelani best, and Biscuit never missed an opportunity to visit the young Kikuyu healer. Jade took the drive slowly, maneuvering Avery's Dodge truck around the rocks, wallows, and occasional termite mound. Her route would have taken her closer to the river not far below the falls, but she saw another truck parked beside it. Assuming that someone was fishing and wouldn't appreciate the noise, she veered away from the Athi until she neared Jelani's village.

She parked the truck at the base of the short hill and walked the narrow, winding path to the huts. On the way she passed several *shambas*, the gardens being hoed by women with sticks. A few had babies strapped to their hips, snuggled in cloth. Most of the women were without children. Jade recalled Jelani's concern that fewer babies were being born, with so many of the men forced to work farther afield in order to pay their hut taxes.

Biscuit padded in front of Jade, the path being too narrow to admit them side by side. The twists and turns gave the Kikuyu a defensive position. It also muffled the village noise, but as they neared the entrance, Jade heard the clamor of angry voices. She nudged Biscuit to hurry.

They entered the compound through a narrow arch in the wooden palisade, low enough that she had to duck her head. She pushed her way past the clusters of women and saw two Kikuyu men engaged in a heated argument. They both wore only castoff khaki shorts, but one man had a necklace of sorts made of a strip of leather threaded through an empty shell casing. A broad scar stretched across his chest from some old wound. A Kikuyu woman wrapped in a dingy ocher cloth wailed behind the other man. The remaining villagers, mostly old men, stood in a crescent around the combatants, clearly enjoying the spectacle.

Jade recognized the two older men seated on logs in the shadows. A plump man swaddled in a new, striped blanket was an elder who served as the village chief as prescribed by the British officials. A thin sort of turban sat perched on his head, and large brass rings dangled from his ears. He held a stout staff the height of a cane.

The other man was the old *mondo-mogo*, the village seer and healer. He appeared to be more shadow and bones than anything substantial, a manifestation of the spirit world that he guarded. Unlike the chief, he wore no adornments beyond a leather pouch around his neck and his threadbare blanket. Behind him stood Jelani, his apprentice. Like his mentor, he also wore a rawhide medicine sack that was draped onto his bare chest. As the two arguing men became locked in a shoving match, the chief raised his voice and called a halt to the squabble. He prodded the pair with his staff, and they separated.

The chief began a lengthy monologue in Kikuyu. Jade caught one word, "police," because it was spoken in English. Immediately, the two combatants turned and pleaded their cases to the chief. To Jade, it appeared that the chief had recommended turning the matter over to the Nairobi justice system, and the two men didn't like that idea at all. Neither, Jade noted, did Jelani. He bent over and whispered in the *mondo-mogo*'s ear. The grizzled old man nodded once and held out his arms to the sides. Jelani placed his own hands under his teacher's upper arms and hoisted him to his feet.

The effect was electric. If the chief represented the British influence in the village, the *mondo-mogo* was the true power. Even the few children fell silent, expressions of awe, expectation, and fear on their waiting faces. He spoke and his voice, cracked with age, carried across the palisade to Jade.

His pronouncement was brief. Jade caught the word for "test" or "ordeal" as well as a dismissal. When he finished, he motioned for Jelani to help him to his hut. The other villagers hurried back to their garden plots or other chores, their children scurrying after them until only the combatants, the wailing woman, the chief, Jade, and Biscuit remained.

Jelani stepped back out of the *mondo-mogo*'s hut and approached the chief, speaking as one equal to another. Each time she saw Jelani, Jade was impressed by how much he'd grown inwardly as well as in stature from the boy she'd befriended nearly two years ago. The chief pushed the two squabblers into the hut. When the woman would have followed, he ordered her with a sharp word to wait outside. But he beckoned Jade to come inside with them. Jelani nodded and fell in beside her, one hand resting on Biscuit's head. The cheetah's throat erupted in a loud and raspy purr.

Entering the hut released a flood of memories in Jade, from her naming ceremony to this past September when the old shaman had warned her of death watching for her on Mount Kilimanjaro. Now it seemed that she was to play the role of witness or perhaps of arbitrator. She didn't relish either prospect any more than she enjoyed sitting in the dark, smoky hut. The scents of dried mud, thatch, and herbs clashed with those of unwashed bodies and the smoldering remains of a fire. Jelani motioned for her to be seated, but the two men were ordered to stand. Biscuit took his place beside Jade, sitting upright with his front paws neatly together, his head level with hers.

Jelani spoke first, in Swahili so that Jade could understand. "This man, Irungu," he said, pointing to the one who had the wailing woman, "has accused this man, Mutahi, of witching him." His finger now pointed to the man who wore the necklace. "This is a serious charge, but it is one for us to decide here and not for the British to decide."

Since no one had been killed, Jade agreed but she said nothing. When her opinion was wanted, she'd be asked for it.

"Why should we not send them to the British?" asked the chief. "We pay hut tax for their protection. They decide what is the law now."

Jade watched Jelani's face. She knew he opposed paying the hut taxes, so she was certain that his opposition here stemmed primarily from accepting those British services. To do so would only enhance the colonial belief that more taxes were owed.

"Some things they do not have laws for," said Jelani. "They do not understand witchery. They will give us mockery. Would you have that? Would you have them shame you?"

He had struck a nerve there, and the chief shook his head vehemently.

Jelani nodded. "I will retell the story now so that all may know what this *shauri* is about. Irungu's wife accepted a gift from Mutahi, a gift of herbs for cooking and drinking. She gave these to her husband, who became so ill that his soul left his body and wandered with the goats. My master made him well again so that he did not die. Now Irungu accuses Mutahi of giving him poison so that he might steal his hut, goats, and wife."

"That is not so," shouted Mutahi. "I do not want his hut. And I do not want his lazy wife. Maybe *she* witched

Irungu." At that accusation, the woman outside started wailing again.

"Silence, woman!" shouted the chief. The sobs and hysterical moans ceased immediately. "Put them to the test. Have them lick a hot knife." Both men protested against facing the ordeal.

"Enough," said the old *mondo-mogo*. "I have no need to hear your yammering mouths. I have talked with my spirit ancestors and they have told me what I need to know. I have seen beyond the village even to Kea-Njahe."

Jade leaned forward to hear better. The old healer spoke Swahili poorly and mixed Kikuyu with it. But she recognized their name for Ol Donyo Sabuk. Kea-Njahe meant the mountain of the big rain, and it was a favorite spot of Ngai, the Maker, second only to his preference for Mount Kenya. She saw that Mutahi trembled, his shell-casing necklace jittering on his scarred chest.

"That man," the *mondo-mogo* said, pointing to Mutahi, "has been there. But he has gone into dark places where he did not belong."

Mutahi's shaking increased but the *mondo-mogo* paid no attention. Instead, he reached for a wooden bowl beside him, shook it, and spilled several bones onto the pounded-dirt floor. He bent low over them, murmuring indecipherable incantations. After poking the bones, he beckoned to Jelani. The youth squatted beside his teacher, his gaze fixed on the bones, his ears attentive to his master's comments. Twice he nodded. Then he stood as the *mondo-mogo* gathered up the bones and put them back in the bowl.

"The *mondo-mogo* has shown me the truth as the bones have shown him," said Jelani. As he spoke for his master, he took on the man's mantle of power, his eyes never wavering, his voice ringing true. "There is witchery here, but it is not Mutahi's doing. Yet all are guilty. First, Mutahi is guilty of stealing and of being a fool."

The accused gasped. "Stealing?" Mutahi said. He fingered his shell casing. "I have worked for many whites on safari. Bwana Nyati knows of me. I do not need to steal. I—"

"You *have* stolen, Mutahi. This poison that you brought was one taken from a dark place. A place that hides in the shadows, not daring to look on Ngai's greatness. That is what the ancestor spirits say through the bones. But you took it as a fool and not with the purpose of evil."

"It is *Irungu* who covets. He desired Mutahi's hut for his lazy wife," continued Jelani. "Mutahi only presented the poison as a gift, for that is what he thought it was, a gift to make Irungu no longer wish Mutahi's hut. Irungu's wife is guilty of laziness and of having a tongue that wears down a man as water wears down a rock."

"Mutahi might have killed me," said Irungu. "Perhaps his witchery is so strong that he clouds the mind of the *mondo-mogo*."

At that, the old healer's head snapped up and his black eyes locked onto Irungu's. "Is it so strong that it clouds the minds of the ancestors? Or has your greed clouded your mind? Perhaps your spirit was better when it went walking from your body. Why has it come back still grasping for what is not yours?" The *mondo-mogo* peered intently into Irungu's eyes. "If you wish for Mutahi to lick the knife and then vomit out his sins, I will prepare a goat for sacrifice." His bony finger quickly aimed at Irungu. "But then *you* must also undergo the cleansing."

Irungu ducked his head. "I am sorry, *mondo-mogo*. Forgive me."

"Yes," said the old healer. "Forgive is what the bones tell me to do. They say to forgive all of you this time, but beware another *shauri* like this. Then you shall be beaten, or worse."

The two Kikuyu hurried out of the hut, nearly colliding in their haste. The chief bowed briefly to the *mondo-mogo* and Jelani, nodded at Jade, and left. Jade remained where she was, sitting on the dirt floor, Biscuit beside her. She'd been called in for some purpose and she waited to see what it was.

She didn't have to wait very long.

"This *shauri* concerns you, Simba Jike," said the old healer. "But I do not know how. My body grows old. Soon I will join my ancestor spirits."

Jade saw Jelani wince at that pronouncement. She knew that, with this old man's passing, Jelani would lose not only a teacher, but also a man who had become a second father to him. He would assume the full mantle of responsibility as healer, a role that apparently carried much weight with the villagers, including the chief.

"Thank you for telling me this," said Jade. She had no idea how she fit into a native squabble, but the old man's warning warranted her gratitude.

The shaman waved a bony hand in dismissal. "Do not thank me, Simba Jike. I am not able to see clearly how it concerns you. But I know I must tell you this." He paused to cough. Jelani retrieved a gourd dipper of water and gave it to his teacher.

"Then know that I have heard what you told me," said Jade. She shifted to rise. This little trial had overtaxed the aged healer and he clearly needed to rest. Before she could get to her knees, he held out his hand, signaling her to wait while he drank.

"You have *not* heard what I must tell you," he said with a wheeze.

Jade sat back down.

"I must tell you that the power of the crocodile is in the water."

CHAPTER 7

*The Swahili word for crocodile is "mamba," not to be confused
with the poisonous snake by the same English name.
Perhaps* mamba *should actually translate into "deadly."*
—The Traveler

"I DON'T UNDERSTAND. What was your teacher telling me?"
Jade and Jelani had left the *mondo-mogo*'s hut and found a
quiet, shady place outside of the palisades to sit and talk. Biscuit had taken his dinner, a scrawny chicken that Jade had
paid dearly for, to an even more secluded spot thirty yards
away.

"When the crocodile is on land, he is not as powerful as
in the water, where he is hidden," said Jelani.

Jade shook her head. "I understand that much. But I
don't understand *why* your teacher told it to me. Is your village being plagued by a crocodile? Has it taken some of the
women when they draw water?"

"We have no trouble with a crocodile. Not now, though
many have died that way in years past. Now the women have
for many months gone down to the river in large groups,
trumpeting like elephants. They beat the water with poles
and they throw rocks while they take turns washing or filling

their jars. They are also instructed not to go to the same spot each time to draw water. Crocodiles watch and learn where people go."

"Clever idea," said Jade. "Yours?"

Jelani shook his head. "Not all of it. I told them to go to different spots each time. The sticks and the trumpeting are my mother's idea. My mother is Mumbi, younger sister of the *mondo-mogo*. She has some of the seer's gift. For many years she has had this idea that the crocodiles do not harm the elephants, but no one would listen to her. Now she has my mouth to speak through and all the villagers call her a wise woman." His lips twitched, and Jade thought the smile was less of pleasure and more of amusement.

"I'm sure your mother's status is well deserved," Jade said. "Your teacher, is he ill?"

"He grows very old, Simba Jike. He has already predicted his own death this year." Jelani's head bowed and his chest rose and fell in a deep sigh. "I am not ready to be *mondo-mogo*."

"How so? Is there more for him to teach you? Can you learn from another man in another village?"

"That is not it. I am not ready to shoulder the burden. But my teacher reminds me that the elephant must carry his own tusks."

"Carrying your own isn't the problem," said Jade. "It's carrying everyone else's. I think you are trying to carry the burden of all your people."

Jelani looked sidewise at her, a wry smile forming on his handsome young face. "And Simba Jike never carries anyone else's burdens, does she?"

He laughed, and Jade could tell it was at her expense.

Somehow, coming from her young friend, it didn't sting and she was happy to hear it. He'd grown so serious in the time she'd known him. Jade joined in his joke. "No, I just run around trying to save elephants and leopards and solve murders."

"And so whose burdens do you carry this time?" Jelani asked.

"Only my own, I think." She told him briefly about the terrible package and the letter she'd received. She omitted her hallucinations and the strange vision in the smoke, for the very fact that he would take them seriously. The last thing Jade wanted was another smelly ointment or medicine pouch to carry. She wanted information.

"I know I have a strong enemy in David's mother," she said. "She is in prison, but she had a lover who came to Africa long ago. I believe he has helped her in the past and is probably still helping her."

"And you do not know who this man is?"

"I know his name, Mathers Pellyn, but I don't even know if he lives in Nairobi. He could be anywhere. Mombassa, perhaps."

Biscuit, finished with his meal, joined them and plopped at her feet, washing himself like some great, spotted house cat. Jade reached down and stroked his head.

"Have you seen anyone new and odd in this area?" Jade asked. "A new settler who doesn't farm or keep animals? Someone who comes and goes a lot?"

Jelani shook his head. "A man from the British Office of Native Affairs," he said with a tinge of loathing in his voice, "comes once each month to see that we are being good Kikuyu. But he is not new. I have seen this man for many years."

"Hmmm," Jade murmured. "Such a man would certainly be able to move about the colony easily."

"And that is all the burdens you are carrying?" Jelani's black eyes locked onto Jade's in a look that bore into her soul.

She didn't flinch. "I found a dead body, if that is what you are wondering. The death is suspicious, but I have no involvement in it beyond telling the inspector what I saw and heard."

Jelani nodded. "That is good, Simba Jike. It gives the police something to do besides look at our *shauris*." He jerked his head towards the village.

"Do you still speak out for self-rule?" Jade asked.

Jelani's eyes opened wide in mock innocence. "Simba Jike, how can you say such a thing? You know that such talk is forbidden. But when I asked you if there was another burden, I did not mean dead men. I asked about your heart. It has been many months since Bwana Mti Mguu left," he said, referring to Sam by his African name meaning "tree leg."

Jade frowned. "Over four months."

The youth's brows furrowed as he shook his head. After a long silence, Jade suddenly felt very foolish talking about a lost love to a lad of no more than fourteen. She hadn't intended to; she only wanted to ask him about strangers in the vicinity and to see how he was faring. She looked up at the sky and gauged the daylight left.

"I'd better be on my way. I'm camping at Fourteen Falls tonight. In less than a week I'll be bringing some girls on safari there."

Jelani nodded. "I will find and send a spirit to watch over you, Simba Jike."

Jade smiled. "Thanks, Jelani. But I think I have enough people watching over me."

"Yes, your Saint Peter and his bait bucket."

"Him, too." She stood and dusted off her trousers. Biscuit rose with her, extending his slender forelegs in a luxuriant stretch. "You shouldn't worry, Jelani. You will be a fine *mondo-mogo* when it is time. And you will have the wisdom of your mother to help you."

As if she heard them speak of her, the woman burst out of the palisade gate and hurried to them. Jade assumed Jelani's mother was no more than forty years old, but a hard life had aged her as it did most of the native women. Her pinched face was creased with wrinkles born of worry, and her spare frame testified to years of hunger. She carried a short digging stick in her right hand. Like many of the Kikuyu who lived this close to Nairobi, the woman wore a more concealing garment than the usual animal-hide apron and beads. Jade recognized the blanket wrapped around her as one that she'd given Jelani as a gift on their return from Kilimanjaro.

"You are Simba Jike," she said in Swahili. It was not a question.

"I am," replied Jade. She'd never spoken with Jelani's mother before. Until a few minutes ago, she hadn't even known her name. The woman had always been at work in her garden or doing other chores. Jade waited, curious as to what this woman would say to her. Would she thank Jade for teaching her son to read or for helping him write and sell articles to the London newspapers? Jade felt compelled to greet her with honor, paraphrasing Ezekiel 19:2–3:

"What a lioness was Jelani's mother! A lion of lions!

Among young lions she couched to rear her whelps. One whelp she raised up, a young lion he became."

The old woman thwacked Jade atop her head with the digging stick. Jade felt the sting even through her thick felt hat.

"Beat foolishness out of your head," said Mumbi. She raised her hand to strike again, but Jelani caught her arm.

"Mother, stop!" he said. His tone was gentle but firm.

"Foolishness in her head," repeated Mumbi. "I have seen the crocodile take hold of the lioness and drag her under. One waits for this one now." She raised her stick again.

"Mother, go back to your hut," ordered Jelani.

Mumbi waved her digging stick in the air as she returned to the gate. She called over her shoulder, "A lioness alone and away from a pride will die. Foolishness!"

"What did I do to earn that?" asked Jade, rubbing her head.

"Be grateful it was not a bigger stick," said Jelani.

JADE'S CAMPFIRE BLAZED, providing warmth in the cool evening air as well as protection from whatever stalked behind glowing eyes. The air was rich with a fine spray, thanks to the arc of falls a few hundred yards downstream. Their muted roar made a backdrop to the jackals yipping in the distance. A few swallows fluttered overhead while she pitched her tent.

A second, smaller ring of stones housed Jade's cooking fire. After photographing the falls from below, she had grabbed her pole and managed to land two large rhino yellowfish below the falls, but not until after they'd both put up a considerable fight. Once back in camp, she'd quickly scaled and filleted one, placing it in her skillet to cook. The other she filleted and gave to Biscuit. A fish eagle, reminiscent of the bald eagle with its great white head, had eyed Jade's catch for a while, even following her up to the top of the falls. It flew away downstream after Jade tossed the head and entrails into the river.

Now the fragrant scent of fish browning in butter filled the air, and Jade inhaled deeply. *This is the life!* She'd known that she'd feel better once she got out of Nairobi. She loved Bev and Avery, but it was getting harder and harder to stay in Parklands. She grabbed a folded cloth and used it to remove the water pot from the fire. Since none of the shops were open on Sunday when she left, she hadn't been able to replace the coffee that Bev took. Jade threw in a handful of spiced red tea and let it steep while she listened to her fish sizzle.

I should go to Lake Victoria and do a story there. Get away. Then, before the thought was finished, another followed on its heels. *And what if Sam comes back when you're gone? Do you expect him to hang around and wait for you?*

She ignored her own question, since it broached the next one: what if he didn't come back? Jade tended her fish instead and tried not to focus on life without Sam. It didn't work. She knew that, ultimately, she'd need to leave Kenya to avoid memories. But with so many painful ones awakened after her trip to Europe, Jade wasn't sure where she could go next. A bit of butter popped and Jade turned her attention to her dinner. After she flipped it over to cook on the other side, she carefully decanted a mug of tea. She took a tentative sip, followed by a second and a third. The brew ran hot and flavorful down her throat. She still missed her coffee, especially the aroma, but this would do for now.

Jade was considering mixing a batch of biscuits when a familiar call drifted down on the evening air from Ol Donyo Sabuk. Jade remained motionless and listened as the male lion hurled his throaty challenge to the last half hour of sunlight. As the call died away in a series of softer *harrumph*s, she felt her throat constrict and her eyes dampen. Her own words to Sam came back to her as clearly as if she'd spoken them aloud.

If you think for one instant that I'm going to forget about you, then you're crazy. I'm going to see you in every sky and hear your voice in every lion's roar.

"Stop it!" she scolded herself out loud. "He left you behind. You're wasting your life fretting over one man." She let her anger deepen in an attempt to drive out more maudlin emotions. "When I do see him, he's getting a piece of my mind!"

In an effort to occupy herself, she decided to make the biscuits. She slid the fish onto her plate, covered it with the heavy cast-iron lid, and opened a box where she stored the wooden bowl, flour canister, lard tin, and baking powder. Her hands trembled and she felt her mind race from Sam to David to Lilith, never staying on one person for more than a few seconds.

Get a grip on yourself!

She tugged at the canister's lid and pulled it off in a jerky movement, spilling some of the flour. *Idiot.* Jade measured the flour using her shaking hand, closed the tin, and reached into the box for the lard can. But when she'd lifted it from the box, she dropped the can and yanked her hand back. Stuck to the bottom of the lard can was a dirty envelope coated with dried mud.

Jade's heart hammered in her chest and ears, and her throat constricted. She tried to swallow the knot growing inside her. Reluctantly, she pulled off the envelope and opened it. Inside was a mud-stained photograph of her and Sam, taken at the Nairobi railway station the day Sam had left. A rent sliced through Sam's face, as if someone had stabbed it with a knife. She turned the photograph over. On the back was written, *You'll never belong to him. You belong to me even if I have to come out of the grave for you.* It was signed, *David.*

Jade's cry pierced the air as the anguish knifed through her chest. She hugged her midsection to stop the sensation that her innards were spilling out. But the visceral pain was as relentless as a pack of wild dogs devouring her alive. She curled into a ball and collapsed on her knees beside the chop box. Biscuit, alerted by her outcry, hurried to his mistress' side. Jade's left hand reached for the cheetah's comforting presence and clamped around his barrel chest. Her other shook as it gripped the haunted memento. Then, in a movement that might have been involuntary, Jade sat up and flicked the offending photograph into the cook fire.

It caught immediately and the reddened flames licked at her face and Sam's.

Forgotten were the fish, the biscuits, the pot of tea. The river's rush and tumble drifted into nothingness. Only her heartbeat was real, beating a rapid staccato. She thought she heard an elephant trumpet somewhere nearby. How many times could a person endure this measure of pain and survive? Each blow struck deeper, twisting her emotions, her body, and her mind.

Jade looked up from the fire with the sudden feeling that she was being watched. Her eyes darted from side to side as she searched the darkness for someone or something that stalked her. The darkness itself shifted and crawled like a giant, creeping maw opening to swallow her.

That was when she saw the wizened old native encased in his gray cloak swaying from side to side as he watched her from across the river.

Boguli?

She felt Biscuit strain against her grip and saw that he, too, was staring across the river. The ephemeral image pointed from his mouth to his head as though trying to tell her something. She tried to reply that she didn't understand, but he vanished into an evening mist much as he'd long ago slipped away into the fog-shrouded forests of Mount Marsabit. Only an elephant's distant trumpeting drifted back to her in the night air.

JADE WOKE TO THE MORNING SUN warming her tent. She didn't recall having entered it. She pulled out her pocket watch and stared at it in disbelief. Seven thirty! She'd *never* slept so late. As she wound her watch and slipped it back in her pocket, she tried to recall what had driven her into her tent so early last evening. She remembered cooking her fish and starting to make biscuits. Beyond that, everything jumbled into a nightmare, the same one she'd fought her way through a half dozen times last night: a fire, Sam burning, a great elephant flailing at a crocodile while women drew water. She didn't even recollect crawling into her bedroll.

When she ran her hand through her matted hair, her scalp prickled and her head hurt. Jade spat, once she could make enough saliva. Her tongue felt thick and the saliva pasty. Biscuit padded forward, a freshly killed grouse in his jaws. He deposited it at Jade's feet and butted her with his big head.

"Thanks," she said, picking up the gift. He'd never brought his kills to her before. "I must really have been in a bad way last night. My mouth tastes like I ate an old shoe." Biscuit responded by licking her hand.

Jade poked at the campfire's ashes and added a bit of kindling to refresh the few remaining coals. When the twigs caught, she carefully added the last of the sticks she'd gathered yesterday, saving one to spit part of the grouse. She drew her knife and skinned the bird, then cut off one leg and thigh. She gave the rest of the bird back to Biscuit and skewered her leg quarter with the remaining stick. After propping it up over some stones at the edge of the fire, Jade wandered off into the brush to relieve herself before returning to the river to wash her face.

The cold water felt good after such a feverish night, and with no danger of crocodiles at the top of the falls, she dunked her head to wash away the sweat from her hair. By then, it was time to turn her grouse leg over. She thought about reheating the leftover tea, then decided she'd dallied too long this morning and settled for several long pulls at her canteen.

The river and the canteen both went a long way towards reviving her, and Jade's stomach growled with renewed hunger. Biscuit glanced up from his breakfast, and Jade apologized.

"Sorry, boy. Didn't mean to startle you. Your food's safe from me." She turned her own portion again, then eyed the tightly covered plate left to one side. When she lifted the cast-iron lid, she saw that the cooked fish had been kept safe from ants and other scavengers. Jade picked it up with her fingers and tasted it.

Still good!

She devoured it before turning her attention to her cooking bird. When it was done, she used her knife to slice chunks off the bone and eat them. Even with the sour taste in her mouth, the roasted meat was delicious.

"Thanks, Biscuit. I needed that, and I don't think I felt like fishing this morning."

A pygmy kingfisher flew past on its way below the falls, as though to mock her fishing abilities. The bright orange head and bill blazed in sharp contrast to the iridescent blue on its back. Jade followed it with her eyes until it disappeared below the falls, then turned her gaze to the opposite shore.

Just what did you see last evening?

It had been sunset when she'd had her vision. Between the strain of receiving that photo and the campfire's flickering glow, she couldn't have seen anything clearly, she reasoned. Perhaps it had been only one of the Kikuyu watching her curiously before hurrying on to the village. But in her heart, she knew what she'd seen and no amount of rationalization could change that. The Kikuyu didn't roam far afield after dark settled.

She'd seen a man, Boguli, who'd never existed to begin with. An old native whom she'd met on Mount Marsabit when she'd been tracking the ivory poachers. A man whom she'd photographed but who only appeared on film as the shadow of an ancient bull elephant, one who'd been shot by those very poachers. Jade had never been able to explain Boguli to herself. It had taken one of the old French priests at the mission to put him in perspective.

Perhaps he was a guardian angel, mademoiselle. One who came in a form that you would trust.

She'd accepted that idea then, mainly because of its comforting nature and because she was sitting at the priest's big wooden refectory table enjoying hot bread and a mug of coffee. Right now with the rushing drone of the falls near her, it seemed eerie. And had she really held a picture of Sam last evening? Or had that been her imagination, too?

Jade took the stick that had held her grouse leg and poked at the fire, pushing the remaining sticks to one side. She rummaged through the ashes, but nothing recognizable appeared. *It wasn't here!* She'd dropped it into last night's cooking fire, not this campfire. She hurried over to that smaller, separate ring of stones and pawed the cold ash. A corner of photographic paper stuck out from where it had wedged between two of the stones. No image was visible, but the paper itself was proof that she hadn't imagined the picture. She stuck the corner into her shirt pocket and wiped her sooty fingers on her handkerchief.

"Someone is playing at some nasty games, Biscuit," she said. "Someone who lives around Nairobi, too."

Suddenly she wanted to return and check her bungalow for any other sign of intrusion. Whoever had left that envelope had left it in her chop box, which meant they'd been inside her home. *Finch warned me to keep my door locked.* The thought made her skin prickle. Jade looked in the box for the envelope but couldn't find it.

"I must have dropped it into the fire, too."

She washed her skillet in the river, and used it to carry water back to the camp to douse the fire. Then, after taking down her tent, she carried the gear in two trips down the rocks to Avery's truck, Biscuit following. As she loaded supplies, she remembered the truck parked downriver that she'd seen yesterday. Maybe someone had come up to her campsite while she was fishing and left the envelope in her box.

"Let's see if this person is still there, Biscuit." Even if they weren't guilty, they might have seen someone nearby. Maybe they saw the native that she mistook for Boguli.

Twenty minutes and many more jolts later, Jade spied the truck she'd seen the other day. It was parked in the same location and, as before, no one was nearby. She turned Avery's Dodge towards the river and parked forty feet away. "Hello," she called as she stepped out. "Anyone here?"

She listened carefully for an answering sound but heard nothing. Jade picked up her rifle, chambered a round, and held it at the ready as she walked slowly towards the abandoned truck, her ears and eyes attentive to anything that hinted of danger. Only the slow murmur of the Athi greeted her. Biscuit padded softly behind her.

A tackle box and a fishing pole lay on the ground, but there was no tent or any other articles of camp about. Neither was there any angler. "This doesn't look right, boy," she said to Biscuit. Jade eyed the truck and took a deep breath, steeling herself to look inside. Her reasoning told her that there was no body in the truck; otherwise the vultures and other scavengers would have been about. Still, she had to look.

She approached the truck and looked first in the bed, then in the cab. All she saw was a pith helmet lying on the ground by the front tire. Jade moved closer to the bank when, at twenty feet away, two warnings stopped her. For one, her left knee throbbed. For another, Biscuit hissed.

"What is it, boy?" she whispered. She took one more wary step towards the riverbank when the cheetah took hold of her leg in his mouth and stopped her in midstep. Caught off balance, Jade tumbled backwards. She landed hard on her rear, her finger jerking back on the trigger.

Her Winchester went off just as the river boiled up in one frenzied roll, and a huge, spectral gray and green crocodile surged out of the water. The bullet struck the side of his skull and ricocheted off. It hit the abandoned truck, shattering the windshield.

"Holy . . ." Jade muttered. She backpedaled, pushing herself farther from the shore before the eerie beast decided to come after her. Jade caught a brief glimpse of a blue-gray eye behind a massive jaw. Then she scrambled to her feet and ran back to her own truck, Biscuit leading the way.

As the croc slid into the water, there was little doubt in Jade's mind as to what had happened to the missing fisherman.

CHAPTER 8

Do not be deceived by a calm, peaceful surface.
Death may well lurk just beneath it in the form of iron jaws.
—The Traveler

"Tie it on good and tight," said Blaney Percival, the colony's chief game warden. "We don't want the bait to slip off the line."

It was Tuesday, and Jade was back at the site of the crocodile attack with an entire retinue. Mr. Percival was present, along with European constable Miller, Constable Singh and his camera, and Harry Hascombe. Two gun bearers attended the hunters, and trailing all of them was a reporter from the *East African Standard*. The only one missing besides a representative from the *Leader* was Biscuit. Jade had left him with Beverly.

Miller poked around the abandoned truck, Singh photographed the scene, and the reporter photographed the constables. Percival and Jade stood by Harry's truck, putting together a line baited with a haunch of zebra, while Harry stood guard with his Holland & Holland .375 in hand. Nakuru, the big Nyamwezi man whom Jade knew from her trips to Mounts Marsabit and Kilimanjaro, carried Harry's heavy rifle, a .416 Rigby.

Jade and Percival finished tying on the bait, and Percival's gun bearer, Mukassa, whirled it over his head and released it to splash into the river. The other end of the rope was attached to a hand-cranked winch nailed to the bed of Harry's truck. The winch was made with a handle on either side of the central spool so that two people could man it if needed. At present, only Jade stood beside it. They settled back to wait for the beast to take the bait.

"If he's still in this area, he'll go for that meat," said Harry.

Percival picked up his .450 Rigby double rifle and chose a position with a clean line of fire to the shore. "It's possible he's gone on to the native village," he suggested. "And you're certain that this was a gray crocodile, Miss del Cameron?"

"I only saw his head, sir," Jade replied. "It was a dull iron gray with a few green and white splotches near the right eye. And the eye was a cloudy blue."

"I know that croc," said Harry. "But when I last saw him five or six years ago, he was a lot farther south. He was a big fellow then, eleven or twelve feet. Ridges along his back were green and so were his legs. The rest of the beast was mostly gray with some patches of olive green. But as bizarre as that beast looked, there was something truly unnatural-looking about those eyes."

"I thought albino animals had red eyes and more yellowed skin rather than gray or white," said Jade.

"They do," said Percival. "This brute's not an albino. He's an odd sort of freak, light overall with his mottled dark green ridges and that white spot behind the eye. I've seen a raven with one white wing before. That bird was always getting chased. Most animals mob the outlier, so it's a wonder this croc survived infancy. Seems he'd have been easy to spot as a youngster by some hungry fish."

"Piebald," said Jade.

"Who's bald?" asked Harry.

"No, *piebald*. It's what we call horses with that sort of mottling."

"Oh, right, piebald. Well, on this beast we call it ugly," Harry replied.

Blaney nodded. "He was an ugly brute at that. I've seen him, too. And you're right, Hascombe; he was a good-sized bull, then, at thirteen feet. Probably fourteen by now."

"How do you know he's a he?" asked Jade.

"When I saw him, he was making a mating bellow," explained Percival.

"Ah. So what's he doing up here?" asked Jade.

"Like as not, an even bigger or more experienced bull chased him out of his territory when he tried to mate with the females," Harry said. "Possibly those same females don't want to mate with him, since he looks different. Hard to say what motivates a croc beyond its stomach."

"That is the truth," said Percival. "They'll take on anything from antelope to zebra, and I hate the ruddy lot of them. They take far too many natives, especially the women."

"Interesting bit of lore there," said Harry. "You'll fancy this, Jade. Some tribes claim when a man or woman dies by another's hand, the soul enters a croc and uses it to seek vengeance. That's why so many native women still wash at the same spot where someone else was taken the day before. They assume that the victim had done someone wrong and, if their conscience is clear, no harm will come to them."

A scratching noise caught their attention and, as one,

they turned to see the reporter hunkered by the truck's bonnet, scribbling away. "Just keep talking," he said. "This will make wonderful copy."

Harry raised his right arm as though to backhand the man. "Get off with you before you get in the way or get eaten."

"I'm waiting to see the croc," the man said. He patted a nearby camera. "Hope to get a shot of it when you've killed it. For once I'll scoop that bloke at the *Leader*. He's too much of a dandy to come out here for a story. Fancies himself a bit of a gentleman."

"*You'll* be shot if you don't get out of the way. Bother the constables while you wait, not us," said Harry. The reporter took the hint and joined Miller as he rooted under the seat for anything of note.

"Do they know who's missing yet?" asked Percival. He kept his gaze on the river, as did Jade and Harry, watching for any sign: a slight ripple, a bump that could be a nostril.

Jade shook her head. "Not that I know. Surely someone back in town will recognize the vehicle if nothing else." She studied the faint ruts behind the truck. "It looks as if there are two sets of tire tracks, but with most of them on the vegetation, there's not much to compare. He might have driven back and forth for that matter." She looked upriver to the falls and caught a glimpse of a rainbow breaking through the spray. "Hard to reconcile such beauty with this place of violent death."

"There's beauty and then there's beauty," said Harry with a sidelong look at Jade. She scowled and he quickly looked to the ground. "*Two* sets of tracks," he said. "Then maybe he went back with someone else."

"But why leave his vehicle here unless it was broken

down?" She jerked her head towards Miller. "It started up fine for him."

"That's true enough," said Harry. "Perhaps—"

"Shh," broke in Percival in a whisper. "I saw a slight V-shaped ripple out to the right. Our friend might be about to take the bait. Get ready."

He spared a brief glance for Jade, who positioned herself at the winch. The crank itself had notches, like a gear, and a ratchet that prevented the wheel from running the other way. Jade had donned leather gloves and took hold of the crank.

"Wind it in nice and slowly at first, miss. We want to lure him up out of the water for a clear shot."

Jade started the crank, listening to the slow *tick-tick* as the ratchet bobbed up and over each of the wheel's wooden notches. The rope line crept along.

"Have you ever shot a crocodile before, Hascombe?" Percival asked.

"Twice."

"Did you kill any?"

"Once."

Percival nodded. "The brainpan is a tiny target even in a big croc."

"And the skull only gets thicker as they grow," Harry added.

The constables stopped their investigation to watch. Miller slipped his sidearm from his holster and held it in front of him like a talisman to ward off evil. His hands trembled, and Jade wondered if he'd ever fired his weapon before. For all she knew, this might be his first look at a crocodile. Not that she'd seen many herself, and none this close.

"Easy, easy," called Percival. "I think he just dove down. Reel it in a little faster."

Jade turned the wheel at double the speed, listening to the ratchets *clack clack*. The rope came up dripping and smelling of fish and ripe organic mud. Bits of vegetation clung in spots.

Suddenly she felt the wheel resist her efforts, no matter how hard she pushed on the handle. "He's taken the bait!" she called. "I can't budge him."

"Nakuru," shouted Harry, "help Simba Jike."

Nakuru, a large man, rested Harry's heavy rifle against the front tire and took hold of the crank opposite Jade. Leaning his entire weight and considerable muscle into it, he forced his lever down as Jade pulled up on hers. The winch spindle jerked around a half turn and locked again. This time Jade felt the jolt reverberate through the truck.

"He's going to drag the truck back!" she shouted. "Somebody shove some rocks behind the wheels."

Mukassa and Constable Singh both raced around, gathering large stones and shoving them behind the rear tires. As soon as Jade and Nakuru felt the slightest release in tension, they turned the crank, managing one and a half revolutions before the handle again refused to budge.

The strength of the crocodile is in the water. Is this what the old man meant by his warning?

Her biceps burned from exertion as she strained into the handle. The groaning of nails ripping through protesting wood sounded as though it came from her own limbs.

"He's pulling the winch out of the truck!" Jade shouted.

"The bait's coming up," yelled Harry. "I can just see the knot we made for the one-foot marker. Nakuru, push!"

The African whom Harry trusted with his life as gun bearer threw himself at the winch with a bellow. Jade's handle flew up at her, tossing her backwards. She hit the ground just as bait, line, and a monstrous mottled demon welled up out of the river.

The beast thrashed, sending spray high into the air. It obscured his head, the dingy water blending with his own washed-out colors.

"I can't get a clear sight on him," shouted Percival. "Reel him in. Get him on shore."

Jade scrambled to her feet and did her utmost to assist Nakuru in turning the winch. The fore nails were exposed by an inch already, bent back from the pressure. They screeched again as the croc fought to retain his prize. From behind her, Jade heard the thrashing and felt droplets of water strike her back. She imagined the creature suddenly lunging towards her exposed back and prayed that Harry and Mr. Percival could get in a kill shot before that happened. She knew that they were closer to the beast than she was, but it didn't make the fear any less real.

The wheel turned another half revolution.

"He's nearly there," yelled Percival. "Hascombe, have you got a shot?"

"Almost," shouted Harry.

Suddenly the rope went slack and Jade knew that the reptile had come ashore. She turned and saw the unnatural-looking animal whose blotches of gray, white, and olive reminded her of a howitzer she'd seen painted in dazzle camouflage during the war. If such patterns were intended to disrupt the outline and confuse a predator, this one was living proof. Jade had a difficult time following the animal's head outline and wondered if Harry was having a similar problem from his angle. The only obvious feature was the chunk of zebra haunch and rope still protruding from the partially open maw. A hiss like a hundred snakes issued from the beast's throat.

"He's going to kill us all!" screamed Miller. He fired three times, striking the bait twice and the croc's jaw once.

"Get back, you idiot," yelled Hascombe. "Jade, get in the truck!"

But the bullets had already served to further irritate the animal, and he jerked his massive head just as Harry and Percival fired. Their shots pierced the nose and the fleshy jowls, respectively. Percival fired again while Harry chambered another round. This shot struck the skull, but hit half an inch behind the brainpan.

By then the croc's head jerk had snapped the rope, and the animal dove back into the water, Harry's last bullet blazing ineffectually at the armored back.

In a moment, the water was still, as though the brute had never been there.

Harry's mouth hung open as he stared at the winch, now attached by one nail. "He's gotten bigger."

"Did we get him?" asked Miller.

Harry's face darkened and he wheeled around with a quickness that belied his big frame. "Damnation!" he roared as he stormed over to Miller. He grabbed him by the shirt collar and shook him like a big dog shaking a rat. "Get him? I *could* have had him. What the hell were you doing?"

"You weren't shooting," Miller squeaked in between shakes.

"I was about to. You don't just shoot at a croc and expect it to fall down dead."

"Harry, let him go," said Jade. She noticed that Miller's face was turning purple.

Harry dropped him, and the constable gasped. "I could have you arrested for that, you know."

While taking a deep breath, Harry's chest expanded until he resembled the Cape buffalo for which he was nicknamed. Miller apparently saw the danger, for he quickly added, "But I won't."

Harry threw a menacing look at the reporter, who was feverishly scratching down every movement and word in his notepad. "And if you print a word about what just happened between the constable and me, I'll—"

The reporter held up his hands in a "don't shoot me" pose. "I promise. You have my word."

"That and a couple rupees wouldn't buy a shot of gin," grumbled Harry.

"You made a foolish mistake there, Constable," said Percival. "Besides ruining our chances at a good shot, you've possibly driven the animal away from here. Now we'll have to watch for it and see where it turns up next. And I don't have the manpower to patrol every foot of this river."

"Do you have any idea where that crocodile will go next?" asked Jade.

Percival shrugged. "It could be anywhere. He could stay here, though I doubt it. He could go back downriver. That's more likely, since it will get shallower up here as the dry season progresses."

"Any chance he'll move to the Kikuyu village?"

"It's a possibility. I'll pay them a visit and warn them." The game warden considered Jade for a moment. "You were planning to take some young ladies out for a safari, weren't you?"

Jade nodded. "We'll be camping above the falls, though." She rubbed her upper arms, trying to ease out the burning pain from her recent exertion. "I'll make certain that they don't come down below."

"You'll be safe enough up there," Percival said. "But stay up top. I can't imagine any croc waiting in those rocks and pools under the falls, but one never knows with animals, especially hungry ones."

"How big was that animal?" asked the reporter. "Fourteen feet, did you say?"

"He's sixteen if he's an inch," said Harry. He moved closer to Jade and placed a hand on her shoulder, giving it a gentle squeeze. "Are you all right, Jade? If I'd known that croc was that big, I'd never have put you at the winch." He smiled. "You're a brave woman. You didn't run. But you should have gotten into the truck." His hand grazed her cheek and hair.

Jade moved away from his touch. "I'm fine, Harry." She turned to Constable Singh and changed the subject. "Did you find anything of interest in or around the vehicle?"

Singh shook his white-turbaned head. "Nothing unusual, memsahib. We shall see if there are any interesting fingerprints when I drive it back to Nairobi. I cannot tell if there was blood on the ground or not. There was a dark spot of dirt there." He pointed to a shallow hole. "I dug it up and put it in a jar. Perhaps we shall see blood under the microscope."

"I'd think there should be a lot of blood," said the reporter.

"Not necessarily," said Percival. "A crocodile is an ambush predator. It lunges forward and pulls the prey into the water, drowning it."

"And then what happens?" asked the reporter, scribbling as fast as he could.

"If he's hungry enough and he can swallow his prey, he'll bolt it down then, but most often he stores his meal in some underwater lair," said Harry. "Tucks it under a root or something until it softens up enough that he can pull off chunks of meat."

"How long does that take?" asked the reporter. His face had paled.

Harry shrugged. "A few days maybe, a week perhaps."

From the river came the sound of rising gas bubbles. They burbled and popped in a frenetic series that ended only when a corpse suddenly bobbed to the surface. Chalky white flesh protruded from torn khaki, and a bloated hand flopped in a mock wave, beckoning them. The body rolled and settled on the surface, one glazed eye staring from the ghoulish face, the swollen lips pulled back in an expression of horror.

They stared at the body in stunned disbelief, mouths agape, eyes wide.

"Unless," Jade said, "a lot of thrashing makes the dinner pop back up."

The reporter was the first to move, hurrying away to gag. "Ulp!"

"Gentlemen," Jade added as she looked at each of them, "I think we found our victim."

CHAPTER 9

Crocodiles do not swim or run down their prey. They ambush,
lying in wait, invisible. Then suddenly, that harmless log attacks
with tremendous speed and power.
—The Traveler

"IRONIC NAME," murmured Inspector Finch later that day. He and Jade were standing outside police headquarters, watching as Constable Singh dusted and photographed fingerprints on the victim's car. The victim, Bradley Waters, lay inside on a table in a back room. He'd been identified by some soggy, folded papers in his pocketbook.

When Jade didn't reply, Finch explained, "Waters. I mean to say that it's rather ironic that he died in the water, drowning in a crocodile's death roll."

Jade only nodded. While she didn't feel as edgy today as she had in previous days, her skin still twitched and crept along her arms and legs. Exhaustion from lack of sleep and this morning's exertion at the winch had also taken its toll. She'd returned to Nairobi with Miller to give her statement, leaving Singh to bring back the victim and his vehicle. Blaney Percival, who'd driven Jade to the river, had gone on to Jelani's village, and Harry—well, frankly Jade had no idea what Harry did afterwards; nor did she care to know. His caress back at the river said that his interest in her hadn't waned. It was as unwelcome as it was unreciprocated.

"We do not know for a fact that he drowned, Inspector," said Dr. Dymant, stepping outside to join them. With Mathews away again for a few weeks, he'd offered his services to perform the autopsy.

"But isn't that what crocodiles do?" asked Finch. "Grab their victims and pull them under until they drown?"

"Yes," said Jade.

Finch nodded, as though he had been vindicated.

"But," continued Jade, musing to herself, "perhaps he was dead before the crocodile pulled him under. Maybe he'd been drinking and passed out in the water. Or maybe . . ." She let her thoughts trail off.

"Maybe what?" asked Finch.

Jade snapped to attention, his question startling her out of her reverie. It wasn't unwelcome either, since she'd started seeing images of David, bloodied and dying, in her mind's eye. "Oh, nothing," she said.

"Miss del Cameron raises some interesting considerations," said Dymant. "The man may have suffered a heart attack and fallen before the crocodile found him. But considering the condition of the body, I'm not at all sure we'll ever know the answers."

"Do what you can with him, Doctor," said Finch. "And quickly. We need to get him in the ground soon enough. Singh, accompany the good doctor."

"I shall get right to it, Inspector," said Dymant. "As you see, I have my medical bag with me. Thank you for entrusting me with this examination."

"I'd like to know what you find out," said Jade. Dymant bowed and hastened inside, leaving Jade and Finch by the vehicles. "You called him in?" asked Jade.

"No. In point of fact, he came and offered his services," said Finch. "Seemed most eager."

"Curious," said Jade.

"How so?"

Jade shrugged. "Well, for one thing, how did he know there was a body to be examined?"

Finch waved a hand in a motion of dismissal. "The question is, who *doesn't* know? Once we made the call earlier for the chief game warden, everyone knew something was up. I had to notify the chief inspector just now and the secret was out." He snorted. "Blasted telephone operators tattle to everyone and their aunt about everything." Finch wagged a finger at Jade. "I swear the newspapers pay them to report anything of note."

"I suppose that explains it," said Jade.

"Yeeeesss," drawled Finch, "but it doesn't explain *your* interest in the results. Somehow I don't think I can put it down to feminine curiosity." He folded his arms over his chest and watched her.

Jade responded with her own question. "You don't think finding a body is enough to warrant interest?"

Finch's lips tightened. "Don't evade my question, Miss del Cameron. Why are you so interested? Months ago, you were furious at being pulled into the investigation when that body was found in your friends' coffee dryer."

She arched one brow. "You tricked me into that one, remember?" She suddenly pictured Sam scowling at her, his arms folded across his chest, unhappy about her tendency to charge into danger. She gave her head a quick shake and sighed. *What difference does it make now?*

"To answer your question, Inspector, I suppose it's because this is the second body I've found this week. I don't like coincidences."

"You suspect foul play then? Is there something in particular that you're not telling me? Because it doesn't matter that you're an American. You're obligated to report to the police everything you know about this incident."

"I told you all I know. I have nothing beyond a . . ." She paused, searching for a way to describe her suspicions. "Call it a gut feeling, if you like. Perhaps I'm reacting as much to these taunts I've received as anything else, but this man Waters' fishing tackle was not left near the shoreline. It was by his truck. So he wasn't standing at the shore fishing when a croc surprised him. And we didn't find any flasks or bottles lying about, so I doubt that he was drunk."

Finch nodded as he pondered her assessment. "Those are good points, miss, and they are the very reasons *I* wanted an examination of the body. Otherwise I would have simply ruled it death by crocodile and moved on."

Jade's brows lifted in surprise. "So you agree with me?"

"Yes. Don't be so shocked, Miss del Cameron. I've come to have some respect for your perspicacity. And since you've brought up those disagreeable items you've received, I must tell you that we've had no luck tracing their origins. Other than those from a postal clerk, there were no other prints on either the letter or the packet with the scarf. Of course, I cannot do anything at all with the last fragment you found in your chop box. It's too charred. And even if there were prints, to what would I compare them? My records are limited."

"Balderdash! You collected prints from half of Nairobi last July," she said. "At the Agricultural Ball, remember?"

Finch looked at his shoes and frowned. "Hmm, yes, well. I was ordered to dispose of most of that collection. A few gentlemen with the ears of the governor were affronted by the entire episode."

"Lord Colridge?"

"I believe he spearheaded the complaint, yes."

Jade smiled. She'd first met the old pioneer settler just after the war. She could imagine him puffing out his bushy white mustache as he broached his concerns to Governor Northey. Even in Colridge's advanced years, he was still a force to be reckoned with.

"What you tell me makes no sense, Inspector," said Jade. "At least one of those parcels came from France, according to the postmark. It should have been handled by any number of people and have innumerable prints on it."

"Which suggests that it didn't actually come from France," summarized Finch. Singh came back outside and Finch ordered him to examine Waters' truck.

Jade considered the implication of Finch's last statement. Someone went to a great deal of trouble to forge a foreign postmark and leave the package with the other mails to be put in the Dunburys' Nairobi box. The dried mud may have been intended to make the items appear sepulchral, and to obscure prints and make the forged postmark less easy to spot.

"Do you think that Scotland Yard has a set of prints for Mathers Pellyn?"

Finch frowned. "And just who in the blazes might that be?"

"He was the lover of Olivia Lilith Worthy, and very likely part of her criminal enterprise. Possibly her partner."

"Explain."

Jade took a deep breath and collected her thoughts. "You know that I drove an ambulance during the war." Finch nodded. "Near the end, a pilot crashed. He died in my arms."

"Yes, David Worthy," said Finch. "This I recall hearing. And I presume this Olivia Lilith Worthy is a relative."

"His mother. She hates me, but not just for David's death. When I came to Africa to find David's brother and uncover who killed their father, I came away with the impression that Lilith had ordered her husband's death. It meant she had an ally here. Later I found that she was using another man to smuggle guns and German East African gold into Abyssinia."

"This Pellyn chap?"

"No. But I stopped that scheme. Then in Morocco, she came after me, kidnapping my mother. She had yet another man helping her move drugs and Roman coins. That time Sam and I captured her."

"Then she's in prison."

"Yes, but these gifts from the dead could come only from her. Who else would have David's bloody scarf? His effects were all sent home to her."

"So you suspect another one of her agents is doing the work for her?"

Jade nodded. "It could be anyone, but Lord Dunbury discovered that she'd had a Cornish lover at one time, a scoundrel who fled to Africa."

"Mathers Pellyn."

"Correct."

Finch uncrossed his arms and shook his head. "Sounds

entirely too implausible. The woman's in prison. You've broken up her schemes."

Jade looked up sharply. "We don't know that. I have no idea what else she might have her fingers in." Jade counted off: "Morocco, Abyssinia, Kenya. I heard Mr. Hamilton from the post office tell of a woman who was an overlord in the Belgian Congo. She cut off the ears of her laborers and branded them. That sounds like something she'd do, and she's always been after gold. Pellyn may have been a part of it."

The sound of an engine interrupted Jade. She looked down the street and recognized Harry's truck. "It's Hascombe," she said. "He appears to be in a hurry, too."

Harry parked beside Waters' truck, narrowly missing constable Singh's backside, which protruded from the open door. "I found something," Hascombe shouted.

He jumped out of his vehicle and, once again, Jade was taken by how quickly he moved. When the Africans had christened him Bwana Nyati, they'd meant more than the buffalo's bulk, power, and temper. They'd had in mind the animal's surprising agility.

"After everyone left," Harry said, "Nakuru and I took some time to reattach the winch in the back of the truck. I decided I didn't care to be that close to the shore in case our scaly friend returned while we were working, so I drove forward a few hundred yards. That's when Nakuru picked up this." He held up an unfired .455 Webley cartridge. "I had parked right on top of it."

"I don't remember a Webley in Waters' truck," said Jade.

"No," said Finch, "but this cartridge could have been dropped by anyone at any time."

"Inspector, quickly. Come!" Singh had extracted himself from the truck's interior. His white-gloved right hand was clenched around something. "I was probing deep into the cushions, Inspector. I found this." He opened his hand, revealing a small gold nugget the size of a cherry pit.

Finch took it, turned it over in his hands, then cast a sidewise glance at Jade.

"Another unbelievable coincidence, right?" she said. Jade walked over to Waters' truck. She squatted down in front of the grillwork and examined the bumpers. "I just noticed these when Harry pulled up. There are fresh scratch marks on the front of this truck," she said.

Finch and Hascombe joined her. "Vehicles are scratched all the time in the bush," said Hascombe. "Look at mine."

"I think Miss del Cameron has something in mind besides rocks and sapling trees, am I correct?"

"Yes," said Jade. "And there were similar marks on the rear bumper of that vehicle you pulled from the Getathuru River. They could easily match up."

"Are you suggesting that this man," Harry said, as he pointed to Waters' truck, "was responsible for pushing Stockton's car into the river?"

Jade nodded.

Harry took off his hat and ran a hand through his hair. "If that's the case, the bastard got what he deserved when the croc took him."

"Unless someone got him before the croc did," said Jade.

"What?" Harry plopped his hat back on his head. "Have you been out without your hat on, Jade? The sun's baked your pretty little head."

"I'm afraid she's quite serious, Hascombe," said Finch.

"Constable Singh," he called. "See if these scratches align with the marks on the rear of that car from the river."

Singh nodded and began taking measurements.

"All right," said Hascombe. "Supposing that this man did push the other into the river. That still doesn't mean that his death was anything other than an animal attack. People get careless when they fish."

"It's entirely possible, Hascombe," said Finch, "but I can't overlook any possibility at present."

"Just who is this Waters?" asked Jade. "What do you know about him?" She addressed the question to both Finch and Harry.

"He's been in the colony for years, but I've never met him," said Harry. "A Cockney, I think. Heard his name mentioned once or twice as a man who was always looking for the next opportunity. But I never heard his name in connection with killing anyone."

"I sent Miller to run down where Waters lived," said Finch. "Seeing if he has a flat above a shop or a room at one of the clubs. If you have any ideas, Hascombe—"

"If I heard, I never paid it any mind, Inspector. But he seemed to be a man who moved about a great deal."

"I think Mr. Holly knew him," Jade added. "He claims to have a share in that gold mine. And if Stockton and Waters were partners . . ." She let the thought trail off. Finch didn't need her help and she shouldn't be getting involved.

Miller returned from his assignment, saluted the inspector, and gave Harry a wide berth. "I found his digs, Inspector. Asked around at the usual watering holes for chaps like him."

"And . . . ?" prodded Finch.

"And one fellow thought he lived south of the rail yards."

"That's where some of the natives live," said Harry. "The ones reestablished after the war."

"Actually, this was a bit east of it, closer to the warehouses," said Miller. "Some Boer has huts he hires out. I hurried back as soon as I heard this, knowing you'd want to inspect the digs yourself."

"The scratches match on the two automobiles," said Singh, consulting his notebook.

Finch nodded. "We'll go now, before his landlord has a chance to clear out his things." He nodded to Jade and Harry. "Thank you both for your help."

"Wait," said Jade. "I'm coming with you."

Finch took a deep breath and exhaled slowly. "Miss del Cameron, as much as I value your mind, I think you've been through quite enough recently. You should go home and rest."

"I saw the scratches on the bumper, didn't I?"

"Yes, but—"

"Inspector, it's possible that this man has some connection to those . . ." She glanced at Harry and thought how to proceed without involving him. "Those parcels I've received. I might see something that relates to them."

"What parcels?" asked Harry.

"I suppose I can't deny that," said Finch.

"What parcels?" repeated Harry, edging closer to Jade.

"Very well, you may come along, Miss del Cameron, but you must promise to follow my orders. Touch nothing."

"I agree," said Jade.

"What bloody parcels?!" roared Harry.

"You haven't told your friend?" asked Finch.

"Harry's . . ." Jade noticed the look of intent concern in Harry's face and stopped herself before finishing the sentence. "No, I hadn't."

"Jade," Harry said, his voice a taut bowstring about to snap. "What's going on?"

"Miss del Cameron has received some unpleasant letters purporting to be from her dead fiancé."

Harry's eyes opened wide. "Featherstone's dead?"

His simple question hit Jade like a heavy blow to the chest, driving the wind from her lungs. She blanched and took a step back to steady herself. "No. David Worthy. The pilot I knew in the war. The one who gave me that odd ring."

Harry stepped in closer and put a protective arm around Jade. "Sorry, Jade. Maybe the inspector's right. Maybe you should go home. I can take you there."

Jade wriggled free of his embrace. "I'm going with the inspector."

Harry clamped his hat tighter on his head. "Then I'm going with Jade."

WATERS' HUT WAS ACTUALLY one of several two-room wood-and-tin shanties that had been tossed together from discarded lumber and crates. Consequently the sides were a hodgepodge of labels and advertisements. *Allenburys' Foods—Your Baby's Welfare* butted against ads for Pears soap and twelve-bore cartridges. Each hut had one window, generally cracked, and was roofed over in galvanized tin. A common latrine and another shack labeled *Bath* stood farther apart from the hovels.

The owner, an old South African named Hartesveldt, seemed glad to see Finch. "Is gut you come. I complain that man Waters leave without notice."

"Didn't pay you, huh?" asked Harry.

Hartesveldt spat on the ground. "Pay before he get room like everyone else. Like he has time before. But this time, he bring damned noisy parrot. All day it talk. All night it talk. Other men complain at me. I feed dat bird and give it water, but I tink maybe I wring dat bird's neck and eat it if Waters not come back soon."

"Waters is dead," said Finch. "We'll take the bird with us after we examine his rooms."

Hartesveldt produced a big skeleton key and unlocked the door to Waters' shack. Finch stood in the doorway first, surveying everything while Jade waited outside, Harry in close attendance. From inside came a shrill voice, repeating again and again:

"Salt! Pile in! Pile in!"

"I can see why the other tenants don't care for that bird," said Harry. "The least it could do is say something else."

"Leopold's an ass!" squawked the bird.

"Happy now?" asked Jade.

"Sorry about that Featherstone comment, Jade," said Harry. "I'm sure you must be hurt by his abandoning you." Jade didn't reply. She was watching Finch, waiting for her chance to enter. "I own," he continued, "I never would have expected it. The blasted man always stuck to you like a drowning man to a life preserver."

"I don't want to talk about it with you, Harry. Please."

"Fine. I can respect that. But what's this about letters from that Worthy chap?"

"Let it be, Harry."

He placed one hand gently on her arm and turned her towards him.

"No, I won't. Something's amiss. I can see it in your face. This could be serious. You need all the allies you can get. . . ." He paused and hung his head. "Even if you don't want them."

"Ah, Harry, knock it off. Blast it. It's not that I didn't want *you* to know. I didn't want *anyone* to know. It complicates matters."

"Then I'll keep my mouth shut about it, Jade, and my eyes and ears open. But someone's playing at a cruel game here, and when I find him, I'm going to rip his ruddy limbs off."

"Miss del Cameron," called Finch, "you may step inside, if you please, but don't touch anything. Miller has gloves. Tell him what you want to see."

Jade slipped in the door, leaving Harry to cool his heels outside. Finch stood inside the doorway with Constable Miller beside a narrow bed with a thin mattress atop what appeared to be a rough, wire framework. A wispy veil of mosquito netting hung from a crossbeam under the tin roof. A three-feet-tall post with a perch stood in one corner next to an upended crate. Two bowls sat on the crate and a large gray parrot occupied the perch. The room was nearly devoid of creature comforts. Smells filled the void: stale sweat, cigarettes, spilled gin, and bird droppings.

"If he hadn't died at the river, living in here would have killed him for certain," said Jade. Every time she took a breath, she nearly choked.

"Miller, see if that window opens," said Finch.

"Right, sir." Miller undid the window latch and tried to swing it open. "It won't budge, sir. Possibly painted shut outside."

Harry bullied his way through the open doorframe and

strode quickly to the window. He shoved Miller out of the way. "Let a man do that." He beat his fist all around the framework, loosening it. On the last punch, the window frame flew open, slamming back into the outside wall. The glass shattered and the frame rebounded with only a few shards remaining.

"Well, at least Jade has some air," Harry said.

"Pile in. Salt," squawked the bird.

"Thanks, Harry," Jade said dryly as he went back outside.

Finch pointed to a stack of wooden crates that served as shelves. "One set of clothes, nothing in the pockets. Some tins of beef, a shaving kit, burlap bag of seeds and nuts."

"For the bird, I suppose. No papers?" asked Jade.

"Not that we've found so far, but we haven't looked everywhere."

Finch jerked his thumb to the bed and Miller went to it. At a nod from the inspector, Miller flipped the mattress over and onto the floor. When it hit, it released a cloud of dust and mold. Jade coughed again. The only thing that kept her from leaving was the sight of a bundle of papers and paper money that had been secreted between the frame mesh and the mattress.

Finch picked up the papers and untied the string that bound them together. "Maps."

"Maps? Of where?" asked Jade, waving away the dust.

Finch flipped through the pages. "Appears to be the Belgian Congo."

"Pile in! Pile in! Leopold's an ass!"

"That would explain the bird," said Harry. "That gray parrot is from the Congo, if I'm not mistaken." When the others looked at him for explanation, he added, "I once took some naturalists on a collecting safari to the lakes. All they talked about was birds."

"You said that Waters was known for looking for opportunities," said Finch. "If that's the case, he may have been scouting about in the Congo for gold before looking up north." He retied the maps and motioned for Miller to replace the mattress.

"We could ask at the land office. See if he staked a claim up north," said Jade.

Both Finch and Harry turned to her, shaking their heads.

"We?" asked Finch. "Your part is done, Miss del Cameron. I've seen nothing here that connects Waters to those packages you've received and, as you haven't indicated anything to the contrary, neither have you. Thank you for your help, but I must insist that you forget about all this."

"The inspector's right, Jade," said Harry. "I'll take you home."

Jade had little choice but to agree. She'd ridden here with Finch, Harry trailing in his truck. She'd never catch a rickshaw or taxi in this part of town.

"And one of you take that bird with you," said Finch.

"It's all yours, Jade," said Harry. "I don't want it."

Jade looked at the parrot, preening itself on its perch. "Biscuit will want to eat it."

"Salt! Salt! Salt!"

"Biscuit has better taste than that," said Harry.

CHAPTER 10

Crocodiles are "fearfully and wonderfully made." Their eyes, nose,
and ear holes perch atop their heads, enabling them to stay
nearly submerged and unseen but seeing. It's as if they invented
a primitive periscope. And they are quick learners, too.
—The Traveler

WEDNESDAY'S ISSUE OF THE *STANDARD* bore a full column elaborating on Mr. Waters' untimely demise. A second page contained photographs of the abandoned truck, Harry aiming his rifle at the water, and the croc's head visible from the emerging spray of water. The article was followed by another on crocodiles in general and the numerous native deaths attributed to them. Thursday's issue added that a .455 Webley cartridge had been found lodged in Mr. Waters' rib and that his right ear was missing.

Thursday's issue of the *Leader* spent a full column on Mr. Waters' possible partnership in a mysterious gold mine with the late Mr. Stockton. A second column speculated on the unlikely coincidence that Jade had discovered both of the recently deceased bodies. By Thursday afternoon, the deaths were the talk of Nairobi, capping all other discussions, including the more recent cases of plague in the Indian district and Lady Northey's latest charitable tea.

"At least the reporter didn't put your photograph in there, Jade," said Beverly. "That reporter from the *Leader* actually took Emily to lunch to probe for information. Luckily my sister knew very little to tell. Imagine the cheek!"

They were seated on the Dunburys' veranda, an hour before the Girl Guide safari meeting. Alice Merrywether cooed happily in her perambulator, sucking on her big toe, which she'd managed to fit into her mouth. Biscuit snoozed at Jade's feet, his head resting on his forepaws.

"Getting her to verify that I'd been involved was bad enough," said Jade. "What was your sister thinking?"

"Emily doesn't have enough experience with men to tell when they're using her," said Beverly. "I think she truly thought that he was a nice gentleman."

"But it's not accurate to say that I found Waters' body. All I really found was the truck and the croc. The body found us. The *Leader*'s implication is that trouble always seems to turn up when I'm around, as if *I* created it."

"It is a pity," agreed Beverly. "I've already had one mother ring me up and tell me that she won't allow her daughter to join us on safari. I told her we were staying atop the falls and would be perfectly safe, but she felt inclined to believe that you would find some other peril for her child."

"I'm sure we'll hear more of that at the meeting," said Jade. Her shoulder twitched involuntarily and she rubbed it.

Beverly caught the movement and frowned. "You're still having nervous disorders, aren't you, Jade." She held up one hand, stalling any protest on Jade's part. "There's no need to answer; I can see it's true. I don't think you should be alone right now. Especially if someone went into your bungalow to hide that terrible letter. Did you ask Farhani if he'd seen anyone about?"

"He saw only Matthew, the cook," said Jade. "I suppose he was bringing me food at your direction."

"Nonsense," said Bev. "Why would you think that?"

"You're already insisting that I eat every meal and take tea with you, Bev, ever since I returned from that crocodile hunt. You *know* I hate tea. You could at least serve that spiced variety." Jade silently cursed the latest corpse and the ensuing investigation for keeping her from buying more coffee.

"I don't care for it much myself," said Beverly. "It's not genuine British tea, and who ever heard of pepper in tea? But you're changing the subject. You should be staying at the house with us."

"Bev, there's no room. Your nanny and the baby take up one bedroom, and Emily has the other spare. It's a hotel here." She nodded towards the barn. "And with that obnoxious parrot, it's turning into a zoo as well."

"It is a dreadful bird," agreed Emily, who just then joined them on the porch. She wore a spring green silk dress in a soft white floral print. "At least it's shut away in the barn, where we don't have to listen to it." She wiggled her fingers at the baby, causing Alice to erupt into giggles.

"What else could I do?" asked Jade. "Biscuit kept eyeing it and licking his chops."

"I'm sure it's driving the horses crazy. I know it's annoying Avery," said Bev. "We'll have to do something with it."

"I'll take care of it," said Jade. "After all, I brought it here."

"That man Waters must have had terrible eating habits," said Emily as she rocked the perambulator to and fro. "'Pile in salt'? What an odd phrase for that bird to overhear. What else could it mean?"

"Are you planning on passing this on to another reporter?" asked Jade. Emily blushed and ducked her head. Jade instantly regretted her accusation. "I'm sorry, Emily. It wasn't your fault. The man used you."

"And he seemed so refined and genteel, too," murmured Emily.

"I can shoot him if you'd like," said Jade. She had the pleasure of seeing Emily smile. "But to answer your question, the bird seems to be giving two separate phrases. At least, I hear the bird yell 'salt' all by itself and 'pile in' at other times."

"Perhaps 'pile in' is a slang phrase," suggested Emily. "Pile in a car?"

"The man must have had an accent that the bird picked up," said Beverly. "'Pile in' actually sounds more like 'pale in' to me. We might be assuming he says 'pile in' because we hear 'salt' afterwards?"

Jade nodded. "Harry said that Waters was Cockney. But those might also be mining terms. Maybe they found a salt bed the first time and Waters was so angry he shouted it. The volume or severity of his tone could have impressed the word on the bird."

"Interesting. I'll have to ask Avery," said Bev. "He's remarkably clever about a great number of things." She looked at her older sister, who was still amusing the baby. "Emily, you look *particularly* lovely today. Are you seeing someone tonight?" The question was innocently asked, but Emily's lips briefly pinched together.

"Perhaps. Nothing has been planned, but I'm hopeful," she replied.

"Oh," said Bev, "someone who is dropping in? But all I know of are the girls and . . ." She paused, her brow scrunched in puzzlement.

"Steven Holly," said Jade. "Mary's uncle."

Beverly's eyes opened wide. "Emily?"

Emily tugged at her elbow-length sleeves and smoothed the skirt. "He has brought his niece to the meetings in the past."

"But Mr. Holly?" Beverly asked.

"There! I knew you would disapprove of him. I don't see that I need my younger sister to act as my guardian," Emily said, half rising from her chair.

"Sit down, Emily!" said Beverly, then quickly added, "Please. You don't need my approval. It's just that you're a smashing girl and you can do much better than Mr. Holly."

Emily sat down again and resumed pushing and pulling the perambulator. "He's not such a bad sort. And he works at a bank. You know as well as I that I wouldn't make a good settler's wife. I'd be terrified to step out of doors. I've never had your dash and daring, Beverly."

"No one's suggesting that you marry a farmer, Emily," said Beverly. She turned to Jade for support. "Are we, Jade?"

"Please don't include me in this discussion, Bev." Jade rubbed her arms again, trying to will away the creeping-flesh feeling.

"Oh, but I want your opinion, Jade," said Emily. "I know you'll speak the truth. Do you think that Mr. Holly is a poor choice?"

Jade sighed. "Yes, I do. He's a skirt chaser, he drinks too much, and he has the intellect of a bug. A very stupid bug."

Emily slumped in her chair. "I suppose you've *both* picked out some nice stodgy old goat for me. I'm too *old* for a spot of fun or a handsome man. Not the sort of thing a skirt chaser, as you called him, would find worth going after." She folded her arms across her chest and looked away, her blue eyes liquid with tears. "Even that silly little reporter only wanted a story out of me."

Bev jumped to her feet and put her arms around her sister. "There, there, Emily. You are too worth chasing."

"No!" Emily choked back a sob. "I couldn't even seduce that reporter."

"What?!" exclaimed Beverly. "When did you . . ."

Emily swiped the back of her hand across her eyes. "This morning. I saw the paper, and I thought I could convince Mr. Smythe, the reporter, to print a retraction. I knew his flat was in the Victoria, so I went there and . . . well, he wouldn't even let me in."

"Of course not, Emily," said Beverly. "What gentleman would?"

"He's probably looking for someone rich," offered Jade, "rather than pretty and smart."

Emily patted her eyes with a lace hankie. "You could be right, Jade. From what I saw of his room, he seemed to have extravagant tastes. Perhaps he prefers men!"

Beverly's eyes opened wider, and Jade wished that she were anywhere but here, imposing on this sad family scene. She turned her gaze from the sisters, giving them some privacy, and spotted a rickshaw coming up the lane.

"We have company, Bev," Jade said.

Emily looked up, her eyes hopeful; then her shoulders sagged again. "It's one of your girls," she said as she dabbed at her eyes with her sleeve. "Excuse me while I patch myself up. It won't do for anyone to see me with red eyes." She ran inside.

"It's Mary," said Bev. "She's two hours early and," she added with a glance at the house, "alone. While I can't say I'm sorry, I do hate to see Emily disappointed."

The rickshaw driver, a Kikuyu on a bicycle, stopped a few feet away, and Mary climbed down from the seat. She wore her Girl Guide uniform and, with great solemnity, opened her little pocketbook and handed a few rupees to the driver.

"Mary," said Bev, after the driver pedaled off and the girl joined them on the veranda, "what are you doing here alone?"

"Oh, madam," said Mary. "I didn't know what else to do."

"What's wrong?" asked Jade. "Has something happened to your mother?"

"No," said Mary. "Mother is at a planning committee for another garden party. It's to raise money for the Lady Northey Home for Children." She looked from Jade to Beverly. "She's to collect me *after* the meeting."

"But she sent you here alone in a rickshaw?" asked Bev.

"Oh, no!" said Mary, her eyes widening. "Mother would never do that. She doesn't know. It's my uncle, Steven. *He* was to bring me here. He promised to help me pick out new boots today, for our safari. But he wasn't at the bank when I stopped after school. And they said he hadn't come in all day."

"He's probably sick and forgot to telephone in," suggested Jade. "Does he have a telephone where he lives?" It occurred to her that she had no idea where a bachelor like Holly would stay.

"He doesn't have one in his rooms, Miss Jade," said Mary.

"Well, there, you see?" said Beverly. "He could hardly telephone then."

"But there is a telephone at the lobby desk," the girl said. "He has rooms at the Victoria Hotel." She fidgeted with her kerchief.

"Sit down, Mary," said Jade as she pointed to the chair that Emily had vacated moments before.

Mary sat, but she continued to fuss with her attire. "I stopped at the bank when I didn't see him at the school and they said that they'd called the hotel. The desk clerk knocked on his door, but no one answered."

"I'll get her something to drink," said Bev. "Keep an eye on the baby, please."

"Your uncle is a grown man, Mary," said Jade. "If he's not well, he might have gone to see a doctor."

"But he would have left a message on his way out," wailed Mary. "I just know something is wrong. Miss Jade, you're clever at solving problems. Please help me find him. I'm afraid he's gotten himself into some trouble."

Beverly rejoined them along with Emily, who had freshly powdered her face. They were soon followed by Farhani, the Dunburys' majordomo. As usual, Farhani was dressed in a long white robe, neatly pressed. He carried a silver tray with four glasses of freshly squeezed lemonade and handed them around using a linen cloth even though he wore white gloves.

"Northey telephoned, memsahib," Farhani said to Bev. "I have told her that you were not at home."

"*Lady* Northey, Farhani," Beverly chided. "You cannot just call her Northey. And thank you. I suppose I'll have to ring her up later."

Emily pulled up another chair and, after Farhani went back into the house, they resumed their conversation.

"As I told Miss Jade," said Mary, "Uncle Steven would surely have answered his door even if it had been to tell the desk clerk to leave him alone. I just know that something is wrong."

At the mention of Steven Holly, Emily sat up straighter in her seat. "Has something happened to Mr. Holly?"

Mary nodded. "He's missing or hurt or something. I just know it."

"Now, Mary," cautioned Beverly, "you don't know that. You are letting your imagination run away with you."

"When did you last see your uncle?" asked Jade.

"Two evenings ago," she said. "He ate dinner with us and talked on and on about his silly gold mine. He was perfectly fine then. And now all this business in the papers about two men dead, both of whom had a share in a mine."

"Did you go to his rooms at the hotel today?" Jade asked.

"Yes, but the clerk wouldn't let me go up alone. He said that children should not be running about disturbing the residents." Her lips pursed together into a pout. "I'm hardly a child. I'm thirteen now, you know."

"We really should see if something is the matter," said Emily. "He may be unconscious."

"I'll ask Avery if he'll stop by the Victoria Hotel," said Beverly. "Will that be satisfactory, Mary?"

"Yes, thank you, madame," said Mary. She sighed. "Uncle Steven *is* rather stupid, but he is family. And we have a duty to family."

"Oh, I couldn't agree with you more," said Jade. When Beverly raised her brows and Emily glowered, Jade hastily explained, "That we have a duty to family."

"That's quite all right, Miss Jade," said Mary. "But do you really think Lord Dunbury will go to town and find him?"

"We shouldn't bother him," said Emily before her sister could answer. "He's in the barn with the horses. *I'll* go into town with Mary and look for her uncle."

Mary and Emily returned two hours later for the Girl Guides meeting, just in time to hear two mothers express their horror over the girls' going anywhere near the "scene of that horrid death." The other girls had gone to the barn to see the horses, and Beverly sent Mary to join them. After Mary left, the mothers launched back into their arguments with great gusto.

To Jade's surprise, Emily came to her defense, reiterating Jade's point that the proposed campsite was above the falls and that the crocodile could not scale the rocks. She announced that with three women, herself included, watching the girls at all times, there would be no danger at all. In the end, the five older girls, the ones the trip was planned for, were allowed to go. When Jade questioned Emily about both her decision to go camping and her search for Mr. Holly, Emily only shrugged at the latter and said she thought an adventure would do her good.

Mary was noticeably quiet during the meeting, which was devoted largely to last-minute details concerning tomorrow's trip. Jade put it down to not having any luck locating her uncle. Considering the man's flighty nature, Jade assumed he'd taken a holiday for himself without bothering to inform anyone else. However, to ease Mary's disappointment and to solve her own problem, Jade made a present of the obnoxious African gray parrot to the girl. Mary was delighted with the gift and named the bird Pepper.

In the morning, Jade regretted her decision when Mary appeared with the parrot.

"He's our mascot," she declared. "I couldn't leave him behind."

"Salt! Pile in!"

Maybe the crocodile will show up and eat this thing. Jade instantly regretted the thought. *Not fair to the croc.*

"I believe everyone is here," said Beverly as she ticked off the girls' names one by one. She wore a split skirt, blouse, and tall boots. Her campaign hat bobbled as she looked around to where Avery was busily tying down the last of the gear onto one of two hired Overlands, whose cloth canopies had been covered in wooden planks to hold the tents. "Emily?" she called.

"I'm here." Emily came from the house with a basket of fresh scones. "Matthew *mpishi* just took these from the oven. There's plenty for everyone."

She passed the basket around and Jade took one of the sweet pastries. "Thanks, Emily." She noted with approval that the woman had opted to wear practical jodhpurs and a linen shirt rather than a dress. "I think you'll enjoy yourself for these two days. The change will be good for you."

"I hope so, Jade," Emily said. "I'm so tired of Nairobi. Why, this morning's papers are filled with news every bit as

awful as that Waters' death. More trouble in the Indian district. There was a knife attack there just yesterday afternoon.
Between that and the plague cases, it's not safe to visit the
bazaars."

"Knife attack?" asked Jade, after she swallowed a mouthful of buttery pastry and raisins.

"Yes. It seems that an unnamed Englishman was caught
up in the middle of a squabble between a shopkeeper and
another Indian. He was stabbed in the leg, according to the
paper."

Jade wondered at Emily's concern. "I hope you're not
worried that it was Mr. Holly. But even if it was, it probably
wasn't serious." Jade nodded towards Mary, who was chat-
tering away with the girls. "Mary doesn't seem anxious this
morning."

"Oh, I'm not worried," said Emily. "On the contrary, I'm
looking forward to this little excursion."

Mary joined them, holding the parrot in a cage. Biscuit
stuck his nose against the bars and sniffed. Pepper let out an
ear-piercing squawk and Biscuit immediately pulled back.

"I must tell you all," said Mary, "that one of our teachers
is coming along as a chaperone."

"A chaperone!" exclaimed Jade. "Why do we need a
chaperone?"

"Um, perhaps that's not the correct word, Miss Jade. Miss
Biddleford is concerned about our having a day off from
school for this outing. I believe she intends to make certain
that we are actually learning something about nature while
we're at the falls."

"Sweet Millard Fillmore on a bicycle," Jade muttered.
"Does Lady Dunbury know?"

"I just informed madame before I told you."

"Well, she'd better get here soon," said Jade, "or we're leaving without her."

Mary pointed to the end of the lane. "I believe she's arriving now."

A taxi pulled up and a dowdy woman stepped out. She wore a heavy brown serge dress that came to her lower calves and old-fashioned woolen stockings. Like many of the Kenya colonists, she must have feared not only the equatorial sun, but insects as well, since her red-lined, broad-brimmed straw hat was swathed with netting like a beekeeper's bonnet. Mary and Elspeth hastened over to help her with her bag.

"I hope I haven't kept you waiting," Miss Biddleford said in a high, crackly voice nearly as piercing as the parrot's.

"I asked Avery to find another cot," whispered Beverly. "But where are we going to put her? Perhaps I should stay at home after all."

"You'll do no such thing, Bev," snapped Jade. "You need time away from the baby, and you're the troop leader. I'll ride my motorcycle. Emily can drive the newer Overland. Put Miss Biddlebody in with Helen and Mary and that blasted parrot."

"Biddleford," corrected Beverly. "The girls told me she's a fine teacher." She shook her head in disbelief as the girls clustered around the woman. "What about Biscuit? If he goes with them, he might eat the parrot."

"One can only hope. He'll ride in the sidecar. He actually enjoys it."

While Jade checked and tightened the sidecars' connectors, Emily escorted the teacher to a shiny green vehicle whose top and sides were laden with camping gear, and helped her into the front passenger seat. Mary sat in the back with Pepper and Helen and several boxes. The other three girls bundled into the older Overland, a black Express model whose rear bench had been removed to hold supplies. After Beverly made a visit to the nursery and the nanny, and gave a parting kiss to Avery, they drove off, Jade and Biscuit taking point.

Jade kept the pace slower than she would have if she had been alone. After all, she reasoned, she wasn't sure just how good a driver Emily was, especially with all the noisy distractions in her car. One of those distractions, the teacher, had piqued Jade's interest, and when they'd finally reached their chosen camping spot on the north side of the river above the falls, Jade grabbed the teacher by the arm and yanked off her hat.

"Okay, Mr. Holly. Just what are you up to now?"

CHAPTER 11

Their nostrils close when they submerge, and they have means of sealing off their throat, too, enabling them to open their jaws and seize prey underwater. It's reminiscent of the Red Riding Hood tale:
"The better to eat you with, my dear."
—The Traveler

"You have to let me stay, Jade," Steven Holly begged as he snatched back the hat and plopped it on his head. "My life is in danger!"

"Control yourself, Mr. Holly!" exclaimed Beverly. She whipped around and faced Mary. "Mary Postlewaithe, shame on you! A Girl Guide does not perpetrate deceptions or tell falsehoods. And you talked all the other girls into assisting you in this fraud."

Mary hung her head. "We're very sorry, madame, but we *had* to help my uncle. When Miss Emily and I found . . ." She stopped abruptly and grimaced.

"Ah, so my sister was in on this, too," said Beverly. She glared at Emily. "I'll deal with *you* later."

"Explain yourself, Mr. Holly," said Jade. She stood in front of him with her arms folded.

"My life is in danger. I'm certain of it," Holly whined.

"First that man Stockton was killed and pushed over the Limuru Bridge; then Waters was fed to a crocodile. I'm next!"

"How well did you know Waters?" asked Jade.

"He's the man who talked me into investing in the gold mine." Holly waved his arms about, accidentally knocking his hat and wig off again. "Don't you see? Someone wants complete control over the mine. They don't want to share any of the gold, so they're eliminating all of the other partners." He plopped his wig back on his head and tugged it into place. "It must be worth a fortune!" he said in a breathy voice.

"Mr. Holly, the police suspect that *Waters* killed Stockton."

"But the papers said that Waters was shot!" exclaimed Holly. "I know I'm next."

Jade frowned, shaking her head. "He could have been killed by someone else whom he tried to get to invest. Someone who didn't like being taken. It doesn't mean you're in danger. And take off that costume. You look positively ridiculous."

Holly shook his head. "I can't risk being seen."

Beverly and Emily stood to one side, listening. "Mr. Holly," said Emily, "tell them what you told me yesterday."

Holly nodded, his wig slipping over his forehead. "I've been threatened."

"Threatened?" exclaimed Beverly. "By whom?"

"I don't know," Holly said. "I returned to the hotel two nights ago and picked up my mail from the desk clerk as usual. There was a parcel with no return name, return address, or postage. Inside was a threatening note. It told me to give up my share in the mine or my life would suffer for it and . . . well, never mind what else. It isn't important."

"Did you take the note to the police?"

Holly shook his head, and his wig slipped around to the side of his face. "Oh, no!" He shuddered. "The message said that I'd be dead very soon and very dreadfully if I did that."

"Did he show you this note, Emily?" asked Jade.

"No, but why should we not believe him?"

Jade could think of a variety of reasons but she kept them to herself, since most stemmed from her dislike of the man and his intemperate habits. She watched his face closely. That he was terrified was obvious. But he was also hiding something. "What else was in your packet, Mr. Holly? You must tell us."

"No! I don't want to endanger you."

"It's too late for that. You already have. Now tell me."

Holly's entire body shook. "It's too horrid."

"Mr. Holly!"

He leaned in closer to Jade. "It was a human ear. A bit dried, rather like one of those tree fungi, but an ear nonetheless."

"Waters was missing an ear," Jade said softly. She looked at Emily. "I assume you had something to do with this getup?" She swept one hand up and down, indicating Holly's disguise.

Emily answered while Holly readjusted his wig and hat. "Yes. When Mary and I went to his hotel, the clerk said that he was not answering and so must be out. Mary and I went to his room. I slipped a note under his door, assuring him that we only wanted to assist him, and to let us know how. As you might suppose, he was hiding in his rooms and he quickly opened the door and pulled us in."

"Emily!" scolded Beverly.

"Don't 'Emily' me," she snapped back. "When Mr. Holly

explained his plight, I offered to purchase some clothes for a disguise. Mary suggested that Mr. Holly pose as one of her teachers, coming along for the safari. We returned with the items, left them with him, and came home in time for last evening's meeting."

"And you slipped out this morning, Mr. Holly?" asked Jade.

"Please, you ladies should all call me Steven."

"We should refer to you as Miss Biddleford in case someone is listening," suggested Emily.

"He can call himself Lord High Queen of the May as far as I'm concerned," said Jade. "I want to know how he managed to get away."

"Why, I donned the disguise and walked out of the hotel," said Holly. "No one would be watching the activities of an elderly woman."

"But someone might wonder about such a woman leaving when none like her was ever seen to go into the hotel. Especially if Emily's two visits were observed. It would certainly look suspicious to me."

"I say, I hadn't really thought about that."

Jade scoffed. "Somehow, *your* not thinking doesn't surprise me. But if you put these girls in trouble with your careless actions, you'll answer to me and you'll wish a croc had you."

"But what can I do?" Holly asked. "I can't go back to Nairobi. Not for a while, at least."

"You certainly can't hide out here forever," said Jade. "You'd do better to go to the police. Talk to Inspector Finch. He's familiar with these other deaths. Take the ear with you."

"I threw it away. Hideous thing."

"Mr. Holly," said Beverly, "we're camping only one night this time and going back to Nairobi late tomorrow afternoon. I can't see that staying here is going to help you."

"But it can't hurt," broke in Emily. "I mean to say, his staying with us for one night isn't going to cause suspicion. When we return, we could escort him safely to the inspector."

"I promise I'll keep out of the way," said Holly. "I'll hide in one of the tents."

"We don't have a tent for you," said Jade. "You can hide in the old Overland, and that's where you'll also sleep."

"Perhaps I shall just take a stroll right now," Holly said, "since I am not wanted about."

"Watch out for lions and crocodiles," said Jade. She was amused to see him suddenly start and look around as though one might be lurking right next to him.

But Holly walked off anyway, tromping through the grasses in his long dress, his big hat bobbing from side to side. Biscuit followed for a few yards before he took off on his own.

Emily looked sheepishly at the other two women, but neither Jade nor Bev scolded her. Instead, Bev commended her sister on her kindhearted feelings and set her to assisting the girls with pitching the three tents. Bev was to share one with Mary and Clarice, Emily with Helen and Lily, and Jade with Elspeth, so that none of the girls was left without adult protection. Once the tents were up and the noisy parrot stowed in his cage in the back of an Overland, the girls began an exercise in tracking according to their handbook.

Lily put on a pair of hobnailed boots and, while the other girls sat in the tents, walked a circuitous route. When she returned, the other four came out and tried to follow her tracks. At first, it was easy; all four of them had heard which way their friend went. But as Lily used some of the rocks as part of her route, they soon lost her obvious footprints. When that happened, they went back to the last set of prints and began making circles around it, each time moving farther out until they came across another set of prints.

Jade observed them for a while, making suggestions when they lost the tracks. She showed them how to tell when their friend was running or, at one point, walking backwards to confuse them. When they were nearly at the finish, she left them in Bev and Emily's care and went to tend to the campfire. At this point, Jade was ready to kill for a cup of coffee. She set the pot of water to boil, threw in enough of her spiced tea for at least three mugsful, and set it aside to steep and cool. While she waited she photographed the falls from the top.

"Miss Jade," called Clarice, "we did it. We tracked her. What shall we do next?"

Jade had just returned to camp and poured a cup of tea for herself when the girl called her attention away from the pot. "Look for other tracks. Don't follow them, but see if you can identify them."

"Do you mean decide if they are lion or elephant or something else?"

"Yes." Jade doubted they'd find anything other than an old set of antelope impressions, but it would keep them occupied for a while.

"I found Mr. Holly's tracks," said Helen. "I think we should follow Mary's uncle and see where he went."

"I think it best that we leave Mr. Holly alone for a while," said Beverly. "I'm sure Mary's intentions for inviting him along were well meant, but the deception was hardly suitable to a Girl Guide."

"What about these tracks, Miss Jade?" called Mary. "Are these lion tracks?"

Jade set her mug of scalding hot tea down on the rock, thought better of it, and poured it back into the pot to stay hot. "No, not lion," she said when she joined the girls and Beverly. "There are claw marks on these tracks. Lions pull their claws in like house cats."

"I know," said Lily. "They're cheetah tracks." She looked around the camp. "Biscuit's gone. These must be his."

"Where did he go?" asked Helen, concern edging her voice. "Should we follow and make certain that he's quite all right?"

"Biscuit is fine," said Jade. "He's probably hunting."

"Should I take them upriver to have a look-see?" asked Beverly. She nodded to the Enfield rifle leaning against her tent. "Avery has been working with me. I'm a good shot."

Jade looked around, her own Winchester slung across her back. The grasses were shorter up here, making it harder for a predator to hide. Still, she felt uneasy. While there were not as many animals here as below the falls, there were a few trees for someone to hide behind. "I'm more concerned about humans now than animals," she said.

Stupid Holly. "I'll walk with you fifty or sixty yards and do a sweep of the area just to be sure it's safe," said Jade. "But, Bev, if you have the slightest hint of trouble, fire a shot in the air. I'll be there on the double-quick."

They walked together above the falls, the girls peering among the rocks and in the dirt for tracks, while Beverly and Jade kept their eyes alert for any sign of danger. Emily, Jade noted, kept straining her eyes to the distance, possibly for some sign of Steven Holly. *She may be a little silly, but she's too nice for him.* Jade knew that Bev had hoped to introduce Emily to Lord Colridge's son, but Edmunde was in Europe at the moment.

"You're fine here, Bev," Jade said. "If the girls can't find anything, they can always practice with their slings. I'm going to enjoy a moment of relative silence."

"You're too late," said Beverly. She nodded towards a small trail of dust coming closer. "We have company."

Jade shielded her eyes with one hand and peered towards the now visible truck. "Oh, spit fire and save the matches! It's Hascombe."

"Hmm," murmured Beverly. "I'll just engage the girls in some footraces or something."

"You do that. I'm going to see what he wants." Jade shouldered her rifle and walked briskly back to camp, returning just as Harry poured a mug of Jade's tea. He downed it in three gulps and poured another.

"Help yourself, Harry," said Jade, not really meaning it.

"Don't mind if I do," he said, and downed the second cup. "This is good. I needed that." To Jade's dismay, he poured a third and set the nearly empty pot back on the rock. "Percival's hired me to help him find that croc. He thinks it went downriver, away from the nearest village, but he needs to be sure." Harry took another gulp of tea. "Nakuru and I've been all over the river below these falls. Haven't seen so much as a ripple in the water or a log on the shore." He finished the drink, wiped his mouth with his sleeve, and set the mug down by the pot. "Thought maybe you might have something to report on the matter."

"Why would I?" Jade asked. "I said we were staying above the falls. I have my hands full as it is without looking for that crocodile."

Harry shifted his position. "Ah, truth be told, I wanted to see how you were after all this mess. I can tell you've not been yourself recently. I blame it all on that damned Featherstone. How in blazes he could go off and leave behind a woman like you is beyond me. I've been worried about you, Jade. Seeing that croc, finding that corpse."

"I'm fine, Harry."

"Don't lie to me, Jade. Not sure who's the bigger fool: Featherstone for abandoning you, or you for waiting for him." He took a step towards her. "Now, you and I are a pair, Jade. We both love Africa and we don't settle well into domesticity. I want you to come with me. We're a good team. I'll take care of you." He reached for her but Jade backed away.

"Are you proposing, Harry? Or just propositioning?"

Harry pulled his hand back. "No. I mean to say—"

"Give it up, Harry. I'd shoot you before a week was out."

His face widened into a big grin. "Ah, that's my girl. But you wouldn't. You'd see. Just you give it some thought." His broad shoulders twitched and he rubbed his arms.

"Drop it, Harry!"

"No. I won't." Harry looked at her, his chin in a mutinous pose. "All I am saying is that he's gone, but I'm still here. And I think you should damn well recognize that."

"Of course you're here, Harry. This is your home." She pointed beyond the hill. "Your old ranch is right around the bend of the mountain."

"Not much there anymore. I sold the cattle." He twitched his shoulders as if the small of his back itched. "A home without a woman isn't much of a home." He reached for her again, but Jade sidestepped him. "I found the woman. You."

"If you're waiting for me, then you should sell the land."

He dropped his arms in defeat before swatting at his head as though an insect was annoying him. "I tried to. No buyers willing to pay anything for it. So I kept it. Sometimes I have an older client who just wants to shoot a little and I take him there. The house is in decent enough repair for someone who doesn't want frills." He took off his hat and swiped at his forehead. "Hell, sometimes I just hire it out to some collector or naturalist to hunt butterflies." He said the last word with a scoffing snort. His voice rose in volume and he started pacing back and forth. "Some of them use my place and don't even pay me for the pleasure."

Jade watched in some alarm, glancing at Bev and the girls finishing a race nearby. She knew Harry had a temper, but she'd never seem him get so angry so easily. "Calm down, Harry," she said. "The girls will hear you and come back to see what's wrong."

Harry started as though her voice was unexpected. "What?" Then he ducked his head and frowned sheepishly. "Sorry, Jade. I didn't mean to sound off like that. But competition for safaris is getting tight, and there are days when I wonder if I made the right decision, quitting the ranch."

"Think nothing of it, Harry."

Harry seemed to notice the girls and the other two women for the first time. "Just you ladies then?" Jade nodded, deciding to keep Holly's secret for a while longer. Harry pointed to Jade's rifle. "Perhaps you might need me to stay around to see that you're all safe?"

Jade heard the hurt in his voice and sighed. *Why are men so blasted complicated?* "We'll be fine, Harry. The best thing you can do for us is to find that crocodile. It would be nice someday to take them fishing below the falls, and I won't feel safe doing that until I know that beast is long gone."

He clamped his hat tightly on his head, his hand shaking slightly. "Right. But I'll be back tomorrow. You'll come around to my idea. You'll see."

He leaned in closer and his shadow over her became a tangible presence. Jade felt his body heat radiating like a power. With it came the scent of the African grasslands, coupled with musk and, most curious, something spicy. The combination was both heady and disturbing. His scent hovered on the edge of her mind, a menacing presence not entirely there and all the more frightening for its vagueness. She shook herself, dispelling the shudder that threatened to race down her spine.

"I don't need you to worry about me, Harry. I'm capable of taking care of myself." Even as she said the words, she questioned their veracity. Recently she felt as if she were losing her grip on her sanity. *Sam doesn't know how lucky he is, jumping ship when he did.*

Harry touched his hat brim in farewell and left just as Beverly, Emily, and the girls filed back into camp. Jade heard their giggles and boisterous calls, and envied them their carefree innocence.

"Who was that man?" asked Helen.

"Was that Mr. Hascombe?" asked Mary.

Biscuit's return distracted the girls, allowing Jade to ignore their questions. The cat strode calmly into camp, a stray feather or two stuck in his whiskers. He sat down and proceeded to wash while the girls petted and made a fuss over him.

"What did Harry want?" asked Beverly in a low voice.

"He's looking for that crocodile." Jade picked up the pot and shook it. "Blast! He left me nothing but the dregs!" She added some water from her canteen and set the pot back on the fire.

"Has Mr. Holly returned yet?" asked Emily.

Jade shook her head. "Probably just as well. I don't think he'd want Hascombe to see him dressed like a woman."

"Oh, he needn't have worried," said Beverly. "He's not Harry's type." She broke out in a melodious giggle.

Jade chuckled at the image of Harry meeting Mr. Holly in woman's clothing. "By now Harry might have wondered how often Miss Biddleford has to shave."

Only Emily didn't see the humor. "Are you sure you can trust this Mr. Hascombe? What if he's the man who threatened Steven? Perhaps he followed him here."

"Harry Hascombe is a rounder and a scoundrel," said Jade, "but I don't think you have to worry about him hurting Holly."

"What Jade means," said Beverly, "is that deep down, Harry is a good man and not a murderer."

"Actually, what I meant," said Jade, "is that he doesn't have the patience to come up with this mining scheme. When Harry's angry, he'd just as soon belt someone then and there. He wouldn't plot out these so-called accidental deaths." Even as she said this, she remembered her first dealings with him when he'd tried to pass off another man as David Worthy's missing half brother. A twinge of doubt, heightened by the sense of danger she'd felt when he came close, gave her pause.

"Jade!" scolded Bev. "You know Harry well enough to trust him with your life."

"I can't trust him with my tea, though," she said as she retrieved the now boiling pot and poured herself half a cup.

"As long as you're certain of him," said Emily, "but I am concerned that Mr. Holly hasn't come back. It's been several hours now."

"I promise if he's not back by the time the girls have our lunch ready, I'll go find him," said Jade. She took a sip of the tea and spat out a mouthful of loose leaves. She tossed the contents from the cup and settled for water from her canteen instead. The next hour was devoted to Beverly's campfire cooking lesson. While Bev took the girls and Emily through the steps of baking a few little flatbreads on a heated stone, Jade wondered where Holly had wandered off to.

I'm not responsible for him. Then she saw Emily's worried frown and mentally chided herself, especially since she'd suspected Holly's disguise even back at the Dunburys' house. *I should have left him behind then.* But she'd wanted to know what had frightened him enough to make a complete fool of himself, hoping it would be a clue to her own problem.

By the time Lily announced that lunch was served, Jade was seriously concerned. She took one of the breads, added some tinned beef, and wolfed it down. She finished it off with more water from her canteen.

"Bev," she called, "I'm going to look for Mr. Holly. You have the camp."

THE CROCODILE'S LAST EMBRACE 151

Beverly came to Jade's side so she could speak in relative privacy. Jade doubted that was possible, considering the attentive faces and the six pairs of ears that seemed to grow larger as heads tilted towards their conversation.

"Where do you plan to look?" asked Bev in a near whisper.

"I'll follow his tracks," said Jade. "I think he went up to the bridge."

"That means he crossed the river."

"Yes, and I wouldn't think he'd do that except I haven't caught sight of him anywhere on the plains. Not that I was looking for him much of the time."

"I wish Harry were going with you. I don't care for your wandering off alone, Jade. Too much has happened."

Jade put a hand on her friend's shoulder and smiled. "I'll be fine, Bev. I've got my Winchester and I'll take Biscuit. If there's any problem, I'll send him back for you. I'll be back before dark, with or without Holly."

Jade picked up Holly's trail quickly enough. He'd stomped off in his ungainly shoes, shuffling and kicking aside debris as he tried to maneuver with the long skirt. Instead of continuing to the bridge, he'd forded the Athi where it broke into a series of serpentine channels winding over themselves. During the rains, the channels filled and merged into one, the falls flowing in a torrent. Now the water level at these upper reaches had diminished to make crossing possible by stepping back and forth on the dry patches until one found a spot to jump the next part of the river. In a few places, the width was such that wading was the only option. It was one Biscuit didn't care for and he told his mistress in a series of discontented churrs and growls. Jade considered going up to the bridge, but then she'd have to work harder to pick up his trail on the other side.

"Come or go back," Jade told him. "I'm going on." She sloshed through the calf-deep water, grateful that she'd recently oiled her boots to make them somewhat waterproof. Still, she could feel the chill through the leather.

Biscuit called to her again, pacing back and forth on his little dry patch. Jade spoke to him, urging him to join her. "It's all right, boy. It's just water. You can make it. Come on."

Finally, when she'd taken two more steps away from him, the cheetah reached a decision and gathered his hind-quarters under him, tensing for a great leap.

He almost made it. One hind foot slipped at the end on a wet rock and dipped into the river. Biscuit trotted to Jade's side and paused to shake the hind foot. He butted her on the thigh and she rewarded him with a scratch behind his ears.

"Looks like we were on the right track, too," she said. A few yards ahead of her lay Holly's straw hat and wig, discarded behind a large black rock. "What do you think, boy? Did he drop them here intentionally or by accident?"

She picked them up in case he'd left a note hidden underneath, but there was nothing. Jade left them and resumed her search for his shoe prints. The moment she found them, she also spied an elephant in the distance, looking at her. The huge bull had one broken tusk. The animal turned away from her and ambled off to skirt the mountain. He turned his head once more and shook it, his great ears flapping.

"What do you think, boy? I don't believe he wants us

around. Not much choice, though. We'll give him a wide berth, right?"

Jade readjusted her rifle in her arms and strode off towards the elephant. When she looked down, she saw that both she and the elephant were on the same track that Holly had taken.

CHAPTER 12

These marvelous adaptations don't stop there. The crocodile has a third, transparent eyelid that allows it to see underwater.
—The Traveler

JADE EASILY PICKED UP HOLLY'S TRAIL. The man must have had a difficult time walking in the borrowed shoes and cumbersome dress, and the smashed grasses, kicked clods, and scrapes were impossible to miss. She was surprised he'd gone so far in the getup, testimony to how afraid he was to remove it and risk being recognized. But what she didn't understand was why he hadn't just turned around and headed back to camp. Of course, it was possible that a city dandy like Holly couldn't follow his own trail back and had gotten lost.

He can't be that stupid. Then she remembered his own niece's assessment of him. *Well, maybe he is at that.*

Across the broad plains, Ol Donyo Sabuk rose in front of Jade, its forests beckoning with the promise of cool shade and interesting wildlife. As befitted its Kikuyu name, the mountain of the big rain, its shape from above was that of a raindrop, with the narrow end pointing north and facing her. Holly's trail skirted it to the west, towards Harry's former ranch. After a short distance, he'd picked up the old dirt track, which still showed signs of use. Not surprising, as hunting was good on the mountain. It was several miles to Harry's house and Jade considered turning back for one of the Overlands, but she'd wasted enough time already.

"I expected to find him sitting under a thorn tree by now, Biscuit."

She picked up her pace, breaking into the easy, loping stride that she'd learned from the Maasai. Biscuit fell into place beside her. If she didn't spot Holly soon, she'd fire a round in the air and then call his name. At least she didn't see any vultures flapping around. She also didn't see that bull elephant, and while those giants hid easily in the forest, Jade couldn't imagine where one would hide out here in the open.

Maybe I imagined him, or else he took off towards the mountain when I wasn't looking. While she preferred to think it was the latter, her recent experiences suggested otherwise. Jade stopped and peered into the distance in all directions, looking for some sign of Holly.

There he is. Ahead, she spied an umbrella-shaped thorn tree and under it she glimpsed a bit of brown shifting slightly. "I told you he'd be under a tree, Biscuit. Probably got too tired to walk back and was hoping someone would drive after him to rescue him." She patted the cheetah's shoulders. "He's going to be very disappointed."

Jade resumed her ground-eating lope, her Winchester gripped in her right hand. But as she neared the tree she could tell she was mistaken. Holly wasn't there. Only the dress, hanging from a lower branch.

"Blast it!" she muttered. "Time to end this now!" She fired once in the air and waited for the report and its echo to fade. "Mr. Holly!" she shouted. Then she listened for an answering call, moan, cry, anything. The only sound was the cry of a bird startled from its roost. "Holly!" she called again, this time facing in another direction. Jade repeated her call to each of the cardinal points, and waited for an answer. There was none.

"He probably went on to Harry's house, looking for someplace to lie down. When I find him, I'm going to kick his backside all the way back to camp."

She pulled out her pocket watch. It was well past three o'clock and she had two and a half hours of daylight left. That alone should have suggested haste, but when she took a step, some inner voice suggested caution instead. There was no pain in her left knee, nothing to warn her of imminent danger, just a gnawing and unidentifiable sense of something being terribly wrong.

Jade was nearly around the mountain's west side, and Harry's house was located just around the bend, perhaps four hundred yards away. She could be there in minutes. Jade checked her rifle and made certain there was a round in the chamber.

"Are you with me, Biscuit?" she asked. She held her rifle at the ready and started off in a slow stalk. Her heart beat a steady rhythm in her chest, strong but slightly fast. Jade took a deep breath to steady herself and took another three steps before stopping dead in her tracks.

From around the bend strode the bull elephant, his one broken tusk nearly crossing the other. Biscuit hissed.

In a small way, the cheetah's reaction calmed Jade. *At least I'm not imagining this.*

In a large way, Biscuit's hiss worried her. Her newer

Winchester .303 British model was better than her old one against a lion or a leopard, but not this monstrous animal. If he charged, she had no place to hide and there would be very little of her left for Beverly to find later.

The bull blocked their path and stood his ground, weaving slightly from side to side. His trunk went up, testing the air, then dropped back to the ground, where it brushed the soil and the grasses. His ears flapped briefly to fan himself, but he didn't hold them out. That was some comfort. Extended ears were a sign of imminent attack. And Jade had seen the results of an elephant attack on a lion before. The rage and destruction were on a scale as large as the beast. She thought about the phrase used by soldiers who'd seen battle. They'd "seen the elephant." It made more sense than most of them realized.

Jade took a careful step back and prayed that the air, now calm, wouldn't suddenly blow in his direction. Step by painfully slow step, Jade inched back until she was near the thorn tree. If she could hide behind it, perhaps the bull would amble off somewhere else without ever having noticed her. He must be terribly old and perhaps his eyes were poor for him to have missed seeing her already.

She gained the tree and, in one quick motion, stepped behind its narrow trunk. The elephant hadn't moved. He just held his ground, a sentry blocking her passage. Jade hoped Holly wouldn't take it into his head to wander back and stumble into the animal from the rear.

She motioned for Biscuit to stay close. "He'll go away soon, boy," she whispered. "I promise." She peered around the tree at it and once again felt as though she recognized him. But common sense told her it couldn't be the old bull from Mount Marsabit. For one thing, that was over two hundred miles away. For another, she'd watched that old bull die.

This one was very much alive and he kept a close eye on her hiding spot, as if he dared her to move. Each time she peeked out, he shook his head, his bulk weaving to and fro as though he were rocking himself to sleep. Only his eyes stayed open.

"Doesn't he have somewhere to go? Some elephant cows to annoy?"

Biscuit paced in a tight circle nearby and uttered soft growls. For a moment, Jade considered sending him racing back to camp. No elephant could outrun a cheetah. But if the bull did charge, it would put him even closer to Jade's position.

That was when she heard a horn honk a number of times and her name being called by several high-pitched voices at once.

"Miss Ja-aade."

"Stop!" she shouted, hoping they'd hear her before the elephant saw them and charged the vehicle. But when she looked around the slender tree to the bull, he'd turned and sauntered off in the opposite direction.

Bev pulled the black Overland Express next to Jade. Crammed inside were Mary, Elspeth, and Helen.

"We're here to rescue you, Miss Jade," said Helen.

"And help you find my uncle," added Mary.

"Clarice and Lily wanted to come, too," added Elspeth, "but there wasn't room for all of us."

"You left them with your sister?" Jade asked Beverly.

Bev shrugged from behind the wheel. "She's perfectly

capable of staying at camp with them for a short while. I left her with my rifle. She can shoot."

"When you didn't come back, we thought there might be trouble," said Helen. She held up a roll of bandages. "We heard your shots and we came prepared to render aid."

"Have you found Mr. Holly yet?" asked Beverly. "We found and picked up his hat and wig."

Jade shook her head. "His trail leads this far." She pointed to the dress, took it down from the branch, and tossed it into the Overland. "I think he went on to Harry's old house, but an elephant blocked my path, so I haven't been able to get much farther. All your noise must have annoyed him, because he left just as you arrived."

"Well, get in and let's go find Mr. Holly," said Bev.

Biscuit jumped up onto the hood and then the roof, where he sprawled out, tongue lolling. Mary, who'd been sitting next to Beverly, slid over and made room for Jade in the front seat. The girl twisted her fingers together and chewed on her lower lip.

"I'm sure your uncle is fine," Jade said to reassure her. "He probably just walked too far and is waiting for us to bring him back. I should have driven one of the vehicles myself instead of setting out on foot." She pointed ahead. "There's Mr. Hascombe's old house now."

Jade stepped out of the vehicle first, making certain that the elephant wasn't loitering. She didn't see him anywhere. Deeming it safe, she motioned for the others to join her.

"Stay behind me," she cautioned. "Bev, take the rear. Biscuit, stay."

That there had been traffic here, Jade could tell by the trampled grasses in front of the door and several fresher prints around the building. They overlapped enough that Jade couldn't tell if they were all made by Holly or if Hascombe had also been here recently. The wooden bar, which had been placed across the door to keep it from blowing open when the house wasn't in use, lay on the ground. A faint breeze stirred and the door creaked open a few inches, then slapped shut.

Jade pulled the door open and took a half step onto the threshold.

"Girls, stay back. I found Mr. Holly, but—"

Mary pushed past her and almost tripped over her uncle. He lay facedown on the floor, his arms thrown out to the sides.

"Uncle Steven!" she called as she knelt beside him.

"Mary, get back," ordered Jade. "Don't do anything until I've made certain that he's—" She bit off the rest of her words when she saw Mary's face blanch.

The girl obeyed her and slipped to Beverly's side. Beverly put a protective arm around Mary while Jade felt for a pulse on Holly's right wrist.

"He's alive," Jade announced. "His pulse is strong." She noticed there was no canteen near him. "He probably needs water."

The three girls scurried forward in one mass, each jabbering at once. "I've got a canteen." "We need to examine him for broken bones." "I have the Girl Guide manual here. We should follow the instructions for treating an unconscious man." They huddled around the manual as Helen flipped to the appropriate page.

"Oooh!" said Helen. "The girl on page one hundred ninety-four is resuscitating a man by pressing on his back with Schafer's system." She peered at the illustration again. "He has no shirt on." She slapped the book shut. "We must take his shirt off first."

"I'll do that," said Elspeth.

"No!" snapped Mary. "This is my *uncle*. You can't take his shirt off. It wouldn't be proper. Besides, that's for drowning victims."

"Then we must check for broken bones and bandage him up," said Elspeth. She knelt down and started feeling Holly's legs, starting at the calf and working up to the thighs.

At that point, Mr. Holly stirred. "I say, where am I?" he muttered as he struggled to sit up despite the three young ladies doing their best to push him back down in a prone position.

"Mary, give your uncle some water," said Beverly. "The rest of you, please allow Mr. Holly some air."

Mary held the canteen for her uncle while the other two girls stepped back, their faces downcast. Jade couldn't decide if they were more disappointed at not being able to practice their nursing skills or at not getting his shirt off. Elspeth and Helen were clearly interested in more than his health.

Thank heaven Emily didn't come with them.

"Can you get up, Mr. Holly?" Jade asked. "We've got a car here to get you back to camp."

"What? Oh, yes. Jolly good of you to think of a car. Dreadful walk, that."

Then why did you go so far? Jade kept her questions to herself. Better to wait until she could talk to him alone. The girls, however, peppered him.

"What happened?" "Did you fall?" "Were you lost?" "Why did you wander off?"

Holly put a hand to his forehead and groaned. "Please, girls. Not now. I have the most horrid headache. So thirsty. Mouth feels as if I ate sand."

"You're dehydrated," said Beverly. "Come along. You can lie down in the back on a blanket."

They led Holly out and assisted him into the rear storage bed of the Overland. Biscuit climbed into the back and stretched out next to him. The three girls piled in next to the cheetah and Beverly took her place behind the wheel. "Come along, Jade," she called.

"Coming," Jade replied. But she took a moment to look around Harry's front room. The dust on the floorboards lay thick in spots, but there were more footprints than just those made by the girls and Holly, some leading to a back storage room, which, if she remembered correctly, also led outside to the separate kitchen. Jade was about to step into what had been Harry's bedroom of his two-room house when she heard the car horn honk.

She stepped out of the house and waved at Bev before replacing the door bar. Jade had been at Harry's house only once, but she remembered him having a good well and pump in the far corner. It was still there. Why hadn't Holly seen that if he needed water?

"Just a moment," Jade called. She trotted over to the pump and noticed the damp soil beneath it. When she took hold of the handle and pumped, water came out after only two primings, hardly what she'd expect if it hadn't been used in a long while.

"Everything in order?" asked Beverly.

"I think a rat ate the fan belt," Jade replied, with an eye on the girls. She hadn't used the phrase since their days in the

Hackett-Lowther ambulance corps. That event had actually happened once, and the phrase had become a code for something inexplicably amiss.

"Indeed?" Bev replied. She arched her brows. "Do you know how large a rat it was? Perhaps only a mouse?" She put the Overland in gear.

"By the marks, I'd say a big one."

"Well, we'll have to flush it out then. Shall we?" said Bev. She focused her attention on turning the car around and driving back along the rough trail.

Jade folded her arms across her chest. Message delivered and understood.

Beverly took the rough terrain slowly and by the time they made it back to camp, the girls had wrapped bandages around Holly's head.

"In case he had a concussion when he fell," explained Helen.

"Help Miss Emily and your friends with dinner," ordered Beverly, sending the three would-be nursemaids out of the way.

"I'll feed Pepper," said Mary. She carried the caged bird over to her tent.

"Leopold's an ass!"

"Lovely girls," said Holly as he rubbed the bandages.

"Knock off the pretense, Mr. Holly," said Jade. She kept her voice low so the girls wouldn't overhear, but it sounded more like a growl. Biscuit detected it and positioned himself beside her, his golden eyes fixed on Holly. "You're not injured, so I want to know what in the name of holy Moses' compass is going on. Why did you wander off so far? Why did you leave the dress on the tree? Why did you pretend to be dehydrated when you'd obviously been at the well?" She punctuated each question with another step closer to him until she was within a few inches of his face.

Holly backed up two steps, tripped on a rock behind him, and fell down, Jade and Biscuit looming over him. He glanced towards Beverly for support, but she folded her arms in front of her and tapped her foot.

Holly scrambled to his feet and dusted off his rear. Then, pulling himself to his full height, he stuck out his chin in defiance. "I don't believe I deserve or appreciate this interrogation. I told you that someone threatened my life. When you made it clear that my presence around the camp was a danger to the girls, I took it upon myself to distance myself from them. I'll admit that I had no idea where I was going. I believe I'd heard of some old ranches in the area and hoped to come across one sooner than later."

He tugged on the bandages around his head and pulled them off in one lump. "It was quite frightening, if you must know. I had no firearm."

"So you intended to hide out in one of the old ranches," Jade said. "Then why advertise yourself by leaving the disguise scattered on your trail like so many bread crumbs?"

Holly flung the bandages onto the ground. "I suppose it was rather unconsciously done. I must have thought I might get lost and have to find my own way back."

"But instead you found an empty house. What were you doing on the floor? Why pretend to be in a faint when we found you?"

"I believe I passed out from dehydration."

"Was that before or after you visited the well pump?"

asked Jade. Her expression of bored disbelief did nothing to put Holly at ease.

"I . . . I have no recollection of any well pump. I barely recall the house."

"Then that cigarette on the floor must have been someone else's," mused Jade. "Were you meeting someone there?"

Holly's pale face blanched even whiter. "No, I was completely alone. I swear. That was *my* cigarette. I remember now. I had been smoking it when I got there. Must have fallen out of my hands when I fell."

"You're very lucky it didn't burn the house down around you then," said Jade. "You're without your disguise now, though. You'd better lie low in the back of the Overland and decide where we can take you tomorrow."

She turned away from him as though she'd just dismissed an underling. Holly shuffled over to the campfire to sit down.

"Into the Overland, Mr. Holly," said Beverly. "We'll bring you supper."

He glowered at Bev and crawled into the backseat of the newer car.

"What was that all about, Jade? I don't recall seeing any cigarette stub."

"There was none. But did you see how he backpedaled to cover his tracks when he thought we found one? He met someone there, or planned to, and he's lying about it."

"Or knows someone was there before him," suggested Beverly. "Maybe he was waiting for this person to return when he heard us."

"And fell into his fake faint to avoid suspicion? Either way, he's up to something. Someone *had* used that well pump recently. That's why I didn't tell him we had his disguise. It's an excuse to keep him shut away in the motorcar. I wish I could lock him in there."

"What shall we do, Jade? It's nearly sundown. I don't care to take him back to Nairobi tonight."

Jade shook her head. "No. But we had better take turns at the watch tonight. Do you think Emily could take a shift?"

Beverly shrugged. "If I ask her to, yes, but she's so besotted by Mr. Holly that he could convince her of anything."

"Then it's up to us, Bev. I wish I had some coffee. I need something to help me stay awake." She rummaged through the supplies and pulled out her tin of South African tea.

"You could drink some of our black tea instead. It keeps Avery awake," said Beverly. Her nose wrinkled as Jade opened the can. "Are you certain that your tin hasn't molded? It smells *much* stronger than ours does."

Jade took a whiff and felt that same inexplicable sensation of danger tingle along her arms and legs and prickle at her neck that she'd felt when Hascombe had been in camp. "You know I hate ordinary tea, Bev. You should have considered that when you took away my coffee. I meant to ask you about . . ." She stopped when she saw Beverly's wide-eyed look of alarm.

"I didn't take your coffee, Jade."

Jade capped the tin and dropped it onto the ground. "Then who did?"

CHAPTER 13

The massive teeth, as horrid and large as they are,
are not used to bite off meat, but to clamp down and hold.
The crocodile resorts to drowning its prey.
—The Traveler

EVERY HOUR OF THE NIGHT WATCH felt like three. Emily had volunteered for part of the watch, so Jade gave her from nine until midnight, but noticed that Beverly kept her company for the last two hours before taking her own shift. The two chatted softly as one might expect of two sisters, their conversation punctuated by occasional laughter. Jade knew in her heart that Bev was staying up so that Jade wouldn't worry about Emily on guard and could catch at least a few hours of sleep. But Jade, restless and ill at ease, relieved her yawning friend at one o'clock instead of three and held the long dawn watch with only Biscuit for company.

She couldn't have asked for a better ally. The cat, though not nocturnal by nature, had a keen sense of hearing that more than made up for a lack of predatory night vision. Twice during the night he growled softly when an elephant trumpeted from across the Athi. And he heard Holly stir from the Overland before she did.

"Only going to see to nature's call," Holly said grumpily when Jade stood by the fire watching him, her rifle cradled across her arms. Biscuit accompanied him at Jade's command of "Guard," escorting the man back to the vehicle before rejoining her. Only when the sun rose and the camp stirred did Biscuit trot off into the brush to find some unsuspecting breakfast.

Biscuit had returned and was eating his usual ground bird as Bev rousted up the girls and Emily. She was assigning them breakfast duty when a Kikuyu man ran into camp. Jade recognized him as one of the men from Jelani's village.

"Memsahib Simba Jike," he said between deep gulps of air. "You must come to village," he continued in Swahili.

Jade answered in the same language. "Why?"

"Bwana Nyati very sick. Speaks out of head."

"Spit fire!" Jade swore in English before replying in Swahili, "I am coming." She expected the man to wait for her, but he simply turned and ran back to his village, splashing across the shallows of the river on the way.

Beverly joined her. "Is there trouble?" she asked softly.

Jade nodded. "Harry's sick at the village. Sounds like he's raving."

"Malaria?"

Jade paused, remembering his visit. "No, I don't think so. He drank my tea. A *lot* of it all at once, and it had brewed even longer than usual."

Beverly gasped. "Your tea was poisoned!"

"I'd bet my rifle on it now. It would certainly go a long way towards explaining my recent hallucinations." She knew it didn't explain her vision of David in France, but at present, she wasn't ready to deal with that. Jade looked long and hard at the old Overland, where Holly still lay in the back. She could hear his soft snores through the closed doors. "I'm taking him with me. I don't trust him out of my sight right now."

"I could have the girls bandage him up like a mummy," Beverly suggested.

The image brought a smile to Jade's face. "Tempting, but you have enough to deal with without him."

Bev nodded, a coy smile playing on her lips. "These little darlings? But what are you going to do about Harry? He should have a proper doctor."

"Who? Dr. Mathews is away. I don't know Dr. Dymant well enough. Most of the others are in the government's employ, except for Burkitt, and his solution would probably be to dump Harry in the river to shock him out of it. Besides, none of them are here. I'd rather trust Jelani's skills right now."

"Wait a minute." Bev raced back to the supplies and returned with a box of her black tea and a tin of crackers. "At least see if you can get some of this down him."

"I might not be back before it's time to take the girls home," Jade said. "Can you manage without me? You'll have to take my motorcycle. Do you remember what I taught you?"

"Of course. It will be fun. I'll take Helen in the sidecar. Take the new Overland. We'll have more room to stow the gear on the top of the old Express. Some of the girls can sit on boxes in the rear if we need to. I'll have them back to town before lights-on," Bev said, referring to the required six-o'clock headlamp law. "And then you and I are going to gather with Avery and sort out this *shauri*." She grinned and nodded to the Overland. "Don't toss him around too much, darling. I'd hate to ding up the car. It's hired, you know."

Jade started up the vehicle with Biscuit on the bench beside her. She took off in a rush, not bothering to go up to the bridge. Instead she took the river at the shallows and made the turn to the village faster than caution dictated. She was gratified to hear Holly's startled yelp in the back followed by some ripe curses.

"Have you gone mad? What the blazes are you doing? I demand you stop this car at once!"

"If I do, it'll only be to leave you behind. As far as I'm concerned, Mr. Holly, you can walk back to Nairobi or Thika or to the devil." She punctuated her statement with another sharp and completely unnecessary turn, slamming him into the side of car. She didn't trust Holly and intended to establish straightaway that she was in charge. "You can hike up the mountain if you'd like and hide out."

"No, thank you. I believe if I—" He bit off the words as his head knocked against the ceiling. "Ouch! If I survive this kidnapping I shall take an extended holiday to the Blue Posts Hotel and hide there."

"Suit yourself." Jade rounded the northernmost part of Ol Donyo Sabuk and followed the river southeast to Jelani's village.

"Where are we going?"

"Kikuyu village. There's a sick man there."

"Oh, dear. Nothing contagious, I hope."

"Never know. But if it is, it's at least a new place for you to hide."

Holly's voice rose to a frightened squeal. "I'm not staying in any stinking native village."

Jade smiled and made another quick turn, ostensibly to avoid a rock. Behind her, Holly banged into the other side. "You should hold on to something back there. Biscuit keeps his seat better than you do."

She passed the Kikuyu messenger, who seemed in no hurry to return to his village. Shortly after that she saw Harry's truck, abandoned farther down the Athi. Jade stopped her car. "Mr. Holly, can you drive?"

Holly twisted around and grabbed hold of the rear bench for support. "Even if I couldn't, I would just to get out of this vehicle alive."

"Good. That's Harry Hascombe's truck. Drive it to the village."

She got out and waited while Holly started the truck and put it into gear without too much grinding. Then she pointed downriver, got back in her Overland, and followed him. They left both vehicles below Jelani's village and, after prodding Holly with her rifle butt, they started into the narrow winding path, Biscuit in the lead. Several village women and their children met them halfway.

"Simba Jike," they cried. "*Kwa haraka!*" Quickly!

They turned and led Jade and Holly along the pathway, pausing to look over their shoulders to make certain that Jade was following. When she nearly collided with the woman directly in front of her, Jade shooed them all on with a flap of her hands.

"Bwana Nyati very sick."

Holly hugged himself and shied away from the palisade sticks, the stray chickens, the goats, and the people. "This is intolerable," he said. "I want to wait outside."

"You're not leaving my sight," Jade replied. "Not after

yesterday's stunt." She took hold of his left elbow and pulled
him along like a recalcitrant child. The women led her to
a hut at the edge of the village. It had the look of abandon-
ment, with missing thatch in the roof, but the added sunlight
and ventilation could only improve Harry's chances.

Harry lay faceup on a mat woven from leaves. His shirt
was missing and his hands were tied at the wrists to two
wooden stakes so that his arms were drawn out to the sides. A
row of long scratches ran across his chest where he'd clawed
at his skin. An old Kikuyu woman knelt beside his head,
dabbing his forehead with a wet cloth. On second glance,
Jade recognized both the woman—Jelani's mother—and
the cloth—Harry's missing shirt. His breathing was shallow
and rapid, more like that of a panting animal than a sleeping man. Biscuit chirped once, then voiced his distress in soft
churring calls.

Mumbi glared at Jade. "Has the crocodile come for you
yet?" she snapped. "She hides from you in full day as a harmless log, waiting to pull you under."

Jelani stepped into the hut, a gourd bowl in his hand.
"Good, you are here, Simba Jike. Mother, you may go." He
nodded to the door and Mumbi left, leaving Harry's shirt in
a bowl of water near him.

"Beware of *mamba jike*," she whispered as she passed
Jade. Jade was glad Mumbi left without striking her on the
head again.

"Why are his hands tied?" asked Holly, his voice edged with
scorn. "What have you done with him, you filthy native?"

"Shut up, Mr. Holly!" snapped Jade. "I suspect Harry
needed to be restrained."

"He tried to harm himself," said Jelani.

Jade knelt down where Jelani's mother had been and picked up the wet shirt. She squeezed out some of the excess water and dabbed Harry's face and neck. Biscuit added his raspy tongue to the cause, licking Harry's arm. "Tell me everything," Jade said.

"It is quickly told. Bwana Nyati was found by his gun bearer wandering along the river, shooting into the water and screaming. The bwana did not even recognize this man. When he had emptied his rifle, Nakuru wrestled the bwana to the ground." Jelani shook his head. "It was a battle to see. Nakuru is a strong man, but Bwana Nyati fought like one possessed. Three of the village men saw this and did not know what to do."

"They just watched?" Jade asked.

"Who should they help?" Jelani asked. "They did not care to find themselves in prison for harming a white man."

"Then Nakuru managed to subdue Mr. Hascombe?" asked Jade. "Did he bring him here?"

Jelani shook his head. "No. When the battle ended, both men lay as fallen warriors on the grass. My people brought them both here." He jerked his head to the side. "Nakuru is resting in another hut, but he bears many bruises and perhaps a broken arm."

"Oh, dear," murmured Jade. "He'll have to see a doctor at that horrible native hospital in Nairobi to have that set." She remembered that Dr. Mathews often visited villages, but she had no idea where he was right now. Fort Hall? Too far. Perhaps Dymant would treat a Nyamwezi man. He was willing to take care of the Indians, and there were few British doctors who cared to do that either.

"I have set Nakuru's arm," said Jelani. When Jade looked

up suddenly, he added, "You forget, Simba Jike, that I am a healer. There were broken bones in our villages long before British doctors came to fix them."

"Yes, of course," Jade said, sorry that she'd touched yet again on the issue of British rule, which rankled Jelani so much. "I didn't mean that—"

Jelani squatted beside her. "Do not distress yourself, Simba Jike," he said with a slight smile. "I know you are my friend." He held out the gourd bowl. "This is a healing drink. It will help him sweat out the rest of the poison. I have gotten one bowlful down him during the night, but perhaps you can get him to take some."

Jade hesitated a moment and sniffed the concoction. It smelled mildly fragrant, reminiscent of lemongrass or sassafras, something cleansing. She took a tentative sip and found it palatable. Biscuit tried to push his nose into it, but Jade elbowed him away.

"It is what I gave to Irungu after Mutahi gave him the same poison," Jelani added.

Jade looked up sharply. "Irungu is the man who accused Mutahi of witching him, isn't he?" Harry stirred and moaned, and she turned her attention back to him, cradling his head and holding the gourd to his lips.

"Yes," said Jelani. "Irungu's actions were those of Bwana Nyati. Fighting things we cannot see, shouting and clawing."

"I would like to talk to that Mutahi again," Jade said, "and find out more about what happened."

"As would I, but Mutahi has gone. Irungu says he had nothing to do with Mutahi's running away, but I am not sure. Irungu was very angry."

Harry moaned and coughed as some of the brew went down the wrong pipe. Jade put the gourd down and wiped his mouth. "Harry," she called softly. "Jelani, I think we can untie his wrists now. I want him to sit up."

Jelani cut the leather cords, leaving them wrapped around his wrists. Jade shifted her hand under Harry's head and propped it up on her knee. Biscuit padded around to the other side and butted his big, blockish head against Harry's shoulder.

"Harry, it's me, Jade. You're safe."

Harry's eyes flashed for a moment, darting wildly from Jelani to Biscuit before settling on Jade's face. They opened wider as though recognition dawned on him. His sun-browned face seemed paler and more drawn, and he started shivering.

"Easy, Harry," Jade said, her voice soft and reassuring. "I need you to drink this." She raised the gourd to his lips again. Harry's lips moved as his mouth reached for the drink. He took several swallows and fell back against Jade's leg. "Don't try to talk."

That suggestion had the opposite effect. He began to blurt out one question after another. "Where am I? What happened? Where's Nakuru?" He looked back at Jelani. "Isn't that the boy who came—"

"Shh," Jade admonished. "Yes, that's Jelani. You're in his village. His people found you and Nakuru injured and brought you here." When Harry heard of Nakuru's injury, he looked wildly at Jade and clutched at her arm. "He's all right," Jade assured him. "His arm may be broken."

"How?"

"As I understand it, *you* did it. Jelani says that you were raving out of your mind, shooting your rifle at the water. Na-kuru tried to restrain you and you fought him."

Harry sat up with Jade's help and ran his hands through his hair and across the back of his neck. His shoulders twitched as though something was tickling them. "I . . . I don't remember. . . ." He stopped when one of the dangling leather straps brushed his face. "What's this?"

"They had to restrain you as well. You would have hurt yourself," Jade said. "Here, hold out your hands and I'll get them off."

The straps had been tied with a little room to spare so that they didn't cut into Harry's wrists when he struggled. Jade pulled her knife from her boot and carefully slid it under the leather, slicing out, away from his arms. The straps fell to the ground and Harry rubbed his wrists.

"I suppose I owe you my life," he said to Jelani.

"No, Bwana Nyati," said Jelani. "You owe it to Na-kuru."

Harry looked around the hut and, for the first time, noticed Mr. Holly standing by the door. "What are you doing here?"

"I should like to know that myself," said Holly. "I feel as though I were abducted."

"Mr. Holly happened to come by the camp, Harry, when the runner came with news of your sickness. I brought him along to drive your truck up to the village."

"Ah, good of you, Holly," said Harry. "But what—"

Jade held up her hand for silence. "That's enough for now, Harry. You look like hell. I need to get you and Na-kuru back to Nairobi." She held the gourd to his lips. "Finish this."

Harry pushed the gourd away. "I'm fine. Just . . . tired and . . ." He flexed his shoulders and arms. "I feel as if I were hit by a rhino."

"That would be Nakuru's doing."

"I should think that this Nakuru would be in line for a beating of sorts," said Holly. "How do you know that he didn't do this just to have a chance to take a swing at a white man? For that matter, these natives—" He shut up when he saw Jade's and Harry's expressions. "Well, it was only a thought."

"A damned stupid one, too," said Jade.

Harry echoed it with a "Hear, hear."

Holly snorted and folded his arms. "Native lovers, I see."

Harry struggled to his feet and stepped to within an inch of Holly's face. "I neither love them nor hate them, but I trust Nakuru with my rifles and that means with my life. I may not like their heathen religions or the way they dress and live, but I know a good man when I see one. At present, I'm not sure I'm looking at one."

Holly stepped back, his eyes wide with alarm. "That's the thanks I receive for driving your vehicle to you." He turned to Jade. "I'll be outside should you need me."

"What the devil was he doing at your camp to begin with, Jade? A dandy like that doesn't generally leave the city."

"He's hiding from someone who threatened to kill him."

Harry nodded once, then put his hand to his head as though to steady it. "*That* makes sense. I can see any number of people wanting to kill *him*. And no great loss, either." He closed his eyes. "I feel bloody awful."

Jelani, who'd stood silently in the background during the exchange, stepped forward. "Your body now remembers what your mind forgot. You will be well enough in another day. But," he added, "if you leave now, you may have another attack. That is what happened to Irungu. Only when your sweat and urine no longer smell like the drug is your body clean."

Harry studied the youth, taking his measure. "Yes, I *do* remember you. Kilimanjaro." Jelani nodded, meeting and returning Harry's gaze. "You were also with Simba Jike on Marsabit. You're the boy who was captured by the slavers." Harry's eyes sought out Jelani's mutilated foot. "I remember now. You freed yourself at some cost."

Jelani simply nodded.

"Jelani is the tribe's new healer," said Jade. "He said that you're not the first person to have this sickness. Another man, one of the villagers, behaved the same way recently after eating some herbs. That's the man he just mentioned, Irungu." She tentatively sniffed at Harry's shirt. "You do smell funny. I noticed it at camp, too."

"I've been hunting crocodile in the bush for two days. What the blazes do you expect me to smell like? Primroses?" Harry snapped.

"Answer this," said Jade. "Did you feel as though your skin were crawling? Did you see things? Hallucinate?"

Harry twitched his shoulders and rubbed his arms, noticing for the first time that he had no shirt. "What the . . . ?" He found his shirt, wet and sopping, and put it on anyway, turning away to button it. "I don't remember everything, Jade, but somehow, all that rings true."

"Well, to a lesser extent, it's been happening to me as

well," said Jade. Both Jelani and Harry stared at her. "I thought it was a mental breakdown, something belated from the war. Then I thought I had malaria. But now I believe it was the tea. *I* never drank more than one cup at a time, but you had three and it had been steeping longer than usual, so it was potent."

"Someone put a drug in your tea?" asked Harry.

"Then the herbs that Irungu ate were the same as what was in your drink, Simba Jike?" asked Jelani.

"Maybe. I'd like to talk to Irungu and get the rest of the herbs from him."

Jelani shook his head. "Irungu burned the herbs just before Mutahi ran off."

"Son of a biscuit!" said Jade. "Whoever replaced my coffee with that spiked brew must have left some lying around and Mutahi found it. Jelani, I know I have asked you this before, but have there been any new hunters or visitors in the area?"

Jelani shook his head. "Not that I have seen. The giant man who lives atop Kea-Njahe," he said, referring to Lord McMillan and using the Kikuyu name for Ol Donyo Sabuk, "used to hire many of our villagers for his farm. But he has gone away again and the farm rests."

"McMillan wouldn't do something like this," said Harry.

"But he might have some guests staying on," said Jade. "I'll ask around about that."

"I'll ask," said Harry. "But who in the bloody blazes would do that to you, Jade?"

"Simba Jike has made enemies before," said Jelani.

"Haven't we all," Harry countered, "but I can't think of

anyone who would stoop to this. Wait a minute," he said. "Didn't that native who stabbed the movie man last September have some drug like this? Do you think some of it was left lying around?"

"That wouldn't explain how it got into that tea."

"Who has visited you, Simba Jike?" asked Jelani.

"No one," said Jade. "Just a group of young girls, and they haven't been in my rooms."

"Not that bloody Holly?" asked Harry.

There was an edge to his voice that Jade couldn't quite place. Jealousy? She lowered her voice in case Holly was close enough to overhear. "No. He didn't even show up when his niece needed him to bring her to one of the Girl Guide meetings."

"He's related to one of those girls?" asked Harry, raising *his* voice. "Maybe he had her slip something in your tea when you weren't looking."

"I resent your implication!" snapped Holly from outside the hut. "And if you don't mind, I should like very much to get out of this . . . this village."

"As would I," mumbled Harry. He nodded once to Jelani. "Thank you for your, er, help, but if you'll take me to my gun bearer, we won't impose on you any longer."

Jelani shook his head. "Bwana Nyati is as stubborn as the buffalo." He looked at Jade. "You must tell him that he is not well enough to leave. He must drink more of the medicine to cleanse his body. As should you, Simba Jike, since you too have had this poison in you."

"I didn't drink any today. I'm fine."

"No, you are not." Jelani's statement brooked no argument. Jade gave him one anyway. The young healer finally settled for getting both of them to drink one gourdful of his healing herbs. He pressed two packets made of folded banana leaves into her hands. "There is medicine in them. The same that you just now gave to the bwana. Pour it into water and drink it. The bwana, too."

Jade took it, if only to allow Jelani to save face. Harry, seeing his opportunity, sidled closer to Jade. "Looks as though you're supposed to take care of me for a while, Jade. Be my nurse. We could use my old house."

Jade slapped a packet against Harry's chest. "You're obviously yourself again. Take this and help me get Nakuru."

Jelani nodded across the compound. "Nakuru is in the hut by the gate. Your rifles are with him."

For all his bluster, Harry was weak from his long battle with the drugs and Nakuru. Jade could see he took a deep breath to steady himself and started slowly across the compound, followed by Jade and the others.

"What have you seen in your visions, Simba Jike?" Jelani asked softly.

Jade decided there was no harm in telling him. "A dead man," she whispered. "And once I thought I saw that old native from Marsabit. The one called Brother to the Elephants."

"Ahhh," said Jelani. When Jade gave him a questioning look, he merely shrugged. Then he nodded to Harry. "Bwana Nyati will get better faster if he drinks more of the medicine. But you, Simba Jike, watch carefully what you eat or drink until you find who has done this."

"I will. And you, my friend, need to find Mutahi. He can tell us where he got the herbs."

Nakuru was delighted to see Harry alive and well and

immediately apologized for all the bruises and pain he'd inflicted on his boss. Harry waved it all off magnanimously and went so far as to express his pleasure that he hadn't killed Nakuru. After a brief conference, Harry decided that Nakuru did require the native hospital in Nairobi. As for himself, he declared that he didn't need to see any bloody doctor and thought he could just hole up downriver at Percival's camp and sleep it off overnight.

"I've still got that croc to find," he finished. "What do you say, Jade? Watch over me tonight?" He stumbled on his next step. "See? I'm still not steady."

Jade deemed it more of an act, despite how sick he'd looked when she'd first arrived. He was a rounder at heart and wouldn't scruple to use any ploy to get her alone. "Then you should stay in the village another night."

Harry scowled and tottered off towards his truck.

In the end, Harry drove off to find the game warden. Jade took Nakuru to Nairobi, Biscuit wedged in beside him in the backseat of the Overland. Holly decided he had little choice but to return with Jade and opted to hide away at the Blue Posts Hotel near Thika. It was late Saturday night when she arrived home. After a cursory report to Avery and Bev, and hearing that the girls had all made it home safely, she crawled onto her own cot.

She lay awake, wondering at what had happened. Mumbi and the old *mondo-mogo* had both warned her of a killer crocodile and she'd certainly seen it. Then she recalled Mumbi's words. The old woman spoke of *mamba jike*, a female crocodile, not the piebald bull. Jade decided that Mumbi had really said her name, Simba Jike, instead, and tried to sleep. She slept poorly, listening for stealthy footsteps, wary of every night noise. When Jade did sleep, she kept dreaming of Harry tied down, ranting. Only instead of Harry's voice, the sounds that came out of his mouth were those of that gray parrot, squawking, "Salt" and "Pile in."

Only this time, Jade heard it as a name, Pellyn, the name of Lilith Worthy's lover.

CHAPTER 14

Once prey is secured, it is often stored in an underwater larder, often on a shelf that the crocodile has dug out of the embankment with its claws.
—The Traveler

"I'm telling you, that parrot has been screeching 'Pellyn,' not 'pile in' or 'pile on,' as we first thought." Jade sat in the Dunburys' sitting room nursing a glass of lemonade. At present, it seemed like the safest thing to drink. At least it was freshly made, if the number of seeds in her glass was any indication. She felt drained, having slept poorly. After Sunday Mass, she tried to sleep again but it eluded her. Jade thought the only way she could gain any peace would be to share her ideas about what had happened.

Beverly cradled baby Alice in her left arm, a bottle of formula in her right. She wore a loose blue linen dress that complemented her fair complexion and corn-silk hair. Bev gently swayed in her chair, a picture of maternal contentment as the baby sucked at the bottle's nipple. Jade, on the other hand, felt as if she were about to explode from frustration.

Why are they treating me as if I'm the one who took sick instead of Harry?

"You're exhausted, Jade," said Beverly. "I knew last night

when you gave us that very thin report on Harry and Na-kuru that there was more to it than you let on, but I thought you needed sleep, so I didn't press it. Now that we're certain you've been drugged these past days, I think you should go back to bed or see a doctor. Let me send for someone."

"I don't want or need a doctor," said Jade, her frustration mounting. "I want you to listen to me."

"Well, I'm having a very difficult time with all of this. Not that I don't believe you, Jade. I do. It's just all too bizarre."

"Not so bizarre, my love," said Avery. He'd come in from training the horses and wore his working clothes of jodhpurs and a cotton shirt open at the neck, the sleeves rolled up past his elbows. He tamped tobacco into his pipe and lit it, puffing. "Only just consider how tormented our poor Jade has been with those packages."

"And the drugged tea," added Jade.

"As to that," said Avery, "I think we should send it off to a chemist in Mombassa to be analyzed. It could go off tomorrow with the down train. Send ours as well for comparison. It doesn't seem to be tainted."

"I don't understand how Jade's *could* have been tainted," said Beverly. She draped a cloth over her shoulder and laid Alice against it, patting her back softly. "Major Bertram sent that to us and to Jade as a gift. Why, Avery's known him since school. Surely he wouldn't have sent something to harm her."

"No, Tony wouldn't have done so," said Avery. "Someone must have come into Jade's rooms and added the poison."

"He took a big chance then," said Jade. "How would anyone know I had this South African tea to begin with? Anyone who knows me knows I drink coffee. But then, that's why this person also took my coffee, making it look as if Bev did it."

"Perhaps they planned to add the drugs to the coffee and then found the tea," suggested Beverly. "The spices in that blend would certainly disguise the taste better than coffee would do." Her tone suggested that she didn't believe her hypothesis herself.

"The alternative is that the tea came already drugged," said Avery. "Which means—"

"Which means that your friend didn't send it," finished Jade. "We're dealing with a decent forger, it seems. I wish I still had the note that came with the tin, Bev. And the one signed by you."

Avery paced around the floor. "I saw the box and the letter inside. I would swear that was Tony's writing."

Beverly wiped Alice's mouth. "I did put the tin and Major Bertram's note on your table, Jade, but *I* didn't write any note, nor did I take your coffee. I'm not that brave. You're positive that it is the tea that was drugged? Not some bad food or medicine?"

"I haven't taken any medicine, and how else would Harry have taken sick like he did? And it would explain my feelings of apprehension, my crawling skin and seeing things that weren't there. I've been drinking that concoction for more than a week."

"Yes, well," said Avery, puffing on his pipe. "As to those hallucinations. I should like to hear more on that account. Just what have you seen?"

He was interrupted by the ring of the telephone. Farhani appeared and picked up the handset, speaking softly. "Northey is telephoning you, bwana."

"The governor?" said Avery. He sounded alarmed.

"No. His missus," said Farhani.

"*Lady* Northey," corrected Beverly. "Farhani, when will you learn to use titles? I'm sure she wants a report on the girls' safari. Farhani, please tell *Lady* Northey that I shall ring her up in an hour." Farhani bowed and spoke softly into the phone before hanging it up. "Now, where were we?" asked Bev. "Hallucinations!"

Jade ticked off the events on her left hand. "That red paint in the target, it looked like it was crawling. And I saw David waving to me one night before his face disappeared into a skull. And I thought that I saw Boguli."

"Boguli?" echoed Beverly. "That old man from Marsabit?" Jade nodded.

"But I thought he didn't actually exist," said Bev. "That photo you took of him . . ."

"The one in which he didn't appear? Yes, that's why seeing him again must be a hallucination," said Jade. "I thought that I was experiencing some belated war trauma, brought on by my recent visit to France."

"But I'm confused," said Avery. "You said that you also saw David in France. That was before you drank this drugged tea."

Jade nodded. "I can't explain that either, unless David was actually trying to warn me."

"Nonsense," said Beverly. "David is safely tucked away in heaven. You saw someone who resembled him. You were overwrought at being in France to begin with and it was accentuated by your fretting over Sam." When Jade glared at her, Beverly raised her chin. "Oh, stop it, Jade. You've been a wreck since he left and you know it."

"Bev," Jade growled.

"My darling wife is quite right, Jade," said Avery. "But all that aside, it seems that it has little to do with the real hallucinations. Someone wanted to torment Jade with those packages and letters."

"But without drugs, our Jade might not have taken the bait, right?" asked Bev.

Avery simply raised his eyebrows and puffed away.

"What am I saying?" asked Bev. "Of course not."

"I'd appreciate it if you didn't speak about me as if I weren't here," said Jade. "I don't know how I might have reacted to those items, and neither do you."

Bev handed Alice Merrywether off to Shilangi, the Seychellois nanny, to be changed and put down for a nap. "Nonsense, Jade," Beverly said when baby and nanny had left for the nursery. "Your usual reaction is to take charge and sort it out." She rang a little bell to summon Farhani and requested that tea be served soon.

"You mean that she'd have—what do the Americans say?—walloped someone by now," Avery said with a chuckle.

"Perhaps," said Jade, "but these packets were very disturbing on their own. The first one, the obituary, upset me without having had the tea. I would swear before Saint Peter that the letters were penned by David. But then I saw his scarf, and that *was* his scarf." She shuddered. "It was enough to disturb anyone."

"True," said Avery, "but if your reputation to charge in—"

"Guns a-blazing," added Beverly.

"Thank you, my dear. Quite right. Well, this person needed to alter your usual behavior."

"Which is why my tea was laced with something," concluded Jade. "It's possible I wasn't supposed to receive the obituary until after the tea arrived. But what's the point of all this?"

"To ruin your credibility with the police?" suggested Avery. "To make you flee the colony?"

"Perhaps to put you in an institution?" offered Bev. "To get you out of the way."

"Or perhaps just for the sake of torturing me," said Jade. "Having me declared mentally unfit and locked away would certainly be a suitable revenge for Lilith."

"But Lilith can't be behind this," said Beverly. "When Avery inquired last September, we learned that she'd seen no one in prison but one Anglican minister, and him only once."

"There's been no other word at all," said Avery, "and I'd left previous instructions to be notified if anything altered with her in any regard."

"And that," said Jade, "is why I think this is the work of her lover, Pellyn. All we know of him is that he's been in Africa for years, possibly since David was a child. We've always suspected that he acted as her right-hand man, carrying out her orders."

"But why wait until now?" asked Beverly. "This Pellyn could have done this any number of times before now. Of course, before now . . ." She paused and looked at Avery as though seeking guidance.

Avery, like many good spouses, seemed to read her mind. "Before now Jade wasn't as vulnerable emotionally."

"She may have been when she first arrived in Africa after the war, but she hadn't done anything to rile Lilith yet," said

Beverly. "And finding David's half brother accomplished two ends. It *did* infuriate Lilith, and it also made Jade stronger."

Jade waved aside their arguments, feeling uncomfortable with the conversation. "We don't know why Pellyn waited," said Jade. "We don't even know who he is or what he looks like." The *mondo-mogo*'s and Mumbi's warnings came back to her. "He could be hiding here in plain sight."

"All I ever found out was that he was from Cornwall," said Avery, "and considered a scoundrel, but as that chestnut came from Lilith's parents, it may have had more to do with his toying with their daughter and continuing the affair after her marriage to Gil Worthy."

"Pellyn would have to be at *least* forty-five by now," said Beverly. "Assuming he was in his early twenties when he started the affair. He may be considerably older than that. And aren't the Cornish usually . . . Jade? What are you thinking?"

Jade stared at the floor, faces playing in her mind. "He could be anyone, but I was thinking of people whom we know. Harry for one, Inspector Finch for another."

"What?" exclaimed both Avery and Beverly.

"Surely not Harry," added Bev.

"Why not?" asked Jade. "He's the right age, and he was involved with passing off another man as Gil's bastard son. He was around in September when that native stabbed the movie producer while intoxicated with datura. He could have learned about it and other drugs then and waited to use them until I was, um, vulnerable, as you put it."

"Hmmm," mumbled Avery around his pipe stem. "And the inspector?"

"Again, the right age, and who better to operate anything

illegal than someone inside the police force? Perhaps it's not true that there were no fingerprints on any of my packets excepting my own and the postal clerk's. It would be easy enough for him to declare it to be so."

Beverly sat up straighter, her eyes wide and her mouth agape. "Oh, Jade, think of what you're saying. To accuse these two men of being—"

"A shifty, low-down, no-good, thieving, murdering forger," finished Jade. "You're right, Harry isn't clever enough. The man can barely lead a safari."

"Jade!" exclaimed Beverly. "You're hardly being fair to Harry. He's quite clever. Only think how he managed your safari in Tsavo on half the budget, and how he was there to help save you from Lilith's gunrunner on Marsabit and—"

"My dear," began Avery with a sidewise glance at Jade's face.

Beverly held up her hand. "Please, darling, don't interrupt me. He's been here since he was a young man and knows Africa very well. He even did some mining in Tsavo. How else could he . . . Oh, dear." She put a hand to her mouth. "I seem to have just put him squarely on the suspect list, haven't I?"

Jade smiled. "You've explained it very nicely, Bev. Harry has been here since Gil Worthy came over. He probably knows enough about mining to perpetrate a fraud, he's been in contact with several of Lilith's confederates in one capacity or another, he travels a lot, he was familiar with that crocodile, and he knows us well enough to gain access to our houses. He could have found a letter from Major Bertram and used it to copy his handwriting."

"But surely you don't think Harry would try to poison you, Jade," said Avery. "He took the drink himself."

"He might not have been as sick as we thought. It could have been a ruse to throw us off track. Remember, he still has property near Ol Donyo Sabuk. He might have known we were there and needed to get us away from it." Jade thought about her earlier meeting with Jelani. Mutahi, the Kikuyu accused of witching the other man, had been around the mountain before he gave his gift of herbs to Irungu and his wife. He could have gone into Harry's old house.

And Harry wanted me to go there with him, too. Was it a ploy to capture me?

"Jade, we've known Harry far too long," said Avery. "There could be any number of men in the colony who would meet the criteria to be suspects. Someone in the land office, a railroad man."

"Or even Inspector Finch," said Jade. "But you have made my point, Avery. We can't trust anyone."

"Well, that's a bad ticket and no mistake," said Avery. "Makes sending a telegram or a letter a bit of a problem."

"Someone in the postal service," suggested Beverly.

"Hamilton is too old and too stout," said Avery. "Hardly a match for Lilith, and the underlings are mostly either young men or Indians. Not that she hasn't employed them," he added. "We suspected before that Jade's letters had been opened."

"I suppose Mr. Holly is too young," mused Beverly.

"Too young to be Pellyn, but not too young to have been recruited by him," said Jade. "He claims that someone sent him an ear. But no one has actually seen it. He heard Hamilton talk about the Congo natives losing ears. It may have given him the idea." She felt exhausted, physically and emotionally. Maybe Bev was right. Maybe she did need to sleep before she started hallucinating again—without the benefit of drugged tea. For that matter, she had no idea how long any residual effect might last. Her skin didn't feel as if it were crawling anymore, but that didn't mean her mind was unaffected.

This is ridiculous. What am I doing here?

"I should leave," Jade said.

"But tea is almost ready to be served," Beverly protested. "Good British tea at that. You can drink it if you put in enough honey. You must eat before you go back to rest. We'll get coffee for you in town later."

"That's not what I mean, Bev. I should leave Kenya, maybe Africa. Go home, or someplace remote like New Guinea or Bora Bora."

"You're speaking nonsense, Jade," said Beverly. The words sounded like a slap. "If you think I'm going to let you go harebraining off to some faraway island to face headhunters or even the French in this state of mind, then you had better think again."

"Hear, hear," said Avery.

"But if I go where Pellyn can't find me—"

"Then *we* won't be able to find you either. And that is not acceptable."

"We are not without resources, Jade," said Avery. "I'll start by seeing if anyone is staying at Lord McMillan's Juja farm. And I think that we should question Mr. Holly more thoroughly."

"He's at the Blue Posts Hotel," said Jade.

"Splendid. I'll drop in and pay him a visit later," said Avery. "Catch him unawares. You see, Jade, now that we know of Pellyn's activity, we shall be on our guard so he can't harm you."

A commotion on the veranda interrupted them, and the three hurried to the door.

"Oh, thank heaven you're home and safe," said Madeline. She clutched her son, Cyril, in her arms as though she feared someone might snatch him away at any moment. Neville followed close on her heels, along with Biscuit.

Beverly led Maddy to a chair.

"My stars, Neville!" exclaimed Avery. "What happened?"

"Someone tried to take our son!"

CHAPTER 15

The Africans have many sayings about crocodiles. One is,
"The strength of the crocodile is in the water." This is true,
but that doesn't mean that one is safe on the riverbank.
—The Traveler

THE ANNOUNCEMENT STUNNED EVERYONE, resulting in a disjointed moment when no one moved, no one so much as breathed, followed quickly by a flurry of activity, as though nature rushed to fill the void.

"You cannot mean it?" said Beverly. "Surely . . ."

Farhani entered with a tea tray loaded with little sandwiches and cakes.

"The devil with tea," said Avery. "What Neville needs is a good gin and soda."

"No," said Neville, raising his hand, "tea will be fine. I need to keep a clear head."

"As you wish," said Avery, but he poured a drink for himself and downed it in one gulp while Beverly ordered a glass of milk for the Thompsons' adopted son.

"Tell us what happened," said Jade.

Maddy set the twenty-two-month-old boy on the floor with a cheese sandwich in his hands. Biscuit, who always seemed intrigued by the little fellow, lay down beside him, a deep raspy purr rumbling from his throat.

"It happened today," said Madeline. "Neville and I had gone to the little prayer meeting at Thika. We left Cyril at home in the care of Samuel."

"He's watched Cyril many times while we were busy on the farm," added Neville.

Beverly and Avery both nodded. Jade knew that hiring a trusted Kikuyu servant to act as a yaya, or nanny, was very common, especially on the farms. Samuel, the son of their head Kikuyu worker, Kimathi, had been with the Thompsons for years as a general house servant.

Neville and Maddy looked at each other, as though they sought in each other's eyes confirmation that they had done nothing wrong in taking care of their child.

Beverly added her own assurance. "Samuel is a fine young man."

"Thank you, yes," continued Maddy. "We returned home and found Samuel positively frantic. It seems that there was a fire in the grasslands behind the coffee orchard. No one knows how it started. Terrible commotion. Samuel put Cyril in his crib and went to help. The fire didn't go far, thanks largely to the longer rainy season we've had. Much of the grass was still fresh. But when Samuel returned, the boy was gone."

"We returned home not long after," said Maddy, her voice breaking. She put her hand to her face, hiding her eyes as she fought back tears.

"There, there," cooed Beverly. "The little tyke is here and safe."

Maddy pulled a white kerchief from her dress pocket

and dabbed at her eyes. "Yes, thank you. It's just that . . ." Neville stood behind his wife and put a comforting hand on her shoulder.

"Where *did* you find him?" asked Jade. "Why do you think someone tried to take him rather than him simply climbing out of his bed and toddling off?"

"We called and called," said Maddy, "and found him curled up asleep inside . . ." Her voice gave way here and she broke into a sob. Cyril, noticing the sound, turned around and offered his half-eaten sandwich to his mother. Maddy scooped him up and hugged him close.

"Point of fact," said Neville, "we found him asleep inside of the coffee dryer."

Beverly gasped and Jade found herself grinding her teeth in fury. The dryer had held a corpse when the Thompsons had first purchased it. Whoever had put the child in there knew the significance of that dryer drum.

"It's actually not the same dryer," said Neville. "We couldn't abide the first one and we sold it up-country. This is a replacement. Still . . ."

"Quite," said Avery. "Damned despicable trick."

"Praise God that whoever did it left the lid open. It's not airtight, of course, but it could have been an oven in short order," finished Neville. Maddy choked back another sob and Neville patted her on the shoulder. "There, there, my dear. He's safe. That's what matters."

Cyril protested the tight embrace and Maddy gradually eased him back down onto the floor. The remains of the sandwich stayed behind, crushed into her dress front. Beverly handed him a slice of sponge cake when he noticed the sandwich's absence.

"Has he told you how he got in there?" asked Jade.

"No," said Neville, "but that's only because he was asleep and, well, we came straight here, too upset to even question any of the workers. Not that anyone had anything to add when we had them all looking for the boy."

"Everyone loves Cyril," protested Maddy. "You know how the Kikuyu dote on children. They're forever giving him some sticky sweetmeat or other."

"Which is why," said Neville as he reached into his pocket and pulled out a leather cord, "it wasn't much of a surprise to find this in Cyril's hands when we found him."

Jade reached out and took the item. It was a necklace of sorts with a spent shell casing hanging from it.

"As you can see," said Neville, "it looks like the sort of trinket that the Africans pick up and wear for an ornament. Heaven knows hunters leave enough of them about. This one looks to have some design scratched onto it, but I couldn't quite make it out. A circle or some such thing. I thought it might help us identify the owner."

Jade didn't reply. Instead, she turned the unlikely charm over in her hands, studying it and the simplistic etching. The hairs on her arms stood on end and tingled at the sight of one circle overlapping another.

"Then you think a native took Cyril?" asked Beverly. "Surely someone on your farm would recognize that necklace and identify the man who did this."

"I know who owned this," said Jade. "A man from Jelani's village named Mutahi. He ran off from the village after being accused of witching one of the other villagers."

Cyril, spying the necklace, reached for it. Jade handed it to Maddy.

Maddy gasped. "How horrid! But why would he do it?"

"I have no idea," said Jade. "But before we jump to conclusions, I think we should ask your son."

All eyes turned towards the little towheaded child. Jade hoped he'd be able to tell them something about his abductor. Presently, he sat giggling as Biscuit licked the remains of smashed cheese and sponge cake from his fingers. "Kitty," he exclaimed. "Biscuit big kitty."

Maddy slipped off her chair and sat on the floor beside her son. "That's right, darling. Biscuit is a big kitty." She dangled the necklace to the side, attracting the child's attention. "Sweetheart, Mummy wants to talk to you about something. Who gave this to you?"

Cyril looked at the scratched and battered casing hanging from the dirty strap, then turned his attention back to Biscuit. "Nice man," he said.

"A man?" echoed Maddy. "Can you tell Mummy about this man? Was he dark like Samuel?"

Cyril shook his head.

"Not a native then," Avery said. "Was he big?"

The boy shrugged.

"I suppose everyone looks big to a little chap like that," said Avery. "Perhaps he can describe his hair. Does he know his colors?"

"Cyril," said Maddy. "Was his hair the color of my hair? Or your aunt Jade's hair? Or Aunt Beverly's hair?"

Cyril's head swiveled back and forth as he looked at each of the grown-ups. His little brow furrowed in puzzlement until he looked at Biscuit. One chubby hand slapped Biscuit in the flank. The hand rested mainly on the cheetah's golden brown base coat, though two fingers touched a dark spot.

"This color," he said with a slight childish lisp. The toddler giggled and poked Biscuit's chin. "Biscuit has fuzzy chin!" He giggled.

"Did the man have a fuzzy chin, too?" asked Jade. Cyril didn't answer.

"What color were his eyes, Cyril?" asked Beverly. "Did he have blue eyes?"

Cyril shook his head. "Big, big, big black eyes."

"'Big, big, big'?" repeated Avery. "That doesn't make sense."

"But it was a white man," said Neville. "This was no native prank."

Madeline reached up one hand and grasped her husband's as it rested on her shoulder. "Oh, Neville, who could it be?"

"It could be any number of men," said Beverly. "Nairobi has gotten very large of late and so has the rest of the colony. It might be someone from Thika or Fort Hall or anywhere."

"But why?" asked Neville. "Do you suppose someone is envious of our new coffee washer going into production?"

Avery headed towards the door to his study. "Whoever it was, this is a matter for the police. I intend to ring them up now."

"Jade, you haven't said much," said Maddy. "What do you think?"

Jade reached for the necklace from Maddy and turned it over in her hands. "I think Avery has the right idea. You need to talk to the police."

Beverly studied her face from under partly lowered lashes. "Jade, I believe you are withholding something from us. Tell us what you know. Why do you keep looking at that necklace?"

In the background, Avery spoke to the operator, summoning the Nairobi police. Jade could tell that he'd reached a particularly chatty operator. She held up one hand as a signal for patience and gave her attention to Avery's conversation.

"This is Avery Dunbury. I need for you to ring up . . . Oh, hello, Nancy. I would like for you to ring up the Nairobi police. Yes, of course I remember you. Quite. No, I don't want the Parklands police. I want the . . . Yes, it was most exciting. I'm well aware that I reside in . . . The baby is just fine." He rolled his eyes.

Jade leaped up and snatched the handset from him. "Listen to me. No, this is not Lord Dunbury. He wants the Nairobi police and he wants them *now*. I don't care if they're busy. This is urgent. Now!" She passed the handset back to Avery. "You are too nice," she told him.

Avery spoke with someone at the station before hanging up. "They are sending one of the constables around soon enough," he told them. "It does appear that they are in a bit of a to-do over at the station. The game director just brought in the remains of another crocodile victim and—"

The telephone rang and Avery picked up. "Hello? Yes, this is he. Ah, good to speak with you, Inspector. Yes, she *is* here." He motioned for Jade to come back to the telephone. "Finch wishes to speak with you."

Jade took the handset again and listened intently without saying anything more than "Hello." When she hung up, all eyes were on her, waiting. "It seems I'm needed at the station."

Avery agreed to accompany Jade, at Beverly's insistence, and for once Jade didn't mind Bev's overprotective attitude. Enough had happened recently that Jade was certain of nothing. Outside of her immediate friends, she didn't even know whom she could trust. Finch was not one of her immediate friends. If he was Pellyn and this was a trick, then she would be grateful for Avery's guarding her flank.

Avery parked the Hupmobile on Eighth Avenue. "Shall I go in with you?"

Jade nodded, expecting to see the inspector pacing outside his office, waiting for her. She wondered if he had new information regarding the murders or her packages, and she'd imagined both on the short trip into town. But whatever scenarios played through her mind, she wasn't prepared to see Blaney Percival, Jelani, and Irungu, the latter two under guard.

"What's going on!?" she demanded. "Why are these men here?"

Finch motioned for her to take a seat, asking Avery to wait outside in the waiting area. "It appears you were present recently at a native court," Finch said. "You were a witness in something that rightly should have been determined by the police. As a result, I've got a mess on my hands."

"As I recall, there was no crime committed," Jade said. "Just one Kikuyu accusing another of witching him. Hardly anything that your courts need to bother with."

"That should be for us to decide, Miss del Cameron. And it may be that you are correct, but because there was no show of the Colony's interest in the matter, a crime may have been committed *after* the fact."

Jade looked at Jelani, hoping to see some hint of what

Finch was talking about. Instead, she only saw a veiled anger in the youth's eyes, directed at Finch. Irungu, on the other hand, stood with his head bowed and his hands clasped before him in a posture of submission.

"What crime?" Jade asked.

"The man Mutahi, the one accused of witchcraft, has disappeared from the village, correct?" asked Finch. Jade nodded. "And you have no idea where he went?"

"None," Jade said. She thought of his necklace and knew she needed to tell Finch about it, but not until she knew what was going on.

"We may have found him. Or rather, Mr. Percival found part of him." He motioned for Jade to approach a table at the back of the room near where Blaney Percival stood. A dingy white cloth covered a short lump on the table.

Jade looked at Finch. "I take it I'm supposed to help identify him?"

Finch nodded. "Your word in this would be greatly appreciated and it seems only fitting, since you've been a part of his story."

"I must protest, Inspector," said Percival. "This is most unseemly."

Finch held up his hand. "I understand your feelings, Mr. Percival, and I'm sure they do you credit. But Miss del Cameron is a most unusual woman. She's seen her share of corpses and has always made it a point to become involved should one cross her path. I should hate to deprive her of this opportunity."

Jade kept her eyes locked on Finch, returning his stare. If this was his way of teaching her a lesson, then she intended to beat him at his own game. And after seeing Waters' corpse bob up out of the Athi, she didn't think anything could be worse.

Finch motioned towards the table again. "If you please?"

Jade went to the table and waited, steeling herself for what she knew would be an unpleasant sight. Finch whipped off the cloth, exposing the head and torso of an African man, the legs and arms missing. The corpse was every bit as disgusting as she'd expected, but she recognized Mutahi by the broad scar across his chest. It showed as a tight line amid the swollen flesh and the places where fish had nibbled. But what sent a shiver down her spine was his head. One ear was gone, neatly sliced away.

"That's Mutahi," she said. "But when I saw him, he wore a tight necklace of leather and an empty shell casing. It's missing. And he had two ears."

"This is true," said Jelani.

"Shut up," snapped a constable. Jade glared at the man, and Finch waved for the constable to leave.

"See if you can't find Dr. Dymant," Finch ordered. "Blasted time for Mathews to be off. I've a mind to telegram Fort Hall and order him back here."

"If I might intrude," said Percival. "Those limbs were torn off by a croc, most likely after the body was submerged for a while. As you know, this isn't the first person that croc has taken." He replaced the cloth over the body and stepped farther away from it. "But no croc could cut off an ear like that. That was done with a *panga* knife."

"I'm well aware of that, Mr. Percival," said Finch. "But the question remains whether the crocodile killed this man or whether he was dead and then thrown in. Theft of the necklace might be enough of a motive for revenge. And *that*," he said, glaring at Jelani and Irungu, "is why I've brought in these two for questioning, as well as you, Miss del Cameron."

"You're assuming that Irungu or one of the other natives killed Mutahi and tossed him to the croc," she said, nodding to the covered corpse.

"When Mr. Percival found the body, he inquired at the village and some women told him the witching tale."

"I didn't look at the body that closely," said Jade, "but all I saw were teeth marks. I didn't see any evidence of a stab to the heart, at least not from the front. No deep cut to the throat or mark made by a rope. The natives aren't allowed to possess firearms. Did you see any marks on the back, Mr. Percival?"

"Possibly a blow to the back of the head but it may have been caused by a fall or by hitting a rock in the water when the croc had him in a death roll."

"The lack of those more obvious marks are why I want a doctor to look at him," said Finch. "He might have been throttled by someone's bare hands. Difficult to see such bruising now, but there may be internal damage from a beating."

Jade sized up Jelani's smaller build. "I can't see Jelani having the ability to do that, and Irungu made no such threats in my presence." She looked back at Finch and folded her arms across her chest. "You must release them."

"So now you are telling me how to conduct my investigation and how to run native affairs?"

"You brought me in here. But I might have information that would interest you."

"Go on," said Finch.

Jade shook her head. "Not until these two men are released back to their village."

Finch glared at Jade, his jaw clenched. "I give you my word, Miss del Cameron, that I won't hold them for this man's death unless I have solid evidence. However, I must detain them until Dymant examines the body."

Jade watched Jelani for a moment before answering. He stood ramrod straight like a soldier, eyes ahead and looking beyond the room. No, not a soldier—a martyr ready and willing to die for a tightly held belief. She knew he wouldn't thank her for gaining his release. Irungu kept his head bowed but his eyes looked up hopefully.

"I have your word?" Jade asked.

"As I said." Finch called a constable and ordered the two men to be taken to a holding cell until the autopsy was completed. "Now," he said when they were gone, "I believe you said you have information for me. Or was that some female ruse?" He motioned for her to leave the room and rejoin him in his office.

Jade wrestled with her fears and suspicions. Could she trust Finch? Other than the fact that his age and position made him eligible, was there any other evidence that he could be Pellyn? She'd need to trust him a little, if only to find out more herself. She waited until he'd offered her tea, which she declined, had poured a cup for himself, and taken a swallow.

"I know what happened to Mutahi's necklace. Someone, a white man, gave it to Neville and Madeline Thompson's little boy just before he tried to abduct him."

Finch choked on the tea and coughed, spraying the papers in front of him. Jade checked her smile. At least his reaction made her less suspicious of him. *Unless his reaction is to my knowing.*

"The Dunburys called for the Nairobi police just before you demanded my presence," Jade said. "Madeline and Neville Thompson are at Lord Dunbury's Parklands estate with their child." She briefly explained what had happened.

"A kidnapping for ransom that went awry when one of the native staff came too close?" suggested Finch.

"Everyone was on the far end of the farm, fighting a grass fire."

They were interrupted by a rap on the doorframe. A European constable poked his head in. "Begging your pardon, Inspector, but we're having a spot of trouble finding Dr. Dymant. He doesn't answer at his office."

"Did you try his residence?"

The man cleared his throat and looked at the far wall. "Actually, sir, I'm not certain where it is. Dr. Mathews is still away. Is there someone else I should fetch?"

Finch pounded his fist on his desk, splattering the rest of the tea. "Use your head, man. Find someone. There has to be at least one government doctor left in Nairobi." He righted his teacup and sponged the mess with his pocket handkerchief. "I'll send someone around to the Thompsons' to make inquiries."

"There's more," said Jade. Finch clenched his jaw. "I saw the shell-casing necklace. Someone, maybe Mutahi, had scratched a design on it. It was simply and crudely done, but I recognized the pattern. Two overlapping circles. It represents a moon eclipsing the sun."

"Likely a design this Mutahi felt had power. He's seen an eclipse, I'm sure. What of it?"

"It's Lilith Worthy's emblem. I ran across it before. Mutahi must have seen it somewhere."

"And you think that it might have something to do with that Pellyn chap then? Very well, I'll collect the necklace for evidence."

"Overlapping circles, you say?" asked Blaney Percival. "There was a circular burn mark on this man's back. Too decomposed to be clear. I thought he may have backed into a torch or something but it could have been a brand."

"The Congo natives were branded," murmured Jade. "And had an ear cut off."

Jade excused herself, but as she joined Avery in the waiting area, she considered Dr. Dymant. Assuming Cyril had been pointing to Biscuit's lighter base fur, the hair bore some resemblance to Dymant's. Dymant also sounded Cornish.

And now Dymant can't be found.

CHAPTER 16

With a sudden explosion of power, a crocodile can shoot out
of the water with amazing speed. Just as quickly, it recedes into the
water with its prey, leaving barely a ripple. Perhaps the entire drama
was imagined? Yet one backs away, and adds twenty more yards
between oneself and the water's edge.
—The Traveler

THE OX-5 MOTOR'S SONG reminded Jade of Biscuit's throaty purr, surrounding her as did the blue sky and the plane's Irish linen. Avery sat in the rear of Sam's Curtiss JN-4, manning the controls, while Jade took over the front of the plane and scouted for anything out of the ordinary on the ground. Avery had offered to let Jade fly, but she'd declined. It was uncomfortable enough being in Sam's beloved Jenny without him. Flying it would have felt dead wrong.

Neville had gone home Sunday to wait for Finch's man and to guard against further attacks on his farm. He'd left Cyril and Madeline at the Dunburys' estate under the Dunburys', Biscuit's, and Farhani's watchful eyes. Jade and Avery took Maddy home later Monday morning to help Neville continue searching the grounds for any sign of an intruder. Beverly had promised to do something nearly unheard of during the day: she'd shut and bolt the doors, admitting no one until Avery returned.

Madeline had been torn between duty to husband and to son, but Beverly had finally convinced her that Cyril would be safe, allowing Madeline to search with Neville. Jade had never seen such a look of determined and controlled fury on Maddy's face. She could still hear Maddy's voice saying, "I want to be the one to find that bastard so that I can shoot him first!"

Avery banked the Jenny and broadened the search circle, moving outward in an ever-increasing spiral. Below them on the Thompsons' farm spread burned grassland, a patchwork of black blotches amid wetter wallows where fresher grass had resisted the blaze. She spotted trampled areas where the men had stood and fought the fire. She pointed down and Avery dropped lower and crisscrossed over the burn. Jade looked carefully for any telltale tracks at the point of origin. She spied some and pointed again.

Avery followed a set of tire tracks as they cut a wide path around the farm nearer to the house. The vehicle had never been any closer than a quarter mile. If they hoped to find where the person had come from or escaped to, they were disappointed. One set of tracks eventually doubled back on the other and all tracks were lost at the road. The vehicle could have come and gone from anywhere.

Below, Maddy and Neville continued their own ground search for anything dropped by the would-be kidnapper. Jade saw them look up and wave. Avery waggled the wings in reply and turned away. With little more to be gained here, they'd continue to fly around the area and especially Ol Donyo Sabuk, hoping to spy a camp or an unknown vehicle.

As they headed southeast, Jade kept her eyes on the land-scape, but her mind played with the morning's first visit to the land office.

The spectacled clerk, a Mr. Lippincott, had insisted that no mining claims had been filed for anyplace in the colony in the past year.

"But that's not a surprise," he'd said. "It's common knowl-edge that the colony is sadly lacking in valuable minerals. Why should anyone even attempt mining? Getting Tanganyika Territory from the Germans might prove useful. Shame we couldn't win the Belgian Congo, right? That Leopold, he sure fell into a rich pot. Copper by the score. Gold too, but some of that is in pretty rough country. But they have a new governor-general running things now, don't they?"

"Yes, but it took long enough," said Avery. "Leopold died in 1909, but the scoundrels in the Congo continued running things for years and the war only aggravated the problems."

"What do *you* know about the mining under Emperor Leopold?" asked Jade.

"Terrible tales," Lippincott said. "Butchery and brutality. Open season on Africans, it was."

"Did you ever hear of anyone named Worthy or Pellyn committing these crimes?"

"Those are English and Cornish names," said Lippincott. "Can't say I recognize them, but I did hear of an Englishman involved in one mine. Put a brand on his workers in case they tried to run away. Oddest part of that story was that once, a white *woman* came into camp and sliced the ears off some men."

"When did you hear these tales?" asked Avery. "Were they reliable?"

"During and just after the war. And reliable enough. Settlers and traders proving up land would swap tales in the office. I heard that one twice after the war."

Now Jade pondered those facts. The Congo was reported to hold gold, especially in the Katanga province. That obnoxious parrot was a species from the Congo. It stood to reason that Waters had been prospecting in the Congo, legally or illegally. The question remained: had he been prospecting in Kenya Colony as well or had he brought gold back and used it to lure gullible settlers into investing in a fake mine?

Salting the mine. Salt!

If that parrot was trying to say "Pellyn" rather than "pile in," then either Waters was actually Pellyn or had worked with him long enough for the bird to have learned the name. Jade didn't think Waters was Pellyn. For one, he wasn't Cornish. He was a Cockney. True, the drugged South African red tea had been given to her before Waters died, but Cyril's abduction pointed to someone still active in the area. Perhaps Waters had run afoul of Pellyn and tried to cheat him. That would explain his death, but why would Pellyn try to take Cyril?

The drugs were meant to either drive me insane or chase me away, possibly so I could be captured away from my friends. If they all thought I was fleeing, it would be months before anyone knew what had become of me and by then I'd be dead.

And it might have worked if Harry hadn't been taken ill, exposing the scheme. Now she was still here and she'd have to play a part, testifying in any inquests or trials concerning the recent deaths. *Is someone now threatening me through my friends? Is their safety the price of my silence? Or does Pellyn hope that my friends will drive me out?* She thought of Mary's plea to help her uncle. Jade had grudgingly agreed, but Holly's suspicious behavior suggested he was involved as more than a victim. *Was he told to lure me to Harry's farmhouse?*

Whatever Pellyn had in mind, he was in for a surprise. Jade didn't run away from a fight. She'd find him and deal with him.

Jade pushed her speculations to the back of her mind and concentrated on studying the landscape. She loved seeing Africa from the air; the distant zebra herds looked like living shadows as they milled and grazed, and she wished she could give herself over to the view. They next followed the Athi downriver from the falls. A tent and a boxy car attracted Jade's notice and she pointed them out to Avery. He passed over them at fifty feet and Jade recognized Blaney Percival's truck. This was where he was camping as he continued to look for the elusive mottled crocodile. They flew over Jelani's village before turning back west for Ol Donyo Sabuk. Several women hunkered over the river, washing broad swaths of cloth. Others stood nearby, throwing rocks and beating the water with sticks to drive off any lurking crocodiles.

She couldn't hear them over the airplane's motor, but she knew they were chanting and singing loudly. Jade prayed their ruse would work, but somehow she doubted it would fool any crocs for long. She'd heard reports of the reptiles savaging migrating herds of wildebeest as they crossed rivers. If all those slashing hooves didn't deter them, a few poles wouldn't either. The Kikuyu's best defense lay in the game warden killing this croc and patrolling the upper reaches of the Athi to keep more away.

They next flew around the mountain, clockwise from the south. Jade leaned over the lowered right side of the plane.

She didn't see Harry's truck or another tent. She wondered if he'd given up looking for the crocodile or if Percival had sent him even farther downriver.

After they circled the mountain once and succeeded in startling one buffalo and two giraffes, Avery turned the plane and reversed the route, heading counterclockwise. Jade had suggested it earlier, hoping that something hidden from view in one direction might be visible from the other. But with so much of Roger's and Harry's land returning to wild growth, it was difficult to spot anything amid the tangle of vegetation. Jade did see old tire tracks here and there, but they might have been made by Harry. Avery had made inquiries and found that McMillan's farm hadn't had visitors for months.

Jade wasn't sure what she'd expected to see. She'd hoped to find someone encamped in the grasslands with a clear trail leading to and from the Thompsons' farm, unrealistic as it had seemed. Avery reached forward and tapped her on the shoulder. When she turned in her seat, he pointed down to his fuel gauge, then back to the Thompsons'. She nodded. They needed to return. Fuel was still difficult to come by and they'd used enough already.

Once they'd landed and tended to the plane, they rejoined Madeline and Neville. Neither of them had anything to report.

"You'd think he'd have dropped a button or something," said Maddy.

"We've questioned every one of the Kikuyu and no one remembers seeing anyone near the house," said Neville.

"But then they wouldn't, would they," said Avery. "That was the intent of the fire."

"I don't suppose you found anything from above?" asked Neville.

Jade shook her head. "Tracks, but we lost them at the road. Still, not seeing any camps tells us that this person most likely came from one of the towns."

"Do you think it's safe for us to bring Cyril back home?" asked Maddy. Jade heard the longing in her voice.

Neville patted his rifle. "We won't let the little chap out of our sight, Maddy," he said. "Anyone who tries anything won't live to try it again. I'll go get him now."

"Jade and I will locate Steven Holly at the Blue Posts," said Avery. "He may know something."

"Very well," said Neville. He shook Avery's hand. "Thank you. I can't imagine a better friend and ally at present." Then, as though he felt embarrassed by this exuberant display of masculine emotion, he coughed and added, "Not excepting you, of course, Jade."

"Will you stay and take lunch before you go?" asked Maddy.

"Thank you, but no," said Avery. He flexed his hands in a manner that bespoke an itching to connect a fist to a jaw.

Jade thought he'd need to get in line after her.

THE BLUE POSTS HOTEL was mainly a large round hut surrounded by a veranda upheld by blue posts, surrounded by several whitewashed sleeping huts and stables. When the hotel first opened in 1908, it boasted only four huts. Now there were more, testimony to the popular Chania Falls, which thundered nearby. But the same nearly deaf manager stood behind a wooden desk. He was known to all as Major Breeches ever since he misunderstood a question as to who made his breeches. Avery did his best to inquire after Holly, but the fall's din, only partially subdued after the end of the rains, did nothing to help the man's hearing.

"Mr. Steven Holly," shouted Avery for the third time.

Jade took a more direct approach and pulled the guest registry towards her. She looked in vain for the name Holly but found the name Smith. She showed this to Avery.

"If he was really afraid someone might find him, he wouldn't use his real name," she said.

Avery pointed to the signature and shouted "Smith" at Major Breeches.

The manager beamed and nodded, his bald pate shining. "Very good, Mr. Smith," he said.

"We want to see him," yelled Avery. He pointed to himself and then to the book.

"Are you newly married?" asked the manager. "How very nice."

Avery shook his head. "No."

Major Breeches' smile evaporated as he looked from Jade to Avery and his mustache drooped as though it had wilted. "I run a respectable hotel, sir. If you're not married, I don't think you should stay here."

Avery sighed. "Any ideas, Jade?"

Jade looked about for paper to write a note and, seeing none, started to write in the registry. The manager immediately snatched it out of her hands. At that point, Jade pantomimed writing and was promptly rewarded with a sheet of paper. She wrote very carefully, *We wish to speak to Mr. Smith*, and handed the message to Major Breeches.

"He's not here. He checked out this morning. Took the omnibus."

"Blast and damn," muttered Avery.

"Did he have any visitors?" asked Jade.

Major Breeches smiled. "Always nice to have visitors here. So many people come to see the falls."

"Now what?" Jade asked Avery when they left. "We can't visit every hotel in the colony."

Avery shook his head. "We've run into a dead end, it seems. I for one want to get back home and make certain that Beverly and Alice are all right."

They drove back to Parklands in silence. Jade felt she'd learned nothing the entire day, and her frustration had reduced her to introspective brooding.

Beverly must have been watching for them from a window, for she met them at the door and hurried them into the front parlor. She explained that Emily was out purchasing a ticket. "She was quite upset that we didn't include her in the search or confide in her. She plans to take the down train to Mombassa tomorrow and stay for a few days. I believe she's over Mr. Holly, at least. What did you two discover today? Why did you let Neville take Cyril so soon?"

Her inquiries were quietly answered by Avery. Jade, tired, waited for an opening so that she could politely excuse herself and go back to her own rooms.

Farhani came to the sitting room door and coughed to announce himself.

"What is it, Farhani?" asked Beverly. "Is Matthew *mpishi* having difficulty with my new recipe?"

"No, memsahib," said Farhani. He stood ramrod straight, his white robe falling in stiff folds. One arm was behind his back. He brought it forward now, his white-gloved hand holding a silver tray. "A boy has delivered this message for the bwana. I have already paid him a rupee and sent him on his way."

Avery took the paper from the tray and thanked their majordomo. Farhani bowed, his white turban nearly brushing Avery's shoulder.

"What is it, Avery, darling?" asked Beverly.

"It's a telegram," he replied.

"Sam!" said Beverly. She smiled broadly. "I knew we'd hear from him soon."

"It's not from Sam," said Avery as he read the return address. "In point of fact, it's from my brother."

"Marcus? Whatever could be so urgent?" Beverly's eyes opened wider. "Oh, I hope he and his family aren't on their way to stay with us. I'm not sure where I can fit any more relations."

Jade felt her neck hairs tingle. Avery could have had any number of estate-related telegrams, but for some reason, she knew this was different. She watched Avery's normally placid face tense as he clenched his teeth. "Avery?"

"For mercy's sake, Avery, don't keep us in suspense. What does it say?" asked Beverly, her hands knotting around her skirt.

"Quite simply, 'The bird has flown.'" He crumbled the paper in his fist and sank into a chair. "It means that Lilith has escaped."

CHAPTER 17

*Some tribes say, "A thirsty frog does not let the crocodile's
threatening eyes keep it from drinking." The message is, "Do not be
intimidated from doing what you must," but frogs don't make much
of a meal and have less to worry about to begin with.*
—The Traveler

"ESCAPED!" shouted Beverly. She jumped to her feet. "Lilith?"

Jade said nothing. She fought down the panic, her heart
pounding as the force of this news hit home. When she closed
her eyes, Jade saw Lilith rise up like a specter, an icy woman
in black silk, a mockery of a grieving widow. *Mamba jike!
The female crocodile.*

Avery smoothed out the telegram and studied it as if
some hidden message would rise out of the paper. "I'll read
it." He cleared his throat. "'In London. Found old telegram
at house. Date December twenty-six. The bird has flown.
Marcus.'" Avery folded the paper and set it on the side table. "That was the code phrase I told my acquaintance at the
prison to use if Lilith escaped."

"Then she escaped over the Christmas holidays two
months ago," said Beverly. "I understand the telegram going
to the London house, but why wasn't the message sent on?"

Avery put his head down and ran one hand across the back of his neck. When he looked up, he seemed older and haggard. Jade had never seen him this way. Avery was always the epitome of British pluck and dash. "I fear this is all my fault," he said. "When I originally arranged for these messages, we were in London awaiting Alice's birth. When we left early for Nairobi, it was rather sudden and"—he looked at his wife—"I confess I had more important concerns on my mind at the time. I neglected to leave notice with the prison warden." He stood up and paced around his chair. "But I never really expected Lilith to escape. To attempt it, perhaps, but—" He broke off and dropped back into his chair.

Beverly hurried to his side, kneeling beside him, her hands on his. "It's not your fault, darling," she said. "I don't understand why the message was not sent on to us from the house."

Avery patted her hands. "The London house was shut up. The only person there was Mrs. Delvin, and that's only because the dear old soul has been with the family for so long that we let her live there in retirement. She probably hasn't employed anyone other than a part-time cook. Marcus must have had business in London and decided to stay at the house rather than the club."

"Does he know what this means?" asked Beverly.

"'The bird has flown'? No. Probably thought it had to do with an aeroplane."

Jade listened to their conversation as if she were eavesdropping from another room. At least, that was how she felt—unconnected. It seemed as if neither of them fully grasped the magnitude of the situation, like someone who smells smoke but doesn't realize that the room they're sitting in is on fire.

"You have to leave," Jade said, "and take the baby with you."

Her voice broke through, but her message did not. "What?" asked Beverly. "The baby's asleep. Why would I wake her?"

"Bev, Avery, listen to me. You have to leave and take the baby with you. Hide. Get Maddy and Cyril to go with you."

Avery sat up straighter. "You're suggesting that they are still in danger. That the attempt on Cyril might be repeated." It was not a question. At least, thought Jade, one of them was grasping the situation. Jade nodded.

"Don't you see?" said Jade. "That attempt was a warning, meant to frighten me. Perhaps to induce you to send me away. The next time will be more serious. She could be anywhere by now. Here, in the colony, maybe even in Nairobi. It's enough to worry about who Pellyn might be masquerading as, but Lilith? For all we know it was Lilith who put Cyril in the coffee dryer. Whoever gave Mutahi's necklace to Cyril did it not to put blame on a native, but to let me know that I'm being watched. This person knew I'd recognize the emblem etched on it."

"Perhaps she never made it out of England. Perhaps they've captured her by now?" suggested Beverly, her tone hopeful.

Avery handed his wife back to her chair. "Until recently, *you* were the only target, Jade. Do you think Lilith took Cyril or would go after anyone else just to make you leave?"

Jade shook her head. "There will be inquests in the recent deaths and she may fear my testimony more than we know. Those deaths were *meant* to look like accidents. Now they're murder. And it would expose the mining scheme. Or she may be trying to get me away so that she can kill me. I can *feel* her behind this. She hates me; *that* much we know for certain. I doubt she'd scruple at hurting my friends just to get to me."

"Oh, dear," said Bev. "Taking the children would be the ultimate blow."

"Exactly," said Jade. "Until we find her, everyone I care about is in danger. You all should go to ground. Someone should alert David's brother, too." Jade looked at Avery. "She hates Pili as much as me simply because he's her husband's illegitimate child."

"More likely she hates him for taking half of Gil Worthy's estate," said Avery. "Rest assured that Pili is safely tucked away. He's in no danger, but he will be if I try to send him a message. You said yourself that we don't know who we can trust, Jade." He held up the crumbled telegram. "The only reason we may have received this is because it's coded. Sending him a telegram could give away his hiding place."

Jade nodded. "I think my parents are safe as well. Their ranch is remote. If Lilith wanted to use someone to capture me, then she'd most likely try for someone close at hand." *At least Sam is safe.* She felt the ache in her chest swell. Her throat tightened and her desire to hear his gravelly voice, to see his angular face and to feel his embrace, swelled into an overwhelming need, one that she had to satisfy or die. She carried this new wound as she did her scarred knee, a constant reminder of an injury, sometimes a dull twinge and at others a searing pain, but always present.

Ah, Sam. Where are you? Why did you leave me? She fought back a sob and clenched her jaw until the moment passed.

"Beverly may be right," said Avery. "The London police would be looking for Lilith. They surely had the docks closely watched. Chances are she's been apprehended and we just haven't heard."

"They'll be looking for a woman," said Jade when she finally felt she could trust her voice. "Lilith has a scar from her nose past her eye. People would comment on it. She's got to stay hidden or else disguise herself as a man, perhaps wear a beard. It wouldn't cover the scar, but it would draw attention away from it. She's done this before, but the London police may not think to look for a small, bearded man."

"Still, at most she could have been in the colony for only a month," said Beverly, "and that's assuming she caught the fastest ship here straightaway. I wish we knew who Pellyn is. Then we could take our own hostage, force her hand."

"I've been thinking about that, too," said Jade. "Avery had the right idea when he suggested interrogating Holly. Only now we don't know where he is." She fixed her gaze on Beverly. "But I was dead serious when I said you need to hide."

Beverly raised her chin and sniffed. "I have no intention of leaving Avery. Or you, for that matter, Jade. Nor do I intend to entrust my baby with the nanny in some strange place. She's safest here, in our own house, where we can keep an eye on her. And what if Pellyn or Lilith spies us catching a train? They'd only have to track us down in Mombassa, where we're completely unprotected." She folded her arms adamantly around her chest. "So no! I'm staying."

Avery smiled. "My brave, stubborn little wife is right,

Jade. We would do better to keep Maddy and Cyril here. Safety in numbers and all that. And then go on the hunt for Holly." He balled one hand into a fist and punched it into the other. "Should we keep Emily here, do you think?"

"Let her enjoy her little holiday, love," said Beverly. "She was most upset today. And she and Jade are not close enough to make her a target. She should be safe enough."

Farhani returned with the announcement that afternoon tea was served. Jade didn't feel like eating anything; her stomach was too unsettled, her nerves too fever pitched. She stood up and paced around the room.

"I'm going to the Thompsons' now," she said. "They need to know. If you don't mind, Avery, I should like to borrow your Hupmobile so I can bring them back with me."

Avery walked up to Jade and put a brotherly hand on her shoulder in what was for him an uncharacteristic gesture of concern. "Forgive me for saying this, but I don't trust you behind the wheel of my car. You are far too distraught. They're already on the alert. Maddy won't let Cyril out of her sight and Neville is probably standing guard with a rifle."

Jade scowled. "I feel fine." She knew she was lying. In truth, she felt as though the walls were closing in on her. She needed to get outside and breathe.

"You look like hell and I mean that in the nicest way." Avery took his hand off her shoulder and slipped it in his trouser pocket. "If you must do something to burn off your restless energy, go and see if there are any letters waiting for us. A mail ship docked Friday. There might be a letter from my brother or the warden with more information."

"Yes, do go," echoed Bev. "Perhaps the fresh air will do you good. And don't worry about Biscuit. I'll find him a nice fresh cut of meat to occupy him while you're gone. Take a rickshaw or let us ring up a taxi for you."

"I'll take my motorcycle, thank you very much."

Jade rode her Indian Power Plus into Nairobi proper. As she motored past the government buildings and shops, she again wondered which of the city's many men might be Mathers Pellyn. *Perhaps someone in the land office?* Such a person would be able to forge a mining claim easily enough. But she had no idea how to catch him at it.

Whatever role Pellyn had chosen, he was skilled at forgery. Who else could have imitated not only David's handwriting but also Major Bertram's and Bev's so well? Could Lilith? The thought gave her pause. She'd been thinking of Pellyn being behind all of her torments. But now that she knew Lilith was free, it opened up an entirely new vista of possibilities.

A horn *oogah*ed at her and she turned aside just in time to avoid colliding with a man driving a new Chalmers automobile.

"Watch where you're going, lady!" he yelled. "Blasted women on motorcycles now. They get a vote and suddenly they think they're free to run loose everywhere." He shoved his car into gear with a grinding screech and puttered off.

The up train that left from Mombassa Sunday afternoon had arrived a few hours before, so Jade had no chance to scan passengers for any small men with beards. Instead, she went directly to the post office and collected the Dunburys' mail. She looked in vain for anything from Sam. In fact, the entire bundle was a paltry assortment of monthlies. Avery's copy of *Flying* sat atop the heap, and Jade scanned the many photos of the newest airplanes. She closed the issue with a sigh, as it made her think too much of Sam. There were no letters, nothing to give them more information regarding Lilith's escape.

Blast! Now what?

The answer came to her quickly. Inquire at the different hotels for someone matching Lilith's probable description: a small man, slightly built, with a beard and a small scar riding up from the nose bridge past the left eye.

And how are you going to do that? Just go up and ask if anyone's seen someone who looks like that? She knew the clerks protected their clients' privacy. They would question the validity of Jade's search. Then they'd warn their tenant that someone was looking for them.

I'll make up a name. When they say no one is registered by that name, I'll describe him. Hopefully, someone would slip and reveal such a person's registered name. *Better pick an odd name so I don't risk getting a legitimate guest.*

She went to the Norfolk, the New Stanley, the Old Stanley, and the Victoria hotels. At each one she adopted the story of looking for a gentleman named Clive Whippoorspool. Each time she was certain he had to be there and described him.

"My height, slender, light brown hair. He had a beard when I last saw him. Very soft-spoken gentleman. Rather shy. He's got a scar he's ashamed of." She traced an imaginary scar line on her own face.

By the time she'd gone to all the hotels, she felt that every clerk must have thought she was a desperate, jilted woman. Especially when she also inquired after Mr. Holly. The clerk at the Victoria had not seen him return. Finally, she debated going to Eliot Street to ask at the YMCA. While she had a hard time imagining either Lilith or Holly gravitating to the association, it made it that much more likely that no one would look for them there.

Perhaps the perfect hiding place?

"There's no gentleman by that name, miss," said the stiff man behind the desk. His scowl did nothing to veil his disgust that a young woman was in this bastion of male sanctity to begin with, much less one in her attire. "As a rule, our members do not sport facial hair. Clean face, clean mind, clean soul, you understand."

"He might have shaved his beard. And this gentleman might not have been here more than a month, maybe less. Perhaps—"

"There are no new residents, miss." The man turned back to his bookkeeping, dismissing Jade.

She left, uncertain where to head next. *Finch? Can I trust him?* Part of her still didn't, but she also wondered if he'd learned anything new about Mutahi's death. Remembering an old adage to hold your friends close but your enemies closer, she decided it was worthwhile checking in with him, especially as she had no idea which of those two categories to put him under.

It's late. He probably won't be there anyway. That idea secured her decision to go to the police. She felt confident that she could wrangle information out of a lowly constable.

She was disappointed. Finch was still there. In fact, she heard him shouting at one of his men. "If you'd inquired more thoroughly for him when I'd ordered, we might not be in this position!" He turned and saw her standing in his doorway. "What the devil do you want? My stars! You remind me of a vulture. Do you smell death?"

Jade stood her ground. She'd planned to ask about Mutahi, but she decided to toss an idea at him and watch his
reaction. Dymant was Cornish and so was Pellyn. His hair
matched Cyril's description and no one really knew the man.
"I think I know who tried to abduct the Thompsons' child."

"Who?"

"Dr. Dymant."

Finch's reaction was as instantaneous as it was unexpected. He laughed in one sharp hoot. "Well, then you'll be
happy to hear this news, Miss del Cameron. Dr. Dymant is
dead."

THE MAN FINGERED HIS BEARD in a way that said he was still
not used to it. It was hot for one, and it itched for another. But
it was necessary if he didn't want to be recognized in Nairobi. His pulled his hat brim down lower and nestled back
into the building's protective shadows. After the woman left
the YMCA, he followed her as far as he could on foot before
he lost her. But his ears tracked the sound of her motorcycle,
and he'd guessed where she was going. It was one place he
couldn't go right now. He'd have to catch her alone. Later.
When it was dark.

CHAPTER 18

Another saying is, "Do not mock the crocodile until you have crossed
the river." It might be a good plan not to mock it even then
in case one has to return later.
—The Traveler

No one spoke. The constable acted as though he were trying to blend into the wall lest his superior yell at him again.
Finch appeared to be deciding whether to throw both Jade
and the constable out of his office. And Jade was too stunned
by Finch's news to speak. She'd been prepared to hear Finch
scoff at her half-baked idea, but to hear that Dymant was
dead?

Jade took a deep breath and broke the silence. "How did
he die?"

"Plague," said Finch. "Found him lying on the floor of
his office this afternoon." He glared at the constable again.
"If Gardner here hadn't been such a bloody damned idiot the
other day and done a more thorough search for the doctor
when he was told to, we might have had him in a hospital.
Dr. Mathews is at Dymant's surgery now, finishing a rather
hasty examination before an even quicker burial."

"He did say he planned to take care of the Indians," Jade

said. She felt ashamed for having suspected someone who'd wanted only to do good.

Finch paced back to his desk, picked up a pencil, and tossed it back down again. "Yes, well, he certainly paid the price for that. He may have been involved in that knife fight reported in the papers a few days ago. The one in the Indian district. A witness said he saw a white man in the thick of it, but as no one ever came forward, we had no idea who he was or his level of involvement. All we have is what some anonymous person told a reporter for the *Leader*."

"And he actually died of the plague?" asked Jade.

"Septicemic plague, to be precise," said Finch. "The variety that gets into the blood. He had a deep gash on his leg and Dr. Mathews speculates that the knife was infected with the plague germ. Probably had tainted blood on it. We've had enough problems with the pneumonic variety in the slums."

Jade nodded. She'd read about it in the *Leader*. Dymant dead! She still couldn't comprehend it. But if he'd been ill, then he was probably not the one who had taken Cyril from the house. Unless he'd started to take sick then and that was why he left the child behind.

"How fast does that form of the plague work?" she asked.

Finch shrugged. "No idea. Well, not much of one, I should say. More quickly than the bubonic form, I believe. Dr. Mathews is the man to ask, though I doubt you'll have the chance. He just returned last evening and already we have him on this case. Chap's hardly had a chance to sleep."

"And did he also examine Mutahi's corpse?"

"Who? Oh, the Kikuyu eaten by the crocodile. No. Corpse too far gone to tell much of anything, there. Brought in another military doctor. He ruled it an accidental death by crocodile." Finch seemed to notice the constable still standing silently at attention. "You're still here? Get the car round, man! We're going to take a look at Dr. Dymant's rooms to see if there's any family we need to notify."

"I'd like to go along," said Jade, as the constable sped past her.

"And why the blazes should you?" demanded Finch.

"As I told you, I thought Dymant might have been the man who tried to kidnap Cyril. I suppose I'm looking for evidence to prove he was or wasn't."

Finch raised his eyebrows. "Indeed? You were serious about that?" He rubbed his chin with a thumb and forefinger, considering her request. "Oh, the devil! Come along then."

Jade followed on her motorcycle as they drove towards the Indian district. She had been there often enough, sometimes to buy trinkets for her parents, once to photograph the area for her magazine. While the streets weren't as mazelike as in Morocco, they still reminded Jade of the souks in Marrakech with their exotic costumes, faces, smells, and sounds. The narrow streets were thronged with humanity as women in colorful saris pulled dusky children in shorts or in tunics past the roughly built shops and residences. The melodic intonations of Hindustani dominated over English, and the scent of sweat collided with sandalwood incense.

Extended families lived crowded in the backs of stores under some of the meanest conditions. The British citizens had expressed disgust at the Indian slums but offered very little in the way of an alternative. The city government still denied the Indians any land in the upland area away from the swamplands. Most Europeans avoided the interior of the district, especially in light of the plague incidents. Dymant had made the same choice as far as his residence went.

Finch's driver stopped at the shop of Harisingh Valjee, a block off Government Road. Several Europeans who'd been doing last-minute business at the store stopped and stared as first Finch and the constable got out of their vehicle and then as Jade parked her motorcycle just inside the alleyway.

"He took rooms upstairs of this shop," said Finch, handing a key to the constable. "Close enough to get to his patients, but far enough to avoid the hazards of living among them. At least, that's what he thought."

The constable opened the door at the end of the building and held it for Finch and Jade. Jade followed the inspector up a steep, narrow flight of stairs to a short hallway. He went past the first door, which opened into the shopkeeper's home, and headed for Dymant's flat at the rear of the building. They waited while the constable fetched a spare key from Mr. Valjee and opened the door. The building was wired for electricity, but the lone, bare ceiling bulb was weak and fitful.

"Please do not touch anything, Miss del Cameron," said Finch. "You are here to look only. And to answer any questions I might care to ask you." He turned away from her and walked into the front room, which served as both a study and a parlor. He lifted the desktop. "Kept his keys in the desk. Trusting chap."

Jade went inside, her gaze taking in the simple appointments: one easy chair and a threadbare ottoman sat next to a small coal stove for heating the room on cold nights. A rolltop desk and wooden chair stood in an opposite corner. The wall facing the stove sported a barrister bookcase, nearly empty, and an end table beside the chair held one brass oil lamp.

Finch struck a match and lit the lamp to add more light. There were no papers atop the desk, just a blotter and a pen-and-ink holder. Jade turned back to the bookcase, noting that a key also sat in the lock, and silently read the book spines: A King James Bible, a tome on tropical diseases, a Hindustani language booklet, and one anatomy text. A tall, leather-bound book propped up the others. *Photograph album?*

"Not many books, but about what one would expect a missionary doctor to have, I suppose," she said. Or were they chosen for that very reason? She longed to flip through them and see if there were any hidden notes tucked in the pages. "His other medical books must be in his office. The album might hold a clue to his family."

"Gardner," barked Finch to the constable, "see to that album."

"Sir!" said Gardner. He opened the case and pulled out the book.

Jade looked over his shoulder long enough to see that there were only photographs of India in it. She peered into the second room and saw, in the gloom, a plain-looking bed, a washstand with an old-fashioned pitcher and ewer, and several open-fronted shelves of clothing. A small door near the washstand led to a tiny lavatory. Stepping in, she noted a dressing gown hanging on a hook, but left checking any pockets to Finch. She didn't want to risk being tossed out before finding out anything she wanted to know.

Instead, she scanned the clothing on the shelves, noting several pairs of trousers and socks on the bottom shelf and a large assortment of shirts on the upper next to a stack of men's drawers and undershirts. A shaving kit sat by the ewer. There was nothing in this room to give any insight into Dymant's personal life. Both rooms were windowless and dismal. Jade rejoined Finch in the parlor and found him rummaging systematically through the desk.

"Have you found anything?" she asked.

"Such as?"

"I believe you said you were looking for the names of relatives." When Finch didn't answer, Jade tried another approach. "Perhaps he kept addresses and other information like that at his office. There aren't any medical supplies here, so he must not have been operating out of his parlor."

Finch slammed a drawer shut. "Thank you for that sterling bit of detective work, Miss del Cameron. I can assure you that I intend to go there as soon as I am finished here." He glared at her as though daring her to interrupt him again. Jade leaned against the doorframe and waited, her hands in her pockets.

But her eyes and mind weren't idle. She watched Finch's face as he leafed through every folder, journal, box, and book. The man was fairly inscrutable. Other than showing some impatience, he gave no evidence of surprise or interest.

"His personal calendar is all but blank," Finch said, slapping it shut. "Engaged to dine with Reverend Wright in two days. Nothing more. I suppose I should notify him. At least to say prayers at his burial."

"How far away is Dymant's office?" Jade asked.

"A mere walk around the corner," said Finch. "Valjee rented out two rooms in a building just behind the store. Mathews should be finished. We might as well go there now. There's nothing here."

Leaving Gardner to lock up the flat, Jade and Finch hastened to the office. The door opened as they arrived and they were met by Dr. Mathews. Jade thought he looked more drawn and tired than when she'd last seen him. She noticed that he was meticulously dressed, including a pair of white gloves, lightly soiled from examining the corpse.

"Ah, Mathews," said Finch. "Finished with the examination?"

"Yes. I was just on my way to your office to relay my report. Too tired to sit and type it myself." He yawned. "The mortician has taken the body away in a coffin. All that can be done for him is to put him in the ground as quickly as possible before he becomes—how shall I say it?—unbearable." He looked at Jade. "I can't say that I approve of your bringing a young lady here, Inspector, even one as inquisitive as Miss del Cameron. She should not be subjected to the smells inside there."

"Is he contagious?" asked Jade.

"No, Miss del Cameron. He is not, nor is the room. Plague is carried by flea bites, or in the case of pneumonic, it seems to go by air. This man had the septicemic variety."

"What is the difference?" Jade asked.

"Any form can become septicemic if it enters the blood, but in his case, it began there. Most likely either from a knife wound I found in his thigh or one on his forearm. The former was a deep enough stab to make it very hard to wash clean. But in any case, he had no fleas on him to leave behind. You are both quite safe, though I would advise burning the rug in the surgery. There looks to be old blood on it." He took a deep breath and released it slowly.

"You look like hell, Mathews," said Finch. "Time to stop galloping all over the colony and leave that to the younger men."

"Perhaps you are right, Inspector," Mathews said. He looked at Finch. "But that is not for me to determine. You know how superiors are. I merely go where I am told to go, when I am told. I'm glad that they didn't need me at Fort Hall and sent me home earlier than usual."

Finch snorted. "Indeed. Well, I shan't call on you again today. Go home." The inspector held out his right hand, but Mathews merely made a lazy salute instead of taking it. "Are you certain you won't reconsider, Miss del Cameron? I could see you home, or call for a rickshaw for you."

"I'll be fine, Doctor." She smiled to reassure him.

Mathews bowed briefly to Jade, took two steps, paused, and turned back. "I nearly forgot. I suppose that's an indication of just how tired I am. But I recall Miss del Cameron telling me that this Dr. Dymant thought he knew me. Before I left for my recent tour of the native villages, I perused my albums from my medical school days. I found a Dymant listed a year behind me, but this wasn't him."

Jade stifled the urge to question him, knowing it would only rile Finch, and she didn't want to risk being sent home.

"You're quite certain?" asked Finch.

"Absolutely," said Mathews. "Mind you, this man had bled a great deal under the skin, so he was quite blackened in spots and very nasty to look at. But the Dymant in *my* album was taller and more slender. He might have put on weight, but unless this man found a way to shorten his height, it's simply not the same Dymant. Perhaps a cousin? I only tell you this because I thought I might be able to help with your search for living relations. But I'm afraid I cannot."

Finch and Jade stepped inside the office, and Jade immediately winced at the stench of death unalloyed by any cleaning. The front room of the two-room suite was a waiting area with three plain wooden chairs lined up along one wall. In front of the chairs lay a threadbare carpet, once brightly colored before countless dirty sandals and feet had ground it down to muted tones. The rest of the room was bare of decoration except the thin cotton cloth that served as a curtain over the lone window. Its saffron color lent a jaundiced glow to the room as the final rays of late-afternoon sun filtered through.

"Dymant was found in his examining room," said Finch as he pushed aside a matching curtain separating the two rooms and turned on the single light. The putrid stench increased as the partition between the surgery and the waiting area was moved.

Jade soldiered on through, disturbed not so much by the odor as by the memories that it conjured: soldiers in muddy trenches side by side with horror. While she'd carried only the living wounded in her ambulance, she'd driven close enough to the front lines to become familiar with the sight and smell of rot that clung leechlike to the living. A stained throw rug told her that Dymant had not only fallen and died there, but lain there long enough to leave his mark. She ignored it and moved on to examining the surgery.

A bookcase matching the one in his parlor stood in a back corner, filled with medical books. Two chairs and a low, strong table occupied the room's center, and a sturdy rolltop desk and chair dominated the other back corner. Dymant's open medical bag sat atop the barrister bookcase. The side wall held a rudely constructed set of shelves, filled with chemicals, powders, bandages, gauze, and other medical accoutrements one expected to see. Jade studied each of the glass vials, looking for anything that resembled her poisoned tea.

"Right," said Finch. "We'll have at that desk, I suppose."

The desk was unlocked, the key still resting in the lock. Finch heaved up the top, revealing a jumble of papers and a leather-bound volume. "Doctor's log," he announced, reading the ledger. "'Catarrh, catarrh, lesions, bad teeth.'" He flipped past the remaining blank pages and slammed the book shut. "Nothing of interest in there." He riffled the loose papers, scanning them as he went. "Bills pending or receipts, mostly the former. Can't say he was making a living as a doctor."

Jade watched as Finch pulled open a drawer. She had no idea what to expect. Obviously no one would write, *Kidnap Thompsons' child* or *Poison Jade's tea* in an appointment diary. "Are all these handwritings the same?"

Finch looked up. "I have yet to find any letters addressed to him, if that is what you mean." He continued looking at her, waiting for her to explain.

"Not entirely. Someone sent letters to me forged in the hand of a dead friend and also left notes forged in Lady Dunbury's hand. If this man was behind it, then perhaps we'll find evidence. Maybe an old letter he'd stolen to copy and practice."

Finch frowned. "Just because Dr. Mathews cannot place this man doesn't mean he's behind those . . . pranks played on you."

Jade's sharp and sudden intake of breath sounded like a hissing snake. Finch paused suddenly as he pulled open a drawer. "My apologies. Poor choice of words," he said. "Ah, here's something." He pulled out a stationery box and set it on the desk. "Might have some addresses written down in here. Siblings perhaps." He removed the lid and tossed it aside. "Looks like he'd begun a letter and never gotten around to posting it. 'My dearest . . . ' " he began, and abruptly stopped.

"What?" demanded Jade. She didn't wait for him to continue, hurrying to his side to see for herself. " 'My dearest Jade!' " she read aloud. " 'You won't have long to wait before I come to take you to join me forever.' " Jade took a half step back and faltered. "And look at the hand, Inspector. It's not the same as on these billings. This is David's hand." She reached for the letter, but Finch stopped her, grabbing her by the wrist.

"Don't," he said. "It will be taken in as evidence. And I owe you an apology."

"What else is in this desk? Check the bottom drawer." She no longer bothered to make herself unobtrusive. She wanted confirmation of what she already surmised.

"It's stuck," said Finch. He yanked at the drawer and it broke free of whatever had jimmied it in place. A small strongbox filled the drawer. Finch felt under the desk blotter and found a key. He let out one low whistle when he opened the box.

"Mining papers," said Jade as Finch took them out one by one. "Maps, a claim, blank forms."

"One of these maps is from the Belgian Congo," said Finch. "And these forms are from the land office but they aren't filled in."

"Waiting for another victim?" asked Jade.

"You're probably right. How he acquired them is what I'd like to know. Here's a claim file with three names." Finch held it up to see them better. "One is Stockton's."

"That's the man I found dead at the base of the Limuru Bridge."

"Yes, and the other name is Waters. He's our first crocodile victim," said Finch. "There's a third name as well."

"Pellyn," said Jade without looking. "Mathers Pellyn."

Finch looked up sharply from the paper. "Yes, Mrs. Worthy's supposed lover, right?"

Jade nodded and sifted through the rest of the maps. She stopped suddenly, a worn photo in her right hand. "Inspector. I think we have our proof that Dymant knew Lilith Worthy." She handed him the picture. It showed several Africans, naked but for loincloths, burdened under heavy loads. But it was the woman standing like a queen to one side that riveted Jade's attention. Lilith. The woman held a chunk of ore in her left hand and, in the right, a *panga* knife.

"Nasty piece of work," said Finch as he placed the picture on the desk. He picked up another stack of papers and read the top. "This appears to be some love letter. Most likely to this Pellyn, since the hand looks feminine. At least it begins with 'My darling.' After that it becomes rather businesslike." Finch read aloud, "'I'm entrusting this task to you and I know you won't fail me. You've never balked at an indelicate task before. Bring all your resources to bear. You know, of course, what I want the most.'" His voice trailed off as he turned the page over. As soon as he did, he gasped.

"What is it?" asked Jade.

Finch hesitated a moment before handing it over to her. "It's a list entitled 'Target and possible resources to use.' Your name is at the top, underlined."

CHAPTER 19

*And yet another: "If you live by the river, make friends with the crocodile." I
do not recommend this, but if you must, do not accept luncheon invitations.*
— The Traveler

THE PAPER READ like an innocent list of invitees to a social:
Jade del Cameron, Lady Avery Dunbury, Madeline Thompson. But the additional *and brat* under both Bev's and Maddy's names said otherwise. Following their names were Pili's
and Sam Featherstone's. Both of these had question marks
beside them.

"They don't know where Pili and Sam are," murmured
Jade.

"This next paper is rather curious," said Finch. "It's a
map. Nothing is labeled but it's fairly obvious that it's the
colony." He showed it to Jade as well.

"Yes, that's the railroad. There's Nairobi, Naivasha,
Mount Longonot to the west of the tracks. That looks like Ol
Donyo Sabuk and Mount Kenya."

"What do you make of the 'x's?" asked Finch.

"One is the Limuru Bridge; the other is on the Athi. That's
where I found the bodies. The 'x' near Mount Longonot could
be an old farmhouse. I remember there being one there."

"That was my guess," said Finch. "The one farther north might be the alleged mining claim." Finch folded the map and tucked it in his jacket pocket along with the letter. "More evidence against Dymant or Pellyn, if that was his name. But perhaps it would help me if you'd explain just why this Pellyn and his female companion are so bent on harming you."

Jade explained in detail what she knew of Olivia Lilith Worthy's past and ended with her not so recent escape from prison. As she spoke, her tone softened towards Finch. She'd suspected him for no good reason other than his age, gender, and the fact that he annoyed her. And while he didn't know that, she still felt that she owed him some courtesy by way of a respect, a sort of unspoken apology.

"And you think this Lilith Worthy has come to the colony? Why?"

"Several reasons, Inspector. For one, her lover was here." She gestured at the room. "For another, she can't very well stay in England. Her business ventures were here as well." She picked up one of the mining claims to illustrate the point. "She's been involved with smuggling guns, drugs, and Roman gold in the past. Now it seems she's involved with gold in the Congo and some scheme to steal from investors, not to mention murder. And finally, *I'm* here."

"And she hates you," Finch said. "That much I've gathered from what you've told me of your Moroccan encounter. But why this elaborate ruse with drugged tea and packages from the dead?"

"I've given that considerable thought," said Jade. "I think Pellyn was supposed to get me out of the way before she arrived. I've interfered with her before, so she'd want to make sure I couldn't do so again."

"And if you weren't frightened away, then you might be *put* away, is that it?" asked Finch.

"Possibly. Harry reacted very strongly to those drugs, from what I was told." She shuddered at the memory of that night when she saw David's ghost beckoning to her, his face melting into a skeletal nightmare. "I should probably thank Harry for providing an end to those hallucinations. Once he took sick, it was obvious to me that I'd been drugged, and that I wasn't losing my mind. Pellyn had to try something else to drive me off: threats to my friends. If I were to leave the protection of my friends, I could be dealt with and who would be the wiser?"

"Which is why young Cyril was only hidden away and not actually taken. It was a message, a warning," said Finch.

"That's what I think. If I leave Kenya Colony, then they won't be harmed, but if I stay or try to interfere . . ." She let the consequences remain unspoken. "Or perhaps it was all Pellyn and not Lilith's doing. He may have been afraid of my testimony in Stockton's and Waters' deaths."

Finch opened the medical bag and pulled out a stethoscope. "So was this Dymant-Pellyn a genuine doctor?"

"Probably," said Jade. "At least, he had enough medical training to pass for one."

"As long as he didn't treat the British colonists? I take your meaning," agreed Finch. "He could manage well enough with the *poorer* class of Indians and no one would question him or where he actually came from."

"And no one would really comment on whether he came or went," added Jade.

Finch went back to the papers and picked one up. "It appears that your Pellyn was in business with this Waters fellow to bilk green colonists out of their money, investing in a mine. Take their money and then the investor conveniently dies in some accident."

"Stockton at the Limuru Bridge. Then why kill his partner?" As soon as she voiced the question, she knew the answer. "Holly!"

"Steven Holly?"

"Correct. Mr. Holly told all and sundry at that garden party that he'd just invested in a gold mine. He bragged about it to anyone with ears," said Jade. "He said Waters brought him into it."

"Dymant was there?"

Jade nodded. "Yes. He left just after you did, I recall." She stared into space, trying to envision the scene. "You didn't find a similar paper in that pile with Holly's name on it, did you?"

Finch flipped through the pile again. "No. So perhaps this Waters decided to go one on his own. Find some other dupe without sharing with Pellyn."

"Pellyn found out and killed him for it. Threw his body to the crocodile to dispose of."

"The body would never be found, and even if it was, it would be just another tragic accident," concluded Finch. "How many other accidental deaths have gone undiscovered, I wonder?" He slapped the papers with his hand. "Only *you* managed to be there for the first murder and heard a second automobile. We probably wouldn't have looked beyond a drunken mishap if it hadn't been for you." He said it with a hint of admiration. Then, as if to cover up any possible display of feelings, he quickly added, "Making more work for us once again."

"Not much more on this one," said Jade. "Pellyn's own disguise ended up killing him."

Finch snorted. "Right. We still don't have anyone apprehended in that knife fight. And unless some witness comes forward to the police, we're not bloody likely to either. Wish I knew what that row was about."

"Another squabble with business partners?" suggested Jade.

"If it was, then what was the business? Someone not get paid their share in killing Stockton or Waters? Blackmail for seeing more than they should have seen?" Finch shook his head. "Gardner!" he shouted.

The constable who'd been standing in the waiting area ran to the doorway. "Sir," he said, executing a sharp salute.

"Gather up all these papers and ledgers. Bring them back to headquarters. You may have the car. I'm going to walk." Finch looked at his watch. "It's late. I'm hungry." He gestured to the door. "You had best get home, too, miss. It's already past lights-on time."

Jade stepped outside and was surprised to see that the sun had already set. One street over, the electric lights maintained Nairobi's sense of power over the wild African night that loomed not far away, like some great beast waiting for its prey to venture beyond its safe confines. She knew that the illusion was deceptive. Some of the greatest predators prowled within the city, striding unknown within the herd of humanity, camouflaged by respectable clothing and money. If there were street lamps in this part of the city, they were broken. Here, blackness swallowed all, held back by only a few dimly lit interiors.

"I know you're an independent woman, Miss del Cameron, so I won't insult you by hovering over you while you get your motorcycle. But you may choose to wait for Constable Gardner to escort you if you like." He saluted her and took off in a fast stride around the corner, heading towards Government Road.

Jade idled a moment just inside the office door, trying to sort through her feelings. Only a few hours ago, she was hell-bent on finding Pellyn before he could strike again. Now he was dead. She was relieved beyond measure. One less adversary to worry over. But his demise also made it more difficult to find Lilith.

We might have been able to follow him and find her. And now? Jade had no idea where to begin. She didn't even know if the woman was in Africa or not. Well, there was time enough to worry later. Right now she needed to get back and let Bev and Avery know the news. *They're probably getting worried.*

Jade headed for her motorcycle, peering into the darkened street and berating herself for not anticipating the evening and choosing a better spot to park. She stepped into the alley, her entire focus on her friends and how she could help protect them. Dymant as Pellyn. Dymant dead. What did it mean? Were they safe now?

No, Lilith is still alive.

But how could she defend her friends against an unseen assailant? Hire more servants to watch their homes and children?

All her plans shattered the instant she felt a masculine arm wrap around her waist and a firm hand clamp over her mouth.

CHAPTER 20

"A log in the water will not become a crocodile" speaks of pretenders to power and the futility of that game. But the trick is to recognize the genuine log, for crocs strive to look harmless.
—The Traveler

THE GRASP WAS FIRM but gentle.

Jade's reaction was not.

She immediately slammed her right elbow back and felt it connect just below a rib cage. A gasp and an *oof* told her that she'd bought a bit of time, and without waiting for a response, she shoved her head back, hoping to hit jaw. She did, but the blow was partially cushioned by a beard.

"Ouch!"

Pellyn's death hadn't fully sunk in yet and a part of her hadn't let go of her suspicions regarding Finch. When the arm around her waist loosened by a fraction, she stomped her right foot down hard, hoping to connect with her attacker's.

She hit wood.

The sensation was unexpected, and for a moment, Jade couldn't reconcile the pain in her own heel. Her assailant released her.

"Dammit, Jade! Cut it out. It's me."

Her mind was not prepared for that voice. She spun around in the darkened alley, one hand gripping her knife, her eyes straining to see. In front of her stood a tall, slender form, but the beard enlarging the lower jaw was all wrong.

"It's me!" the form repeated.

"Sam!"

Jade launched herself at him, wrapping both arms around his neck and flinging her legs around his thighs. She felt him stagger momentarily under the impact, but he quickly grabbed hold of her, one arm tightly around her back, the other supporting her rear.

Her lips found his and pressed against them, forcing their way past the bristling beard and mustache. She let go of every thought save one, and relished the moment. His surprised *ooh* quickly turned into a husky groan of increasing need. Jade's senses were alive with the feel of his warm muscles against her, his musky scent filling her nostrils and his taste in her mouth. She was Persephone rising up from nearly half a year in hell, a starving person awakening to a feast, and she couldn't get her fill. She wrapped her legs tighter around him, pressing closer.

"I'm glad to see you, too," Sam said when Jade finally took a breath. "But your knife keeps hitting me in the back of the head. Do you mind putting it away?"

With those practical and unromantic words, all at once the despair and loneliness of those past months filled her mind. Every second of her time in hell, every endless day without him, and each nightmarish night burst out from her soul: a dam releasing a flood of pain. Jade pulled back and dropped her feet to the ground. She sheathed her knife, letting her anger purge away the passion and fill the void left behind.

"Sorry to have startled you the way I—" Sam began, reaching for her.

"You sorry son of a . . ." she growled. Her hands clenched into fists as she threw a one-two punch at his stomach. The first hit hard muscle; the second was caught and held in an iron grip. "Let go of me, you low-down coyote," she snapped. "Is this your new trademark? Rush in at the eleventh hour like you did in Morocco? How dare you leave me for five months without any word and then have the nerve to—"

Sam pulled her in and stifled her outburst with another kiss. She fought against him at first, assaulting him physically and verbally for every nightmare she'd had, every moment when she thought she'd never see him again. He met each jab, every kick with an unrelenting gentleness emanating from his voice and his embrace. Then the solid warmth of his body took over and she fell against him with a sob.

"Sam," she whispered into his chest. "Are you really back? Or am I having another hallucination?" After having seen Boguli and David, she wasn't ready to trust her eyes. Something hard pressed against her temple and her fingers groped for it.

The Berber talisman. That was something tangible. *He is real!*

"I'm here," he whispered into her ear, kissing her hair. "But no one else can know it. Your life depends on it." He pulled her deeper into the alley with a "Shush," as the constable locked up the medical office and walked, whistling, to the police car. They listened to him drive away.

Everything was happening too fast for Jade: Dymant's death, Dymant as Pellyn, Sam's unexpected return. Even his whispered warning seemed unreal. The talisman did not. She felt the silver box, cool against her fingertips.

"You're still wearing the charm I gave you," she said.

"Yes, and I swear the blasted thing really is haunted. I haven't had a moment's peace since I put it on. All I could think of was you. I'm sure I heard you one night, but all around you was the sound of wind and the moaning of the dead."

"I went to France to see the battlefields. I remember hearing those sounds. I even saw . . ." Jade wanted to tell him more, but just then something scuttled along the alleyway. *Rat.* Thoughts of plague popped into her mind. "We can't stay here; it's not healthy or safe. Where are you staying?"

"Nowhere at present. I thought about getting a room at the YMCA when I saw you. I hid and eavesdropped, then followed you as best I could."

Jade took his arm and pulled him out of the alley onto the dusty walkway. With no lights it was still dark, but the distant glow from Government Road's street lamp let Jade see Sam and convince herself it really was him beside her. "You're on foot?" she asked.

Sam nodded.

"Get a rickshaw and meet me at the Dunburys'. You can stay there or at Maddy and Neville's."

"No," Sam said. "I was not exaggerating when I said no one can know I'm here. I definitely can't stay at the Thompsons'. The Kikuyu talk. I don't want word to go around that Bwana Tree Leg is back. When I'm seen, I have to be a different person."

"How will you disguise your voice? Or your leg? Another wounded American is going to get noticed!"

"I'll be an Australian." Sam pronounced it with the broad

"ale" in the middle and followed it all with a reasonably convincing, "G-day, mate." When Jade's brows rose up in wonder, he added, "I met one on the boat back here. Interesting man. Saw a lot of action in Turkey. He was hoping to start fresh here in Africa, so I bought his old uniform from him to help. I'll just become him. Easy enough accent to mimic. And he's already gone north to Lake Victoria."

"As long as you don't talk to too many people asking too many questions."

"That's the beauty of this disguise. When you smell like the back end of a barn for a while, no one wants to get too close." He shushed her with a finger to her lips. "Listen. I know about our friend's escape. When I left, I sent word to Avery's contact and told him to also keep me informed of any change. Call it a hunch or a premonition, but I couldn't imagine that witch submitting to prison for long. I told him to send any word care of my family in Indiana. I knew within a week of her escape and took the first ship to Africa after I . . ." He bit off his words as though he'd nearly revealed a deep secret. "Never mind that. I'm here now." He stroked her hair and let his fingertips sweep around to caress her cheek. "I got your telegram, too."

Jade studied his face and shook her head. "I don't think anyone would recognize you straight off, especially in the dark. And you sure can't sleep in the streets. You'll be thrown in jail and then your secret's out. I know I can sneak you into the Dunburys' tonight and . . . Oh, damn, Biscuit will know you."

Sam rubbed his neck and winced. "Fine job I'm doing, riding to your rescue. I *am* a horse's patoot. My plan depends on secrecy and your cheetah might wreck it immediately."

"You let me worry about Biscuit. Just get to the Dunburys' tonight. Avery can hire you as a down-on-his-luck man to muck out stalls and sleep in the loft. That should help out the aromatic part of your disguise. One horse's patoot with the others." She grinned.

He pulled Jade in tighter and looked around at the silent neighborhood, all the shops long closed and everyone inside. From a few blocks over, the nightlife of European Nairobi echoed in honking horns, puttering motors, and snatches of indistinguishable conversation. Sam took Jade's hands in his.

"You still have the ring," he said. "On your right hand."

"Is there a reason I should move it?" she asked. Jade wondered if he'd have come back to her otherwise. Did she have Lilith to thank for this? She waited expectantly, straining to read his features in the dim alley light.

He kissed her fingertips and the lion's-tooth tattoo on her left wrist. Jade shivered as his whiskers brushed her skin. "We'll talk about that when this is over. For now, you need to go before someone sees us. Since I'm a drifter, I'll start walking to Parklands, but I won't show up until late."

"Then shall I tell Avery and Beverly to expect you?"

Sam hesitated a moment. "Yes, but only when you know that no one is going to overhear. Beverly especially. She's likely to exclaim something."

"Her sister is staying with them," Jade said, suddenly remembering Emily. "She's looking for a husband, too."

"Damn," muttered Sam. "I hate to be rude but—"

"If she sees you, you'll have to be a bit brusque and maybe a bit stinkier than you'd planned," finished Jade. "But not for long. She's going down to Mombassa for a day or two."

Jade reached up and kissed him on the lips. "And don't think that smelly horse manure or this horrible beard will deter me either."

Sam's dark eyes bore deeply into hers and she felt a warm flush rush down her arms, and her stomach did a curious flip-flop. "You will have to deter yourself. We're going to have to be aloof with each other anyway so as to avoid speculation. Remember, I'm your ace in the hole. Lilith can't know I'm here."

"I'm ashamed that I didn't ask this earlier, but did you sell your movie about the coffee farmers?"

Sam brushed back the curls from her forehead, exposing her tiny indigo lion's-paw tattoo given to her by the Berbers. He touched it gently and smiled. "I did, but I think the studio bought it mainly to cut and use as background footage for their own adventure movies. But this is no place to talk." He smacked her on the rump. "Now skedaddle like a good little varmint."

She hadn't taken but one step to her motorcycle when Sam grabbed her wrist. "I forgot to ask. How's my plane?"

Jade smiled. "Jenny's fine. Avery flew her this morning." Jade left ruefully before he could cause her to lose the last of her self-control. But as she motored off to Parklands, she couldn't help but feel wryly grateful that Sam had asked after her first, then his plane.

AVERY, BEV, AND EMILY were all waiting on the veranda for Jade's return, after which they immediately sat down to dinner. As gently as she could, Jade divulged first Dr. Dymant's death and then his true identity. All in all, she thought it went very well. Beverly choked on her food only twice and Avery muttered, "Damn," only once. Emily, who was not familiar with the tales of Lilith Worthy and Mathers Pellyn, concentrated more on the fact that an eligible bachelor was not only a criminal but also dead.

Jade noticed that Beverly kept watching her expectantly, as though she could tell there was something else that Jade hadn't revealed. For the first time in her life, Jade found herself hard-pressed to maintain a solid poker face. She made one sidewise nod to Emily, who was involved in receiving a fruit compote for dessert. Avery caught his wife's look and provided Jade with an opportunity.

"Jade, your motorcycle sounded rough when you drove it in this evening. If you like, we can take it to the barn and have a quick look at it."

"Thank you, Avery. That would be good."

Jade spilled the news of Sam's return to Avery in the privacy of the barn. He reacted by biting the stem of his unlit pipe in two. Soon after, Avery called Beverly to walk with him, and if her reaction to the news was more exuberant, the household simply put it down to the master and mistress being in a frisky mood. Jade kept Biscuit shut in her bungalow and watched out of the Dunburys' drawing room window.

Sam appeared walking down their drive by eleven o'clock, and even Jade didn't recognize him at first except for the familiar slight limp. He'd managed to turn himself into such a down-and-out reprobate that the limp was one of the last traits anyone noticed. His brown hair was longer than last September, hanging down to his eyebrows in front. His beard was a full-blown bush that obscured his lower face and distorted the jawline. As he came closer, Jade noticed that his hair was darker, too. In the shadows of the alley, she hadn't noticed. But then, she'd been too preoccupied for details.

He stained it with walnut or tea.

Most compelling for his new persona was his attire. Jade got a good look at it for the first time. He wore the ragged brown trousers and threadbare tunic of a former Australian Light Horse regiment man. One ragged duffel and a squared-off canvas pack across his back and a beat-up slouch hat atop his head completed his disguise. If ever a man painted a picture of hard luck and a veneer of disrepute, Sam had mastered it. His eyes shifted constantly under his thick brows like those of a man always on the watch for trouble.

Emily immediately declared that she never wanted to see that "creature" in the house with the baby.

"I'm sure he's harmless," said Avery. "Just another chap struggling since the war."

"The war ended over two years ago," said Emily, "and I'm through trusting men."

"The war hasn't ended for everyone, my dear," said Beverly softly. "Some will never be free of it unless we assist them. But let both of us go inside and allow Avery to deal with him. Have you finished packing for Mombassa? You'll enjoy yourself so much. You should stay for a week. Perhaps take a steamer to Zanzibar."

Jade didn't trust herself and walked away. A half an hour later, Avery told them all that he had hired a Mr. Oliver Fairley, formerly of the 2nd Light Horse Regiment, to do the stable work, and that he'd be sleeping in the loft and taking his meals in the barn.

CHAPTER 21

*As these reptiles grow in length, they reach a point where they
begin to add massive weight to themselves, becoming bulkier
and more muscular, veritable machines of death.*
—The Traveler

JADE ROSE AT FOUR THIRTY Tuesday morning and slipped out
to the barn, hoping to talk to Sam without the *mpishi*, Matthew, or any of the other hired help finding out. She even left
Biscuit tied behind her bungalow, an act that her pet found
less than desirable. He let her know it with a series of plain-
tive *rowr*s. Jade ignored him. Her face grew warm as she
thought about seeing Sam alone.

Perhaps talking can wait? Her hopes received a shock
when she discovered Avery and Sam sitting on a bench with
their heads together.

"Ah, Jade," said Avery. "Good of you to join us."

"Hello, Avery," Jade said. It was not the warmest greeting she'd ever given him.

After sleeping in the barn, Sam looked even more dis-
reputable than yesterday. His clothes smelled of horse and
straw, his hair was matted, and his face was pinched. But to

Jade he looked irresistible and she wished Avery would leave so she could let him know.

"We were just discussing what to do next," said Sam.

"Hard to decide when we don't even know if Lilith is in Kenya or not," said Avery. He pulled a pipe from his pocket, then, as if he realized he shouldn't smoke in the barn, frowned and stuck the stem in his mouth to chew on.

"Oh, she's here," said Jade. When they both looked to her for elaboration, she shrugged and plunked down on an overturned bucket. "She can't stay in England and she's not going to bide her time in Europe. She didn't do that when Mother was kidnapped. She won't now. But she will keep to her hideaway for as long as she can. She'll be close so that she can get information and give orders."

"With Pellyn dead, she might decide to cut her losses and leave," suggested Avery.

"Or hole up until she can find another minion to replace him," said Sam. "We can't let her do either. Now we have the advantage and we need to act on it."

"'The strength of the crocodile is in the water,'" murmured Jade.

"Say what?" asked Sam. "You haven't been drinking any more of that drugged tea that Avery told me about, have you?"

"No. I'm just remembering something the *mondo-mogo* told me. 'The strength of the crocodile is in the water.' Lilith's strength is in her disguise, her hideaway. From there she can see and watch and orchestrate. A croc hides in plain sight, looking harmless. We need to flush her out."

"And how do we do that?" asked Avery.

"Bait," said Jade. "I know she was part of a gold mining labor camp in the Congo. I've seen a photo. It was probably shut down when Belgian rule finally changed hands. And as a fallback plan, she and Pellyn took to showing bits of gold to potential investors here, just to rake in some capital before starting some other major operation. Lilith never does anything by small turns."

"And Pellyn was running it with Waters while Lilith was in prison?" asked Sam.

"Yes," said Jade. "I think Waters was killed when he started acting on his own. So let's imagine that Holly wasn't the first dupe; there were others. Let's lure Lilith with a notice in the dailies saying that the interested party now has the rest of the money for the mining investment. We'll pick a place to meet. Then we'll lie in wait for Lilith and catch her."

"You *have* been drinking that tea again," said Avery. "I can't see Lilith just waltzing into a meeting. It would destroy her cover."

"But if she does have another minion, as you termed him, waiting by her side, she might send him instead of herself. The more we can diminish her forces, the better off we are."

Avery pointed at Jade with his pipe. "You might have something there. Especially if we make it sound as though this person had incriminating information. We can address it to Waters' boss."

"Good. Make it seem as if he knows something that he could use to blackmail her with," added Sam. He ran his fingers over his beard and stroked it. "I don't suppose we have anything to lose. If we do catch someone else, we might be able to turn him on Lilith and find out where she's holed up."

"I would have guessed that old farm of Roger Forster's," said Avery, "except that everything burned not long after he died. We flew over it and saw nothing."

"There's an outbuilding, but the area is overgrown and the door is blocked by trees," said Jade.

"You've been there?" asked Sam. His brows furrowed.

"It was before most of this mess began," said Jade. "Harry says it's empty and it didn't look as if anyone had lived there for a long time."

"Harry," repeated Sam flatly. He looked into her eyes and she felt the power behind those coffee brown orbs. For a moment, it gave her a taste of what others experienced when she stared them down.

"Yes, Harry," she repeated. "His land is next door." Then, to get Sam's mind away from his perceived rival, she asked, "So where shall our patsy tell Waters' boss to meet him?"

"Why not on the Limuru Bridge?" said Avery. "That in itself might sound incriminating, considering Stockton was killed there. Catch a murderer with news of the murder."

In the end the notice read, *I want into the mine, as Waters promised. I have the money. Meet at eleven p.m. tonight where the first investor dropped out.*

Jade took it to both the *Leader* and the *Standard* to run in the Wednesday and Thursday dailies. She spent the rest of Tuesday keeping Biscuit and herself occupied by taking Avery's truck and driving the cheetah to the Thompsons' for a run. There she privately passed on the news concerning Dymant and Sam. Madeline's reaction to Dymant as Pellyn and his horrific death was a grim smile. Her reaction to Lilith was renewed fear, and to Sam's return, joy. Jade left Biscuit behind to help watch Cyril and, as she returned to Nairobi, she saw Emily leave in a taxi for the train station.

One less person to worry about.

Jade longed to see Sam, and the barn was a terrible draw for her. But she knew that he was right. As long as no one knew he was back, he was an ace in the hole. Literally, she thought with amusement. A flying ace. So in order to distance herself from him and avoid temptation, she took her motorcycle and rode along the Athi, looking for Blaney Percival and Harry. She found the game warden not far from Jelani's village, breaking camp.

"There's no sign of that crocodile," he said. "We can only hope that it's gone far downriver."

"And have you seen anyone else here? Someone possibly new to the Colony?" Jade asked.

"We have hundreds of new people in the Colony, but if you mean out here . . ." He waved his hands. "Only the usual traffic, which is to say, not much. But I must move on to other problems. The elephants near Mount Kenya are into the *shambas* and eating the sweet potatoes, so I need to sort that out."

That made Jade think about the big bull elephant she'd seen near Harry's land. Elephants were no strangers to Ol Donyo Sabuk, but this one had stuck in her memory, hauntingly familiar. A look at her fuel gauge told her she needed to return home soon, so she drove back to Parklands, keeping one eye open for anything out of the ordinary.

Wednesday was spent much the same way, keeping herself occupied. She stayed in the darkroom that Avery had built for her, developing photographs of Fourteen Falls. Next, she cleaned her rifle and tried to write an article on the falls for *The*

Traveler. She found herself making more notes on crocodiles instead and began a second article on the huge reptiles. That evening, Beverly centered the dinner conversation around the Girl Guides and the Ladies' Revolver Club, avoiding any mention of the new hired hand, Lilith, or Pellyn. Sam kept to the barn, and by ten o'clock Jade had paced herself to a fever pitch outside her bungalow. That was where Avery found her. He carried a Remington shotgun slung across his arm and wore a dark brown shooting jacket, the better for hiding. Jade had also opted for darker clothing, settling for a pair of deep blue dungarees and an indigo linen shirt.

"Shall we keep our appointment?" he said.

"Where's Sam?"

Avery nodded to the road. "He's already left for the bridge. He said it will look more authentic if he appears alone and on foot in case someone is watching. We'll drive over the bridge and, if no one is about, hide the truck in the brush and get in position. If we see someone already there, we'll warn Sam by laying on the horn."

"Is Sam armed?"

Avery nodded. "He has his Colt revolver. Don't worry. We'll have him well covered before anyone shows."

His calm demeanor didn't fool Jade for one moment. She saw how he patted the shotgun and knew he wanted a chance to capture anyone involved with Lilith. The fact that she was behind at least two recent murders and possibly Mutahi's as well paled next to her threats against Cyril Thompson.

"Remember, Avery," Jade said, "we want this person alive so we can find out where Lilith is hiding."

"Of course. But that's not to say that I won't have to fire a warning shot . . . in the leg."

They drove past the bridge, meeting only one other vehicle, a hired taxi coming back into town with no fare. Avery pulled the car off the road, following the belt of trees that lined the river. A hundred yards farther on, he stopped and they made their way back up towards the bridge, secreting themselves in the shadows. Jade chose a thornless tree on the far bank whose leaves resembled a locust's. It afforded sturdy enough branches to support her, but was open enough to allow her to see. She shinnied up into the lower branches and gained a clear view of the bridge from end to end. Avery crossed over to the side nearest town and slipped into the shadows by the bridge's abutment.

Twenty minutes later, they heard footsteps. Sam strode up the road in plain sight, his left hand in his pockets. He whistled a tune, and Jade recognized "Waltzing Matilda." He paused at the end of the bridge and surveyed the area, peering deep into the timber. Jade resisted the urge to whistle back. For all she knew, someone might be in hearing range.

She took a deep breath to steady her nerves. She was fairly certain that no one had gotten to the bridge before them, but that didn't mean that Sam wasn't in danger. What if someone decided it was better not to even negotiate for silence? Lilith or her lackey could simply drive up to the site and shoot Sam without a thought. Or no one might rise to the bait. And while Jade didn't relish Sam's being in danger, she dreaded the thought of repeating this charade tomorrow night.

Another sound intruded in the night and Sam broke off his tune. From the south came the purr of a motorcar. Jade looked for a headlight and saw none even though the vehicle was close enough that lamps should appear. She heard the car chug to the opposite end of the bridge and stop, idling. Immediately, the headlamps came on, flooding the scene in an attempt to blind Sam.

Sam shot out the headlamp on the left, the one opposite the spot where Avery was hiding.

"Get out of the car, mate," Sam shouted. He held his revolver ready. "The next thing I shoot won't be the ruddy headlamp."

Jade marveled at how he'd managed to capture an Australian's accent and wondered why she'd ever thought he could be in danger. He seemed to have the situation well in hand. She raised her rifle and sighted down the barrel at the car, waiting for a driver to exit.

She heard the hand brake set before the driver's door opened and a man stepped out. At least, Jade assumed it was a man. The form was certainly too tall to be Lilith. He looked to be unarmed at first, but when he reached back into the car, Sam ordered him to stop.

The man said something and Jade strained to catch the words. There was something naggingly familiar about the voice, but the idling automobile prevented her from hearing him clearly. Sam, who was closer to her, was more audible.

"Then bring it out slowly," growled Sam. "Put it on the bonnet."

As Jade watched, the man took out a leather attaché and set it on the car's hood. Then he opened it.

But his right hand moved too quickly for someone extracting a document. He whipped out a gun and aimed for Sam. He was too slow. No sooner had the little revolver cleared the case than Sam shot it out of the man's hand. The bullet ricocheted off the gun and into the window glass.

"Bloody hell," yelped the man. "I hired the loan of that car."

Now Jade recognized the voice and she shouted down to Sam and Avery, who'd come up to join Sam. "Just shoot him. It's Steven Holly."

"No!" yelped Holly. "Miss del Cameron?" he asked, peering into the trees. "Is that you?"

Jade scrambled down from the tree and joined Avery. She held her rifle across her chest.

"Yes, it is, Mr. Holly," Avery said. "Now, what in the name of the king's knickers are *you* doing here?"

"Is this a robbery?" Holly asked, looking from her to Sam and then over his shoulder to Avery. "Lord Dunbury? Is that you?" He swiveled his head around to face Sam. "Who is this?"

"A new friend," said Jade. "Consider him to be just another one of the many that your friend Waters cheated out of his hard-earned money in that preposterous investment." She patted her rifle stock. "But you haven't answered *my* question. Why are you here?"

"Are you with the police?" Holly asked.

"Mr. Holly, you are sorely trying my patience," growled Jade. As if to punctuate it, Avery stepped up and poked Holly on the thigh with his shotgun.

"Very well!" Holly exclaimed. "I came here hoping to recoup my own losses. I thought perhaps if I showed my copy of the mining partnership, I could pretend to represent the group and take the money."

Jade watched him closely. As a poker player, she'd learned how to tell when someone was bluffing. She'd since applied that skill to ferreting out liars. Holly's lack of eye contact when he spoke told her that he was lying and also afraid. He had good cause to be. He was surrounded by three people with loaded firearms, all of whom looked like they'd just as soon shoot as talk. But when Holly's gaze kept shifting down to his jacket's lower pocket, Jade knew he was afraid of something or someone else, too. Sam seemed to guess as much.

"Missy," he said, using his thick accent, "you promised me *I'd* get every ruddy pound of my money back. Now I'm looking to get stiffed again. Is this some sort of trick?"

"Not on our part, I assure you," said Avery. "If this man doesn't have your money, then I told you I'd pay you myself to make good your loss in return for helping capture the man who tried to abduct that child."

"Abduct a child?" wailed Holly. He turned to face Avery, then whirled back around to face Sam. "I never tried to abduct a child. Someone threatened to kill *me*! Remember?"

"This man's jumpier than a kangaroo and dumber than a doorless dunny," said Sam. "I knew I should've taken that job cutting timber in Tasmania."

"And you can go take the train south tomorrow and get on the first boat to Sidney," promised Avery. "After you help me find who I want even if we have to beat it out of this man."

Sam grinned, his eyes glowing wickedly in the lone headlamp. "Fair dinkum, mate. That might be a corker at that."

"No, please," whimpered Holly. "What I said was true."

"Then why are you so jumpy?" asked Jade. "What's in your pocket?"

Avery slapped Holly's leg again with his shotgun barrel. "Best to spill it all, Mr. Holly."

"Very well. It wasn't my idea to come here. After you left

me at the Blue Posts, I stayed there one night. Place was as inviting as stale ale. I decided to try my chances again at my own digs and rode back into town with some farmer. I paid the hotel clerk to tell everyone that I was away. Everything was fine until this morning. I woke up to find a box outside my door. A typewritten note was attached telling me that I had to come here and see who was larking about trying to get a go at the mine or I'd be the next to die." He shifted nervously from side to side. "Odd thing is, I think someone suspected you, Miss del Cameron."

"Why?" asked Jade.

"Because the note told me I was supposed to give you this." He pulled a small box wrapped in brown paper from his pocket and handed it over to Jade. *For del Cameron*, was printed on the paper.

Jade shouldered her rifle and tore open the box. Inside, nestled atop a scrap of ocher cloth, was a Girl Guide pin, a barrette, and a note addressed to Jade del Cameron.

"'So easily taken! So trusting a child. Come alone to the house near Longonot. Try any tricks and she could lose an ear.'" She gripped the note more tightly. "It's signed with a drawing of a moon eclipsing the sun. That's Lilith's emblem."

"There's something else in the box," said Avery. He pulled up the cloth, a folded square of blanket like those the Kikuyu wore. With painstaking care, he lifted one end of the dirty fabric, revealing a large dark brown ear.

CHAPTER 22

One could possibly pick up and tote an eight-foot crocodile,
whereas a fifteen-foot one might weigh more than a ton. The armor
is stronger, too, and with that extra mass come ages of experience
and cunning. Now the beast is nearly unstoppable.
—The Traveler

SAM'S FIST HIT HOLLY'S FACE with a resounding *thwack*.
Holly fell back, crashing into the car. Jade stepped in before
Sam could say anything in the heat of anger and destroy his
masquerade.

"That's enough, Mr. Fairley," she said, reminding Sam of
his alias. "Who gave this to you?" she demanded of Holly.

Holly struggled to right himself. He passed the back of
his hand across his nose, smearing blood across his hand and
his face. "I don't know! I didn't even know what was in the
box."

"Liar!" she shouted.

"Please, I don't want to die." He put his head in his hands
and began to sob hysterically.

"He's no good," said Avery. "I say we turn him over to
Finch."

Jade took Avery aside and whispered, "And perhaps get

ourselves arrested in the bargain for this charade? If Lilith really has taken one of the Girl Guides, she might kill her. Plus, how will we explain Sam?" She paced back and forth briefly. "We either need to keep Holly locked away or turn him loose and hope he leads us to Lilith."

"I hope you're planning how to get rid of this bloody dingo's body once I've shot him," said Sam loudly enough for Holly to hear. "The likes of this one's not worth keeping about."

Avery shook his head. "We won't be able to follow him, Jade. We couldn't even find him when we wanted him. But you're correct that we can't turn him over to Finch without everyone finding out about Sam."

"But if Holly goes off tonight we may never find him again," Jade argued.

"Then we'd better take him prisoner," said Avery. He went to Sam and whispered to him for a moment.

Sam nodded and sighted down his revolver barrel. "Happy to oblige, mate," he said. "Since you won't talk to us, you're about as much use as a pouch on a male roo."

It was all the incentive Holly needed. He rolled to the side as Sam fired into the right front tire. "Don't kill me," he screamed. "I'll say whatever you want; just don't kill me."

"That's a right clever choice, mate. Now, you've just had a nasty puncture and got yourself stranded. Lucky for you that I'm a Good Samaritan come to help you out. You're coming with me. I'll keep you nice and safe and in return for all your bloomin' gratitude, you're going to tell us everything you know."

Holly stood still, his hands in the air and his legs shaking. "I swear, I don't know anything." He looked pleadingly at

Jade. "You've got to help me, Jade. Lord Dunbury, don't let this man kill me."

Avery stepped up to Holly and clapped him on the back before grabbing hold of his shirt collar. "Mr. Fairley wouldn't kill you, Mr. Holly. Why, he's worked for me for an entire day and I'd swear to his even temper. Now you just come with us and we'll keep you all nice and safe locked in one of my sheds. No one will get to you there."

Sam pushed Holly into the rear of Avery's truck and sat beside him as Avery drove them back to Parklands. Jade emptied out the stone building that was used as a darkroom and shoved Holly inside with a lantern, a mat, and a bucket of water.

"I can't stay in here under these conditions," Holly wailed.

Sam cracked his knuckles and growled, "I can put you in there under different conditions, mate."

"Be a good lad," said Avery, "and I won't let him hurt you. But you know the Australians; they're a rather hot-tempered lot."

"I've told you everything," cried Holly with a whimper. "I swear. I didn't know what was in the box."

Jade used the cloth to hold up the ear and thrust it under Holly's nose. "Someone cut off a native's ear and now is threatening to take one of the girls. Maybe has already. If any of them are hurt and I find out that you had anything to do with it, a crazy Australian is going to be the least of your worries, because, so help me, *I'll* shoot you myself and toss you to the crocodile."

Holly gasped and looked to Avery for help. Avery simply shrugged and pulled a pipe from his pocket along with a pouch of tobacco. "Don't look at me, Mr. Holly. I have no control over Miss Jade. Barely have control over my own wife, and none at all over my hired hand here. I suggest you cooperate with us and enjoy our protection rather than our wrath." Sam took a step forward to emphasize the point.

"Surely you don't think I'd hurt a girl," Holly wailed. "I *did* hope to get my money back just now and I like to chase a pretty skirt or two, but I'm not a kidnapper." He looked at the barrette again and winced.

"You know who it belongs to, don't you," said Jade. "Is it Mary's? Did you help someone take your own niece, you low-down piece of hyena dung?"

"It is Mary's. I admit it. I told you on safari that I'd been given a parcel message telling me to give up my share of the mine. And there was an ear in it, too. A white ear." He jiggled on his seat. "Oh, I was also told to take something of Mary's to use as a joke on someone. I didn't know what this person had planned. I just knew I'd be hurt or worse if I didn't comply. I took the barrettes and the badge when we were on safari and left them in a post-office box." He stumbled backwards against the far wall and started sobbing.

"What box number?" demanded Jade.

"One forty-six."

"Do we believe him?" asked Avery as he lit his pipe and took a puff.

"He's telling the truth," said Sam, dropping his accent. "At least in part. He's too spineless to lie when he's that terrified. But I think he's still holding back."

Suddenly Holly looked up and ran forward. "You're not an Australian. I know who you are now. You're that American pilot, Featherstone, aren't you?"

Sam launched a solid right jab to Holly's jaw, knocking him back into the wall. Holly hit with a thud and fell to the floor. "Pleased to meet you, Mr. Holly," he said, rubbing his knuckles. He looked at Avery. "Keep that trash locked up and don't let him out for anything."

Avery put some food in the darkroom, locked the door, and pocketed the key. Then, after alerting Beverly, they all went to the stables for a private council.

"Should we turn him over to Finch?" asked Avery. "If we turn him loose, he may lead us to Lilith."

"No," said Sam. "We can't let it out that I'm back yet. He has to stay locked up here. Besides, Holly's a dead end. Lilith has used him, and if she's got half the brains that we give her credit for, she won't show up anywhere near his hotel again." He took Jade's hand and squeezed it. "Do you think she really took this girl Mary?"

"That's the implication with that pin and barrette. We should know quickly enough. Beverly is ringing up Mary's mother now," said Jade. "But whose ear was that? Mutahi was missing an ear. Could it have been his?"

Before anyone could answer, Beverly joined them. "I spoke with Mrs. Postlewaithe. She said that Mary is staying the night with Helen at the school. Helen boards there. I rang up the school but the headmistress was not willing to rouse any of the girls in their rooms just to see if one was missing. She didn't seem to believe me when I said this was serious." She sniffed. "As if I'd telephone anyone in the middle of the night for something frivolous. We'll have to get the police to find out for us."

"Did the headmistress at least verify that Mary was sleeping over?" asked Jade.

"She didn't seem to know one way or another," said Beverly. "It appears that she was away today. The school was left in the care of another teacher who has gone for the night."

"That ass Holly is really Mary's uncle?" asked Sam. The others nodded.

"Her mother is widowed," said Beverly. "Mary's father passed on last October. That's why she looks to her uncle so much. Quite tragic."

Sam took the box and stared at the contents, his lips in a taut line.

"Sam?" asked Beverly. "What is it?"

"It's too easy," he said.

"What is?" asked Avery.

"Finding out if Mary was abducted. We telephone her mother, telephone her school."

"But we still don't know for certain," said Jade.

"A ruse," murmured Avery.

"It could be," said Sam. "To get Jade to go off to that farmhouse and rescue Mary."

"That's my reputation, isn't it," said Jade, keeping her head bowed. "To go harrowing off like that." She felt Sam's eyes boring into her soul and blushed for the times she'd argued with him about her escapades.

"Making it very easy to capture you," said Sam. "You thought the drugged tea and packages were part of a plan to get you to leave the safety of your friends. Holly was probably ordered to lead you to Harry's for that very reason."

"We must ring up Finch," said Avery. "He could go out to that farmhouse now and possibly capture Lilith. If he uses Jade's motorcycle, Lilith might think it's Jade. Then Finch would have an element of surprise. He can also convince the headmistress to look in on the girls, too. We won't rest easy until we know that Mary is safe."

"There's another possibility," said Jade. "Lilith's plan to get me away could be another, more serious attempt to actually abduct one of you for revenge."

"The children," whispered Beverly, her hand to her mouth. "We sent Cyril back home with Madeline."

"The Thompsons won't let him out of their sight that easily," said Avery. "But I would feel much better if we removed the baby and you, my love, to safety along with Madeline and Cyril."

"Avery," pleaded Beverly, "how can you ask me to leave you and Jade to that fiend? You must all come with me then."

"Bev," said Jade, "my running off with you won't help. She'll only pursue me."

Beverly took a deep breath. "You and Avery are right, of course. But where can we go that's safe? We decided before that Lilith might see us board a train or follow our Hupmobile."

"I think I know a place," said Jade.

"Where?" asked Sam.

"St. Austin's, the French Catholic mission in Ngong. I know the fathers there very well. They could put you all in the convent. We just tell Finch and everyone else that you're going north instead."

"It *is* a good spot," agreed Avery. "But how do we get them there without anyone knowing? As my wife said, our movements may be watched."

"We take a convoluted route," said Sam. "I have an idea there, but this only postpones the final situation. Lilith may not have Mary or any of us now, but she is not going to stop until she has what she really wants, and that's Jade, dead or alive!"

"So what do you propose, Sam?" asked Avery.

Sam stroked his beard, his gaze never leaving Jade's face. "I have a thought on that as well. It came to me when I first learned of Lilith's escape. Do you trust me?"

"Sam!" exclaimed Jade. "I always have. You know that has never been the issue." She ducked her head. "It's always been me that's the problem."

"No," Sam said. "No. I realize that now. And you'll have to trust me on that as well."

THAT FINCH WAS NOT HAPPY about being rousted out of bed at two in the morning was an understatement. That he was surprised by the reason was another. And while he hated to disturb the citizens, he agreed that it was imperative to ascertain whether Mary had been abducted. He also felt they should see to the other girls in case this threat was yet another deception.

Many hours and several distraught parents and a grumpy head schoolmistress later, they learned that all the girls were where they should be and, as Mary's mother had said, that meant she was spending the night with Helen at the school. The headmistress herself tiptoed into the dormitory and found an extra head beside Helen's on her pillow.

A search of Steven Holly's rooms in the Victoria ensued. They found no trace of any other communications that could connect him with a kidnapping plot. Jade and Avery insisted on going along with Finch while Sam stayed hidden behind to guard Beverly and Alice.

"If it weren't for that ear," said Finch, "I'd say that Holly made up the entire threat. I've known him for several years. He hasn't got it in him to cut off a man's ear. A shame he ran off." He studied Jade's face. "I'd have expected you to have shot him before you'd let that happen."

Jade maintained her best poker face and said nothing about Holly's presence in the darkroom. "Is there any way to tell if that was Mutahi's ear?"

Finch shook his head. "Mutahi's in the ground."

Jade pointed to the drawing of a moon eclipsing the sun on the note. "That's Lilith's trademark. I saw it often enough in Morocco to recognize it. How would Holly know that?"

Finch frowned. "Perhaps he read it in one of Mrs. Thompson's fictional accounts of your adventures. Wasn't her latest book, *The Kahina's Hand*, set in Morocco?" He pocketed the note without waiting for a reply. "So what do you plan to do?" Finch asked Jade and Avery.

"Now that I know Mary is unharmed," said Jade, "I'm going to fly Lady Dunbury and the baby to safety in the north, and then come back and take Mrs. Thompson and her son out next. They should be safe at the hotel at Naivasha with all of the people around."

"And you, Lord Dunbury?"

"I intend to drive with you to that house at Longonot and capture this woman. I can't have her threatening anyone else."

"Out of the question, Lord Dunbury," said Finch. "If she is there, she won't be alone. I cannot put a civilian in harm's way."

Jade scoffed, remembering when she'd been nearly killed while investigating for Finch.

Avery persisted. "I know more about this woman than

you do, Inspector. And I'm not going to sit passively and wait for someone else to do the job of keeping my family safe. I'll go with or without your permission."

"Very well," agreed Finch. "But Miss del Cameron, you must remain at Naivasha with the other women and children."

"The hell I will," said Jade. "If I'm Lilith Worthy's target, then my proximity to them will only put them in danger again."

"Then stay at the Thompsons' coffee farm. By tomorrow this time, we should have this woman recaptured and all will be safe."

AVERY HAD RISEN EARLY and sent word to a neighbor saying he had to leave for several days and to please see to his horses. Then he took Jade, Beverly, and Alice in his truck to Sam's hangar before joining Finch in town. Sam had already left on Jade's motorcycle, going first into town, then to the hangar, where he was waiting for them. He cautioned Avery to make certain that people saw him leave with Finch.

"There must be no doubt as to who is flying the plane," Sam had said.

It was now time for Jade to go into action. Neville drove out to the hangar shortly after seven, bringing Maddy, Cyril, and Biscuit. Cyril wore a little cap tied under his chin, and both Maddy and Bev carried blankets to swaddle their children.

Sam had just finished the preflight inspection but he continued to test the wires and check the wings. His own Indian motorcycle stood by the hangar with several bundles tied onto the back. It had been repainted from the scratched army drab to a flat black just before Sam had left. It was a fortuitous decision, as motorcycles were common, but Mr. Fairley could hardly have been seen on Mr. Featherstone's machine. Neville delayed long enough to kiss his wife and son good-bye, then loaded a reluctant Biscuit into the old box-bodied car along with Jade's Winchester, Beverly's and Madeline's valises, and satchels of baby clothing, bottles, and diapers. He drove northwest towards their proposed landing strip. Madeline had held on to Cyril's hand when he'd tried to run after his father.

Jade pointed to the bundles on Sam's cycle. "What's in there?"

"Supplies," he said. "Madeline, do you and Cyril want to go first?"

Jade knew that her question was being evaded, but she stifled a retort, mentally scolding herself for questioning Sam. Instead, she retrieved the leather aviator's caps and goggles from the rear cockpit and handed one set to Madeline.

Madeline pushed them away. "Let Beverly go first with the baby. I hate to see them wait out here in the sun very long."

Jade helped Bev don the goggles as Sam gave the plane one final check.

"I'll leave on my motorcycle as soon as you take off on your second run," Sam said. "Remember, we *want* people to see you, just like we want people to see Avery. Fly west first and get close to Nairobi. Then act like you have to follow the railroad to find your way north. There's a good spot to land near Kinangop just east of Naivasha. Neville will meet you there." He took hold of her by the shoulders. "Can you do this?"

Jade nodded. "Yes." She slipped a leather helmet over her black curls and tightened the strap below her chin.

"Then let's move the children."

Sam helped Beverly up onto the wing walk and into the front cockpit. When she was settled and had pulled down the goggles, he handed up Alice Merrywether, bundled in a blanket against the wind and the engine's oil spray.

Jade stepped up onto the recessed stirrup and climbed into the rear cockpit. She pulled down her own goggles from atop her head, retarded the magneto switch, and primed the engine. Next she turned on the switch and cracked the throttle.

"Contact!" she shouted.

Sam swung the propeller, moving quickly aside as the engine caught and purred. As she opened up the throttle, the plane raced down the makeshift runway, gaining speed. At fourteen hundred rpms, Jade pulled back on the stick and let the Jenny have her head. She felt the seat press into her spine, making her one with the machine as the plane sped forward. Then the rough jostling gave way to a smooth glide and the slight sensation of floating that came when she first leveled off.

As she peered over the side at the neat rows of coffee trees and the Thika River, Jade couldn't believe that so much danger lurked in the landscape. Only this time it wasn't a crocodile or a hungry lion; it was a human. *If one can consider Lilith a human.*

Jade had soloed only once before, and that time *another* human had interfered and nearly cost Jade her life and Sam his beloved plane. She pushed those memories to the recesses of her mind and focused on the task at hand. She turned west, the still-rising sun to her back, and flew in low over the Muthaiga and Parklands estates before heading northwest along the railroad.

Below her, many people stopped and looked up, pointing at the yellow Jenny. *I've been seen, Sam*. Sam! He was actually back. She still couldn't believe it. *Wait until he's shaved off that hideous beard and his hair has returned to normal.*

The memory of the flight when he'd proposed marriage to her flooded her mind. Even though she now sat where he had, she could feel him behind her, watching her as she opened the ring box and read his proposal, waiting expectantly for her reply.

And what the hell did you do, you idiot? You put him off! When he left, she'd made a vow to win him back. Now he was here, but with his return came a fresh danger, threatening everything she held dear: her future with Sam, her friends, her life.

Africa!

Lilith had already spread bloodshed and evil in Kenya, Morocco, Abyssinia, and the Congo. The woman was a disease, a foul, festering pestilence tainting everything she touched. Jade's fresh vow was made before the heavens with all of Africa as her witness.

I swear I'll see her in her grave before I let her harm anyone else!

Movement in the front cockpit caught Jade's attention. Beverly pointed to the left and Jade broke out of her reverie to look. Ahead at eleven o'clock lay the lovely Lake Naivasha. Jade gave Bev a thumbs-up and turned the plane east to Kinangop. South of that little town was a fairly level patch of land. Jade buzzed by it once to make certain there were no hidden dangers such as a napping rhinoceros before she set down the Jenny.

Fifteen minutes after she landed, Neville's old box-bodied

car came bouncing along the ground towards them. He took the baby from Beverly and carried her to the car while Bev climbed over the side. Jade was glad to note that Neville had his rifle over his shoulder and a revolver stuck into his side pocket. Biscuit strained against his lead, but Neville had him tied securely to the steering column, keeping the big cat out of harm's way.

"I'll be waiting here for you," said Neville. "Bring Maddy and my son back safely." He swung the prop, and the Jenny's motor roared into life.

"Jade, be careful," shouted Beverly. She held Alice tightly in one arm against her chest and waved at Jade with the other.

Jade replied with a thumbs-up sign, taxied off, and rose into the sky. This time, she took a compass bearing and headed directly back to Thika. Once she was there, Sam helped Madeline into the front cockpit and handed up a wiggly toddler to her. The instant Jade was aloft, Sam mounted his motorcycle and roared off on a more direct route to Kinangop.

The second trip was much like the first but for the passengers. Madeline, who'd never flown before despite Sam's offers, clutched Cyril tightly with both arms. The little boy, clearly excited by this new adventure, squealed with both frustration and delight as he squirmed for a better look. Jade knew that with her indirect route Sam would arrive shortly after she landed. All he'd told her was that he wanted her to go on to the mission with the others and that he'd fly the plane back. When pressed as to why, he'd replied with his enigmatic, "Trust me."

Now, as Sam took the goggles, leather cap, and the leather jacket she'd worn, she felt a queer twinge in the pit of her stomach. She'd shut the engine down completely while Sam took a few bundles of his own from Neville's truck and plopped them into the rear cockpit. The sight of them told her that Sam had plans she didn't know about, and her throat tightened. She forced the feeling down as they gathered around the old car and Sam's motorcycle for last-minute plans.

"Do you think Finch and Avery will capture Lilith?" asked Madeline. She held Cyril's hand as he bounced around her, singing out, "I flew up, up, up," his voice rising with each word.

Jade shook her head. "She's too clever. That land is very exposed and it's hard to sneak up on anyone. I doubt she's even there, but if she is, she'll see Finch coming, turn tail, and run. Finch should have listened to me and set up an Apache camp."

"An Apache camp?" asked Beverly.

"Yes," said Jade. "It's what the Indian Geronimo used to do. He made a small encampment with a few lame or worn-out horses to draw in the cavalry. Then he attacked from the rear or made a raid elsewhere. I could have camped nearby and drawn Lilith out while Finch and Avery came around from behind."

"It's a decoy," summarized Sam, "and a bit like what we're doing here. We're making it look as if you are all going to Naivasha to hide."

"I see," said Madeline. "So you expect Lilith to come for us there?"

"That's our hope," said Neville. "And we'll be watching in turn to capture her. In the meantime, you will be safely tucked away elsewhere."

"But she'll still go after Jade," said Beverly. "Or is Jade staying at the mission, too?"

"Jade won't be an option for her anymore," said Sam.

"What do you mean?" asked Jade. Suddenly, she had an idea just what he planned to do. "Sam, you're not—"

He put a finger to her lips. "I told you to trust me. But once you are not there for her anymore, then there's only one person I can think of that she wants as much as she wants you."

"Pili," murmured Jade.

"Yes, her late husband's illegitimate son and heir," said Sam. He brushed the curls from her forehead, revealed a tiny blue Berber tattoo, and kissed it. "And Mr. Fairley," he added, pointing to himself, "will promise him to her if she makes him a partner." He spoke quietly and kissed her again, this time on the lips. "Now get in the car. Neville, help me; then get them out of here. After you have them safely away, meet me at your farm."

The plane was turned so that the mounting step was on the opposite side. Jade couldn't see Sam, but in her heart, she knew what he was doing and what at least one of those carefully hidden bundles contained.

And she knew she could never make it up to him.

CHAPTER 23

This animal is an ancient species, one that saw the monstrous dinosaurs
and watched them disappear. It is said to have an equally long memory.
—The Traveler

SAM HAD FALLEN IN LOVE ONLY TWICE IN HIS LIFE, once with his Jenny and once with a woman who defied every notion he'd ever had of women. And now he had to break the heart of one of them. *What's that aphorism? You only hurt the one you love?* He was getting good at it, too. This time it was going to hurt him as well. But feeling pain meant you were still alive.

He'd considered his plan for days, ever since he'd set foot on the boat to Africa and perhaps even earlier, when his parents had first handed him the cryptic telegram. As he'd expected, everyone else had assumed "the bird has flown" referred to an airplane, but he'd immediately set to making plans to rescue Jade whether she liked it or not. She might toss him out on his ear when he was done, but at least she'd be alive to do it. He'd left Indiana for Dayton, where his two engineering friends, affectionately known as the Bert boys, had gone to pursue their aviation dreams. Gilbert and Robert hadn't failed him. They'd not only listened to his half-formed plans; they'd made suggestions of their own.

Meeting the Aussie on the last ship had been a godsend. It gave his plan the structure that it had lacked. A plan that he was about to put into action.

Sam watched Neville drive off with the women, children, cheetah, and his motorcycle before he banked his Jenny and headed towards Thika. For this to work, he needed witnesses, and the Kikuyu who worked the farms were the best ones he could think of. They knew that Bwana Mti Mguu, that is to say himself, had left and not returned. Avery had been seen going off with Finch to Longonot. Jade was the only other person who could fly the plane. Simba Jike would be flying now. And as Sam had tried to explain to her as gently as he could earlier, Simba Jike had to die, or Lilith would never come out of her stronghold. Very early this morning he'd put part of that lure into action while Jade was helping Bev pack the baby.

He'd gone to the offices of the *Leader of British East Africa* before anyone was on the streets and left an envelope in the after-hours slot. It contained money and a note that read: *Run this notice in tomorrow's personal column. Put it in the weekly edition as well as the daily.*

The notice was simple: *I've taken care of the lioness for you. I can give you the worthy cub as well if you make me a partner. I'll be camped where Waters went for a swim. Come alone at sunset tonight. O. Fairley.*

He'd next walked to the offices of the *East African Standard* and repeated the procedure.

So with the notice due to appear in the papers as word of Jade's death hit, the bait would be set. He hoped it would be tantalizing enough to lure Lilith.

Sam thought about the look of disbelief on Jade's face

when he'd quietly suggested the plan before he took off, her mind unaccepting. Of course, he admitted to himself in retrospect, he'd never actually come out and said, "Jade, you have to die." Even the pretense had seemed horrific, and he couldn't bring himself to actually say it. Instead, he'd danced around the notion.

"As long as you are here in Kenya, Jade, you are a threat to Lilith. You have been ever since you came to Africa. And as long as there are people you love and care about, she will use them as pawns to torture you or to draw you out. Add your interference in Waters' and Stockton's deaths and you could seriously ruin her mining scheme or even hang her. She has a strong motive for revenge."

"I know that, Sam," Jade had replied. "That's why we're moving people to the mission but making it look as though we're taking them farther north. Then, if she wants me, she'll have to come and get me. She must be out of minions. She's never kept more than one or two on any scheme before. And once she's out, she'll be like the crocodile out of water. We'll have her."

Sam had shaken his head. "Somehow I think a croc out of water is still dangerous." And Jade had admitted that to be true based on her recent experience. "You can't use yourself as bait, Jade," he'd said, taking her hands in his. "She could simply shoot you with a rifle. Instead, we need to have something to either bargain or threaten her with. Once the children are safe and you are . . . gone, there's only one thing she'll want, and that's her husband's bastard son."

"But you don't know where Pili . . . You *do* know?"

Sam had nodded and Jade guessed that Avery and Sam had kept Pili safe somewhere in the States. Jade frowned, her fine lips tight and her eyes flashing. "You can't give up Pili! I won't allow it!"

"He won't be in any danger. But I have to let Lilith know that Oliver Fairley is a force to be reckoned with. Since she lost Pellyn, she'll need a new ally anyway."

"And you think she'll take you on to help her get me?" asked Jade.

Jade had studied him with those gorgeous eyes, glowing green fire. He knew she hadn't seen his latest missive to the newspaper. *Wait until she discovers what I'm about to do.*

He'd hoped she hadn't read his thoughts. *She'll kill me.* Of course, taming that angry outburst was something he looked forward to. He caught himself smiling at the fantasy playing in his head and quickly stifled it.

"Trust me, Jade," he'd said. Then he'd added softly so no one else could overhear, "You *will* get your chance. I'm going to need you before this is over. You need to ride with the others to the mission. Neville's got my motorcycle strapped to the back of his car, hidden under that tarp. He's going to take it back to the hangar. You aren't going to the hangar yet. You'll go to the mission until Neville can sneak you back to the hangar after dark."

She'd looked deep into his eyes, and he'd felt his innards melt under that look. He'd longed to grab hold of her and kiss her every fear away. But Neville and the others were too close and Sam knew time was wasting.

"So you plan to fly off and make it look like I'm flying somewhere else to hide?" asked Jade. "Lilith's going to know that I have limited fuel and can't go far." Jade searched his face again for clues to his plan.

Sam didn't answer. Instead he kissed her gently on the

brow, then thought better of it. *The hell with the others. I may not survive this.* He pulled her into a tight embrace and kissed her hard on the lips. His right hand searched her back and hair, settling onto the nape of her neck. She'd tasted slightly of the engine oil that had sprayed back over the windshield from the engine, but he'd relished the flavor mingled with her own sweet mouth. It was everything he loved combined into one.

Finally, he'd released her. "Stay by the car and guard the others," he ordered and, without another word, he'd picked up his smaller bundle and joined Neville on the far side of the plane. Neville had carried over the bulky parachute while Sam had kept Jade's attention focused on him. With the fuselage and wings blocking Jade's view, Sam stepped into the cumbersome parachute harness, praying that his buddies, Gilbert and Robert, had packed the chute carefully. They'd assured him that the Irving Air Chute Company combined all the best features of the new military chutes, and Leslie Irvin used only the finest silk in mainsail and lines.

Not that they'd ever bothered with parachutes in the war. Not unless you were in a balloon. Pilots were told to trust in their machine and ride it down like a glider. Having a chute would only give pilots an excuse to ditch rather than stick it out. He'd heard of more than one pilot who'd carried a sidearm, not to avoid enemy capture but to avoid the more horrific death by fire in a crash.

And what would I have done with a chute? Could I have bailed sooner and avoided being taken prisoner? Would I still have my leg? It wasn't worth thinking about, but he couldn't help it as he tightened the last strap and climbed into the rear cockpit, clipping the static line in place.

"Forgive me, old girl," he'd whispered to his plane. "I guess a man always has to choose between the two loves in his life, and much as I love you, I love her more."

Neville had swung the prop for him when the time came and he'd roared off into the sky without hesitation.

Below him, he'd seen Neville gently herd Jade into his old car. She'd hung back, her face upturned, watching him. Did she know? Had she guessed?

Of course she's guessed. She's too clever for her own good. The real question was, would she forgive him?

She damn well better! He just prayed that he'd be alive to demand it of her. Enough things could go wrong. The chute might not open. The drag line or the harnessing might snag on the rudder, dragging him down with the plane. The chute might have a rip.

I could land on a damn pride of lions, hidden in the grass.

In a way, that was also part of the plan. And now that he'd climbed to fifteen hundred feet, it was time to put it into action. He'd already flown in a wide circle until he was nearly out of fuel. Sam checked his harnesses one last time and stood up, swinging his good leg over the side and into the stirrup on the fuselage. Clinging to a wing post with one hand, he lifted his right leg over and, at the same time, cut the throttle.

And then he jumped.

FATHER JACQUINET EXTENDED BOTH HANDS in welcome. "Monsieur, mesdames, and Mademoiselle Jade, allow me to express our joy in serving you in this hour of need. The sisters will make you all as comfortable as their humble dwelling allows. Come, I am certain the children are hungry, and we will find room for all of you to sleep."

"Thank you, Father," said Jade, as one of the sisters silently pointed the way to the mission's convent. "But I won't be here long." Biscuit leaned against her, resting his powerful shoulders against her thigh. She reached down and stroked his head, scratching him behind the ears. "Biscuit should stay, though."

Beverly's attention was immediately captured by Jade's statement and she turned around. "Jade? What are you doing? You're supposed to hide away while Sam hunts out Lilith. He's flying back to do that now, isn't he?"

"Not entirely," said Jade. "He's crashing his plane so that everyone will presume I'm dead."

"What?" Bev exclaimed. Madeline stood by, her eyes widening with shock. Neville, standing to one side with Cyril, verified Jade's statement with a nod.

Father Jacquinet studied Jade for a few moments in silence. "This is the American pilot, Featherstone, no? He has come back?"

Jade didn't answer, suddenly feeling sheepish. She'd told the fathers about Sam when she'd returned from Morocco and they'd expressed their interest in meeting him. But once he'd left, Jade couldn't bring herself to face their penetrating looks and polite questions. She knew now how foolish she'd been. These men knew how to keep secrets and they understood the human heart. As if Father Jacquinet could read Jade's mind, he expressed her discomfort in his own gentle manner.

"Mademoiselle Jade, it is very clear to me. This man is in your life but you did not know how much of your life you wished to share. Maybe you will no longer be free, no? Then he gives you this freedom and suddenly it is a gift you do not

want. You hide away and we do not see you. But he is a true
man, your Featherstone. He comes back to help you and he
gives everything for your life. Is this not so?"

"Yes, Father, it is," said Jade. "If I'm right, then at this
moment, he's jumping from his plane in a parachute and
crashing the Jenny. His *Jenny*, Father. That plane means
everything to him. And what if he gets hurt? Or killed?"
She shook her head. "I don't deserve him. There is no way in
hell . . . Excuse me. There's no way I can ever repay him."

Father Jacquinet took her right hand in his and patted
it. "Ah, but that is where you are wrong, my dear. That is
where you are very wrong." He smiled. "He does this because you do deserve him and he knows this. And this Jenny.
It does not mean *everything* to him." He chuckled. "I think
your young man will be safe. And when this is finished, then
perhaps we will meet him?"

"I promise," said Jade. "*If* we survive this, we'll both come
back to get the others." She turned aside, lost in her fears.

"Then your pet is very welcome to stay here," said Father
Jacquinet as Biscuit rubbed up against his robe, leaving a gift
of golden hairs behind on the black cloth. The nun holding
Cyril looked less than enthusiastic. Father Jacquinet stepped
close to Jade and took her hand. "And you will succeed, Mademoiselle Jade," he said. "Because you, like your brave Sam,
are willing to risk and give all."

TIME HALTED THE INSTANT SAM STEPPED OFF the plane and
into emptiness. He closed his eyes, feeling the air buffet his
clothes. He heard his plane sputter once and then go silent.
When he opened his eyes, he saw his Jenny blur away from
him and he fought the urge to call to her.

Then a sudden jerk grabbed at his groin and chest. The static line reached the end of its brief tether, snapping taut. He might have heard a brief rip; he wasn't sure with the wind and his heart in his ears. A clear *whoomp* reached him as his parachute silk burst forth from the open pack and unfurled. Sam felt as though he were being pulled upwards and then released to float motionless in the sky. Now all his attention was focused on his plane as she stalled and plummeted, spinning as if the entire plane were a propeller desperately trying to keep itself aloft.

"Good-bye, my friend," he whispered. The wind swept the words away.

The Jenny sped downward, eager to fulfill her part of the sacrifice. She became a pale yellow blur of wings and wood, turning in a graceful pirouette, dancing with the sky. Sam watched as she struck the ground and shattered into an ir- reparable mess. He heard the spruce wood crack and splinter like so many bones snapping and felt the phantom pain sear into his own wooden leg. Sam noted with growing concern that the wrecked Jenny and the ground were rising to meet him faster and faster.

How could that be? He was hovering, wasn't he? But that illusion of floating disappeared as he approached the ground. Quickly he searched his memory for everything the Bert boys had told him.

Don't keep your legs stiff. Roll when you fall.

He was pretty sure his wooden leg could take the shock, but he didn't think he wanted the prosthetic pushed up any higher into his knee.

The ground leaped up towards him, a green and golden blur. He flexed his legs, felt the force striking his left foot and his right knee, and quickly rolled, the chute drifting over him and swaddling him in silk.

Sam lay still for a moment, forcing himself to breathe and waiting for his pounding pulse to slow down.

I did it!

His pulse quickened, but this time with exhilaration rather than fear. Did this make him a member of Irvin's caterpillar club? Probably not, since one needed to jump from a disabled plane. Did it count if he'd disabled it himself? It didn't matter. He was alive.

"Whoo-hoo!" he shouted from under the silk. He pulled and tugged at the chute, crawling out from under, and stood. Another shout swelled within his chest, then died out as he beheld his beautiful plane lying in a crumpled heap not far away. The rush from the danger turned into grief for a lover. Sam gathered up the silks and walked the few hundred yards to his plane.

He found the tail first. Farther away the nose, or what was left of it, had ended up pointing skyward after her roll and flip. Now the propeller spun with squeaking groans as though she were breathing her last. Sam pulled his sidearm, took aim at the fuselage, and fired.

"Rest in peace."

Then he dropped the chute and climbed out of his harness. Sam pulled the tightly packed bundle from inside of his leather jacket and opened it. He took out a pair of Jade's jodhpurs and her white linen shirt, each ripped and shredded. Sam arranged them inside of and under the harness and snagged one of the lines on the rudder.

He pulled out a file and worried the rudder cable until he could snap it. *That should make it look like sabotage and give a reason for Jade's jump.* Finally Sam opened his canteen and poured goat's blood over the clothes. He tossed part of a boot complete with a knife beside the entire mess and drizzled the rest of the blood on it. He stepped back to evaluate the results.

Wild animals rarely left much for remains, sometimes even eating the clothing. If his illusion worked, it would appear that Jade hadn't survived the jump and that a passing lion had devoured her body. With any luck, jackals or other scavengers would soon smell the blood and finish the job, adding that last touch of verisimilitude to his scene. There was time for that. The search wouldn't begin until tomorrow morning.

And the scavengers may be here sooner than you'd like. Sam scanned the horizon, searching for movement. Seeing none, he holstered his revolver, took his bearings, and headed towards Thika and the Thompsons' farm.

CHAPTER 24

Hunters report finding everything inside of a croc's stomach: antelope horn, porcupine quills, stones, and, sadly, necklaces and bracelets.
—The Traveler

WHEN AVERY JOINED THEM AT THE MISSION, he had little to report. Jade met him outside the convent door with a cup of coffee, a chicken leg, and a loaf of bread that Bev had saved for him. Bev, Maddy, and the children were effectively cloistered within, away from prying eyes.

"Finch and I found nothing at that Longonot farmhouse," Avery said.

Jade hardly had ears for what she'd already surmised. "I just hope Sam made it back safely," she said.

"I should imagine he's fine," Avery said after downing the coffee. "I haven't heard to the contrary. Why would you think otherwise?" He bit into the chicken.

"Because he crashed his plane to make it seem that I'm dead."

Avery nearly choked on the chicken. "Bloody hell. I should have seen that myself. And now that you're gone Lilith has no target."

"Sam said that he had a plan to draw her out now. A

combination of information and blackmail. We plan to flush that mongrel hyena's whelp out of wherever she's hiding."

"I take it you are not surprised that we found nothing at Longonot. Not sure she was ever there."

"Such an open place," Jade said with a shrug. "She'd have a hard time escaping unnoticed and she could hardly expect that the police wouldn't show. Do you know what Finch's plans are?"

Avery shook his head. "He was still searching the area when I left. I believe he was actually quite happy to see me off. I made him nervous. I did overhear him order one of his men to remain behind until he sent for him. In case Lilith did show. I doubt they'll leave him there for long. The force is spread too thinly as it is, and there's more trouble in the Indian district over the sanitation and plague problems. If the newspapers are correct, I expect riots any day. And if *you* crashed, then Finch will probably be involved in the search for your remains. Ah," he added as he heard footsteps, "here's Neville now. Perhaps he's privy to Sam's plans."

Neville joined them. "I'm supposed to go home tonight," he said, "and see that Jade isn't back. I'm to organize a search tomorrow morning at first light."

"And I'm supposed to stay at Naivasha as if my family were there and watch for Lilith," said Avery.

"I'll join you there once I finish the search," said Neville. "I just hope that woman comes looking for us." He flexed an arm muscle as he clenched his fist.

"I wonder if Lilith will be part of your search party, Neville," said Jade.

"I can't imagine that," said Avery. "But word travels fast

in Nairobi, so she'll find out soon enough. Should make the papers by Saturday."

"I'll say something on the telephone," said Neville. "The story will certainly spread then. Lilith may even be one of the hello girls," he added, using the colony's pet name for the telephone operators, a term left over from the war.

Jade didn't join in the conversation. She closed her eyes and took a deep breath, her left hand fingering the sapphire ring on her right. Avery nudged her. "I'm certain that Sam's fine."

"I wish I could say that I knew he was alive, that I could feel it, but all I can do is trust in him and God."

Avery pointed at Jade's left knee. "I say, your knee there. It doesn't pain you, does it?"

Jade's lips curved in the faintest smile. "No, as a matter of fact it doesn't."

"Well, there you have it. Your knee always hurts when death is imminent. I should think it would have hurt when Sam took off if anything was to happen."

Jade didn't have the heart to contradict him, possibly because she wanted desperately to believe it herself. But her knee's gift for predicting danger didn't always extend beyond that to herself, and even then, it gave *very* little warning, tending towards the imminent side of things, as Avery had put it. She only hoped it gave her enough notice when she faced Lilith.

By THE TIME SAM COMPLETED HIS TREK TO THE HANGAR, all traces of exhilaration from the jump had vanished. During the last mile he'd moved like an automaton, putting one foot in front of the other, flesh and wood, determined to see this

through. Reaching the hangar didn't provide any mental relief. Coming back to the vacant space within the thorn *boma*
felt like coming home to an empty house after a funeral.

Neville hadn't returned yet with the motorcycle and
Jade. Sam looked at the long shadows. It wouldn't be too
long now. He dropped to the ground inside the thorn bar-
rier and took a few minutes to rest. He cleaned his Colt New
Service revolver one more time. Sam had no illusions about
capturing Lilith alive. His disguise wouldn't fool her for long
and then it would be his life or hers. He clicked the newly
reloaded barrel into place. Sam knew he might get only one
shot. He'd make sure it was lethal.

BY SUNSET, Jade felt like a mortar shell, ready to explode
at the slightest provocation. She pressed her big slouch hat
firmly on her head, slipped out of the mission, and headed
for Neville's battered car. She hunkered down beside Sam's
motorcycle, and Neville adjusted the tarp to cover them both
before he drove home. Next to her lay her Winchester and
she drew comfort from its presence. Once they passed Thika,
Neville turned off the main road and stopped. Jade crawled
out from the back and brushed the dust off her hair. Neither
of them spoke until after he'd bounced along the rutted path
past his house and headed to the hangar.

"Are you supposed to keep watch near Naivasha tonight?" she asked.

"Yes, I get the watch from midnight until four. I'm going back there as soon as I leave you at the hangar. You don't
agree?"

"It seems to me that we're spreading *our* forces too
thinly," Jade said.

"On the contrary, Jade. *We're* positioning our troops. The net is tightening. Avery and I will keep watch at Naivasha. It will be difficult for Lilith to make a move without being seen by someone."

"Which may simply mean she won't move. And that makes me wonder just what in tarnation Sam is planning."

"I don't know," said Neville, "but I say, Jade, this is exciting. I've never been part of your adventures before. I feel like one of the characters in Maddy's books."

The nearly full moon hovered above the horizon, an iridescent orb that scaled the horizon and silhouetted the flat-topped acacia trees, transforming them into black parasols over the grassland. Neville deposited her near the empty hangar. The sight brought on a fresh wave of her grief and fear. She prayed that Sam had survived the jump. But even if he had, his beloved Jenny had not. The sacrifice was humbling. Jade helped Neville unload Sam's motorcycle.

Why did Sam do it? She knew one thing. Sam had just proven himself to be as reckless as she ever was. This stunt clearly exceeded her time spent as leopard bait or charging the young lion on her motorcycle. *Well, maybe not charging the lion, but it certainly matched it.*

Now the playing field was even and it made her love him even more. It also made her want to yell at him. *He crashed the Jenny! He proposed to me in that plane. If he thinks this voids his marriage proposal, he's got another thought coming to him!*

"Where is he?" she asked Neville.

Neville shrugged. "He may be hiding in case someone came here looking for the plane. Do you want me to wait with you?"

Jade shook her head. "No. You'd better get back to

Naivasha and rest before your watch. It's late enough and you have a search to lead tomorrow."

After Neville left, Jade paced the interior of the thorn brush hangar like a caged cat while she considered her next move. Should she walk on to the house? In the rising moonlight she spied Sam's motorcycle parked beside the gate. *Where is he? He should be here.* But he wasn't.

A cold fear gripped her stomach and her pace quickened. Maybe Sam was injured in the jump. He could be lying somewhere wounded, bleeding, waiting. *Waiting for me.* She had started for the gate to leave when a slender figure caught her eye.

Sam! She resisted the urge to run to him, once again aware of the need for secrecy. She'd made herself too visible already.

He came strolling from the east, a tall silhouette against the low moon with a faint shadow towing him forward. His softly limping stride appeared slow at first; then it quickened as he spied her.

"I couldn't sit and wait anymore," he said. "I took a stroll."

Jade watched for only a moment before she fumbled to open the gate and ran the last forty feet to him.

"You're alive!" she exclaimed as she threw her arms around him and hugged him tightly. "Oh, Sam. How could you do it?"

Sam pulled her in closer and kissed the nape of her neck. She felt his bristly beard scrape against her skin, a tangible reminder of their dangerous deception.

"Not hard. You just jump. Static line does the rest."

Jade pushed him an arm's length away, watching his

features in the moonlight. The beard made it impossible to tell if he was frowning or smiling. "That's not what I meant and you know it. You destroyed your plane. You loved that plane."

"It's only an airplane, Jade." He moved over to a rough wooden bench and sat down, motioning for her to join him. "I'm tired. I need to sit. Shouldn't have taken that last stroll."

"How far away did you crash? Did you have to walk all the way back?"

Sam waved off her questions, then put his arm around her, drawing her close. "We don't have much time. When the sun comes up, we mustn't be seen around here."

"I presume you've got a plan?" Jade asked. "You went to a lot of trouble getting everyone out of the way, including Neville and Avery."

"You noticed that, did you? The fewer people actually involved, the better. I'd have kept them all at the mission, but I knew neither Avery nor Neville would have stood for it. As it is, they're busy but not in the line of fire."

"And you will be?"

"We both will be. Jade, I'm counting on you."

Jade lunged at him, nearly knocking him off the bench. Her lips locked onto his, forcing their way past that dreadful bush of a beard. He tasted of grit and hay and smelled strongly of horses. Jade didn't care. She pressed closer to him. He responded by wrapping his arms around her waist and pulling her tightly against him. She felt a strong shudder run down his chest and wasn't sure if it came from him or her.

"You're welcome," Sam said when he regained his balance and breath.

"I'd thank you some more if you didn't have that shrub on the bottom half of your face."

Sam rubbed his beard. "It's not too comfortable for me, either. It's hot. But after another day, it shouldn't be necessary. I left a notice in the morning's papers challenging Lilith to meet me tomorrow night. It's one that I hope will lure her out, especially when news of your untimely demise circulates. You see, I took credit for killing you." One hand lightly caressed Jade's cheek. "Neville will go into town at first light to get Finch and some others to go search for you. They should come across the wreckage easily enough. Word will spread like a wildfire."

"But there won't be a body. Won't they assume I walked away?"

"I sawed through the rudder cable to make it look like the plane was sabotaged. And I left the chute snagged on the tail. There's enough bloody clothing lying about to attract the usual scavengers. If they find anything, it will be a stray boot fragment and knife and a broken pair of goggles. Remember, predators and scavengers rarely leave anything behind."

Jade nodded. It was true enough. Animals cracked and consumed bones as well as clothing. Often when some hunter went missing, all that was ever retrieved was a gun.

"And Lilith," continued Sam, "wherever she is, will eventually see it or hear of it. It gives us one day to get ready, if that. I have a feeling she's been under our noses for a while. How else could she manage things so well?"

"If by 'things' you mean Mr. Holly, you may be right. And with her lover, Pellyn, dead, she'd have to stay closer to town to know what's going on."

Sam shifted on the bench, clasping his hands in front of

him. "Where the devil can she be hiding? She could be anywhere, but what I'm afraid of is that this pretense of abducting that girl, Mary, had another purpose than drawing you out west to Longonot."

Jade shuddered. "It was a decoy! Sam, we weren't thinking this through. We thought that Lilith was diverting our attention so she could snatch one of the children. But as you noted before, it was too easy to find out whether Mary was taken. So why else would she have Holly give us that box?"

"She could move around unnoticed while we were scrambling to save the children."

Jade shook her head. "She could've been planning to strike somewhere else. But who?"

Sam sucked in his breath. "Blast and damn. That list you found in Dymant's room. Maybe Lilith *intended* for you or Finch to eventually see it, just not so soon. Pellyn's death forced her hand. Ask yourself who's *not* on the list."

Jade ran through the list in her mind. "Harry wasn't on the list and neither was Jelani." She gasped. "Jelani! We need to get to his village."

SAM FELT JADE'S ARMS WRAPPED AROUND HIS MIDDLE, solid and warm as they sped on his motorcycle towards Jelani's village in the cool Kenyan night. It was all he could do to keep from simply riding off with her to Fort Hall or some other safe haven and locking her away. But if he'd learned anything in his self-imposed exile back in the States, it was that you couldn't lock away a wild animal like Jade and expect her to thrive. He'd always known it in his heart. Now he knew it in his head.

It had nearly driven him mad, being apart from her,

wondering if she'd actually forgive him and take him back. Then came word of Lilith's escape and he knew that it didn't matter whether she forgave him or not. He was not going to let her face that bitch alone. And wonder of wonders, she was actually happy to see him. It made him feel as if he were flying all over again, this time without needing a plane.

Which is a good thing, since you just destroyed yours.

It would be worth it, though, if they could pull off this ruse. He revved the cycle a bit faster and sailed over a small rise, reveling in the open country. Nairobi had grown so much that the streets were nearly flooded with cars and cycles. Jade was right. Wild Africa had better run for its very life around here.

And so had Lilith! As a war veteran, Sam had no qualms about killing her. She was as much the enemy as those German fighters he'd shot down. But he also knew that killing her outright could mean his own incarceration for murder. He hoped she'd strike first so he could justifiably claim self-defense. Somehow, he didn't think that would be a problem. Satan had more of a conscience than she did. He'd been taught that anyone could be redeemed if they had a true change of heart. The trouble was, Lilith didn't have one.

What concerned him more was Jade. He'd convinced her once before on Mount Marsabit that she wasn't a killer. He hoped it was still true. It wasn't that he didn't want Lilith dead. He did, but by *his* hand and not by Jade's. But he also knew that she was a sure shot, something he was counting on to protect his own life. Lilith was pure evil and had to be destroyed. His dad called homely animals "ugly as homemade sin," but Sam knew that evil often put on a beautiful face to lure in more victims. And Lilith was beautiful.

Was!

He'd seen her after Morocco, when Jade's knife had slashed up from the woman's nose past her eye. The wound hadn't been deep and, in a younger woman, it might have healed clean. But Lilith was no girl. Age and harsh prison conditions would have also marred her beauty. Like a cracked vase, Lilith was severely flawed. He shuddered to think of her plans for Jade.

If Dymant hadn't died . . . Sam let the thought disappear as Jelani's village came into view. Over the palisade, he could just make out the tops of the huts, like hulking beasts curled up asleep. He stopped the cycle and shut off the engine.

"You mustn't be seen," he whispered. "Hide by the goat pen until I get back."

Jade slid off the rear of the cycle and ducked low, her movements and bowed form making her resemble some scurrying night creature. When she reached the palisade wall, she hugged it, keeping in its shadows. Sam took his flashlight from a pannier and, switching it on, wended his way up the path and approached the gate. As he got closer, a Kikuyu man stopped him, holding a spear point to Sam's chest.

Sam held his hands out to his sides. "I see young *mondo-mogo*," he said in broken Swahili spoken with the fake Australian accent, bending the "o"s. "Jelani," he added in case none of it made any sense to the guard. The guard hesitated, trying to see Sam's face. "*Rafiki*," Sam added, giving the Swahili for "friend."

The guard nodded and led the way to a hut. He motioned with outstretched palm for Sam to wait outside while he ducked his head near the leather curtain and whispered inside.

An angry, snarling voice answered, and soon after an elder wrapped in a striped blanket stepped out. "Who are you and what do you want?" the man said in English.

"I've come to see the young healer, Jelani," said Sam. "I think he may be in danger."

The man snorted. "You are too late. He is not here. He has been taken."

CHAPTER 25

Animism teaches that souls can enter crocodiles. There are tales of crocs shifting from animal to human and even of marriages between humans and transformed crocs.
—The Traveler

JADE MOVED FARTHER BACK FROM THE VILLAGE ENTRANCE, pressing flat against the wooden fence. On the other side she heard a deep *maa* and knew she was outside the animal pen. The strong smell of goat wafted through the spaces between the poles. Suddenly her mind swept back to June 1919, and a shudder born of memory rippled down her spine and legs.

She'd spent a harrowing night in this same pen then, waiting with Madeline and Jelani during a hunt for a man-eating hyena that had plagued this very village. The three of them had been put in with the goats where it was safe, while the men, including Hascombe, sat in an elevated blind for the brute to take their staked-out bait. The hyena came, but passed by the bait in preference for human flesh. It had forced its way into the *boma*, stalking Jelani and uttering that horrid, maniacal laughing call—a call that still reminded Jade of shell-shocked soldiers. She'd relived that night time and again in her dreams.

There were no hyenas around tonight. At least, none that she'd heard. A lone jackal barked in the distance, and somewhere farther off yet, a male lion voiced his deep-chested, groaning roars as he announced his territory and challenged all comers. The roars settled into the final coughing harrumphs and died into silence.

What's keeping Sam so long? It'll be dawn in five hours. Think about something else.

She stifled a yawn, only to have her stomach growl. She couldn't decide what she needed more, a decent sleep or a hot cup of coffee and a half dozen biscuits loaded down with smoked bacon. She settled for a drink from her canteen.

A soft cough alerted her that Sam had returned. He knelt down beside her.

"Is Jelani all right?" she whispered.

"He's not here. The village chief says that Finch arrested him."

Jade's "What!" was hushed by Sam's hand over her mouth. When he pulled it away, she whispered, "That arrest was about the time when you showed up, Sam. They found the body of another Kikuyu, Mutahi. Finch had Jelani and Irungu brought in on suspicion of murder. But Finch promised he'd release Jelani as soon as there was an autopsy and . . ." She clenched her fists. "That damned jackal Finch! He said he wouldn't charge them with Mutahi's death. But he must have planned all along to hold him on some other charge. Jelani's too political for Finch's taste, speaking out against British rule like he does. Did Irungu come back?"

"According to the chief, Irungu was only fined for not having a *kipande*," said Sam, referring to the case and the required government documents that one was required to wear around his neck. "But Jelani never returned. The old *mondo-mogo* has taken ill so he's of no help to them. The village is worried." Sam inhaled deeply. "But Finch may have done us and Jelani a favor. *If* Lilith planned to kidnap him, he's safer in a native prison than in his own village."

"You may be right," said Jade.

"Right now, we need to get some sleep. In the morning, I want to take a look at Hascombe's old haunts. If Steven Holly lured you there, there must be a reason."

"You suspect Harry?"

"I would," said Sam "except we know Pellyn's dead, and Harry's sure as hell not Lilith. But she may have used his house. Holly did try to lure you there. If we don't find her there, we'll set up my trap. In my newspaper ad, I told Lilith to meet me where Waters took a swim."

"Just downriver from the falls," said Jade. She yawned.

Sam looked at the palisade behind her. "The goat pen should do for us for tonight, right? We'll be well chaperoned, too. I told the chief I'd sleep there tonight. We just need to be out before anyone sees you."

Jade shifted position, pushing the persistent nanny goat off her lap. The acrid scent of goat wafted up and assaulted her as much as a bottle of smelling salts. Jade had spent enough time tending sheep and new lambs on her parents' New Mexico ranch, but goats were an entirely different aroma. She stretched her legs in front of her and looked at Sam.

Sound asleep.

For a moment after they'd entered the goat kraal, Jade had actually thought the stay might be enjoyable. She'd imagined snuggling up to Sam, his strong arms around her.

And then some blasted nanny actually butted herself between them like a hairy old matron. Sam had chuckled and shifted, using the goat's back as a pillow.

Jade tried it, but the odor was too strong. She sat up instead, her back against the palisade and her legs drawn up. That was, until another nanny scrambled onto her lap, *maa*-ing softly. But something other than goats kept her awake: concern for Jelani. Why was Finch keeping him? If they hadn't already found Pellyn, she'd have suspected him more than ever.

She pulled her legs back up and wrapped her arms around her knees. Sleep finally overtook her, and she dreamed of Boguli, the old gray man from Mount Marsabit, the brother to the elephants. The soul of an elephant, if she believed the evidence of her last photograph on Marsabit.

In Jade's dream he stood before her next to Jelani's mother. The old woman kept saying, "*Mamba*," and both of them pointed to Ol Donyo Sabuk. Just as Jade was about to turn in her dream and see what they wanted to show her, a pair of sharp little hooves dug into her thigh and she woke.

Jade could have sworn, as she shoved the persistent goat away, that she heard an elephant trumpet, but this time it sounded frustrated, as though a message had been interrupted.

HARRY HAD BEEN UNABLE TO FIND any sign of the crocodile, and had gone back into town Thursday, opting to spend his evening at the Norfolk hotel bar before going back to his own room and falling asleep. He woke on his bunk, fully dressed, his mouth tasting sour and his head throbbing. He splashed cold water on his face and decided some breakfast at the New Stanley hotel was in order.

That was where he ran into Neville Thompson.

"Hascombe," called Neville. "Thank heaven. I need you to join us."

Harry took one look at Neville's face and gave up any hope of having a decent breakfast. "Cripes, man. What happened? Don't tell me that bloody croc has struck again."

"Worse," said Neville. "Jade's missing. She was flying yesterday and—"

Harry grabbed Neville's shirtfront in both hands and yanked him closer. "What happened to Jade?"

"She didn't come back. Inspector Finch is calling up Dr. Mathews and I'm rounding up a search party."

Harry stifled a ripe swear. Somehow he couldn't imagine Jade being in any serious trouble. But Thompson was a level-headed man and he was clearly agitated. "Likely she ran out of fuel and had to put down somewhere. Do you have any idea where she was headed?"

"She was flying back to my farm from Kinangop," said Neville. "Is Blaney Percival about?"

Harry shook his head, but stopped when it only made his headache worse. "No. Still on Mount Kenya taking care of that elephant problem. I'll grab some coffee and get my gun and truck. We'll find the little minx, Thompson."

By the time Harry returned in his vehicle, Neville had netted nine other men, including Finch, Mathews, and two reporters anxious for a scoop. The eleven men drove off to Kinangop, where they regrouped around Thompson.

"Miss del Cameron took off from here," said Neville. "That was yesterday afternoon and she should have arrived back at the hangar within half an hour. I noticed she was still gone when I returned home last night, but by then it was too dark to do a proper search."

"Mr. Thompson," said the reporter with the big sun-shades and wide straw boater, "I represent the *Leader*. What was Miss del Cameron doing out here, and how do you know that this is where she'd been?" The man asked deferentially, but his counterpart from the *Standard* licked the tip of his pencil, waiting to write every word of what promised to be a good story.

Neville pointed to the flattened grasses. "You can see the marks of the aeroplane's wheels and the tail skid. That proves she took off from here."

"Right," said Finch, elbowing his way past the reporters. "And I happen to know that she was making some deliveries to Naivasha."

"I saw the plane yesterday," said the reporter from the *Standard*. "It looked to have someone sitting in the front seats. Is that correct, Mr. Thompson?"

"None of that matters," snapped Finch. "We're here to find Miss del Cameron, not to write stories. Thompson, you say she'd have headed straight back to your farm? No chance that she'd have diverted course?"

"None, Inspector," said Neville. "As I understood it, she had adequate petrol for the trips she made and to return, but not much extra. She'd have to have landed and refueled. I checked the petrol drum this morning. It was at the same level as yesterday when I helped her fuel the plane."

"Very well," said Finch. "I want each of you to fan out your vehicles into a wide line and hold in that position un-less you come to a ravine or something that you need to go around. Once you're around, resume your proper place in the line. We want to cover as much ground as possible in one pass." He pointed to Neville and Harry. "I want you two to take the ends of the line. You're the most experienced in the bush. You can keep an eye on the others, keep them from straying. No one should be more than twenty yards from the man next in line."

"Where do you want me, Inspector?" asked Dr. Mathews.

"You and I will take center point positions. And you reporters," Finch barked. "You're not here for a story. I expect you to assist in this search or I'll throw you into prison for interfering with a rescue. We're here to find this woman and, if possible, rescue her."

Harry took his position on the north end of the line, clenching his jaw to bite back his distress. What optimism he'd first felt quickly fled like antelope in the presence of a lion pride. Jade was many things—foolhardy, brave, reckless—but she was also trustworthy. She'd never have taken Featherstone's plane nor left her friends without a damned good reason.

Damned Featherstone! It's his fault for leaving the bloody plane there to begin with.

Twenty minutes into the search, two cars had stalled out when their oil pans hit rocks. The line of vehicles collapsed to take up the slack. Harry checked every ravine before he drove around it, but so far all anyone had managed was to flush out several bush pigs and to panic a mongoose.

Then he spied a patch of yellow.

"I see something ahead," Harry shouted, the words nearly choking him.

News of his discovery passed down the line and every man converged on the distant point where a bit of yellow stuck up above the grass like a guidon. Harry's heart raced as he watched for any movement, any sign of life. He saw none.

"It's a wing," exclaimed the reporter from the *Standard*. He removed a large camera and a tripod from his Buick's rear seat and began setting up a shot.

Harry fought the urge to smash the camera.

"There's the propeller," said Dr. Mathews. "That crumpled mess must be the wings, but I don't see Miss del Cameron's body anywhere in this debris."

"There!" exclaimed Harry. He pointed north towards a patch of white and another bit of yellow. "Could that be a parachute? Thompson, did Jade have a parachute?"

Neville nodded. "She wore something bulky strapped around her when she left the farm. It hung rather low, as though she might sit on it. I thought it might be a cushion to elevate her for better visibility so I asked her about it. She said that Featherstone had left a parachute behind so she decided to keep it handy . . . in case."

"In case," repeated Harry. His jaws worked again, clenching and unclenching. "I thought she knew how to fly Featherstone's damned machine. What was she doing up in it to begin with?"

Harry moved in closer to Thompson. Dr. Mathews joined them and Neville lowered his voice. "She was taking my wife and child to safety, along with Lady Dunbury and her baby."

"To safety? From what, for the love of Pete?" roared Harry.

"Keep your voice down, Hascombe," cautioned Neville. "From an old enemy."

"An enemy!" Harry's voice rang out. He looked from

Thompson to Mathews, waiting for someone to explain. He saw the two reporters pull out their notebooks.

"Tell us about this enemy," said the *Leader* reporter.

"Just what or who was she taking to safety?" asked the hatless and sunburned *Standard* reporter with the camera.

"Someone tried to kidnap my son," said Neville. "We feared another attempt."

Harry wanted to ask where Jade had taken the children, but the reporters had closed in like jackals on a carcass, Mathews following close behind.

Finch called over from the wreckage, "You should have a look at this."

Harry and the others trotted over to where he stood by the rudder. Finch poked at the parachute silk with his foot, nudging it gently aside.

Harry's breath caught in his throat.

"IT'S TRUE!" whispered Jade. "It's as if that elephant had kept me away until Bev and the girls arrived. "Father Jacquinet thinks he's a guardian angel."

They walked the rest of the way in to Harry's ranch, Sam pushing the cycle. They kept their conversation low as Jade related her account of seeing Boguli and the old elephant.

Sam snorted in disbelief. "Well, if he's protecting you, he'd better let us know whether or not Lilith is holed up in Harry's house before she shoots us."

There was no sign of activity in or around the building except for a few rodents that skittered away. If Harry or anyone had been back here recently, Jade saw no fresh evidence.

Sam drifted around the rooms, his lean, muscular body shifting like a slow-stalking wolf. He checked every shelf and every cupboard and peered into the side rooms, examining the floors for dust and footprints. "If she was here," he said after two hours of intense searching, "she hasn't been in here since you found Holly. And neither has Harry, by the looks of it."

"Even my footprints are partially obscured by dust," said Jade. "This can't have been her headquarters."

"Wasn't there a second farm near here?" Sam asked.

"There's Roger Forster's place around to the east. If the tales are true, it burned just after a woman bought it. I always suspected it was Lilith's doing to remove evidence incriminating her in her husband's death. But I've already been there. There's nothing but one storage shed and it's got a tree growing right up against the door."

Sam's boot toe nudged aside a pile of rags, revealing several small wriggling pink and hairless bodies. He quickly pushed the rags back into place over the little mice and slipped past Jade to the door. "The only rats in here are the honest ones. Probably scared the mother away when we came in. Let's go on to Forster's. I want to see it."

HARRY STARED AT THE MEAGER REMAINS, struggling to maintain control.

"Is she dead?" asked one of the searchers, hanging back.

"Very likely, yes," said Finch. "There are no actual human remains, but judging by the shredded clothing, it would appear that our young lady did not survive her jump or, if she did, she was seriously injured and couldn't move. Wild animals found her and . . . well, you can imagine the rest."

"It appears that the parachute lines snagged on the rear of the plane," said Neville.

"Are you *absolutely* certain?" asked the *Leader* reporter. "I mean, isn't it more likely that she left that rigging behind and walked off? Perhaps she's waiting for us somewhere? Surely we can track her." Several of the other men murmured agreement.

Harry tried not to listen to them. They reminded him of ghouls, voraciously discussing the events. Instead he inspected a loose cable.

"I know you think tracking is easy," said Finch, "but the plain fact is, we haven't had rain for two weeks now and the ground is hard. We're not likely to find any footprints, especially," he added, "since we do have one of her boots here."

Harry lunged forward, following the inspector's line of sight, and stumbled. There, below his feet, was a solitary boot, or what remained of one. Little was left of the leather beyond the heel, sole, and a few inches of the legging. A few feet away lay a knife.

"Here's her knife," exclaimed Neville. "She always carried one in her boot."

"Predators and scavengers leave very little behind," said Finch. Harry watched him put a hand on Thompson's shoulder. "I'm very sorry," said Finch. "She was a fine woman."

"Wait a minute!" growled Harry. "Jade carried a knife with a bone hilt. This one is different. And where's her rifle? She never went anywhere without that Winchester."

Neville cleared his throat. "The Winchester wouldn't fit in the cockpit. As to the knife? I don't know why she changed blades, but I did see her use *that* one to scrape discharge off a piston yesterday."

"This was no accident," said Harry. "I found a broken cable that worked the tail. It looked to have been filed thin."

He showed Finch. "You can see a shininess where a file or something worried it down."

"So you think someone tried to kill her?" asked Finch as he examined the cable. "Don't pilots check their aeroplanes, Thompson? Would something like this show up?"

"I don't know if she did a full preflight," said Neville. "I know she worked on the plane earlier in the week. Maybe someone did this when we had the fire at my farm."

Most of the men milled around the pitiful remains, hands in their trouser pockets, eyes downcast. The reporter for the *Leader* accosted Dr. Mathews for a few minutes, as though he expected the doctor to provide some explanation or evidence. Mathews said little, only nodding or shaking his head at times. The thought of Jade's death being turned into a story angered Harry and he roused them all into action again.

"Spread out and gather what we can for a burial. It's little enough, but we can do her that much honor." The men fanned out on foot, stooping to retrieve a scrap of fabric, a button, a pair of goggles. Harry watched for a moment but he didn't join them. He grabbed Neville's arm and pulled him farther aside.

"Now what the devil was Jade doing?" Harry demanded. "Who was she running from? And what's this about a fire?"

Neville put his hand on Harry's and pushed it from his arm. "I don't know what I can tell you, Hascombe. Jade said she wasn't certain who she could trust."

"The hell you say!" shouted Harry, then quickly lowered his voice before anyone else overheard. "Jade knew she could always count on me. Who was after her?"

"She had some old enemy, a woman with connections in the colony."

"Worthy's widow?"

Neville nodded. "You knew of her?"

"There was talk of it when Jade first came to Africa, after that business with the native witch doctors and the man-eating hyenas. And you think this Worthy woman is here in Kenya?"

"We don't know that," said Neville, "but we do know she had an accomplice. He's dead now."

"Who?"

"Dr. Dymant," said Neville, after a moment's hesitation. "But his real name was Pellyn. Just before he died, someone started a fire on my farm and tried to take my son."

"If he's dead, then who was Jade running from?"

"Hell, Hascombe. If we knew that, we'd have the bastard brought to book."

Harry stepped away, one hand rubbing his chin stubble. "Someone hiding around in the colony then." His shoulders slumped. "Ah, Jade," he murmured. He hung his head and swayed on his feet. From his right, he heard Finch call to Thompson. Then to his left, as from a distance, he heard the reporter from the *Standard* make an offhand comment.

"I wonder if this had anything to do with a strange personal notice running in this morning's newspaper? Someone claimed to have taken care of the lioness. Wasn't Miss del Cameron called 'lioness' by the natives?"

Harry lunged for the reporter. "What did the notice say?"

The reporter's sunburned face turned a deeper red. "I picked up a fresh copy of the paper on my way out. It's in my Austin."

Harry ran to the reporter's car. He found the notice and read it silently. "Who is this O. Fairley?" he demanded, his voice low and menacing.

"An Australian," said one of the other searchers. "I heard from my kitchen boy that Dunbury hired him to help with his—"

Harry didn't stay to listen. He strode rapidly to his car.

Dr. Mathews ran after him. "Hascombe, stop. You look apoplectic. I know you were close to Miss del Cameron. Stay here for now. Allow me to give you something to calm yourself. Something to help you sleep when you get home."

"I don't want any of your damn pills," growled Harry. He swatted the doctor like he would a mosquito. "I want to get my hands around the neck of whoever pushed Jade to this end."

"As would I," said Mathews. "She was a fine woman, but this is something for the police to handle."

"Finch is probably just as relieved to be rid of Jade," Harry said, his anger taking control. "She is . . . She was too clever by half for the likes of him. I'm going to find this Fairley, and when I do . . ."

The rest of his words disappeared behind the roar of his engine.

BOTH HARRY'S AND ROGER FORSTER'S HOUSES had stood at the edges of their property, so they were, at most, two miles apart. Jade and Sam hiked silently, pushing the motorcycle, leery of alerting anyone to their presence. As they neared Forster's, Sam held out an arm to halt Jade. Then he quietly laid his cycle down in the grass, unshipped his Colt revolver, and took a few steps forward. After he'd gone forty yards, he motioned her to follow.

Jade joined him, Winchester in hand, keeping her eyes and ears on the surrounding landscape. A striped skink raced across their path, the minuscule lizard scurrying for cover. A few red-billed firefinches squeaked and chittered in the trees, which went a long way toward easing Jade's fears that the shed on Forster's property was occupied. Silence from the woods would have been more worrisome. A clump of swallowtail butterflies exploded in a spray of gold at their approach, revealing a broken well base near where the house had once stood. The pump and handle lay rusting to the side, partly blackened from the fire.

They paused in front of the shed, taking in the tall sapling and the smaller scrubby brush in front of the bare wood door. The entire structure was no wider than eight feet. "Doesn't look like much," whispered Sam. "Does the door open out or in?"

An interesting question. Jade mentally chided herself for not thinking of it herself. All of Neville's and Avery's buildings opened out, as did Harry's doorway, and she'd assumed this one worked the same way. That was why she'd dismissed the building as unusable.

"Only one way to find out," she said, and quickly marched up to the door, bullying her way past the brush. She turned the knob and pulled. The door opened four inches before hitting the sapling. "Out," she announced. "No one could get in here." But as she turned, she paused and studied the brush to the side. In this light, she could make out a faint path. It might be only a game trail made by a small antelope but its deliberate skirting of the shed looked more purposeful.

Human.

A blue-eared starling burst out the door.

Jade shut the door and rejoined Sam. "I can imagine rodents gnawing their way inside, but a bird? How did it get in there?"

"Hole in the roof?"

"Then why not fly out that same way? I think it got trapped in there the last time this building was opened. And that had to be relatively recently for it to be alive. I found what looks like a path to the back."

Sam leaned his angular body so as to catch the same shadows that had first alerted Jade. She heard a soft click as he cocked the hammer on his Colt. He moved onto the trail, Jade right behind him. The trail had been well hidden with brush piled in front to obscure it. She turned and walked backwards, covering his back with her Winchester. Jade felt her pulse accelerate and took a deep breath, forcing her body to calm down.

Lilith won't be in there, Jade told herself. *She'd have shot through the door at us by now.*

Or would she? This was a woman it didn't pay to underestimate. She could still be lying in wait, hoping for a better chance at a more certain shot.

The shed was larger than it appeared from the front, nearly fifteen feet deep, and the back seven feet was a more recent construction than the front. To the casual eye, the rear wall was covered in fallen debris, but Jade detected the outline of another door under the limbs.

"I'll be dipped," said Sam. "Very clever."

"Can't be anyone home," said Jade. "Otherwise the brush would be shifted aside. Unless . . ." She found a latch made to look like a branch and pulled the door open. The rest of the limbs followed with it. "The branches are fastened to the door itself."

"She's clever. You've got to give her that."

Jade wished she'd brought her flashlight as she peered into the gloomy interior, waiting for her eyes to adjust to the dim light. She heard Sam rummage in his pockets and soon a bright beam pierced the blackness. "Good going, Sam."

They went inside, leaving the door open so as to hear if anyone approached. Sam played his light over a well-stocked hideaway complete with a cot, a spirit stove, a small table and chair, and shelves nailed to the wall. A threadbare rug lay beside the cot and the shelves were stocked with canned goods and a coil of rope hung from a nail.

"Plenty of food," said Sam. "Water's another issue, though."

"The well at Harry's still works. When I found Holly there, I noticed that the pump had been primed recently."

"So someone's using that for their water source." Sam looked around the floor. "There's a tin bucket. Dry now."

"Over here," said Jade, directing Sam's light to a heavy sheet of canvas on the far wall. "Let's see what she's got here." She pulled aside the curtain to see rows of metal boxes, not unlike ammunition tins. Slinging her rifle onto her back, she reached for a box when Sam stopped her.

"Wait," he called. "Use your handkerchief if you touch something. We don't want Finch finding our prints all over everything."

Jade nodded and fished out her large, white handkerchief, wrapping it around her right-hand fingers. She opened one of the boxes and whistled. "Saint Peter's little fishes, will you look at that!" Inside were large nuggets of gold, winking back in the light's beam. A paper inside identified them as coming from Katanga province in the Belgian Congo.

"Open another," said Sam.

Jade complied and, one by one, looked into each of the eight boxes. Five held gold nuggets, but others held papers. Jade leafed past maps, many of the northern territory. Underneath was a mining claim form, with the location penned in, deeded to some as yet unpicked name.

"This must be for her mining scheme." Jade opened yet another box. "Pellyn filled in some names and then he had Waters look for someone to invest in it with him. We found a few of those in Pellyn's medical office. Look, here's a pile of business contracts they've accumulated over the years. They go back three years at least." She did a quick tally. "Fourteen! That's a lot of partners. Some went in for a hundred pounds, some for five hundred, others more. What do you bet they're all dead, too?"

"Of convenient accidents," added Sam. "Lilith was in prison for some of that time. Pellyn must have been running the game from here. This place is too rough for Lilith, I should think," said Sam.

Jade nodded. "I saw a photo of Lilith with a work gang. She brought gold out of the Congo—illegally, I would imagine. I don't think old Leopold would have let anyone take anything out of his private realm."

"There was always a lot of graft and backstabbing involved with the men he left to run his fiefdom," said Sam. "Especially soon after he died. It might have been easier than you think to mine illegally. As long as you were willing to use the native labor ruthlessly, you could get hired on to manage an area. The more brutal, the better."

"Leaving the manager free and clear to skim off the top," concluded Jade.

"But recently, the new Belgian government changed some of the rules. Pellyn and Lilith probably lost their opportunity. That's when they went to falsifying documents to dupe would-be investors in a Kenyan mine."

"How did she get the form?" asked Jade. "Could she have had a contact in the land office?"

Sam shrugged. "It would only take one form," he said, "and it might even have been from a genuine claim. After that, they could find someone with a press to make a master and forge copies. But I think if you look at this, you'll find another answer." He pointed to some bottles on the shelf and a signed contract bearing Waters' name. The name was barely visible now, the ink having been lifted with the various solvents in the bottles.

"So they could've reused a deed once they got rid of Waters' name and filled in some other name."

"Lilith has lost both her partners now," said Sam. "Pellyn killed Stockton for cheating on him and now he's dead, too. I don't doubt she'll soon find another."

"What's in here?" Jade asked as she pulled down a wooden chop box. Sam held the flashlight over her shoulder as she opened the lid. "Son of a biscuit!"

"They could've poisoned all Nairobi with this," Jade exclaimed as she examined the array of bottles, each labeled as some drug.

"Quite a pharmacy," said Sam.

"Arsenic!" exclaimed Jade as she lifted a bottle.

Sam took out his own handkerchief and held up several bottles, reading them off. "'Antimony, potassium iodide, chaulmoogra oil.'" He carefully lowered the last one into the box. "Wait a minute. I don't think these are meant to be poisons. I recognize that last one." He paused, eyes closed as though he were searching his memory. "It's a leprosy treatment. All of these are leprosy treatments. Chaulmoogra was first found in India, I believe."

"Dymant—I mean Pellyn—was a physician," said Jade. "He said he'd worked in India. If he went into the Congo to smuggle out gold, he might have gone in as a doctor rather than as a mine overseer. He'd need to carry the tools of the trade to pass. That would include leprosy treatments."

She lifted out a square tin and carefully pried it open. The spicy scent smacked her nostrils and she broke into a cold sweat. "This is my tea! It always seemed a bit too coincidental that I managed to get a gift of spiced red tea and then someone drugged it. This proves that the gift didn't come from Avery's friend. It was sent already poisoned."

Sam took the tin and sniffed. "Hard to say what all is in this. The spices would disguise a lot, I should think. I smell nutmeg. In strong enough quantities, it's a poison, too." He started to close the lid. "Look at the design burned into the bottom. Isn't that Lilith's symbol?"

Jade gingerly touched the moon eclipsing the sun. "This is where Mutahi saw it."

"And why he had to die," added Sam. "We have plenty of evidence here to link Pellyn to your hallucinations, the gold mine scheme, and with the murders, but very little to link Lilith. She covers her tracks well," said Sam. "And I'm sure she learned from her mistakes in Morocco."

"If we only had an idea of where she's been hiding. Surely not in here." Jade tried to run through everyone she'd had contact with in Nairobi and came up blank. "I can't recall anyone with a scar."

"Lilith would be subtle, Jade." Sam smiled and stroked her smooth cheek with the back of his fingers.

Jade felt something akin to an electric tingle. Then she realized what Sam was driving at. "Of course. She probably disguised the scar with some face paints or creams. Good heavens, after that last safari with the actors, I should be used to makeup being used as a deception. You can do anything with it. Appear young, old. Why didn't I think of that?"

"Because you don't use any artifice. Large glasses might hide much of it, too."

"Sun protectors! Of course," said Jade. "Cyril said his kidnapper had *very* big black eyes."

Sam touched her cheek again, then pulled his hand back. "I'd bet my plane, if I still had it, that Lilith is in the search party for you."

"A constable?" Jade paused, considering her idea. "No, wait!" She snapped her fingers. "A reporter! Bev's sister, Emily, met with the reporter from the *Leader*. He's a small man and he wears very large sun protectors, as I recall. Emily said he had rooms in the Victoria and they looked opulent."

"If that was Lilith, it would explain how she was able to leave notes and packets for Steven Holly so easily," said Sam. "She lived in the same hotel. And reporter is a job that would give her access to a lot of people and places."

"Spit fire!" Jade said. "*The Leader* is the paper running most of the articles on riots and problems in the Indian district. Good lord, you don't suppose she actually fomented a riot to have Pellyn killed, do you?" But even as she said it, she knew the woman was capable of throwing away anyone, even her own lover. "Should we go back into town, Sam, and confront her?"

"Too risky. She'll be in that search party for you. After reading my notice, she'd want to see for herself that you were dead. Then she'll come for my rendezvous. If we go into town, we might miss her or, worse yet, alert her that we're onto her."

Jade's head was still reeling from the insight. As she turned around, another object, tucked into a darker corner, caught Jade's eyes as Sam's flashlight brushed past it. She took hold of his hand and carefully swung the light back.

"Well, dip me in phosphorus and call me a match," he said. "It's a lantern. An old magic lantern."

Jade reached for it with the handkerchief and brought it down for a better look. The lantern was a large one, nearly the size of her old Graflex camera, with a space inside for a candle. "When I first stopped by this place, I saw a monkey here. I thought she had some white root in her hand, but it was a candle stub. Lilith or Pellyn must have dropped it when they brought back the lantern."

Inside the lantern was a flat packet wrapped in brown paper. Jade set the lantern on the table and opened the packet, exposing glass photo disks with transparent photographic images. Each image was carefully tinted, but the images themselves made Jade shudder. The body in each was the same, David in his uniform, but where David's smiling face showed on one, a skeletal head showed on another, and in between, half skeletal and half flesh. Rotating the disk at the right speed would give the illusion of the face melting into a skull, especially when projected onto wavering smoke. Add a mind distorted by drugs and one got a convincing ghost.

"That explains the image of David by the barn," Jade said. "How could she do that to her own son's picture?"

"Would you expect anything less of her? She's Lilith," said Sam. "But it gives me an idea." He took Jade by the shoulders. "Now listen up. I told you once that you weren't a killer, and you aren't. But this plan of mine, of ours, might put us in a position where one of us has to shoot to kill."

"You're not a killer either, Sam."

"But I did shoot down men in the war. *This* is war and *we* are on the side of good. So if it comes to it, just remember these words: 'Be sure that you are right, and then go ahead.'"

"Abe Lincoln?"

Sam shook his head. "Davy Crockett."

"Well, blast. We know how the Alamo turned out."

Sam eyed the magic lantern. "This gives me an idea. I'm going to create my own diversion to fool Lilith when she comes tonight." He examined the glass disk with David's images. "Amazing in a warped sort of way. That shows a great deal of planning."

Jade shuddered, remembering that nightmarish vision. "It shows a complete lack of moral scruples. What's your plan?"

He lit one of the candles. "There's room between the pictures of David. I'm going to make a silhouette of a seated man and shine it inside my tent."

"Ah, to make it seem that you're inside when you're not. Won't she just shoot?"

"She might, in which case I'm not the target," Sam said.

"But I'm betting that her ravenous desire for vengeance on Pili outweighs her need for killing a blackmailer."

Jade shivered and Sam put his arm around her. "Worried?"

"Yes, and I've been thinking about Neville leading that search party today. Everyone thinks I'm dead. It's a bit unnerving. Lilith should be gloating by now."

"I imagine she's furious that you escaped that easily. I'm sure she had big plans for you." Sam took down a tin mug from a shelf and held it over the flame, collecting soot. "Can you find another mug or a bowl? Oh, and a bottle of alcohol. I saw one by the medicines."

Jade brought the items to him. Sam scraped the accumulated soot from the bottom of the mug into the dish. Next he added a few drops of alcohol, enough to make a slurry. When he had enough, he used his knife tip to painstakingly apply the ink to the glass. "This should make a decent image. I'll put the lantern in my tent and shine it on the canvas flap. It will look like I'm sitting in a chair, waiting."

"Where am I going to be?" asked Jade.

Sam looked up from his work. "I'd planned for you to be atop the falls with a clear line of fire, but now I'm having second thoughts."

"Sam! You promised me that I'd be a partner in this."

He applied a bit more ink and surveyed the result. "That was before we found this hideout. What if she comes here to collect or destroy evidence? She'll know we've been in here. She might just flee the country, or she might come to my camp even warier."

"You want me to stay here, then?"

Sam blew gently on the image he'd made and nodded.

"Looks rather contemplative, doesn't he?" He set the disk aside and took Jade's hands in his. "If she comes here, you'll be waiting for her. We can't risk letting her escape again."

"Somehow, I don't see her trying to. As far-reaching as the British Empire is, she's running out of places to go. All right, Sam. I'll stay here. And between the two of us, we'll finish this tonight."

CHAPTER 26

*We often fear what we can't see, the hidden dangers.
It's the lion hiding in the tall grass, the rhino or buffalo asleep in the
ravine. But nothing tops the terror of a lurking crocodile.*
—The Traveler

HARRY DROVE AT A BREAKNECK SPEED towards Parklands, pushing his truck past forty miles per hour in the open grasslands. Considering the hidden wallows and rocks as well as the brush, it was a risky act, but Harry was beyond any thoughts or emotions save a burning need for revenge. Like smoke from a brushfire, it filled his nostrils, tainted his mouth, and stung his eyes. The accompanying blaze scorched across his soul, leaving a blackened and raw wasteland.

How could Dunbury be such a damned fool? He hired some wastrel and, soon after, there were threats against the children. Couldn't he see the connection? The newcomer had obviously duped him and driven Jade to fly an injured plane to her death.

Her death!

Harry ground his teeth and bit his lower lip. *Jade!* Except possibly for Dunbury's own wife, Harry had never met a woman with the pluck and daring of Jade. And he'd never wanted a woman in the way he'd wanted her. In his head, he knew he could never have her, but it was enough to know she existed and to have her dance in and out of his life, refreshing it and all of Africa like the rains after a drought.

He'd find this Fairley and kill him.

AN HOUR AFTER SAM LEFT, Jade couldn't abide the shack any longer. True, from within, she'd have an element of surprise and a clear shot at Lilith when she came through the door, but that was only if it was still light when Lilith arrived. And Jade felt as confined as when she'd sat in a cage as leopard bait. There had to be a better place to make a stand.

She listened at the door and, hearing nothing, pushed it open, her Winchester in hand. The shifting shadows told her that the day had moved on into afternoon. Sam should be putting his tent up now. He'd promised Jade that he'd first motor into Nairobi and leave word with Finch to arrest the reporter from the *Leader*. They'd argued that point for nearly thirty minutes before Sam had conceded.

"You can leave some of these documents for him with an anonymous note," she'd argued.

"But if he doesn't arrest her, and she finds out, she'll be warier. She may go to ground," Sam had countered.

"Or it will drive her to your rendezvous more quickly. But we need to plug *all* the holes, Sam. I'll be here at the shack, you'll be back at the falls, and Finch can watch Nairobi." He'd finally agreed, but Jade could tell he wasn't happy with the idea.

He wants her dead, not recaptured.

To a large extent, Jade agreed. But she told herself that they had to make the moral effort to take her alive. Shooting Lilith had to be a last resort.

"The croc isn't getting that chance," argued Sam. "Why should she?"

Sam's question had been rhetorical, but Jade kept trying to answer it in her mind. So far she hadn't succeeded.

The tree line stood a few yards from the shed. Jade eyed the stand, looking for a tree that would provide decent cover and conceal her while giving her a clear view of the building. After fifteen minutes of deliberation, she chose the one that the little vervet monkey had climbed. But just as Jade reached it, she saw something sticking out from the brush below.

A rawhide pouch! It was the kind worn by both Jelani and his mentor. Neither of them would have left it without an excellent reason. It was a mark of their office.

Jelani left it as a sign. He's here. She looked back at the shack. *But where?* They'd searched the entire place. Or had they? If this outer door had been hidden, might another one also be hidden inside?

Jade stuck the pouch in her pocket and went back in. Sam had left his flashlight with her and she played it over every surface, looking intently for a hidden door. There were no scrapes on the floor, nothing to show that a set of shelves swung out.

She stepped outside and paced the building's dimensions, then measured the interior. *Nothing!*

She paced it again and this time she felt more than heard the echo of a hollow space. The sound was as faint as a breath, but it was real.

Under the floor!

Jade grabbed the worn rug and threw it back, revealing an inset door. There was no handle, only a wooden bolt that fit into a recess in the floor. She drew back the bolt, then used it to hoist the door, propping it against the bed frame. Jade shone the light into the Stygian darkness.

"Jelani?" she called.

No one answered. Slinging her rifle across her back, Jade descended the wooden ladder. The air below was suffocatingly close, dank and ripe with the scent of stale sweat and urine. But it didn't smell of death or decay, and that gave Jade hope. She drew on it as she turned, willing it to steady her hand as she ran the beam over the cellar.

Jelani!

He lay in a corner, his hands bound to his feet behind his back. Jade leaned her rifle against the wall and knelt beside him, feeling for a pulse. It was there, faint but steady. She pulled her knife from her boot and sliced his bonds. Then she gently massaged his wrists and ankles.

"I've got to get you out of here," she murmured. "But how?" Unless he regained consciousness and could cling to her back, she couldn't see a way clear. It was too far to try to lift him and there was nothing to stand on.

Rope! She remembered seeing a coil. She could tie it around his chest, under his arms, and haul him up like a sack of meal.

Jelani moaned faintly. "Lie still," she said. "I'll be right back with some water."

Jade went up top, picked up her canteen, and took the rope. When she reached the cellar floor, she gently lifted Jelani's head and let the water trickle down his throat. He swallowed once, then coughed, his chest and shoulders jerking with each spasm. His eyes flickered open.

"Easy," she whispered, shifting her leg to ease the cramp in her left knee. "Did Finch put you in here?"

Jelani shook his head weakly. "He released me. Taken on way home."

"Who?" She offered more water, but Jelani had fainted again.

That was when she heard the elephant trumpet.

We've got to get out of here now! Jade leaped for the ladder but before she could reach the second rung, the trapdoor above her slammed shut.

SAM HEARD THE COMMOTION all the way up to the police station. Glass shattering, shouts, screams, and general pandemonium erupted from somewhere in the Indian district. A phalanx of European curiosity seekers—mostly men—hurried down Government Road, eager to catch a glimpse of the riot.

There was no one manning the police station desk.

"Damn!" Sam rummaged for paper and a pencil, then wrote a quick note for Finch.

Inspector. Have reason to believe that the reporter from the Leader, *the small man with the large sunglasses, is actually Lilith Worthy in disguise. Do not let her leave Nairobi.*

After a moment's hesitation, Sam signed it as Lord Dunbury, hoping Finch would pay more heed to that name than to an anonymous note. He folded the note in half with the mining forms inside and wrote *FINCH* on the outside.

As he exited the station, Sam collided with a young man hurrying down the street. "What's going on?" Sam asked.

The man brandished a stout stick. "Some Indians said that the plague is a government plot to kill them. The district's in an uproar. I'm going to establish order before they attack us."

He hurried away, seemingly anxious to get into the fray.

Sam felt an uneasy twinge in his chest as he started his motorcycle. What better way to occupy the police today than to pay someone to foment a riot? There was no way he could count on Finch to find Lilith in town now, not with all this mess. But Sam wondered if he could himself. He made his way around the gathering throngs and headed for the Victoria Hotel. The street and lobby were nearly empty and Sam asked the clerk for the reporter's room number.

"That fellow's gone, sir. Checked out two days ago, he did. Not sure where he moved to. Didn't leave any forwarding notice here."

Sam thanked the clerk and hurried back to his motorcycle. He needed to get to the falls, set up his decoy tent, and hide. At least, he mused, Jade was safely out of the way. There was no way that a woman like Lilith, one who kept extravagantly appointed rooms, would stay in that dumpy shack.

HARRY DROVE STRAIGHT FOR AVERY'S STABLES. If that Fairley was on-site, then that was where he'd be. He didn't even shut the truck door when he got out. He just grabbed his Holland & Holland and drew back the bolt, putting a cartridge in the chamber.

The first shot in the leg. After he tells me why he killed Jade, I'll put a second in his black heart.

But other than the horses peacefully munching hay in their clean stalls, the barn was empty. Harry hadn't expected that. For a moment, he stood in the center aisle, uncertain what to do next. Then he heard the sputter of a badly maintained motorcycle coming up the drive.

He ran around the paddock towards the house in time to see a pale woman alight from a rickshaw and approach the house, carrying a small valise. The rickshaw driver hurried after her with another, larger suitcase. The woman was met at the door by a servant dressed in immaculate white. Harry recognized the servant as Farhani, who bowed to the woman.

"Memsahib Heathington," Farhani said, "it is good you are home. Everyone is fled."

"Fled!" The woman stood rooted to the veranda, her gaze darting every which way. She spotted Harry. "I recognize you. You came to our camp. Jade said you took sick afterwards."

Harry approached and touched his hat brim. "Harry Hascombe, Miss Heathington. Dunbury knows me."

Emily looked at Farhani for confirmation. He nodded. "Then," she demanded, "perhaps you can be so good as to tell me what the devil is Farhani talking about? Where is my sister?"

Before Harry could answer, Farhani broke in. "They are fled to escape an evil kidnapper that threatened a Guiding Girl and the children. Memsahib left a letter for you." He stepped aside as Emily led the way into the house.

"You are Lady Dunbury's sister?" asked Harry.

"I am." She offered her hand for him to shake. "Emily Heathington, Mr. Hascombe. I've heard your name mentioned."

Farhani handed a sealed envelope to Emily, who ripped it open, scattering shreds of the envelope onto the carpet. The note inside, written in Beverly's neat hand on fine linen rag, was brief. Emily read it aloud.

"'Emily, so sorry to cause you fright. We're safe, but we fear someone may harm the children. Threats were made against Mary Postlewaithe. We'd hoped to have this resolved before your return, but if you are reading this, then you may also be in some danger. You should return to Mombassa until I can send word to you. Love, Beverly.'

"Return to Mombassa," Emily said. "What sort of nonsense is this?" The clock chimed two in the background. Emily looked to Farhani. "Do you know anything else?"

"Yes. Memsahib Jade is dead."

Emily shrieked and would have fallen if Harry hadn't caught her. She covered her mouth with her hands and stared, horrified at the white-robed man before them, looking at him as though he were the angel of death. "Dead?" she breathed.

Harry guided her to a chair and poured a glass of brandy for her. "Afraid so," he said.

"Indeed," said Farhani. "That is what the egg peddler told the cook."

Harry pressed the glass into her hand. "The aeroplane she was flying was tampered with and she crashed. And someone put a notice in this morning's paper saying that the lioness was dead."

Emily drank the brandy in two gulps. "Then it was premeditated murder." She looked at Harry. "You came here to tell Avery?"

Harry looked sidewise at Farhani without answering.

"You can speak in front of him," said Emily.

"No," said Harry. "I came here to . . . to find a man named Fairley. But he's not here."

"Fairley? That disreputable-looking Australian whom Avery hired? Why?"

"He's the one who tampered with Jade's plane. It's in to-day's paper."

Emily found the day's newspapers and flipped through them, looking for the personal advertisements. "Horrid," she said after reading it.

Harry studied Emily for a moment, assessing her. "What do you know of him? How did Dunbury come to hire him?"

Emily related the tale and added that she seemed to be the only one who didn't trust him. "As to where he is, who can say? I took the down train to Mombassa on Tuesday. He was here then." She looked at her valises, placed just inside the door. "I returned after only one night. At first a trip sounded like an adventure, but when I got to Mombassa, it only seemed noisy."

Harry nodded. "It is at that." He rose and paced. "And now we learn that Dunbury and your sister have fled somewhere. Neville Thompson said that his wife and son were hiding, too. Jade had flown them someplace."

"Do you have any idea where they went?" asked Emily.

"Thompson started the search near Kinangop, not far from Naivasha."

Emily stood and went for the telephone, a candlestick contraption on the side table. After jiggling the receiver several times, she spoke into the handset. "Operator, hello. Connect me to— No, this is not Lady Dunbury. Yes, very tragic, now please connect me to—" She immediately replaced the earpiece into the handset and stepped back, her hands clasped in front of her. "If I ask for them in Naivasha, I might give away their hiding place."

"Like as not, they took the train farther north," said Harry. "But it's a clever thought."

"Should we call the police?"

"Inspector Finch already knows about this," Harry said.

"And he's probably got his hands full with the riot in the Indian district," said Emily. "I heard of it when I got off the train. It sounded like a war." She looked at Harry. "Well, Mr. Hascombe, it appears it's up to us to find this blackguard Fairley."

"Begging your pardon, miss, but—"

Emily held up her hand for silence. "Mr. Hascombe, I beg you to listen. My sister is in hiding. Beverly does not hide. She has always been a fighter. It was a trait that, as her older sister, I tried to soften. I was wrong, and it's high time that another Heathington signed up to fight." She lifted her chin. "No one threatens my little niece and gets away with it. And no one who destroys a brave woman like Jade deserves to live."

Harry smiled. "Very well, Miss Heathington."

"Emily," she corrected.

"All right, Emily. But unless you are privy to more information, I have no idea where to look." He heard a quiet cough at his elbow and turned. Farhani stood at attention.

"Pardon, memsahib, bwana. I have overheard. Are you speaking of the man locked in the darkness room? I take him food two times a day. Bwana Dunbury says he is there to keep safe, but I think that he has perhaps gone afoul of God."

Emily and Harry stood motionless for a moment before Harry bolted for the door.

THE SLAM OF WOOD ON WOOD echoed in the stagnant air. Jade felt the reverberation shudder down the ladder. It rattled under her hand and feet as a wave of dust pulsed across her face and the noise slapped her ears. She instinctively ducked as from a blow before resuming her frantic climb. She took the rungs two at a time and pushed with one hand against the door. It gave an inch before a force on the other side pounded back. If she'd harbored any hope that the door had fallen on its own, it was gone now.

Jade heard the soft scrape as the wooden bolt slid home. For a moment, Jade froze. Maybe the person on the other side didn't know she was down here. Perhaps someone thought that Jelani had gotten loose and tried to escape. The thought vanished, an idea made of mist. There was no doubt that the person up top was Lilith, and Lilith was no fool. She'd know that Jelani couldn't have opened the door from below. *She knows she's trapped someone. But she doesn't know who.*

Jade eyed her rifle, leaning against the wall. *Lilith wants me. Could I lure her down the ladder?*

"You'd better get back down the ladder now, before I decide to shoot you." The voice from above was a woman's, as harsh as sleet.

Jade complied without speaking. She stepped back towards her Winchester. If she shot, the bullet would likely pass through the inch-thick wood, but would it hit Lilith? Jade decided to wait. When Lilith left, she'd shoot around the bolt to break it loose. But Lilith had to leave first.

"Now," said Lilith, "you're going to tell me who you are."

Jade didn't answer, her mind racing for a solution. Mutahi had come here and found some of the poison tea. Perhaps she could convince Lilith that she was yet another Kikuyu.

"I asked a question!" snapped Lilith. "Who is down there?"

Jade looked at Jelani and had a sudden flash of inspiration. She twisted her voice to sound old. *"Saidia haraka!"* she wailed. *Get help quickly.* "*Niko pamojana mtoto.*" *I'm with my child.*

For a moment, Jade held her breath. Would her ruse work? Would Lilith believe that Jelani's mother had come to find him?

The answer chilled Jade's heart.

"Ah, Jade. I cannot tell you how it gladdens my heart that you're not dead. Yet! That was a very good try just now. I almost believed you to be a native woman, but your voice is burned into my memory."

Lilith laughed, the sound of a glacial river tumbling over a rock, freezing whatever it touched while it inexorably ground away at the stone beneath it. "I'm not certain how you managed to fake your own death, but it was most convincing. I trust you are the O. Fairley in the newspaper. Or is it Lord Dunbury? No matter. I'll make a quick check along the river this evening in case. If there is someone waiting, I'll have another nice hostage to keep you from trying anything foolish when I return. And then I'll repay you for *everything* and with interest."

The last sound Jade heard from atop was that of something heavy being dragged across the floor on top of the door.

HARRY REACHED THE DARKROOM BEFORE EMILY, only to realize that he didn't have the keys to unlock it. He heard a gentle jingling behind him and turned.

"You'll need these," Emily said, holding up a set of keys. "I got them from Farhani."

"Good thinking," Harry said, taking them from her hand. "You'd better wait outside."

"I will not," she snapped.

Harry sighed. He'd never met so many temperamental women as he had since Jade had moved here. "Very well, but let *me* interrogate him."

A soft *hmph* told Harry that he'd have no luck getting this woman to comply either. But he no sooner had the keys than three girls with very determined faces raced to join them. They were dressed in their Girl Guide uniforms and wore canvas bags slung over their shoulders.

"Mary, Elspeth, Helen!" said Emily. "Why aren't you girls in school?"

"We dismissed ourselves," said Mary, "as soon as we heard the news about the riots."

"We told the headmistress that we were needed to minister to any wounded," added Helen. She reached in a cloth pouch and pulled out a roll of bandages.

"But when we got to the police," continued Elspeth, "we learned about Lieutenant Jade, so we came here straightaway. Where is Captain Dunbury?"

"She's gone," said Emily. "She's hiding with the baby."

"You girls go home or back to school," ordered Harry. He flapped a hand at them as though he were shooing chickens. The girls didn't budge.

"We can tell that you're in the middle of something important," said Helen. "And we plan to help you." The other girls nodded once, emphatically.

"It's our sworn duty," added Mary.

"Be damned," muttered Harry. "Miss Heathington, tend to these girls."

Emily grabbed the keys as Harry slipped one into the lock. "Mr. Hascombe, I intend to find out what this prisoner knows."

"Prisoner!" echoed the girls in unison. Their eyes widened.

"You must interrogate," said Elspeth. "We'll be witnesses."

Harry growled at them. "Then stay back!"

The four females jumped back a half pace, enough for Harry to regain control of the keys and unlock the door. He wasn't certain who or what to expect inside, but it certainly wasn't the sight of Steven Holly sitting placidly on a cot, reading a book. The darkroom had been wired for electricity and a lamp burned brightly on a table near his elbow. Opposite him were the wet sinks used for developing film. Avery had spared no expense for Jade, even to the point of installing a lavatory at one end. Before Harry could recover from his surprise, Emily pushed past him.

Steven Holly didn't raise his face above his book. "I say, Farhani. About time you served lunch. I'm starved."

"Mr. Holly!" Emily exclaimed. "What is the meaning of this?"

Holly dropped the book and scrambled to his feet. "Miss Heathington? What an unexpected surprise." Then he saw Harry and the girls. "Oh, dear. And Hascombe and . . . Mary?"

Mary elbowed her way to the front, fists on her hips. "Uncle Steven! What did you do? And why did someone tell Mother that I might have been kidnapped?"

Holly blinked back at them like an owl struggling with sudden daylight. "Mary? What are you doing here? Does your mother know?"

"Does my mother know that her brother is locked up in Captain Beverly's outbuilding?" Mary sniffed and tipped up her chin. "No, thank heaven, she does not. It would break her heart." She wagged a finger at him. "But *you* haven't answered my question. Why are you in here?"

Harry was about to physically remove the lot of them when he noted that Holly looked more worried about seeing the girls than seeing him. He folded his arms across his chest and glowered. "Answer the girl!"

"Well . . . I . . . you see . . ." Holly stammered.

Harry stepped in close. Holly shrank back onto the cot, pulling his head down like a turtle drawing into his shell. "Someone damaged the aeroplane Jade was flying and it crashed," said Harry. "She's dead and I think you did it!" He cracked his knuckles by Holly's ear.

"No!" cried Holly. "I admit I've done things I'm not proud of. It's all because of that gold mine. Since then, my life has been threatened more than once." His gaze darted past Harry to his niece and Emily. "I was told I'd be crocodile food if I didn't help someone get hold of Jade. I thought someone only wanted to hold her for ransom. I swear," he added after their shocked gasps, "that I didn't expect anyone to kill her."

"You didn't think at all!" roared Harry.

"You'd better tell us everything, Mr. Holly," said Emily. "Or I'll see to it that you spend the rest of your miserable life in a prison cell."

"Please," moaned Holly. He clasped his hands together in entreaty. "Just let me leave the colony. Jade's already dead. Nothing I can say will bring her back, and if I help you, *I'll* be killed."

Harry whispered in Holly's ear, "I'll kill you myself if you don't tell me everything."

Holly nodded, his body shaking. "It started after Mary's birthday party. I was approached that evening by a man dressed in black and muffled up to his eyes. He wasn't particularly large, perhaps Miss Heathington's height, but he had a presence that one does not defy. There was something about his face, the part I could see. A thin scar running up from the nose and across the eyelid, and those cold eyes." Holly shuddered again. "Look at me! I'm not a fighter. I work in a ruddy bank. I was terrified. I couldn't even tell Jade when she caught me."

Holly shook his finger at each of them. "Do you know, he told me that he could kill me just for mouthing to everyone about the mine. It was to have been a secret, he said, but he'd spare me the fate of the others if I helped him." He put his head in his hands and sobbed. "I didn't want to be thrown to a crocodile!"

"Continue, Mr. Holly," said Emily, her voice cool and subdued.

Holly pulled out a wrinkled handkerchief and blew his nose. "I was ordered to lure Jade to Hascombe's old house, where I'd pretend to be in a faint. But Lady Dunbury and you girls came after her, spoiling the plan. This man cleared out as soon as he heard the Overland." He looked at Harry. "I was glad. I didn't want Jade to come to harm. She was a swell girl."

"Was," said Harry.

"And the barrettes?" asked Mary. "How did you get my barrettes and pin?"

"Yes, well. I was told to collect something from one of the girls in case Jade got away on this first attempt. Something to lure her again. You were just the easiest, since you're my niece. You can imagine my horror when I was given those barrettes and the pin back with that terrible ear thrown in with them. I couldn't let anything happen to you, Mary."

"But now our Lieutenant Jade is dead," said Mary softly.

"And innocent children have been threatened," added Emily. "This is . . . it's unconscionable, Mr. Holly!" She turned to Harry. "Do you think we should go to the police with this information? Perhaps that fiend is again at your farm. After all, Mr. Holly lured Jade there once before."

"I can take you there," said Holly. "If you let me leave the colony afterwards. I think I know where he's hiding."

Harry motioned for Emily to follow him outside, where they could talk without Holly overhearing. "It's a sure bet that the police are too busy right now to do anything," said Harry.

"The notice in the paper," whispered Emily, "said that this Fairley was to meet someone tonight. That he wanted to become a partner."

Harry looked at Emily with fresh admiration. "You're right. If I can get there first, I can capture Fairley and whoever else is involved."

"*I?*" asked Emily. "Don't you mean *we?* You can't keep an eye on Mr. Holly *and* shoot these murderers."

"And we're going, too," said Mary, who'd been listening in with the other girls. She reached into her satchel and pulled out her sling. "We can provide cover."

"Absolutely not!" shouted Harry. "I draw the line at children coming along." He went back inside, jerked Holly to his feet, and dragged him to his truck. The girls and Emily followed. Harry snapped at them, "I'm taking Mr. Holly with me. I am not taking any of you."

He shoved Holly into the vehicle and climbed in, spraying gravel as he raced away.

CHAPTER 27

*As long as animals need to drink, they will come to the water
and brave the danger. They have little choice.*
—The Traveler

SAM INHALED DEEPLY, striving to remain calm. The sun had
moved farther west, well into afternoon, increasing the
chances that someone would spot his shifting shadow. He'd
never developed the level of patience that true hunters possessed. He'd always preferred to stalk prey rather than sit
long hours in a blind or up a tree. And thank heaven he'd
never had to spend months waiting in a muck-filled trench.
His had been a world of activity, of moving gears and flying
machines.

So far everything was quiet, as he expected. At least, all
he'd heard was one lone fish splash downriver, and the falls
muted any noise from upriver. He had little doubt that Lilith
had started that riot today. All her recent plans in Nairobi
were unraveling, thanks to Jade. Stockton's and Waters'
deaths, made to look like accidents, had been uncovered as
murder. The gold mine scheme was exposed, thanks to Waters' greed and Steven Holly's big mouth. And now with Pellyn dead, the best Lilith could hope for would be to escape.

She had to know that the police were interested in finding her now. The riot would keep them busy while she tied up loose ends.

Even the riot had been masterfully orchestrated. A long series of articles in the *Leader*, decrying the horrid squalor of the Indian district and the lack of response from the government to provide alternate home sites, made the resulting plague look like a brutal attempt at reducing the Asian population. The tinder laid, all Lilith had to do was light the spark. A word to a shopkeeper who'd lost a child would do it.

Anyone other than Lilith would have taken the opportunity to leave. And inadvertently, faking Jade's death might have hastened Lilith's departure. But Sam had given her one last reason to stay. He'd let it be known that someone knew about her and could bring her the full revenge she desired or he could bring her down.

Sam was counting on Lilith's bloodlust. She wanted to find her husband's bastard child. But just in case all she wanted was to tie up a last loose end by killing him, he provided her with a target. A few minutes ago he had lit the magic lantern, creating the image of the patiently seated man inside the tent. Then he had taken up his position in the boulders with the falls to his back. Now he waited.

HARRY KEPT ONE EYE ON THE ROAD and another on the sniveling man cowering in the seat beside him. He didn't believe that Holly could show him anything he couldn't find himself, but he didn't intend to let the man out of his sight. If nothing else, Harry wanted to beat the man to jelly for his involvement in Jade's death, and he couldn't very well do that in front of all those females.

He still couldn't. Hot on his tail in Dunbury's Hupmobile was that Heathington woman and those three girls. If he hadn't been so angry at them for following him, he might have admitted to a grudging admiration for their bravery and persistence.

Harry swerved around a Wakamba woman in the road who was carrying a basket of yams. He made the turn by Thika and skidded onto the track heading towards the new Athi Bridge. His tires spewed rust-colored dust but still he made out the Hupmobile. He wasn't going to lose them; that much was clear. He'd have to divert their attention to someplace safe.

Maybe I can convince them to stand watch at the ranch house while I go on.

A family of warthogs stood in a cluster on the other side of the bridge. Harry sounded the horn. It reminded him of a sick goose, and he couldn't imagine any animal taking fright at it.

"Get out of the way!" he bellowed out his open window.

The sow turned tail and bolted, her babies trotting hard on her heels, tails up like the poles on an electric tram. Harry shot off the bridge at a heart-stopping forty-five miles per hour. Then he left the road and went cross-country towards his ranch. His truck lurched and jolted over the ruts and brush.

She won't be able to follow now. A glance spared over his shoulder proved him wrong. If anything, Emily was gaining on him.

"That Heathington woman is persistent," Harry said.

Holly nodded dumbly, his face pale.

Harry hit the brakes hard at the ranch, spinning the truck and causing Holly to lurch forward and slam his shoulder against the doorframe. It gave Harry enough time to get out and seize Holly before he could recover and try to escape. "Now, where is this person hiding?" Harry demanded.

"Inside," said Holly.

Harry kept one hand on Holly's arm and grabbed his rifle from the truck as Emily and the girls pulled up. He shoved Holly towards the house. "Go on in then."

Holly stumbled once towards the door, then stopped, refusing to go any farther. Harry shoved his rifle at Holly's chest. "Move, man! And you ladies, stay clear!"

Harry followed Holly inside and made a quick search of the house. As he had suspected and feared, there was no sign of anyone else there. Not that he'd expected anyone. His best hope lay in going to Waters' campsite on the river. According to the notice in the paper, that was where this rendezvous would take place.

He grabbed Holly's shirt collar and shook him anyway. "Where is this mystery man, Holly? Tell me, or I swear, girls or no, I'll shoot you in the legs and leave you here to find your own way out."

"Please," begged Holly. "Just let me leave unhurt. I won't bother any of you again. I promise."

"Harry," called Emily from outside, "the girls found something." Harry joined them, dragging Holly with him.

"See here, Mr. Hascombe?" said Helen, pointing to some tire imprints. "Another motorcar or truck has been this way not so long ago. It went that way." She pointed east. "It may have gone around the mountain."

"It could have been anyone, right?" asked Holly, his voice squeaking as it took on an increased edge of nervousness. "It's probably not . . . him."

"These tracks were made recently," said Mary. "The grass has yet to spring all the way back up."

"Lieutenant Jade taught us that," added Elspeth.

Harry squatted beside the tracks. "You're right." He stood and stared at Holly. "How about it? Shall we go have a look?"

"I'll stay here with the ladies, if you don't mind," said Holly.

Harry pushed him towards the still-idling truck. "Oh, but I do. And this time, *you* drive so I can keep my eye on you." He patted his rifle and started to slide into the seat. "Emily, you and the girls should—"

The slam of automobile doors interrupted him as Emily and the girls got back into their car, which was also still running. *Blasted women! It's like having Lady Dunbury and three miniature Jades tagging along.*

Harry directed Holly to follow the trail. He expected it to continue on the eastern side, circumnavigating the mountain. To his surprise, the tracks turned into Forster's land. That they'd left again was also clear, but before he followed them, he wanted to have a look around.

"Stop here," he ordered. "Shut off the engine and get out. Maybe that Fairley is still here."

Harry was halfway out the door when he heard a muffled rifle shot coming from inside a shed. In his haste to get out, his own rifle strap caught on the door handle. But before he could free himself, the truck lurched forwards, dragging him with it.

JADE HAD NO INTENTION OF WAITING for Lilith to come back, and if that witch had one consistent chink in her armor, it was that she kept underestimating Jade's resourcefulness. *If she thinks a door bolt and a bunch of crates are going to stop me . . .*

Actually, Jade had to admit that the crates had her more worried than the bolt. She was counting on Lilith's age and smaller stature to stop the woman from moving more than Jade could lift. *All I have to do is break that bolt; then I can put my back into it.*

She took a long draw from the canteen, apologizing to the unconscious Jelani at her feet. "Sorry, but right now, I need this more than you. Otherwise, neither of us will need it." Then she took up her Winchester and aimed at the latch. The first shot hit the wooden bolt itself and Jade heard it career off the rounded surface. The whine of the ricochet was followed by shattering glass. She'd hit one of the bottles lining the shelf. She aimed her next shot a fraction behind the first, hoping to weaken the wooden bolt so it would snap when she pushed up against it. If that failed, she intended to keep shooting around it until she made a hole.

Not a bad plan, except that she had limited ammunition. "I only need one shot to get Lilith."

HARRY TRIED DESPERATELY TO FREE HIMSELF, but his rifle was around his neck with the strap caught in the door. "Holly!" he shouted, but the cry was choked off by a mouthful of dust sprayed up by the tire. Didn't the bastard know he was caught?

The open door swung back as Holly tried to turn. It slammed against Harry's head, and he went down under the blow. It became all too clear that Holly *did* know that he was caught and was doing everything in his power to shake him loose in order to escape. Harry rolled, trying to keep his legs out from under the rear tires as Holly spun in the opposite direction.

The next sight Harry saw was of Emily running after the truck, trying to stop Holly. It was topped by a glimpse of three girls standing in a line like a military formation, each whirling a strip of leather in the air. As the truck twisted again, Harry saw the girls release their slings and let fly their stones. He heard a bang as one struck the truck, but two solid thunks and a curse told him that two of them had met their mark. As he struggled, he saw the girls calmly reload and fire. Emily had given up trying to grab the wheel and had taken to throwing rocks at Holly by hand.

Looking under the truck as he was dragged along, Harry spied a solid-looking tree ahead. It was getting closer by the second. The truck hit with a crunch. The rear of the truck jerked up, throwing Harry's head against the running board just before everything went black.

JADE STOOD FIVE RUNGS FROM THE BOTTOM with her knees bent, her head bowed, and her back pressed against the floor. She straightened her legs and pushed as hard as she could against the door. She heard the groan of wood; then something splintered and cracked. The door gave an inch before slamming against her upper back. Whatever Lilith had put on top was heavy.

You continue to underestimate her as well.

She was about to try again when she heard footsteps running above her. They stopped and a feminine voice called, "Is somebody there?"

Emily!

"I'm under the floor. I'm trapped!" Jade shouted.

"Jade? Jade, is that really you?"

"Yes, it's me. Get me out of here. My friend's down here, too. He's injured." Jade heard a grunt and then the slow, scraping slide as the boxes were pushed away. "Just a moment," Emily said. "The latch is shattered. There's a piece wedged and—"

Jade didn't wait. With the load off the door, she pushed using her legs again and felt the door give way. Emily grabbed hold and pulled it up.

"Here, give me your hand," Emily said. "Oh, Jade. We thought you were dead!" She knelt on the floor and hugged Jade, who was only half out of the cellar.

"Sorry about that. It was a plan to lure the enemy out. I didn't mean to worry you. I thought you were in Mombassa."

"I came back early, and it's a good thing I did, too. What is all this about?"

"I promise I'll explain later, Emily. Can you help me lift my friend out of here?"

Emily peered into the cellar, which was dimly lit by Sam's flashlight. "It's a boy."

Jade smiled ruefully. "No, not in his culture. He's a man and a Kikuyu leader. I've got a rope down here. If I lift, can you pull?"

"Yes. But the girls can help me."

"The girls?" Jade couldn't believe her ears.

Emily beamed back at her. "Yes. This was a revenge mission at first. We followed Harry and Mr. Holly, but—"

"Harry's here? Good. He can bring up Jelani."

Emily shook her head. "He's been injured. The girls are tending to him now."

Jade could only imagine that scene. *They'll have his shirt off for sure.* "I'll get the rope around Jelani and bring it up to you."

After a quarter hour of struggling and pushing, Jade and Emily managed to free Jelani and bring him outdoors. The girls immediately set to work on him, giving him water and washing a nasty head wound. Harry, Jade noted, *had* lost his shirt, but his head and most of his torso were covered in bandages. A trace of blood stained the one on his forehead. Jade stopped them before the girls could cauterize a slight leg wound with ignited black powder. The five of them manhandled Harry into the rear of his truck alongside Jelani. Both were heavily cushioned with the cot and any blankets that the shed had to offer. Steven Holly, on the other hand, was left sitting on the ground, tied to a tree.

"You can send a constable back for him," Jade said. "The truck is drivable, but you'll have to take it slow. Don't try to go all the way into Nairobi. You should be able to get help at the Blue Posts Hotel in Thika."

"Where are you going?" Emily asked.

Jade pulled down the lever on her rifle and heard the satisfying *clack-clack* as she ejected a spent cartridge and sent another round into the chamber. "I'm taking the Hup and heading after the witch who started all of this."

THE MAN CHECKED HIS SPEED, lest an officer stop him. He wanted nothing to postpone this long-awaited reunion. After years of waiting for her, she was here. Years of hearing of her other men, her other schemes. Maddening years in which he'd faithfully, blindly, devotedly done her bidding. He'd followed every request, including the last, fateful trip back into the Congo to retrieve a stash of gold they'd been forced to leave behind when they'd fled. He'd been given the order when he'd visited her in prison, posing as a minister and setting in motion the events for her escape. He had tried to say no, but one look at her beautiful face, marred by a thin, red scar from her delicate nose and across her eye, and he had relented. Relented as he always did. Her will was a blaze that either cleansed the dross from you or left you as smoldering ash.

He'd given everything for her: his country, his family, his soul. It looked now as if he might even be giving his life. But he couldn't help himself. He was a man besotted and on fire. Yet all this time that she was here, close enough to touch, he'd had to stay away from her to maintain her disguise. It had maddened him. But soon, all his patient waiting and sacrifice would end and they'd be free. The plans had already formed in his mind. They'd flee to Rio de Janeiro. He'd get treatment. They'd be safe. And he was on his way to meet her now for one final job.

If he could only survive this bloodlust of hers that threatened to ruin them both.

JADE GAVE HER APPROACH as much thought as she could spare in the short time available to her. Go up the mountain's east or west side? Which way? It wasn't just a matter of speed, but also of stealth. In the end, she opted for the west. Tire tracks went that way, and while she had no hope of overtaking her, Jade prayed that she could sneak up from behind. She left the Hupmobile a half mile back, tucked away in the shelter of the forest, and walked the rest of the way. But when she arrived at the falls, there was no sign of Lilith. Where had she gone? Only Sam's lonely tent with its flat little silhouette of a seated man remained. In this last hour before sunset, it almost fooled her.

And where's Sam? Jade couldn't very well call out for him, not if Lilith was lurking nearby. *Where's Boguli when I need him?* That answer lay with Jelani. If he had conjured Boguli as a protective spirit, then she wasn't likely to see or hear from him again unless Jelani regained consciousness.

The tent is the rendezvous point. Find a spot where you can look down on it and have a clear shot. She opted to work her way upriver to the falls. She'd hide in the rocks there. Jade kept to the protective shadows for as long as she could before dropping to a crouch at the edge of the grasses where the trees were much farther apart. From there she went painstakingly from tree to tree, keeping low. At one point she was forced to half slither, half crawl through the tall grass. Finally, she reached the rocks and climbed them, grateful for the protective din of the falls. She made the summit as the sun set.

There, she spied Sam. *He's alive and unharmed.* Her heart practically sang the thought. She considered giving him a sign, but knew that whatever he could see or hear, Lilith could, too. She was somewhere nearby, biding her time until the evening cloaked her approach.

The elephant's bellow came from beyond the mountain. *Boguli?* Had Jelani recovered enough to request his spirit? The rational part of Jade denied such superstitions. Her Catholic, spiritual side acknowledged Father Jacquinet's hypothesis that her guardian angel was working in whatever form it took to get her attention. In Africa, that was Boguli and elephants. Jade's practical nature was willing to take advantage of whatever would help her catch Lilith. The animal bellowed again. Maybe it was simply a real elephant. It certainly sounded real and it sounded angry. Perhaps Lilith had disturbed it.

If that was the case, then she was on her way from the eastern side of the mountain. Jade looked that way and faced the moonrise, swollen and white. So intent was she that she didn't hear anyone approach until an overjoyed voice called to her.

"Jade! Thank heaven you're alive. I'd given you up for dead."

Jade jumped to her feet as her reflexes kicked in. She recognized the speaker, but it took time for relief to overcome the heart-pounding rush of fear. Now that same reaction coupled with her intense fatigue washed over her in a wave of trembling legs. She slid to the ground, still clutching her Winchester.

"Dr. Mathews, my stars, you gave me a fright. What are you doing here?"

The doctor scrambled from boulder to boulder towards Jade. He cradled a Webley revolver, which didn't surprise Jade. There was always a chance of meeting up with an ill-tempered buffalo around Ol Donyo Sabuk, or possibly a lion, not that a handgun had enough stopping power against either of those menaces.

"You're alive!" Dr. Mathew's voice was hushed and gentle, blending into the muted roar of the falls. "Did you know that everyone was looking for you yesterday? You crashed. Don't you remember?" He reached out a gloved hand towards her arm. "You must be hurt. What are you doing all the way down here? Good heavens, you must have hit your head and wandered aimlessly all day."

Jade slipped aside just before he could reach her and Mathews lost his balance, his right hand landing hard, palm open on a pointed chunk of black basalt. She heard the thin kid leather rip as the rock sliced through his glove, saw the fresh splotch of red. "You cut your hand! What are you doing here?"

He didn't wince, didn't even look at it. "I need your help. Harry Hascombe went a bit insane when he saw the plane wreck. He drove off in a fury." Mathews stared at her, his mouth open in astonishment. "I can't believe you're alive. How fortunate that I found you." He pointed to the southeast. "I . . . I was on my way to find Hascombe. You could help me look."

A bit of movement; a faint moon shadow shifted among the trees and in the distance. She saw Sam slip out from the rocks to one of the few large trees by the river. The elephant trumpeted again. Everything about this scene felt wrong. Her brain screamed a warning, but she was looking at Mathews sideways and he was so close that she couldn't swing her rifle around. "You should leave, Dr. Mathews."

He trained his Webley on her. "I'm afraid, my dear, I must insist that you come with me."

CHAPTER 28

This may be why people hate crocodiles more than any other predator. They use the ultimate need of any animal, for water, to their advantage.
—The Traveler

"DON'T YOU FIND THAT BEARD to be terribly hot and irritating, Mr. Featherstone?"

The voice was low and breathy, like a whisper, but its coolness was far from comforting. It reminded Sam of how a corpse would sound. The speaker was small and of slender build. The loose-fitting, multipocketed hunting jacket and pressed trousers said it was a man, but the smooth, sinuous movements shouted woman.

Lilith came from the east, the rising moon behind her, her boater-style straw hat pushed low over her light brown hair. She'd removed the oversized, gogglelike dark glasses and put them in a coat pocket. She held a pistol aimed at Sam's chest. Sam had reciprocated, raising his Colt.

"I loathed having even that mustache in Morocco and I find the fake sideburns most aggravating, but necessary," she said.

"They detract from your scar, don't they, Lilith," said Sam, no longer pretending to be an Australian. "And the sun protectors did the rest."

"Ah, so you do remember me," Lilith said. "So much the better. No more need for charades. You came to bargain for your friends, didn't you?" She laughed. "Very clever, being O. Fairley in the paper. I thought it was Dunbury."

Sam stepped forward for better aim, holding his Colt with two hands. "It seems you didn't learn enough in your time as a reporter."

Lilith chuckled. "Indeed, but try to shoot me and you'll die first. For one, I have a man up top. And I believe you know something that I want to know. You *do* know where that bastard Pili is at, don't you? Tell me. Tell me now, and I'll let you live."

Sam worried about the "man up top," but did his level best not to let it show. He gauged the distance to the rocks. Could he shoot her and make it to cover in time? "Why should I trust you?"

"You can't. Your little bitch, Jade, made enough of a mess for me here, ruining a perfectly good identity and scheme. So if I'm to leave, I'm going to do so with whatever information you have. Or I'll be forced to get it from Dunbury. I'm sure he knows, too. Your choice, Mr. Featherstone."

Sam had come so far to reclaim Jade. To die now and lose her for good was not his first choice. Did Lilith have a man up top? If she did, the moon would provide enough illumination to shoot by. Sam drifted backwards, closer to cover. *Can't move too quickly or she'll catch on.* "You can keep me as a security until you have Pili. I'll take you to him," he said.

"Ah, I'm certain of that, Mr. Featherstone, because, you see, I also have Jade, and she'll die very slowly and painfully if you try anything."

Rage welled up in Sam's chest. He'd kill her now and be

done with it. "To hell with this!" Sam roared, but the shot he heard was not his. His right leg flew out from beneath him and dropped him to the ground, his Colt firing high.

IN AN INSTANT, the gloved hands and the lack of pain when Mathews fell against the rock made perfect sense to Jade. He had leprosy, contracted in the Congo. The drugs in the shed were for him. The disease had already deadened his fingers. In her mind she saw him try to pet Biscuit and avoid shaking hands. He had had access to Dymant's surgery to plant the suspicious documents and divert their attention. Jade now also understood that Farhani had not meant the cook, Matthew, when she'd asked if anyone had been to her bungalow. He'd meant the doctor, but his indifference to titles before names had misled her. She drew breath to shout for Sam, but Mathews prodded her back with his gun.

"Shh," he whispered. "No noise or you die." He took Jade's Winchester with his left hand and slipped it across his back. Then he motioned for her to walk farther upstream to a place where they could climb unseen down the slope. "I'm going to take you to her. I was supposed to meet her to provide cover for her rendezvous, but I think this will please her more."

No, it won't. She thinks I'm locked in her cellar. Her mind reeled under the new revelation. *Mathews. Mathers! Mathers Pellyn! And leprosy!* He, not Dymant, had been in the Belgian Congo on one of his many supposed tours to the outposts. He'd also been back in England for a few months, and Jade recalled that a minister had visited Lilith in prison last August. She had no doubt now that it was Mathews, arranging for her escape. She remembered he was freshly back in

Kenya in September, helping Sam during the Kilimanjaro murders.

His disguise had been perfect. As a doctor he had access to poisons. As a medical officer assisting the police, he could easily withhold information when the victim was one who'd died by his hand. But he hadn't been around when Waters was examined. *Waters had been shot with a Webley.* It was because Dr. Dymant had stepped in that they knew this.

And Dr. Dymant said he knew Dr. Mathews. Jade had little doubt that Pellyn, who may or may not have finished medical training, had long ago killed the real Dr. Mathews and conveniently taken over his identity. Perhaps that man had no family or few friends to miss him. But there had been one, Dymant. And for that, Dymant had had to die. How convenient that a knife fight broke out in the Indian district when Dymant was there ministering. And with plague already a problem, who would be the wiser that the knife was tainted with diseased blood?

When they were out of earshot, the man pushed her east to the falls. "What do you plan to do with me, Mathews, or should I call you Pellyn?" Jade asked. "You really didn't expect me, did you?"

"Ah, you have divined my real name. Then I'm certain you can guess what will ultimately happen. My Lilith wants you dead, but by her hand. You disappointed her by dying in that crash, but now she'll have the pleasure of killing you. Still, I promise I'll do my utmost to make it a quick death. Even at the risk of displeasing her."

"Why? Developing a conscience after all these years?"

Pellyn chuckled. "Not one that you would approve of,

my dear. But I do have a sense of honor, nonetheless. I've come to admire you. You don't deserve to suffer any more than you already have, and our son did love you."

Jade halted in her tracks and spun around. "*Our* son! David was *your* son?"

Pellyn prodded her in the side with his gun. "Yes. Sadly I never met him, but from what Lilith told me, he was one to make a father proud. And, unlike Lilith, I do not hold you responsible for his death."

He pushed her with the gun barrel. "Now move along, my dear. This will be a lovely surprise for my lady."

Jade again thought of screaming a warning to Sam, but she knew the intervening land and the falls' muted roar would only block her cry. *And Pellyn will shoot me.* To be sure, the shot would warn Sam, but it was a risk she didn't care to take. Not unless she had no other option. Better to get to Lilith and take them both. Pellyn's diseased hand already suggested one idea to her.

"I can't imagine she'll keep you around much longer, Pellyn. Not with your leprosy." Jade heard him sigh as they moved among the rocks, always heading back towards the falls. "She's used plenty of other men before, on Mount Marsabit, in Morocco. Does she know yet? Or is that another surprise in store for her? I think she'd wonder when you start to caress her with gloves on."

"Stop it!" hissed Pellyn. He punctuated his command with a glancing blow to the back of Jade's head. "Those other men were only tools for her to use. *I'm* her love. I always have been."

"Is your disease affecting your brain? The only person she's *ever* loved is herself," said Jade. "I thought she loved

David, but now I see that even he was just a symbol, proof that she duped her husband."

Mathers grabbed Jade and spun her around, his face inches from hers. "*I'm* her husband. She married *me* before she married Worthy. We kept it a secret."

Jade shrugged. "So she adds bigamy to her list of crimes. I'm not surprised. But I am surprised at your blindness, *Dr. Pellyn*."

He pushed her forward. "Silence!"

They were nearly to the falls. Another half dozen steps and they'd break the thin line of trees that hugged the lower rocks. From her vantage point, she could just make out Sam. Jade took the last steps slowly, as though she were picking her way carefully among the damp stones. She heard Sam's voice not too far in front of her.

"You can keep me as a security until you have Pili," he said. "I'll take you to him."

Sam was keeping his Colt trained on someone, but Jade couldn't see Lilith. She hoped it meant that Lilith hadn't spotted them yet, either.

It's now or never!

Jade spun around, her elbow slamming back and up into Pellyn's chest with a resounding thump followed by an explosive "Oof!" Anyone else could have reacted instantly, pulling the trigger, but Jade counted on Pellyn's disease to diminish his abilities. She had no idea how far the leprosy had progressed, but if his fall was any indication, he probably couldn't even feel the trigger.

She was only partially correct. The damage in his left hand was considerable. Unfortunately, Pellyn was right-handed.

As he doubled over, Jade darted down and to the side, keeping under his Webley's firing line. She grabbed his wrist with both hands and twisted, trying to break his grip on the revolver.

The shot rang close to her ear. Besides its nearly deafening echo, she heard another shot from near Sam's tent.

Pellyn kept his grasp on the gun despite Jade's best attempts to twist it free. Perhaps he couldn't feel her blows, or maybe he was incapable of relaxing his grip. All Jade knew was that the blasted thing went off. She thought she yelled, "Sam!" but if she did, she couldn't hear her own voice over the percussive echo in her ear. And when she saw Sam fall thirty yards away from her, she shouted again, using the fear and anger to fuel her movements.

Again and again she stomped on Pellyn's right foot while she wrestled with him for the Webley. He was twice her age, and even though he was riddled with one of the more horrifying diseases known to man, he fought with the strength of a madman.

From her vantage point, Jade saw Sam roll behind a rock.

He's alive!

But so was Lilith and she was advancing, her revolver held in front of her. Sam fired once and Lilith ducked for cover. Jade could see Lilith, nearly fifty yards away, edging her way through the rocks towards Sam, keeping low. Jade redoubled her efforts and raised Pellyn's Webley.

"If you won't let go, then shoot your bitch," she growled as she squeezed his finger, which was still on the trigger.

The shot struck Lilith in her left arm, breaking it above the elbow. Her scream rang through the air, a harpy's cry.

Jade remembered that sound and, for a moment, she saw herself in a ruined palace in Marrakech, grappling with her assailant for a knife, the knife that had scarred Lilith's face.

The outcry electrified Pellyn, and he lashed back at Jade with greater intensity, knocking her down. Jade fell to her side, the Webley flying away from them. It landed on the rocks with a clatter. Jade reached for Pellyn's boots before he could either run to Lilith's aid or remember that he still had hold of her Winchester across his back. She was nearly too late. He'd already unshipped the rifle and was looking for the expected bolt action.

"Wrong kind of rifle, mister," she said as she yanked on one leg.

Pellyn, caught off balance, spread his arms to regain it. His damaged hands had a poor grip on the Winchester and he dropped it. It fell away from Jade's reach and within Pellyn's. His foot lashed out and kicked Jade squarely in the stomach, just below the ribs. Her breath rushed out of her and tears welled as the gagging pain shot through her. Jade fought to regain control of her breath. She needed to get to her rifle and help Sam. He'd scrambled into a kneeling stance behind a rock and was waiting for a clear shot at Lilith. It was Lilith's charge that distracted Pellyn and bought for Jade a little of the time that she needed to recover.

Lilith seemed oblivious to her shattered arm. Jade had seen it before in animals from wounded rhinos to elephants. Pain and rage fueled the body beyond normal endurance, overcoming all but the need for revenge and destruction. There was no time for agony or even for death, only the desire to take all others down with them.

Lilith charged at Sam, her own pistol sending a steady

barrage of death. But what drive her pain lent to her fury, it took away in her ability to focus on her target. Her shots struck the rock in front of Sam, spraying chips of hardened basalt and granite around him. Sam steadied his Colt on the rock and fired once, striking Lilith in her lower chest. She fell to the ground, skidding along the grass and gravel until she lay still in a pool of blood.

"No!" shrieked Pellyn. "You've killed her, damn you!" With a roar, he snatched Jade's rifle and ran for Sam. He pulled down on the lever action to chamber a round and snapped the rifle to his shoulder.

"Sam!" Jade yelled as she struggled to her feet.

Sam turned in time to duck behind the rock near the shoreline as the bullet whizzed over his head. Pellyn rapidly closed the distance and hefted the Winchester as a club, ready to swing down at Sam's head. Jade saw Sam take aim, then hesitate.

He's afraid he'll hit me!

Sam turned his Colt into a club as well, his body tensing to meet and ward off the blow.

Sam struck first, launching himself up using his left leg, slamming Pellyn in the jaw. Pellyn's head snapped back and, before he had a chance to recover, Jade was behind him, pulling the rifle from his grasp.

Despite his disease, Pellyn held on tenaciously, but the distraction gave Sam the time to hit him again with a left jab to the thorax. "See how you like it!" Sam shouted. Pellyn's breath went out in a whoosh as he doubled over. Then, tumbling forward, he toppled with a splash.

The splash was echoed by a softer one farther downstream.

"Help!" Pellyn shouted as he floundered in the river.

"Dr. Mathews?" yelled Sam. Surprise riddled his voice, as if he'd just then perceived the identity of his other assailant.

For a split second, Jade considered letting him drown. But it was Lilith, more than Pellyn, who'd orchestrated all the crimes. And they needed Pellyn to stand trial or too many deaths would go unexplained.

"Grab this," Jade called. She held out her rifle, butt first, for Pellyn to grab. But his gloves, slippery with the Athi's mud, slid off. "His hands are useless, Sam. We've got to get him."

Sam and Jade both reached for Pellyn. Sam managed to grab his left wrist and pull him up far enough for Jade to catch hold of his jacket. Together they hauled with all their remaining strength, dragging him from the river. They didn't quit until they'd put over forty feet between themselves and the bank where he lay unconscious.

"We need to tie him up," said Jade.

"That's Dr. Mathews!" exclaimed Sam.

"His real name is Mathers Pellyn." Jade knelt down and removed Pellyn's boot laces and deftly secured his wrists behind his back. "Lilith trapped me in a cellar at the shed. She had Jelani there. But Emily, Harry, and some of the girls found us." She pointed towards the far side of the mountain. "Avery's car is that way. We can load him up and take him back to stand trial." She finished tying the bonds and leaned back on her heels, panting. "As to Lilith? Let the hyenas have her, as far as I'm concerned. I'll tell Finch to pick up the remains."

Jade thought of what Pellyn had said about David being

his son by Lilith. At one time, the realization would have staggered her. Now it didn't. She'd seen a vision of David in France, his face sorrowful, as if he now knew about his parents. She bowed her head. *It's all right, David. You were not like them. Rest in peace now.*

She felt a pair of strong arms lift her from behind and encircle her waist. Here was love. Here was a man! She turned in Sam's embrace. Fatigue, relief, and sorrow over the unnecessary deaths took them both and they each braced against the other, giving and receiving support. For a few minutes, neither of them spoke, letting their heartbeats speak for them. Jade closed her eyes and inhaled deeply, drinking in Sam's scent.

"It's over," she said finally. She grabbed hold of his arms with hers, gripping tightly. "You're not going to leave again, are you?"

"No," he murmured into her ear. "I couldn't live without you and your wild escapades. So if you'll still have me, I'm yours. Only," he added with a touch of sadness in his voice, "I can't promise you the sky anymore."

"We'll get another plane," she said. "In the meantime, I have this." She broke away from him and took the brilliant sapphire from her right hand. Sam put it on her left.

"Good thing you said yes, too," said Sam. "Because I already told my parents to get ready to come out to Africa for a wedding. We are going to have such adventures, Jade!"

"Well, if you were planning on leaving me again, I was going to keep you here even if I had to shoot you to do it. Wait a minute," she said. "Didn't you get shot when Pellyn's gun went off? I saw you fall."

"Hit my wooden leg." He pointed to his boot. There

was a neat hole in the front and a splintered one at the exit. "Suspect it's cracked now and I'll have to get a new one." He leaned in for a kiss.

Jade tasted his lips and mouth, felt that blasted beard scratching at her cheeks, and decided even that felt like a caress. She was a starved prisoner, newly released and desperate for food, for comfort, for Sam.

And then the throbbing began in her left knee. From the mountain's base came the trumpeting blast of an angry elephant. Jade pushed Sam away. "Something's wrong . . ." she began.

That was when she saw Boguli over Sam's shoulder. But this time he was not swaying gently from side to side. He stood erect, as might a younger, proud warrior, and pointed towards the riverbank. There lay Lilith, blood dribbling from her nostrils and mouth, her clothes caked in red. She'd struggled to her right elbow and now to her knees, her right hand gripping her Webley. Her eyes were glazed with a fanatical hatred as she clenched her teeth and took aim, her right hand trembling.

"Lilith!" Jade shouted. She looked for her Winchester, but it lay on the ground out of reach. Her hand reached down to her right boot and found her knife. Without thinking, she pulled it, drew back, and launched. The knife spun three and a half times before implanting deeply in Lilith's chest.

Sam drew his Colt, but before he could fire, the Athi came alive with a boiling froth. A hideous monstrosity of dappled green and ghostly gray lunged from the water and surged onto the bank. In an instant the beast clamped its massive jaws on Lilith's waist and hefted her as easily as it would a rag doll. She screamed and beat at its eyes, but nothing would break the animal's deadly embrace.

Sam fired, the bullets ricocheting off the monster's head. The crocodile spun around and pushed off into the river. Within a matter of moments, the surface waters were calm.

CHAPTER 29

But one shouldn't read ulterior motives and designs into a
crocodile's behavior. It, too, needs to stay alive.
It seeks no more than any other animal.
—The Traveler

"You'll be wanted for yet another inquest," said Finch.
"Both of you." Jade and Sam sat in the inspector's office.
Sam had shaved his beard, leaving a slightly paler chin and a
pencil-thin mustache gracing his upper lip.

"How will Pellyn be charged?" asked Sam.

"Well, that's going to be up to the chief magistrate in the
end, but I'm pushing for murder. I confess there may not be
enough evidence to make it stick, though."

"How is that?" asked Sam.

This time Jade answered. "Because Waters probably
killed Stockton and pushed him and his car off the Limuru
Bridge."

"That is correct," said Finch. "Of course, we believe your
Pellyn killed Waters for taking on another victim without
him. Dymant did find that .455 in Waters' rib. But Dymant
is dead and his report is missing."

"But Pellyn killed Dymant, too, and he probably killed Mutahi."

Finch shrugged. "Most likely, but we have no evidence." He shook his head. "I still am finding it hard to believe that this man was a criminal. I've known him as Dr. Mathews for so long. He's performed numerous examinations on bodies for us."

"I wonder how many he reported as deaths by accidents or natural causes," said Jade. "People whom he'd killed or had arranged to be killed. In his role, he had ample opportunity to hide evidence."

"Sadly we will never know that," said Finch, "and the jury has known Mathews for so long that they'll be hard to convince otherwise."

"You have the documents from that shed. Surely you can link him to the mining schemes," argued Sam. "You cannot let that man run free."

"I hardly think that will happen, Mr. Featherstone," said Finch. "With his leprosy, he'll be confined to a leper colony, at least." He looked at Jade. "Why are you staring at me, Miss del Cameron?"

"I'm thinking of how I suspected you of being Mathers Pellyn, although in hindsight, I can hardly picture you with Lilith."

"You suspected Hascombe, too, didn't you?" asked Sam.

"For a while." She smiled. "After rescuing Harry, Emily seems quite taken with him, and he with her. That should be fun."

The Dunburys and the Thompsons met Sam and Jade for lunch at the New Stanley after the visit with Finch. Emily joined them, looking more vibrant and alive after her adventure. Jade doubted that she'd have any trouble finding suitors with her revived beauty, but perhaps she'd be less inclined to settle down right away. *I think she's discovered the Heathington spirit of adventure.*

"I imagine, Bev, that the mothers are calling for your resignation as leader of the Girl Guides after their recent escapades," said Jade. "Sorry."

Beverly laughed. "And Lady Northey and Mrs. Archibald would lead the pack against me, too, if it weren't for Avery's doings."

"Yes," said Avery. "I decided the girls needed recognition for their bravery and service, so I sent a telegram to His Highness, the Prince of Wales. He was impressed enough to send them something suitably bright and shiny to pin on their uniforms."

"How is Jelani?" asked Beverly.

"Well," said Jade. "He insisted on going back to his village so the old *mondo-mogo* could care for him. He won't abide the British hospital for natives."

A polite cough interrupted their conversation. Blaney Percival stood beside their table. "Begging your pardon, but I thought you and our friends here would like to know that the crocodile is dead."

"Dead!" they exclaimed.

"Stone-cold dead this time," said Percival. "His body floated belly-up this morning, that woman still clamped in his jaws."

"Indigestion?" suggested Sam.

"Hardly," said Percival. He placed a knife on their table. "Found that in the beast's skull, piercing the brain."

"That's my knife!" exclaimed Jade. "The last I saw it was in Lilith's chest."

"She used it to try to kill the beast," said Percival.

"Crocs are hard to kill," said Jade, and when she looked at Sam, she could see that he knew to whom she was referring. Lilith, like the croc, had not gone down easily.

"I heard about the fight near the falls," said Percival. "I'm thinking that, because Stockton was killed near there, this crocodile learned to associate gunshots with a victim and came to the site during your battle."

Jade shook her head. "The croc didn't kill Lilith. Ask the Africans. They will all tell you that the souls of past victims enter a crocodile, seeking vengeance. Waters, Stockton, and possibly Mutahi killed Lilith."

"Hmm, that poses an interesting problem," said Avery. "Lilith's soul was tormented. It might look for another croc and try for our Jade again."

"I think I'll stay clear of rivers for a while," said Jade.

Sam took Jade's hands in his. "After we're married, we can go anywhere you'd like, Jade: Abyssinia, the Congo. We'll make motion pictures of tribes and places that few people have seen. I love you as you are, Jade, and I don't ever want you to change."

Jade heard Beverly's happy "Oh!" but her attention stayed fixed on Sam. "I love you, too, Sam, and I can safely promise you that I'll *never* make a proper housewife. But we need to get a new plane. I'm marrying a pilot."

"Well, Beverly, my dear," said Avery, "looks like you and Maddy have a wedding to plan."

AUTHOR'S NOTES

Readers might take issue with the book's crocodile staying alive after being shot in the head. The late big-game hunter Peter Hathaway Capstick backs me up in *Death in the Long Grass*, chapter six: "Crocodiles." Crocs, it seems, do not go gently into that good night.

As a disclaimer, Jade is a professional, so don't try her stunts at home. Igniting black powder in a deep wound to cauterize it and stop the bleeding was actually recommended in some earlier books such as *Modern Surgery: General and Operative* by John Chalmers Da Costa, 1910. It was especially recommended after bleeding a wound after a victim was bitten by a rabid animal. One might assume that ripping up a shirt and making a tourniquet to stop bleeding would be less painful, but perhaps the sulfur in some of the powder actually acted as an antiseptic, too. The advice still appeared in the 1926 edition of *Handbook for Boys*, the official boy scout handbook, in chapter seven, written by Major Charles Lynch of the American National Red Cross, as a recommendation after rattlesnake bite. Modern gunpowder wouldn't do the trick.

Sam's Colt .45 New Service double-action revolver was adopted by the U.S. Armed Forces as a Model 1917 U.S. Army and used to make up for the lack of M1911 Colt .45

pistols in World War I. Sam would have been issued one as a pilot and could have purchased it after the war. The intent was to defend oneself if caught in enemy territory. World War I pilot Lt. Frank Luke carried the M1911, and when he crashed behind enemy lines, he used it to open fire on the Germans rather than be taken prisoner. Lieutenant Luke was killed in the return fire. I chose to give Sam the New Service revolver rather than the M1911 pistol carried by Lieutenant Luke simply because I felt the revolver better epitomized Sam. It had more of an American Old West look to it. Call me a romantic.

The Girl Guides formed in Nairobi in early 1921. Reports in the newspapers summarized badges in nursing and horsemanship among others. Often they met at Lady Northey's residence on Government Hill. While the Girl Guides was intended for younger girls up to fourteen years, a Girl Guide Ranger program for young ladies fifteen years and older was proposed in January 1922. Descriptions of the uniforms and activities are taken from their original handbook.

If anyone doubts Biscuit's willingness to wade the Athi, cheetahs have been photographed swimming in Botswana as floodwaters forced them to cross bodies of water to reach their prey.

The Irving Air Chute Company is not a typographical error. At least, not here. Leslie Irvin founded the company, but a clerical error resulted in a "g" being added to the name. It stayed until 1970, so I've used the variation that Sam would have known.

Some readers may question the spelling of McMillan's name. While some books give it as MacMillan, Isak Dinesen uses this spelling. McMillan's farm, Juja, sprawled around

much of Ol Donyo Sabuk, but his wife didn't care for it, so he
didn't often live there. By 1921, McMillan was suffering from
illnesses and lived abroad more than in Africa. His farm was
largely unattended then.

And as noted in previous books, the excerpts at the top
of each chapter are not from a real magazine. The clips are
part of Jade's articles and I write her copy. Readers interested
in more tidbits of historical interest are invited to visit my
weekly blog, "Through Jade's Eyes," at http://suzannearruda
.blogspot.com/. A new post shows up each Monday, barring
unforeseen circumstances.

Photo by Joe Arruda

Suzanne Arruda, a zookeeper turned science teacher and freelance writer, is also the author of several biographies for young adults as well as science and nature articles for adults and children. An avid hiker, outdoorswoman, and a member of Women in the Outdoors, she lives in Kansas with her husband. You can reach her at www.suzannearruda.com.